NAIROBI
TO
Shenzhen

NAIROBI
TO
Shenzhen

A NOVEL OF LOVE IN THE EAST

MARK OBAMA NDESANDJO

Aventine Press

This edition published 2009 by Aventine Publishing

Nairobi To Shenzhen

Author: Mark O. Ndesandjo

Aventine Publishing, 2009
750 State St. #319
San Diego CA, 92101
www.aventinepress.com

United States Copyright Registration Number: TXu 1-607-143

ISBN: 1-59330-623-7

www.markobamandesandjo.com

FOREWORD

The characters and events portrayed and the names herein are fictitious, and any similarity to the name, character and history of any person is entirely coincidental and unintentional. Any actual persons and events which are in this novel are included solely for realism and are entirely unrelated to the fictional characters and events.

The completion of this book would not have been possible without the assistance of family and friends and I particularly want to thank Auntie, Barack, Greta, Harley, Hilary, Jun Da, Lisa, Mark, Paul, my parents, Reggie and many others.

I thank my loving wife for her invaluable advice and support in writing this novel.

I dedicate this book to the two most important people in my life, my mother and my wife, and to the memory of my brother David Opiyo.

Mark Okoth Obama Ndesandjo
Shenzhen 2009

Note About the Chinese Language:

In parts of this book Chinese words are written using the 'PinYin' system of pronunciation. Chinese pronunciation uses 4 tones in pronouncing syllables. Depending upon the tones the same syllable will have different meanings.

First tone (-). This is a flat, level high-pitched tone.
Second tone (^) This is a deep, centered pitch.
Third tone (/) This is an ascending pitch.
Fourth tone (\) This is a sharp pitch, like a quick accent.
For example, the original Chinese from a poem by the great Tang Dynasty poet Li Bai
Before my bed, the bright moonlight
Casts its frost onto the ground):

may be written in the PinYin system using English characters for ease of pronunciation.
Chung/ qian/ ming/ yue\ guang-/ Yi/ shi\ di\ shang^ shuang-

In Shangri La as the sunset falls
Gold dust is sprinkled over the tops of naked trees
A great smoldering flame steals glances at me from behind the clouds.
The rainbow arches over the highest points
At once neither an entrance nor an exit.
When I quench my loneliness
Could you be that inner light from which everything glows,
When it is not the time to have,
Just the time to be?

- Mark O. Ndesandjo

CONTENTS

"*I will always remember the day my mother left me. I was about 5 or 6 years old then. Many things that happened that long ago are unclear but some are as clear as yesterday. I can imagine some of the things she said and what my father and I said. I mostly remember the wetness of her face when she said goodbye.*"

- From David's father's journal

THE BEGINNING

It was the angst that roused him from sleep.

He rubbed his eyes. Outside the window the autumn wind gently rustled the dying leaves. In the far distance, one could see gray clouds over Lian Hua Park. From above the morning mist, the tops of hills could be seen gently weaving around the city like soft green pillows. At this early hour the birds were silent, as though praying for a silent benediction. He could hear the sounds of falling leaves. Their crackling sounds washed over his breast like cleansing water. Infused with a bittersweet merriment, he was at once content and sad. The urge within was profound. He indulged in his sadness, as one who has lost all hope.

Yet there was that ineffable something that seemed to say, *Behold yourself. Go and distinguish what is outside of you.* Questions and opinions were familiar friends, for he was a clever man, and could retort as well as any. Yet to this *Go... outside of you* he had no answer.

I'm in the middle of my life. Jumbled words and scattered thoughts passed through his mind. Questions lingered. *I'm no longer young. Where can I go? What did I come to do in China?* At times like this, one knows what one must do, yet the decision to take action awaits articulation. It is vague and unformed, mute and dumb. It takes an event such as a crisis of conscience, a death of someone close, a close friend's counsel, even a child's innocent laugh for it to become clear. It may take just the sound of rustling leaves on a quiet autumn morning. All is suffused with a sense of solitude.

He couldn't sleep. Neither was he awake. He was somewhere in between. He didn't know why, but within him there was that drumbeat of unease. *I'm in the middle of my life.* There are times in a man's life when everything seems to stop. Things must be re-evaluated. There is profound turmoil within. Like a beating heart it throbs and never stops. Like the unceasing pounding of waves upon the beach, it is unreasonable, unwilling to leave. Like a ship's fog horn within the mist, it rouses one from sleep. Yet the fog remains. All one knows is that one must find a clear path, otherwise all will be lost.

Yesterday was his birthday. Or perhaps it was the day before. He wasn't sure. "I have fewer friends these days.", his stepfather had said to him over the phone as they discussed the phenomenon of birthdays. He had replied with something completely irrelevant, but he knew what the other man meant to say – that with the passing of time, life becomes more precious even as it grows more physically distant.

He lay quietly on his bed. The turmoil roiled within him like a vast formless ether. He was not happy, yet in his solitude he welcomed the discomfort. Perhaps, he thought, this bittersweet feeling might sting him into action.

He remembered some old lines of poetry from Dante's *Inferno*,

"We were sullen in the wet air that is gladdened by the sun, bearing in our hearts a sluggish smoke; now we are sullen in the black mire."

Some more lines bounced around in his mind, this time from Rilke,

"...for here there is no place
that does not see you. You must change your life."

He marveled at how these long forgotten verses from high school were so clear in his mind. He had a gift for remembering phrases from classical literature. At emotional moments they would ebb and flow, enter and exit his consciousness, and sometimes reveal his true thoughts. *You must change your life.* This was the needle that jabbed David awake.

It was 6:51 in the morning.

He had already gotten out of bed. The room was small for such a big man. Mosquito netting sloppily hung over the small pallet of a bed. Newly arrived from the local Wal-Mart, the sheets were clean and the pillow a neon purple. The desk was littered with stray pieces of paper and, together with the bed, swallowed up at least half the small studio. Away from the door, the only window in the apartment was by the kitchen hearth and toilet. It looked out over miles of rooftops and buildings. Outside, a warm rosy glow lay suspended over the distant hills. A kite, or maybe a bird, lazily drifted in the upper currents high above the green slopes. He sensed daylight was fast approaching.

The sense of misgiving that had roused David was still upon him, though less intense. These periods of intense reflection and undefined levity, he somewhat regretfully realized, appeared less frequently since he had arrived in Shenzhen, China. For him ignorance was bliss, but bliss wasn't always welcome. Pain and sadness were sometimes stimulating, and even liberating. The bird was still circling. It was definitely a bird, he thought. It was too agile, too nimble for a kite. He remembered the birds back home in Nairobi. Back home they were loud but not seen. Here they were seen but hardly ever heard, as though they held precious secrets that could be whispered only to a favored few.

Forty three, he thought. *Forty three measures.* He remembered a Rachmaninoff piano piece that he loved. Like a murmur the left hand's melodic runs sweep up and down the piano keys in ever more agitated communication with the right hand. Like the famous themes from Richard Wagner's great opera *Tristan and Isolde*, the right hand motif evolves from a state of hesitation to an orgasmic climax. *Even the greatest pianists*, he thought, *are unable to express all the passion within this forty three measure prelude.* He too could not articulate what he felt. All he sensed was a great cry of execration leveled against him.

He looked at the deepening rose of the clouds and sky that hung suspended like a frozen spray over the city. Instinctively he moved to the desk and switched on the computer. The urge to do something, he realized, could be temporarily satisfied in two ways; by playing the piano (which the apartment lacked), or writing. He lazily scrolled through some of the early entries.

The Beginning *I lost my job due to a corporate downsizing. The world had changed after 9/11. The USA, once a place of hope and eternal optimism, had become a place of systematic and growing suspicion. Greek magnanimity had been replaced by the Roman Empire. Rather than seek another dead-end, I decided to travel to the far end of the earth, a place of spiritual and economic change. I decided to go to the East and seek a rebirth.*

One Thousand Miles, The First Step *In life's moments of loss, one has 3 choices: become one's own disciple, or another's, or scavenge hopelessly in the ruins. It was then that my soul looked eastwards. To live in solitude, with some money and the great soul of the dreamer - a more perfect confluence cannot be imagined.*

The Senseless Man *In about a month I'll be starting a new life in China. As the date of departure gets closer I notice that I desensitize myself to the things around me: my house, my car, even my piano. I take to the Internet with an almost maniacal obsession, in particular soaking in news about Al-Qaeda and the latest exploits of Police Fest USA. Vast amounts of free time abound, and I'm pressed to fill them up.*

Today he added the following:

Searching for the distant beloved China occupies my mind at first like a hazy image of people and places — distant, in some hidden valley of my consciousness. Even as I get closer to defining it, it steps away. Like the veil of Maya, I strip away the folds and find yet more allure, more mystery. Capitalist? Communist? Smoky and polluted? Spiritual? Barren of comfort? The women? And the women are another story. Can I have Chinese girlfriends — or is it illegal? From what I've seen even in white bread Orlando, they are of all types — small, large, different complexions, athletic, tubby. I sometimes wonder if my travels are a perennial search for the distant beloved. Perhaps every lone traveler is in search of his or her other half.

Bashert This future love is sometimes referred to by this Yiddish word (transliterated besherte, beshert or besherter). My grandmother often said "Oy Ve" or "Oy Gevalt" to express "My God" or such like, but I never heard her mention this word. It means "destiny", and often refers to one's pre-ordained soul mate. Jewish singles will say that they are looking for their bashert, meaning they are looking for that person who will complement them perfectly. A clunky sounding word with a deep meaning.

David never dated his entries. He intended them to be a stream of thoughts and impressions, without reason, without goals. They were to be read backwards, forwards, upside down, sideways, and they would still make sense. Direction was a metaphor. Goals and dreams were nebulous things that represented other nebulous things.

He once more reviewed the letter he was sending to his mother. The two of them communicated regularly, sometimes by email, other times with letters. His often dense, wordy missives (he even consulted classic texts sometimes) would contrast with her cryptic, succinct phrases. Recently they had started communicating more frequently.

Liebe Mutter!

You recently asked me why I came to China. Perhaps my answer was imperfect. It was no doubt incomplete. I just said I needed to leave for someplace new. I listed many specific reasons. America had become too familiar. There was the constant battle to ratchet up the career ladder as well as the profound disillusion that set in after 9/11.

What did I mean? I meant America was no longer the America I remembered. Once it was a place of innocence and optimism, it had made fear a rule, not just an *aberration. I couldn't take it. I also told you I wanted to go someplace very foreign, almost mystical, where I could reach some actual spiritual tranquility, not just a semblance of stability. But I didn't tell you the whole story.*

Anyway, I needed to be in a place that would force me out of myself. Some novel place, rooted in ancient myths and dreams. Whether it was the cumulative influence of David Carradine's **Kung Fu** *or the analects of Confucius, the ascetics of Buddhism or the economic juggernaught of China, I don't know what specifically made me come here.*

Since I have arrived, I have discovered so much, the people, the land, the art, and above all the language. Once so cryptic and strange, so convoluted and baroque, mandarin is now a passion and China is a home.

But there remains one thing I must know. In my luggage the other day I found a photo of my father and me. It was taken when I was very young. I don't know why, but know I want to know more about this man who we left when I was so young. I want to know how you met him, what he was like and what happened before you divorced. I realize there are some things I need to know.

Socrates said,
know yourself
Others have said
through others will you discover yourself.
There is another Chinese saying,
"The place you fall is the place from where you pick yourself up."
So the journey begins.
Until the next missive,
Your loving Son
Marcus Antoninus Gaius Esquire (AKA David)
P.S Don't forget to send me the Kenyan coffee. It is my elixir of the heart.

He could not write anymore. *What meaningless drivel*, he thought. He remembered reading an interview with the great Canadian pianist Glenn Gould. Gould had said something like

"There are two major problems with musicians. They can only talk about music and to them music is just a vehicle for emoting. Dumb emotion begets dumb emotion".

He clicked the send button, drank some milk and flopped back onto the bed.

He looked again at the photograph he had found yesterday. It was an old Kodak color print, about 3 by 4 inches. Two people were in the photograph, a man and a young boy. They were standing on a grassy field with a hedge in the background. The background was dark, as though the print had been overexposed. The man was tall. His skin was very black. He wore long white slacks and a turtleneck sweater. Huge spectacles were perched on a large fleshy nose. His dark skin roiled with perspiration or oil and a huge pipe seemed about to fall from his lips. And those lips were thick and sensual. They seemed the lips of a man who loved sounds, sights, shapes and colors, a man who is born to command and enjoy life. One hand was casually draped across the boy's thin shoulders and the other nursed his pipe as he looked into the distance behind the photographer through piercing, unsmiling eyes.

The boy was about 8 or 9 years of age. His skin was much lighter, a milky coffee color that seemed almost white against the dark skin of his father. He was wearing a scruffy shirt that was unbuttoned in places. His long tan slacks were muddy and disheveled. A soccer ball was lying on the grass before them. The contrast between the untidiness of the boy and the almost Etonian *bon ton* of the man was striking. The boy's face was uncomfortable as though he was both pulling away from his father's huge hand and cringing from what lay before him. His deep brown eyes stared in mild confusion and bemusement under sharply arched eyebrows.

David wondered again. *Was this I? Who is this child? Who was that man?* His mind went back to those early years.

He remembered his family, far, far away; his mother back in Kenya and his long dead father, particularly his father. "A brilliant man, but a social failure" his mother often said. She would say so carefully - as though balancing oranges on a scale, making sure nothing tipped over. She hadn't needed to defend or assail anyone. David easily remembered the hulking man whose breath reeked of cheap Pilsner beer who had often beaten his mother. He had long searched for good memories of his father but had found none. He had been born in abject poverty in the western Kenyan province of Siaya before the Second World War.

Back then the green and wet hills of Siaya province wrapped voluptuously around the clusters of single-roomed thatched huts. The land was rich with oaks, fig, euphorbia, sadry and blue gum trees. The grand baobab, known all over Africa for its medicinal and life healing properties, and known locally as *mirembe*, often spread its wide canopy to cool the land. These days the lush forests and vegetation in many places seem diminished. Cut and cleared before the relentless march of development projects and the search for land, once lofty boughs have been turned into charcoal or cheap furniture. Where once there were mango trees birds now dart through empty spaces. Overloaded *matatus* deliver passengers from place to place. A gob of spit from a weary conductor spins like a lost raindrop through clouds of dust. Murram and tarmac roads now snake like long gray tongues through the small plots of tea, pyrethrum, sweet potato, cotton, maize and sugar cane, past villages, green fields and some fuelwood and timber trees.

"Your grandfather was an *askari* for the colonial government. He had often beaten your father and left him for long periods of time." Someone had told him long ago, probably his mother.

"He beat me because he too had been beaten. It must have been hard growing up like that.", she would say, as if it would partly expiate his father's sins.

In the decades leading up to the Second World War food was sometimes in short supply. Once his father told David of how hungry he had been when the man of the house was not there to provide for them. When they were hungry he and his friends occasionally had had to forage, eating the scrawny tiny birds unlucky enough to fall into their traps.

"We got those birds but it was hard sometimes", he would say in a deep voice. "We took a dustbin lid and put a stick under it with a long, long string attached. We put a little *kwon* inside", the father told his son, referring to the corn staple known elsewhere in Kenya as *ugali*. "Then we hid under bushes and waited. The bird would fly down and go inside. We pulled the string, but sometimes it fell this way or that and *OOOYYYYYYYYYYYYOOOOOO* the bird would escape. But sometimes they were trapped." He laughed harshly. "They were so much more tasty than just eating *kwon!*" The two would laugh.

David was reminded of the bird's nest soup in China that went for hundreds of dollars a bowl and was a measure of one's wealth. He remembered seeing and, like his father, trapping those African birds. They were scrawny things, thin, bony, virtually tasteless. *Would Chinese eat them?* he wondered.

David recalled the story with some tenderness. Father and son had briefly bonded during storytelling, but such moments were rare. In general, he felt his father and he had a bond borne more of respect than love, something that was almost *feminine* in its undercurrent of fear. David remembered, soon after such reflective moments, how his father, after a bad day at the office, would return home from a night of drinking at the Norfolk Hotel. When he saw the boy and his doting mother he would bellow, "This place is filthy! Do something about it. Give me food and stop tending to that brat." In a Dionysian rage he would thrash his white wife and terrify his coffee colored child. If he tried he could still hear the screams.

How *random these thoughts are*, he said to himself. No logic, no order, just streams of memories cascading down like confetti from a rooftop. From the streets of Shenzhen some strains from a popular children's song drifted into his room.

Xiao yan zi chuan hua yi
Nian nian chun tian lai zhe li

Little Swallow Wearing Pretty Clothes
Every Spring You Fly Here

He remembered the bugler of Alego. *Why the bugler? Why tonight?*

As he was growing up in Nairobi there would be three important school breaks, each about a month in duration. During these breaks, at least once a year, his father would drive his white American wife and son back to the town of Alego to visit the ancestral home. Each night his father would visit the local pub, a grimy two room brick house where the locals gathered. Under the smoky haze and heat of bare 200W light bulbs beads of sweat glistened like rivulets of miniature diamonds: in the mock grimaces of their gleaming ebony faces and moist cracks and wreaths of their smiles the whites of men's eyes would turn into a devilish pink. The after-effects of these African bacchanals could be seen across the country in the narcoleptic walks and bloodied eyes that attached themselves like stigmata to these drinkers, Kenya's fat-cats, corrupt politicians, wife-beaters, lazy do nothing lotharios- well into the lucent blue of the following midday.

David idly fingered the photo between his thumb and index finger. He remembered the thick voluptuous, oily smell of local fermented maize *kong'o* and the noise of the rock and roll from the local radio station, low key and seeping everywhere like an invisible ether. The boy was used to going to sleep at 9 or 10 each night. The father would forget the boy and the woman as he drank into the night. David's mother would sneak away to the smaller adjoining storage room and tuck him onto the tiny iron framed bed.

"You can sleep here a bit and when we go I'll wake you."

But it was always too loud to sleep in this alien commotion and the mosquitoes would bite him when he dozed off. One night the clamor was so loud he had no choice but to come out. He stood glumly next to his father and mother and the women and men who sat happily gossiping and chattering on white plastic chairs before simple, wet wooden tables filled with beer bottles and glasses. Among them, weaving like a black Santa without reindeer was the bugler of Alego. Dressed in his straw loin clothes, long bead necklaces and traditional Luo hat, his distended bare potbelly and jolly face were a terrifying sight. When he lifted his wooden clarinet-like horn to his fleshy lips, his cheeks blew up, in a Dizzy Gillespie fashion, to an incredible size. It was as though both sides of his face had been hijacked by shining, coffee colored footballs. The child looked in amazement at the two glistening orbs as though afraid they would burst, so tight was the bulging skin. From behind the obscene cheeks small eyes were narrowed to slits that shone with a maniacal intensity. And then that sound issued forth; high pitched and yodeling as if to the very gates of hell or heaven. It was deep, throaty, feminine, masculine all at once as it leaped from the pub and towards the gorges and valleys, thrusting through the secrets of nighttime Alego like a hell-driven banshee. And just as suddenly, the sound would cease and the face would shrink – back to the jovial, blubbery visage of the old bugler.

Back in Shenzhen David's eyes grew heavy and he slept. Outside the bird had long left its lofty vantage point and the warm pink flood of morning flowed like a stream of honey into the black cracks of the city below.

David had been in Shenzhen just a few weeks. The day he arrived, on his way from the Shenzhen airport by taxi, the other red Jettas careered crazily about the streets. On the highway, or broad roads such as Shennan Lu, carts and bicycles and even a lone motorcycle carting two passengers moved in opposite directions. He pointed this out to the driver who just laughed like someone who doesn't see the point of the question. They arrived at the hotel where he was to be picked up by the teaching school representatives. While he waited several people in the lobby looked at him curiously. It was as though he were a circus curiosity. Their looks were concentrated and direct, neither hostile nor friendly. Occasionally they were sensual, leering, paternalistic or solicitous. Most of all they were *zoo-like*, like the look of a child licking an ice cream bar while peering at the creature behind the cage. In much of China the foreigner is a curiosity and the source of myths, legends and superstition. To the simple citizen, or villager, foreigners have strange appearances and stranger fashions. Their bodies are often bigger and broader next to the generally slim Chinese.

And they have hair on their arms.

A friend of David's had almost resigned from his $200,000 a year expatriate job because he had hairy arms. At a corporate lunch in Shenzhen, (so his friend had recounted to David) one of the Chinese guests had made a joke to an associate, who then broke into a broad smile. Not understanding the Chinese but hearing the reference to foreigners (disparagingly referred to as *LaoWai*), David's friend had asked someone sitting next to him to translate what had just been said.

"Oh, they are joking about your arms. They say the hair is a sign of primitive development."

"Well, you can just tell him that Chinese women need to shave their armpits. Chinese women have hair in their noses, not to mention zero asses and no tits. But it's the hair that freaks me dude. Every time I have a date with one of them I have to bring along my Norelco."

David's friend had responded tartly, half miffed, half in jest, not realizing that one of the guests understood English. This businessman complained to a VP at the party, with the result that a row ensued behind the scenes. Even the New York headquarters were involved in what became known as the "Battle of the Hairs". A faction within the law office in New York defended his comment as an innocent joke, while another branch, local to Shenzhen and with many native Chinese employees, insisted he had defamed the fair face of Chinese womanhood. Finally, some higher up is reputed to have solved the matter with a brief (never discovered) memo, which said

"Foreigners will always be barbarians, so just give him a reprimand, reduce his bonus and let's go on with making money! *TaiWu Liao!*"

And having declared the matter as not worth his time, the higher up turned his attention back to making money and playing golf. Per his memo, action was taken and the matter was not discussed again.

It would take David years to get used to this *otherness*. Yet whether it was the sentry trying to stop him entering a building, while letting locals glide by, or the instinctive pulling away of some local women when he drew near, or the occasional taunts of children crying the words for *Black Foreigner!* (*Hei LaoWai*) nevertheless he felt immensely privileged to be living in China. He remained convinced of the essential goodness of these people. It was an optimism ringed with caution, sprinkled with some small dislike, but fueled by an overwhelming curiosity and attraction to Chinese culture. Other foreigners despised this in your face *otherness* - so profoundly did they feel like animals in a zoo. But he was, unlike most, an exile who had long been habituated to being a stranger in all lands. He was a Jew who didn't like *borscht*, he was black, and he had survived living in Georgia.

In addition he had the benefit of an almost profound obliviousness to slights. In most cases, for his thick skin to be breached, no less than a physical push or the forceful and omnipotent word *no* would be required. Yet here in

China *no* was a powerful and slippery concept for him to grasp. To the Chinese, it was the ultimate relationship breaker, a word so fraught with power that it was rarely said. "I have something else to do that day…" they might politely say in refusing an invitation. "This might be hard to do….I do not know…" might be said in declining to do something. All these comments were hints and allusions. And to fully understand them, one had oneself to be skilled in hints and allusions. There were many reasons for this culture of veils. In a society of hundreds of millions of people, keeping secrets while maintaining social harmony quickly becomes a matter of personal survival. China has always had its own internet. Words fly fast and thousands of infinitely complex sensations and gossip items are available to all those with a subscription. Hence *no* was too direct a sound. Furthermore, among the more educated it lacked what the French call *bon ton*. Some had said to David that Chinese are inscrutable actors. He would begin to see that although they had many masks, often all these masks were true.

At a computer bar one day David sat across from a girl who was using her computer's skype software to talk to 4 people separately and simultaneously. Although he did not understand exactly what she was saying he knew enough to see that she had developed a different persona for each person she was talking to.

"Let's go shopping, hit *Hua Cheng Bei* street. And then get some drinks."

Her speech was rapid fire, staccato like as she used the local Guangdong dialect.

"Hold it," she then said, and switched to the other caller.

" I think I can convince him to buy more, but it's hard."

This time her speech was in bland Mandarin, slower and business-like. Then she switched into English for another caller.

"You are so BAAAAD. You teach me OKAY" and she giggled a lot. Then she launched into some simple Chinese sentences, very slowly and without the Chinese accents, just like foreigners speak bad Chinese. She giggled flirtatiously.

"Hold on."

Switch 4. She was back to the Guangdong dialect.

"*Shu Shu*, I bought some juicy raisins and plums from *Xin Jiang* for you, *Tai Tai* and little *Mei Mei*. They are so sweet and tasty. Tell auntie and my little sister I'll be there soon."

Then she switched back to the sales talk in Mandarin. In each case, her face and speech was quite different. Realizing that David was looking at her she glared at him accusingly. He quickly turned back to his computer. David knew that these masks were genuine each in their own way. He had come to realize that, like most good actors, the Chinese lose themselves in their roles, until they become a contiguous whole. What he didn't know, but would find out soon, was that a *no* could become a *yes*, a smile would hide sharp teeth. a *maybe* could mean certainty. In Chinese culture the goal becomes the means. And the means is a circuitous path, drawn out by *maybe* and double negatives. "Who does not know..."replaces "Everyone knows." "I really cannot not do this.." becomes "I must...". At the end of the day, when words evolve into actions, the actions themselves are performed within an unstated timeline and seem purposeless. Words, actions, speech – all stood on the periphery of one's consciousness. David would realize he was unschooled in such things. It was a catch 22 situation. To understand China one had to artfully conceal. But for that one had to be Chinese. This meant one must take pains to understand the language, the culture, and the women, particularly the women.

"Chairman Deng Xiao Ping discussed the issue of developing special economic zones and stimulating economic development with his associates. He said:We will set up a special economic zone, put it into practice, develop some clear ideas, not just about receiving things, but about doing things proactively. The special zones will be a window, a technology window, a management window, a window of knowledge, even of foreign strategies. Outside of the special zones, we can consider developing a number of ports, such as at Dalian, Qingdao...let some places start to flourish...
These words were uttered from Jan 24 to Jan 29, 1984, when he inspected the Special Economic Zones (SEZ) of Shenzhen and Zhuhai."

-Adapted from the *Xian Three Qin Capital City News*, July 2008

CITY AND SCHOOL

7:30 am. It was time to go to class.

First he had an appointment with the assistant headmaster of the school.

The Shenzhen International Bilingual School was situated on a quiet street near a busy intersection, its white and green walls were almost hidden behind the tall leafy trees. On the long and broad boulevard beside the school mangrove and cypress trees cast deep and soothing blankets of shade over pedestrians and cyclists. Protected by leafy branches several meters high one could wait at a bus stop without fear of the harsh noonday sun. On certain evenings the wind rustled through the leaves, mourning unintelligible hymns and delivering sweet scents as if from a divine place. He had fallen in love with these trees the first time he had seen them. He found them grand, profound, slaked in history. Their chocolate boughs and green arbors seemed like thousands of fingers stretched across the sky, casually sweeping away unclean sounds, harsh lights and ugly shapes, leaving behind a place of stillness and placid repose. Their beaten, weatherworn and husky trunks were in some places black with soot from passing cars — but to him these smudges were emblems of honor, signposts of history in a city that lacked it.

Like most Chinese public schools, high walls circumscribed the buildings. The main gate stood state-like and solemn. Across the street a little mom and pop store sold the chocolate ice-cream bars loved by the foreign teachers. On one side of the gate were small stores selling Japanese sweets and confectionaries, bottled water and package tours to Hong Kong. The other side was a short quiet walk to the busy intersection. The barred iron gate was about two meters tall and was opened only for official vehicles. Cut into its left side was a small pedestrian entrance, next to which was a guardhouse whose blue uniformed guard stood ramrod straight under a yellow canopy.

Proceeding into the school, one would first see the looming six story tall green and white painted buildings on the left and right. The vast quadrangle would then open up before one like a placid white sea. The large quadrangle reminded David of another school he had briefly visited, the Shenzhen Foreign Languages School. Situated on Hong Li Road, it was one of the oldest and most respected schools in Shenzhen. As one entered the gates, one would see on the right a lofty marble like wall inscribed with embossed calligraphy of Deng Xiao Ping.

Education Must Meet The Needs Of Modernization, The World And The Future

ran in English beneath the flowing Chinese text. The calligraphy was bold and flowing, and made a strong impression on Chinese and foreigner visitors alike. A huge green banner about two meters in height ringed the quadrangle ahead. On it an exhortation proudly rang out in large white English letters:

A foreign language is a weapon in the struggle of life.

The *e* of *language* was partially obscured by a hastily constructed basketball hoop. The effect was that when he first saw it it read like:

A foreigner engaged is a weapon in the struggle of life.

"I guess I should get a Chinese girlfriend so I can defend myself!" he had joked at the time. His Chinese hosts did not understand the joke and smiled condescendingly.

In this school there was no such quotation. Just a large quadrangle. There was, however, a basketball hoop. The top two floors held apartments for senior teachers and foreigners. The lower two classroom floors bustled with middle school students and teachers. Domestics and low seniority Chinese teachers lived on the middle two floors, sometimes packed four to a room.

After he lost his job the American University had hired him. By that time he had already resolved to go to China. While browsing in a bookstore in Morristown, New Jersey, he had come across a magazine article about English teachers living and working abroad. A short phone call, a brief but impressive emailed resume, an eloquent explanation of his dream – and he was in the teaching program. The school had provided free housing (with bathroom, kitchen, and air conditioning), RMB 5,000 per month salary, two weeks holiday for Chinese New Year, no more than 8 classes a week, the work visa, and airfare to and from China. Most importantly, the teachers and students were his initial shoehorn into China. Through them he learned about living in the country and would make important friends and contacts.

The foreign teachers of the teaching program were all Americans and lived in various schools around the city. They were a mixed lot, in their twenties and thirties. His apartment was next to that of Eric, at 20 the youngest teacher in the program. Eric was quiet and modest, and made extra money teaching 'business English' (so he called it) to Shenzhen businessmen. In his spare time he could also be seen, like a white banshee in yellow hot pants, racing his bicycle along the city sidewalks (The street traffic wasn't safe) to his appointments and local soccer games. For one so young he was deadly serious, rarely smiled and if he did, awkwardly, as if it was a courtesy.

"Don't bother with the TV."

he pointed out as he showed off his apartment to David.

"Just 2 English channels and a lot of hair and shampoo commercials."

His face had that hard to read un-demonstrativeness that is typically middle American. It was a healthy jock look, almost disarming —at once gently smiling and softly weeping - without the facial tics and nervous features of the stressed and vulnerable, like the French and Italians. The American face, particularly the mid-western face, is a study in blandness. Inside a cauldron of passion may boil, yet the features outside imperceptibly, reluctantly creak.

The other American teachers in the program were also each distinct and aloof in their energetic, ambitious, clean-linened, sweaty, khaki coutured, sexual, wide-eyed, earnest, idealistic, youthful way. The pimply blond from New Jersey boasted of the job offers she was balancing without committing. The Hispanic from New York shaved his own head ("no good barbers here") and couldn't wait to get back to America to drive his hot rod.

And then there was Ronald. He had been in the country for longer than any of the other teachers. While he had started out at the same school as David, he now juggled teaching with sales training at an electronics exporting company in the Bao An District. An African American from New York, he had that lightness of spirit that is uniquely American, that is to say, guileless, naïve, optimistic, but also wildly opinionated.

Some days back David had dropped and damaged his notebook computer. Ever since then he had looked for someone to help repair the screen.

"Ask Ronald, he'll know exactly what to do."

someone had suggested, tone muted, as though passing on the location of the night's rave party. And Ronald had been happy to help. They had set off to look for a repair shop.

They took the minibus from Cai Tian Road to the bus stop on Shennan Boulevard. Once off the bus the two set off at a fast walk towards the market.

The sight of the lanky, feline Ronald barreling down the street, his head pointed ahead, almost overshooting his feet, his long dreadlocks swatting his ears and cheeks, two bright and luminous eyes sucking in the sights and shapes around him, often drew stares, smirks and occasional hoots. Frequently pretty schoolgirls, their white teeth beaming, red lips softly parted, would flash him a playful wink or a coquettish smile. Ronald was a free spirit in every sense of the word. He was flabbergasted and amazed, admiring of and at the same time repelled by China. He explored China's nooks and crevices, sought the palatable and not so palatable, made of its bizarre terrain a habitation and a temporary home. As for those who frowned upon his willingness to explore the unseemly, he shrugged and gave his "What me worry?" Alfred E. Neumann look.

"Girls, girls, pretty massage!"

A short middle aged woman in a red shirt with a huge pot belly shoved brochures of pretty women in front of him. For a fleeting moment, he was filled with a powerful desire to get laid. There were so many gorgeous woman all around. Everyone said they were all looking for foreign men. He sighed and suspended the thought.

"How's work coming along?" David asked.

"Dude, Foreigners working for Chinese get a shitload of scrutiny. Their threads, their bags, it's all about status. Chinese are so fucking conservative. The foreigner must fit in."

"It's true.", David nodded, "They don't say it to your face, but they are always looking closely at everything you do. Even the way you eat! "

"The other day the Chinese GM told me I couldn't wear jeans because they were too informal. Yet the day after he said this I counted several staffers wearing jeans. I said to him "Hey man, all these other guys are wearing jeans. What gives? Why single out me?" He just shrugged dude and said, "No, it is not true. It's our company rule." I pointed out someone wearing jeans, and he just shrugged, "You're a foreigner. It's different""

Ronald went on, he was just warming up.

"The other month, he wouldn't pay me my salary. He asked me to wait a few weeks – gave some excuse. Shit. I wouldn't take that. I refused to leave his office. "I am not going to leave this office until you pay me." I told him."

"What did he do?"

"He had no choice. I would have stayed overnight. Shamed him. He paid me, but was unhappy about it. And dude, it's not how good your work is, it's the *way* you work, and *how long*. And the hours you work. If you come in early, leave late, that is a good sign. If you come in late, leave early, but do your work brilliantly, you're a bad worker. I wrote down the following DO NOT list. You want to hear it? I'll put it on my web site. "

Without waiting for David's answer he stopped in his tracks, fished in his khaki pant pockets and pulled out a piece of paper.

"This is my first draft

DO NOT wear jeans

DO NOT wear any form of headdress, even on weekends

DO NOT leave before the boss leaves

DO NOT arrive after the boss arrives

DO NOT send emails that directly criticize someone

DO NOT waste electricity

DO NOT call out to employees in the office

DO NOT criticize racist, anti-Japanese, xenophobic emails

DO NOT be black

OK the last one was a bit of an exaggeration. "

The two continued to make small talk. Soon they had reached the famous electronics market on Hua Cheng Bei Road.

Shenzhen's most famous electronic market sits like a huge white marshmallow astride the intersection of two of Shenzhen's busiest streets, Hua Cheng Bei Road and Shennan Boulevard. Imagine Ebay's electronics section transformed into a huge physical supermarket, and that's the Electronics Market of Shenzhen. Over 13 floors are jam packed with kiosks, booths and showrooms selling every imaginable electronic appliance, microprocessors, battery chargers, cell phones, computers, PDAs, CDs, DVDs, plasma display panels and hundreds of other electronic parts and devices. Outside on the street the human waves of Chinese pedestrians and hawkers resemble a Wall Street rush hour compressed into minutes. David was reminded of the Nairobi open air supermarket at Westlands, where spinach, mangoes, lettuce, potatoes, tilapia fish, slabs of beef, oranges, and other produce and viands were sold in unregulated abandon, the ground filthy with mud and squashed and rotting vegetables. Here the floor was cleaner but the chaotic environment was similar.

Entering the mall is an experience for any stranger. Shoppers and hawkers here are decidedly more upscale than their Kenyan, and more downscale than their American, counterparts. They bustle and bargain at an almost hyperkinetic pace for blocks on end. In the blazing heat of summer, the crowd pushes away from the street inwards towards the open shop doors from which billow cool and comforting air-conditioned gusts of wind. On circular brick benches wrapped like orange plastic lips around tall palm trees, people lounge and chatter. Each have their myriad reasons, but it seems they sit down most of all to just look at life's miracle in all its flourishing, decadent, irrepressible glory.

As one heads towards the huge marshmallow ahead, it is as though one is swept up like a surfboard on the crest of a wave. Yet, unlike the surfer, one is almost exhausted at the maneuvering, strategizing, ducking, twisting, weaving, and stepping required to get through the crowd. Miraculously, however, perhaps due to the fluidity and instinctive agility of the Chinese, one almost never makes skin contact or bumps into anyone. The crowd grows thicker. One knows one is closer as the vendors more insistently shove their DVDs in front of the foreigner, yelling,

"DVD, DVD. Good movie. Have fun. Hello! Hello!"

Finally, as if with a great belch, one is suddenly propelled from the open mouth of the street into the cooler confines of the great electronics bazaar. 5000 people, 5000 square meters on each level, connected only by 30 moving escalators and, further within the labyrinth of stalls and shops, 15 elevators and innumerable staircases. One often wonders how people actually locate specific vendors. The first time visitor can search for a floor plan in vain. Then, many visits later, after experiencing the sheer multitude of shops, one finally realizes that directions here are an unconscious thing. Locations stay in place for months, even years, and people eventually grow used to the two or three stalls where they want to do business – and that's enough knowledge. Any more is best left to curious foreigners, like David and Ronald.

This great eastern bazaar gave them a taste of the miracle of modern China. Here circuit boards and binary codes mixed with flesh and sinew in a great digital ecosystem whose plankton were the cold, hard currencies of renminbi, dollars and euros.

Amid the noise and din, the two of them were swept up the escalators to the third floor. The football field size open space was filled with rows of small booths each about one to two meters wide and deep, with a counter in front and merchandise piled up behind. Two or three salespeople sat before each counter, haggling with customers, dozing, observing, surfing the internet or slurping noodles from plastic foam containers. High above them, rows of neon lights harshly shone down on the sales floor.

They stopped in front of a small booth pressed against a back wall.

"Hello *Lao Ban*." Ronald greeted a man who was bent over a desk, peering at the innards of a circuit board.

He looked up with some irritation at being distracted and tossed back his tousled rusty hair. Adjusting his glasses he recognized Ronald and gave a weak smile. He nodded courteously and looked inquiringly at David.

"This is my friend, also from America."

Ronald quickly said.

"Very good, very good!" The man replied in rapid Chinese, his glasses trembling on his oily nose.

"You want to give him a good deal on a computer screen. His laptop is broken."

"Me see, let me see. "

He looked at the Dell notebook.

"Very hard to get this! Made in America yes? "

"Yes."

"Hard to find, hard to get!"

"*Lao Ban*, how much to get a new screen? "

The man picked up a calculator whose numbers were faded from frequent use and punched in some numbers. Then he placed the screen right in front of David's nose.

"Money, money, OK, OK?" he said in English.

David and Ronald looked at the screen. Before David could say anything, Ronald chipped in.

"Man, 800! That's *too* expensive. You can give us a big discount. I know. "

"No, no, no. This is the price. "The older man shook his head.

"600."

"No, no."

"*Lao Ban* you have to make it less. I'm an old customer, or we go. "

Ronald made a motion as if to leave. The shopkeeper hesitated, shook his head.

"750."

"700."

"OK."

Quite proud, Ronald turned to David.

"That's a good price man. His products are also covered by a year guarantee. And you can trust there aren't shoddy materials."

David paid the shopkeeper. He would return in a few days for the notebook. He felt the price was still a tad high but shrugged.

Ronald had just returned from a trip to nearby Guangzhou City's famous open market. Over cappuccinos at the local Shanghai Hotel they discussed the trip. Ronald had documented everything he saw, including the sorry poodles, pigs, snakes, turtles, cats caged and on sale.

"All those animals were about to be *eaten*! Dude, I photographed this old lady who was selling cats, dogs and turtles. She thought I was photographing this huge turtle man but it was her *feet* dude...her feet were on the turtle's back and they were so fucking ugly man I just...I just had to get it. Then she got sort of suspicious and stopped smiling and removed them. But it was too late. You can see the pics on my web site. Take a look!"

And Ronald smiled with such proud bravura no one would have had the heart to chastise him.

At the school there were a few people from the American University program who he was in regular contact with. Apart from some friends like Ronald, there was his adviser Tracy, director Helene Sadek and the assistant headmaster Mr Deng. Like moons circling around his planet, they whizzed in and out of David's orbit from day to day, week to week.

David had a Chinese teacher assigned to him. Tracy advised him on the dos and don'ts. If he had questions about where to go shopping or, in particular, how to modify his class teaching schedule (for teaching to him was a diversion, an unimportant thing), he would just ask Tracy. If she didn't have a ready answer, she would whisk out her cell phone from her fake *Vuitton* handbag, clasp it to her chubby ears, tweak her nose, adjust her eyeglasses (all with one hand) and shoot a staccato like stream of Chinese into the handset. Every so often she nodded her head in agreement and said *Hao De, Hao De*, sometimes in an unbroken streak until it sounded like the guttural mating call of a marshland bird.

Tracy hardly ever smiled, or perhaps she just smiled too much for David to actually notice. Many Chinese smiles are instinctive and unfelt. Westerners tend to smile when they are happy. Chinese, on the other hand, smile whether they are happy or not. To them a smile is above all a courtesy, and, at minimum, a Pavlovian knee kick - but always helps break the ice with foreigners. Conversely, Tracy never seemed put out by David's seemingly selfish and unreasonable demands. At the eleventh hour he might want to change the class schedule, and although this was simply not done and almost impossible to manage, she would at least try.

Tracy was an ambitious and smart teacher. Her mother and father had raised her in poverty in distant Hunan province, breaking their backs in construction yards and knitting mills to save college money for their daughter. In China, there is little or no government aid or scholarships for students. They must not only compete against thousands of others for limited places, but also dig deep into family savings. She viewed foreigners as tools for her advancement. It was not that she did not have feelings or empathy. In fact when dealing with the *Lao Wai* she was very understanding and almost motherly. But there was no real relationship. Relationships, what the Chinese call *guanxi*, is a product of family or of years of mutual friendship and experience. When it came to work, how much money she made was key. She made 3000 *Yuan* a month, including housing which was gratis. In a year she would probably be promoted and her salary would increase to five or six thousand. All she needed to do was make no mistakes.

She also had a work ethic that inevitably, like a bone deep power, led her to exceed expectations. She was young, but she wasn't naïve. She knew that a well-placed comment from a foreigner had a powerful resonance in Chinese society, whether negative or positive, reasonable or unreasonable. What foreigners said or wrote was like the invisible trail of paper that worked chameleon-like through the strata of society. The Kafkian trail would never reveal itself in its entirety, but always be part of a cause or an effect. Foreigners had outsized influence in China. They could be hated, loved, praised, demonized, brutalized, criticized, cursed, but they could not be ignored. For the ambitious Chinese who worked among them, it was always as though they were climbing two mountains at once, one foot on a ladder of Confucian values, and the other on a steep cliff of Western constructs, precariously and fatally balanced.

Helene Sadek was the resident director. A fast speaking Californian, she was the mother hen of the group, always bustling around in her wrap around silk dresses, her fleshy red face puffed up and anxious as she tended to her brood. She was also a Coptic Orthodox with a PhD in education. Her parents had immigrated with her as a child to the United States. She still had a slight accent that she stressed whenever she raised her voice or was agitated.

"Now don't forget," she told him over lunch at a vegetarian restaurant, "Shenzhen is a place where you can get laid just because you're an American. I would definitely not recommend sleeping around with the AIDS thing everywhere. But these girls will do anything to get married for a quick passage back to America."

David sat up in his chair. He had visions of lines and lines of beautiful Chinese women queuing up to meet him and saying "Can you teach me English? I'll teach you Chinese. Then we can make love, get married and go to America, OK?" He was 'OK' with all of the above, except the getting married part. He liked being single. He cleared his throat and took a sip of tea.

Helene gulped down a tofu crab cake as though she were plugging a hole in her throat, using her whole hand rather than the fingers to push the food down.

"And don't be taken in by their courtesy and smiles. They are always observing you. It will *never* change. Just smile and say yes. Yes. Yes."

She said something to the waiter and leaned over to another teacher, a handsome blond Iowan who just smiled sweetly.

"Yes, Jackie love, don't you start showing him around to all your pretty girlfriends. But he's smart," she slyly winked at David, "He's no *lucky ducky!*"

She absorbed and eliminated the second crab cake.

She was not David's boss, and wisely did not pretend to be. In any case, he had no boss. For him that boss thing was left behind in America. To David, Helene was a helpful associate, and sometimes a friend.

Helene was a fierce combination of intellect and physique, mentally robust and empowered, and always in pursuit of a holistic lifestyle. She was a facilitator par excellence. She made China easier for the expatriates, and was proud of her 10 years of living in China and ability to get along with the locals.

"Someone once told me," she said, "Helene you're more Chinese that many Chinese!", this said without an inkling of arrogance but with a touch of pride, as though remarking on a treasured teacup, or explaining her family's passed down salad tossing technique. In Helene's playbook language was about nuance and gesture, the purposeful use of body and vocals. She never said *no* in the presence of others. Denials were low-grade affirmations. In this strange place, the two of them fashioned their speech in the familiar tenses, he black and she white, pressed together in their state of exile. Alone with him, she was more direct, and he welcomed that, as a man lost in the desert who heads straight for the oasis. There was camaraderie of sorts in their conversations.

It reminded him of how African Americans living in white society had, over the generations, developed their own flavors of intimacy, saying things among themselves they would never say to whites.

He reached the assistant headmaster's office on the second floor.

He knocked on the door and walked in the large room. A man was quietly sitting at his desk, several feet from the door, as though hiding from the sounds of children and the glare of sunlight.

"Oh, Mr. David, you're here for our little chat. Please, please sit down."

Mr Deng waved David to a chair in front of the desk and smiled cryptically. This was their third or fourth interview. The assistant headmaster called them his 'little chats', just the two men discussing the work. To David, however, it was clearly one of a series of interviews in which the assistant headmaster could probe the American's weaknesses and strengths.

"Don't worry, you'll fit in here.", Mr Deng said without enthusiasm. He stayed seated.

Mr Deng was a short man. How short, no one seemed to know, because he never seemed to leave his desk and stand up. He had a large mop of black hair, almost like an Elvis do, that arched over his wide square glasses. Like a modern mandarin, he sat with arms crossed behind his office desk, listening and speaking slowly, as if mentally processing every word beforehand. He was something of a cipher - like the school headmaster, whom no-one ever seemed to see - and cautious and deliberate. He was a man who gave and took sparingly, from the words and thoughts he shared, the crisp and careful manner in which he walked, the money he reluctantly spent and even, it seemed, the air he breathed. He would purse his lips tightly, like a fish, as though inhaling with great care and with the utmost intention of absorbing just enough oxygen to survive, and not a whit more. As he looked at the black man sitting across from him he noticed the hair on the forearms and mentally logged this phenomenon as another reason to distrust foreigners.

"They may be technologically ahead of us", Mr Deng remembered his mother saying while wagging her finger, "but they don't wash enough, they refuse to shave correctly and they insist on using tissue paper and towels for wiping their asses. They don't throw away their tissue paper, they have sex before marriage, and do not look after their old people."

The assistant headmaster had categorized these life observations into four basic groupings that to him summarized the failings of Western Society : 1) Rampant sex (Chinese were discreet and more efficient), 2) Sloppy appearances

restaurants, the continual hum and din – and yet to him it was so delicious. A green street sign loomed over a nearby road, its three Chinese characters atop their pin yin transliteration Ai Hua Lu. *The first character is beautiful*, he thought, *like three dominos tumbling onto the roof of a house*. He absent-mindedly wondered what character it was.

David was now living in a country on the move and Shenzhen was its avatar. Finally unburdened by the shackles of war or the excesses of ideology, China had poured billions into its cities, infrastructure and people. To walk on the streets of its newest city, Shenzhen, just over thirty years old, was to see a place that reached for the stars. The new conference center with its wave like curves that washed colors of gold, white and orange over the city at night, the gleaming subways that shot its metal bullets through the innards of the city from dawn to late at night, the soaring banks and hospitals whose windows, like encrusted diamonds, sparkled in the rarefied air, all said to the world *Look At Me*. In all of this gleaming metal and marble, rough stone and wet concrete and loam, clean linen clothes and cellphones galore, even in the filth and garbage that streamed from the shanty towns to the streams and in the hard-scrabble canteens and worker dormitories that leached pain and desperation, there was still the unmistakable rush of hope and promise, and belief, that not only to be rich was a glorious thing, but that hard work would always be rewarded,

And there was no harder worker than the Chinese of Shenzhen who often toiled 14 to 15 hours a day, six days a week. From 4 or 5 in the morning, when the sounds of cars and buses would slowly increase in intensity to 8, even 10 at night. From the Luo Hu Station with its brand new passenger terminals to the *Window of The World* theme parks, from Shennan boulevard to Hong Li Road, from Futian district to Bao An, they would stream forth in their daily lust for wealth. The murmur of a city wakening, galloping and cantering would throb through high-rise windows and bedroom doors from morning through evening. China was loud, not occasionally loud, but persistently, abrasively, extremely loud. It was as though the Chinese had finally found their Munch's *Scream*. Wherever one went, people would scream into their cell phones, cars would honk at leaves falling in their paths, drinkers would toast each other in stentorian tones. TVs would be turned on full blast. Hearing was acutely sensitive, such that a bus driver could hear an old woman's question from half the length of the bus behind him without shouting "What? What did you say?" Thus their vocal range covered the entire spectrum, from *piano* through *triple fortissimo*. This loudness was rooted in a fear of being isolated and rejected, a brash *look at me for I exist*. It was also part of a self-absorption that ignores strangers and is prevalent in modern culture. Thus in villages and apartment blocks people would heap their smelly socks and shoes right outside their doors, their laundry and household offal on every available balcony, for all to see. It was not about being purposely rude. It was about having no relationship with strangers, no *guanxi*.

But David forgave all these things. He looked around with bright, curious eyes. At times he was seized with the thrill of this land. A shiver would travel up his legs and through his arms, and give him a jolt of energy. How wonderful to live in a place that was all about expectations and promise. At these times, the storyline wasn't about China or its advance in the world. It was about personal possibilities. It was about the future and the desire to live a better life than one's parents. When he had had enough of the future, there was always the present to nourish him. And when culture wasn't enough, there was love to be had. And he needed love. Not the love that finds sweet, brief relief in a sweaty bed, but something more enduring, more rooted. He sought balance and was starting to find it in the language and the traditional culture of China. The experience was like a fugue of Bach's. The people, the language, their dreams, their calligraphy and art, their interactions with foreigners, even their architecture were all musical melodies. Melodies in four, five even six parts would intertwine like snakes between one's fingers, sometimes dissonant, other times consonant, but with direction, perpetual motion, and, occasionally, a superb grace.

A road sweeper on an old dilapidated bike trundled by him, her head covered with a huge conical sunshade in Burberry patterns. Ahead of him on the sidewalk, a man stood beside his loaded bicycle. It was heaped from saddle to tray with at least two to three meters of bulging plastic bags and cartons that wobbled like a totem on a balloon. Dressed in plain blue shirt, trousers and plastic sandals, the elderly man gingerly steered inch-by-inch, foot-by-foot past the curbs, potholes and flashing metal. *Look how we persevere*, David thought. *This man has spent half an hour navigating a few meters of road, but he will get to his destination. Focus on the next few steps, and forget about everything else. This is life.*

All of a sudden he felt quite happy. Why happy? Why now? People paid attention to him. The girls standing in front of the restaurants on the streets looked at him with some interest. He knew he was in good health and had a reasonable sum of money in his bank account. He anticipated the pleasant warmth of a cup of green tea resting against his fingers. *But is there another reason*, he thought, *has it something to do with this road sweeper?* He often ascribed his optimism to some inner refusal to be beaten down, like a buoy that refuses to sink in a vast sea. He knew that inclement things were not innately hostile to him. God (if he existed), the weather, the weavings of fate – these things were not necessarily *against* him – they were just *indifferent* to him. So in the face of this pantheistic nonchalance, he only had hope to rely upon. And hope filled him like water saturates a sponge.

Even when he visited Hong Kong.

"I've been there before." a Hong Kong girl shop assistant once told David, speaking of the mainland, "It's frightening."

David had visited Hong Kong a few times since arriving in Shenzhen.

Although it reverted back to Chinese control in 1995, this former British colony reflects the effects of class distinction in subtle ways. The use of English rather than the national language Mandarin, the border controls that wall off the populous mainlanders, and the occasional disparaging comment towards the territory "on the other side" – all these serve to reinforce the separation of the two territories.

Although Hong Kong lies just across the narrow bay from Shenzhen, the ostensibly simple trip is complicated by border checks and slow trains. To travel from Shenzhen to Hong Kong, one typically crosses the border checkpoint at Luo Hu in Shenzhen, then takes the special train to one of the crossover points, such as Tsim Tsa Shui station, and finally takes the city subway (or bus) to one's destination.

When one exits the subway into Hong Kong one may be forgiven for feeling one is stepping into a sloppy, though relatively, clean mouth. The walls and narrow streets are crammed close. The shopping arcades and modern looking shops and restaurants are crowded. Like fleshy projectiles, people dart in every direction, skillfully, as in Shenzhen, avoiding body contact. Above one's head the pale blue sky is impaled by the hard edges of lofty buildings.

David preferred Shenzhen. There was a world weariness about Hong Kong that sterilized it. In his opinion Shenzhenites, as he called them, embodied his dreams and aspirations. Hong Kong, on the other hand, was all about *been there*, *done that*. There were physical irritations too. In the city buses he would constantly bump his head on the low roofs and feel claustrophobic on the packed streets.

Nevertheless, since many of the government visa offices were located in Hong Kong he had no choice but to visit.

On one Saturday visit he had stopped by a local culture fair in Yong Leow, a suburb of Hong Kong. He sat before the proscenium that afternoon watching various musical skits and performances in Cantonese. Cantonese is a Chinese variant native to upwards of eighty million people in southern China, Hong Kong and Taiwan. The announcer, a young woman with tight jeans that often slipped sideways on her rump, suddenly broke from her Cantonese and yelled in English,

"Hello, any tourists here?"

All of a sudden there was a rush of movement around David. Various pockets of the crowd made (to him) unintelligible sounds and pointed at him. Shocked out of his anonymity he timidly raised his hand.

"Hello, where are you from?"

She spoke in a stentorian voice, waving her free hand, the other clutching the mike.

"Mei Guo, Mei Guo!"

he said, using the mandarin term for the United States.

"America, American!"

some in the crowd roared. The people sitting in front of David, a couple with their daughter, turned around and looked at him, smiling, and the grannies next to him did the same. The little girl looked at David as if in shock and hid behind her father.

"Do you like it here?" the announcer mercilessly continued.

"Tai Bang Le!" (Very much!) he bellowed.

"Great!" she laughed and with that turned to other matters. The crowd laughed good naturedly.

Meanwhile the little girl kept scowling at him until he took her photo with the digital camera, at which she flipped out and finally smiled.

Later that afternoon he managed to process his visa fairly quickly and headed back to Shenzhen. On the train back to Luo Hu, the train was packed with weekend commuters and families heading back home. Tired from walking and standing much of the day, he grabbed a seat before a woman and her two kids could seize it. Although the train was crowded and he had been courteous up to that moment, he was gripped by a desire to have things his way. *By God, I am going to have that seat*, he said to himself. As a result, one of the kids, a five or six year old, had to stand, refusing to squeeze onto the seat between his mother and David. Feelings of guilt weighed upon him all the way back to Shenzhen. *Seats are golden*, he thought, *why should I have to be so damn courteous?*

At the border crossing on the Shenzhen side, he wasn't sure how to fill the paper work so he headed to the local visa office, also situated inside the terminal. It was a brightly lit office the size of a large living room with surprisingly comfortable leather chairs. Behind windowed partitions sat border officers, with their heads constantly bent down so that, were it not for the grim scowls on their faces, one might think they were praying.

"Which form should I fill?"

The officer ignored him, peering at a mysterious spot somewhere on his counter.

A man came up to David, smiling nervously. He had a mop of black hair, was dressed in a casual shirt and shorts. David guessed he was in his late thirties.

"You should fill it in here and just hand it to the officer at the window counter, with your passport of course., "

He had a strong American accent. He was probably Chinese American, David thought. The man showed David which parts to fill in.

"Thanks."

They made some small talk.

"Where are you from?" David asked.

"San Francisco. I live in Hong Kong and am trying to get into Shenzhen."

"Why are you going into Shenzhen?"

"To work but..." And he suddenly leaned his head forward until it was almost touching David's. He spoke quietly, almost confidentially,

"I shouldn't be telling you this...here... but I'm not sure I'm going to get my visa."

"Why not?"

"When I filled in the paper work they asked me why I didn't use my Chinese name or spell it out in Chinese characters. Then they said I couldn't get it today."

"What, because you didn't spell out the Chinese!"

"Yeah, they were suspicious. As for me, It been so long since I spoke Chinese I can't remember. So I asked them where in the rules it said that..."

"And..."

"And they got really upset and told me that I was not allowed to ask them anything about the rules, and for that I would not get my passport. So anyway, I've been very nice to them since then. But I may have to go back to HK tonight if they don't give it to me."

David wished him luck and headed back to Shenzhen. The other man just gave him a weak smile.

At the counter the customs officer looked bemused, peered at David, and then at his passport picture. He gave a half leer and showed the passport to a woman officer next to him. She nodded uncommittedly. He then let the officer in the booth on his left take a look.

"Yea it's OK, He looks young, that's all!" the other replied.

"Yeah, I look like a young man!" David said, smiling good naturedly.

The officer gave him an icy I-haven't-finished-yet-so-please-continue-to-look-scared-and-shut-up-when-I'm working type of look. He held up the passport to the light and again scanned him. David rolled his eyes. He sensed how the officer hungered for something, however small, to detain him with. But there was nothing. He finally let him through.

Later that evening he reviewed his diary, as he did every day, and added some more notes.

The New China As once posted on streets during the early days of Shekou, the port district of Shenzhen, the slogans **Zeit Is Geld** *(German for* **Time is Money**) *and* **Efficiency is Life** *continue to be the mantras of latter day Shenzhenites. At the time the bold pursuit of wealth was anathema to adherents of conservative communist doctrine. How things change!*

The New Wild West As a city grows, so do its people. To many who first arrived in Shenzhen over twenty years ago, the dream has been realized. There is no single culture in Shenzhen. It is a mix of people from different parts of China, each imbuing the city with its unique vitality. From the vast reaches of Tibet and Shangri La to the bookstores and narrow streets of Beijing and Hangzhou, from the villages of Lijiang to the clay mines of Henan, a new multi-cultural phenomenon has arrived. The dreams and vigor of its ever-varying inhabitants create a cycle of energy that constantly rejuvenates itself. Shenzhen is the mill and the Chinese people are the rushing water that drives the wheel around.

I stride far from the land of right angles As America is full of right angles, Shenzhen's streets are full of twists and turns. With the exception of two or three major thoroughfares, the streets and alleys of this otherwise modern city are the finest examples of metropolitan obfuscation China has to offer.

A Boom City's Soul Shenzhen's soul is like its immigrant inhabitants, at once dispersed and congealed, radiating outwards and flowing inwards, like the ever changing facets of a kaleidoscope.

He had received emails from some American friends. There was nothing from his mother. He wrote her a short email.

Liebe Mutter!
    This may be a bit of a surprise but...
    *It's as though being in a strange place has opened me up a bit. Or a part of me
has wanted to open up. This land is amazing. To visit China must be like when the
settlers first arrived in the New World. Perhaps it's like a movie I saw. A guy had a
heart attack and almost died. Afterwards he saw things very differently. He sought
deeper relationships with others, particularly women. I feel I am in the Wild West, or
should I say Wild East. Shenzhen is like a frontier town. Dynamic, young, exciting,
and a little dangerous. As Nietzsche once said, it is time to re-evaluate all values.*
    *Recently I found an old photograph of my father. I had forgotten what he
looked like. It had been so long. I don't even remember where this photo came from.
A whole host of memories suddenly bubbled up. These memories cascaded down on
me and I was overwhelmed. Which were true? Which were false? Many places were
dark. Some were light. Maybe someday you can help me separate the truth from the
fiction?*
More later,
D.

On impulse he reached for the US passport sitting on his desk. He flipped
open the little blue book. Most of the pages were filled with visas from the
various countries he had been to. All were small, unpretentious seals stamped
in red or black. The Chinese seal was the only one that occupied a full page.
He was relieved to finally have his China visa. It had been a hard slog through
the Kafka-like morass of Chinese bureaucracy. It was only a temporary 30-day
visa, but it was a certification of sorts, an official brand of his legitimacy. He
sent the following email to some friends in the United States:

Hi Guys:
    *The latest from the front. Finally got my multiple entry visa. While the school
is getting me a work visa I need a temporary visa and it was no joke getting it!
Here's the process I followed.*
    *Yesterday afternoon Sara (the Shenzhen Bureau of Education contact) and the
assistant headmaster, Mr Deng, called me at the school. Sara suggests I meet her on
Friday, which is when we believe my 5-day visa will expire. She says the medical
exam is much less important for now but that it will be good if I have it before we
meet.*
    *At the school Tracy (my contact teacher) tells me there has been a change in
plans and that the assistant headmaster wants me to go to Hong Kong on Thursday*

to get a 5-day visa again. I'm confused so I suggest I talk to Sara and find out 1) if we're still on track for Friday and 2) whether I really need to go all the way back to Hong Kong. I tell Tracy that I will call her as soon as I hear from Sara and she agrees. OK, I'm just getting started. This process ain't for the squeamish!

Later Wednesday I call Sara. She is on a train to Guangzhou (a neighboring city) and tells me that she cannot meet on Friday but suggests Monday. She also says the visa will expire on Thursday so I get a 5 day visa or a 1 month visa. She advises me the 1-month is better since the 5 day extension raises more questions in people's minds as to whether I'm a tourist or an employee. She doesn't know whether I need to go to Hong Kong or whether I can get the visa in Shenzhen or any more specifics (and complains that if I had come in September none of this would have happened.). Suggests I talk to Helene to decide on the 1-month or the 5-day. Later I discuss with Tracy. Tracy says Helene knows the specifics on how to get a visa. Helene sends me an email suggesting 1 month.

Thursday morning I call Helene and we determine options to get the 1-month visa. I should either go to HK or get it in Shenzhen at the DiWang building (this is one of the largest buildings in China). Incidentally Ronald (another teacher here) had told me that visas were available at Di Wang. But that's another story. I also suggest, and Helene agrees, that I get the health examination done in the morning and in the afternoon go to the Shenzhen office for the visa.

I get lost on the way to the hospital. Helene helps me direct the taxi driver over the phone. Once there I find out that there is a 500-Yuan charge, which is way beyond anything I expected. I don't think anyone had told me just how expensive this whole process is. Anyway, I don't have the money so I take another taxi and look for the bank. With no bank in the vicinity I am at a loss on what to tell the taxi driver. Helene on the mobile helps again. I spot a bank, pull the taxi over, find out that the bank machine doesn't accept my card and return to find the taxi has left. I get another taxi. The taxi driver fortunately understands some of my Chinese and gestures. We find the bank. I get the money and return to the hospital (by 'magic' taxi).

The rest of the examination goes OK (I have to return in the next few days to pick up the certificate.)

Next step: The Shenzhen Public Security bureau. This is not in the Di Wang building, as Ronald had said, but about two blocks down from it. About eleven o'clock I pull up in another taxi (I must have spent about twenty bucks on taxis today). The clerk informs me (after ignoring a very irate man who is teething and foaming over some red passports on the counter in front of him while his wife and infant baby look on) that they do not issue 30 day or 5 day visas, only work visas.

He gives me the address in Hong Kong (written in Chinese characters which I can give any taxi driver). He does not provide a phone number for me to call them in advance.

About 2 o'clock I arrive by taxi at the border crossing. The trip into HK is uneventful except that the address I was given is being renovated (so an elderly, fastidiously uniformed guard tells me) and the visa office is now on Kennedy Street. So I take another taxi to Kennedy street where, fortunate to already have the required photos in hand, I go through the application process.

The clerk at the window questions my address at the school and forces me to say a blatant lie that I'm not working there. I do not know what repercussions this will have. I'm concerned that someone will investigate and maybe throw me out of the country. Anyway the lie is said and she tells me to return about 5pm. She also informs me that the charge for the 1-day processing will be 400 Hong Kong dollars (another surprise).

After some yummy noodles for lunch and a little tourist exploring I head back and pick up the visa, hit the border crossing and head home with a 1-month visa.

Ain't it simple? Food for thought.

Until the next, stay in touch
David

"I started to cry. Later my father came to me as I stood alone on the street. I don't remember what he said but I think it was something like 'Don't worry. Be strong. She was no good. The woman who bore you will soon be forgotten. You are older now and do not need her. She will be forgotten, for that is the way of our people.'"

- From David's father's journal

THE DANCER

"You're best suited for the younger children. They listen to you. They are obedient when you teach. That is very good."

Mr Deng decided early on that David would not teach at the main middle school, but in one of the nearby smaller, satellite schools. David had felt a little miffed. *Why are they wasting my time with small children*, he asked himself. He took some comfort in reasoning he wouldn't teach forever. In time he would get some other job. Secondly, if he made mistakes teaching, the younger students would be less critical.

One day, after observing David in class, Mr Deng invited him for lunch. They set off together to a nearby restaurant, about a ten-minute walk. During the entire stroll the assistant headmaster was uncharacteristically mum. His lips pursed, his eyes were cast down aiming somewhere just in front of his Italian made leather loafers. He suddenly made a comment. David didn't hear him clearly. He was looking at a short message on his cell phone someone had translated for him.

> *People don't say the truth*
> *They say stocks are drugs but they play the market*
> *They say money is evil but will do anything to have some*
> *They say beautiful women are unlucky but go after them anyway*
> *They say smoking and drinking are unhealthy yet don't stop*
> *They say heaven is beautiful, yet never get there*
> *In today's society, the poor eat meat, the rich eat shrimp and political*
> *leaders eat each other*

"Pardon me?" He looked up apologetically at Mr Deng.

"Book 2. The students must understand it entirely." The assistant headmaster gently chided. He seemed to take almost a personal interest in the new teacher, as though he were a prodigal child.

Science Book 2 was the officially sanctioned school text. Slavishly adhered to by thousands of elementary scool teachers in Southern China, it is prepared by the GBELC-CTFLESS (Greater Guangdong Board of Education in liaison with the Committee for the Teaching of Foreign Languages in Elementary Schools for Shenzhen). David thought the committee born text was boring, lifeless and too rigorous for children.

Mr Deng thought otherwise. His interest was more than intellectual. His brother in law was a member of the committee and had just been arrested for soliciting sexual favors from a woman who desperately wanted her child to pass an examination managed by the board. That morning he had heard the news. His first reaction had been to wash his hands, his second to berate his wife for not replenishing his favorite bottled soap, his third to rub his hands nervously, his fourth, to call his sister and berate her for not being able to control her husband, and his fifth, to review with his new teacher, in detail and with utmost urgency, the two imperatives: Science Book 2 and the importance of being on time for class.

Mr Deng's attention switched to the bustling restaurant. A young women at the restaurant entrance welcomed guests inside. Various live animals and fish in pots, pans, cages and tanks were displayed besides the door. He didn't say anything but waited until they were seated.

"Yes, Book 2." Mr Deng continued,

"And there is no substitute for being on time." he added.

He took a very small portion of the mushroom dish before him. He fastidiously leaned his head just centimeters above the dish, chopsticks delicately clicking, placing food in almost slow motion between his tight, pursed lips.

"Everything else must be subordinated to this. I'm sure it's very different in America. Please eat. Please enjoy."

His guest dipped with abandon into the bamboo shoots, dumplings, fried corn and beans, pumpkin pancakes, sautéed string beans, diced chicken with spicy sauce and fried bean curd. The waitresses looked over his shoulders with interest as he gulped down the food with a large fork, dropping morsels onto the table.

"Have some tea."

And then, to his astonishment, Mr. Deng gently took the teapot, stood up and walked around the circular table and poured out his tea for him. David remembered Helene's comments from a few days back,

"The Chinese take great pride in subordinating themselves. The person who humbles himself most is greatly respected."

After lunch he headed back to the teacher's lounge. He wouldn't be teaching anymore today. It was a large sunlit room, neatly filled with white metal desks arranged in a long row by the windows and in a cluster in the center of the room. He sat down heavily at his own small desk, glad to be away from Mr Deng's paternalistic attention. Several teachers were milling around, some at their desks chatting, others helping a student or two resolve a problem. Bored he decided to go to a local tea house close by.

"Where are you going, David?" Laurie, a fellow Chinese teacher, asked him. Laurie was short and plump and held her hair tightly wrapped in a bun. She spoke the King's English, was a covert Christian (her church was not officially sanctioned), and always held a secret smile on her face. She liked foreigners even though one of their most visible imports, the huge WalMart stores, had worked her to the bone until she quit. She had decided to help David fit in with the school and looked upon him almost tenderly, as though he were a younger brother. In fact he was much older than her.

"I'm going to visit a teahouse and study a bit." He said somewhat reluctantly.

Laurie's eyes lighted up.

"Oh that sounds like fun. It's so boring here." She giggled. David knew that was her way of saying she wanted to come along. He had hoped for some solitude but he sighed.

"Would you like to come?"

Laurie leaped at the opportunity. Soon Laurie, her best friend Miss Hu and David left for the small and elegant tea house situated on the second floor of an apartment block. On the landing below was a Kodak photo shop run by a young man and his wife, and next to it a beauty parlor where the wealthy Shenzhen mistresses of Hong Kong businessmen went to get their feet waxed and fingers manicured. Large red silk curtains with calligraphic prints bordered the large wooden doors. Inside it was cool and relaxing. A small spring in the corner of the large room tinkled in the silence. In the middle of the afternoon there were few customers. They sat down in the expansive cushioned wooden seats and ordered their tea.

He did not see her at first, but then became aware that someone was looking at him. From the corner of his eye he saw a woman standing by the entrance, discreetly observing him. When she saw him looking away she quickly turned away and half seriously, half casually, said something inconsequential to another woman standing next to her. From the manner in which she talked David guessed that she was perhaps a team leader or manager. Laurie noticed David looking at her.

"Isn't she beautiful?"

Laurie said this to him that day not just because Laurie saw the good in everybody and everything (which she did), but because she felt David was lonely (which he was). Sensing her kindness he had put down the book he was reading and repeated her phrase mechanically.

"Yes, she is beautiful" almost with nonchalance.

Then he had looked at the woman again. She had a way of staring at people when they were not looking and she was staring directly at him. Her face was impassive, but her posture, extended forward in the direction of her subject, like a crane about to seize a fish, her beautiful ivory neck ramrod stiff and straight, revealed her intense interest. She had looked at him with that unique gaze just for an instant. Even if her face was wax, her body spoke volumes. Like a dancer, the face and head were exotic appendages. The arch of the neck, though mostly straight, the light tilt of the torso, and the gentle slope of arms were held slightly away from the body. He saw her as if she were an eagle perched for flight on the edge of a cliff, facing him, with curious eyes, but with the slightest hint of disdain.

"Very beautiful person."

But it was as though he was commenting on some abstract painting. To him she was a curiosity, beautiful in a classical Chinese way, with round features, narrow eyes, perfect skin and a very thin body. He saw her as if on the periphery of his consciousness. And the woman, hearing what they said, looked at him as though for the first time, perhaps because he said it with a measure of nonchalance, and with an oblique allusiveness that an imaginative person could read the world into.

And he had smiled broadly, all the time looking at her. She had quickly flushed and turned her head away. Nevertheless , there wasn't much work to do and she looked at him closely when he was talking to Laurie and Miss Hu. She noticed the expensive, but shabby clothes, the wrinkles beneath his eyes that betrayed his age, and at first saw nothing special. She saw but did not see. She saw a foreigner, a man who laughed often and heartily with these other two woman, but also was inscrutable. He was not that interested in her, so she thought, and *that* was unusual for a man. Few men were capable of ignoring her. She decided to come over. She would practice her English. She didn't have to say anything because David saw her coming and immediately greeted her.

"Hi!"

She did not know what to say. Flustered she replied in Chinese.

"*Ni Hao!*"

She wondered why she was nervous. *Foreigners always make me nervous*, she angrily scolded herself.

"I like your tea." David said. She corrected his Chinese.

"Thanks, my Chinese is very poor!"

"No, very good!" She smiled, holding up her thumb.

"David do you want something to eat?" Laurie interrupted, avoiding the other woman's eyes.

"Yes, I'll eat some food." He attempted to say in Chinese.

The women all laughed. Laurie explained.

"No," that does not mean "I'm going to eat food". It means "I want to beg for money"

He looked around, embarrassed. The woman's eyes saw a flash of fear. *He's afraid*, she thought. *He wants so much to be accepted. He's afraid their laughter will turn against him.* Suddenly, she wanted to know more about him.

The first day they had exchanged some small talk. She spoke enough English to carry a simple conversation. Afterwards he came back more frequently, this time alone. She would serve him tea and a small meal. From that first day that David called her beautiful she had started to pay more attention to him. She was curious about him. He had arrived at the tea house suddenly and mysteriously, bringing the freshness, allure and romance of America. He tended to speak directly, without the emotional distance that formalizes and characterizes Chinese relations. As though instinctively, she would not let the other girls tend to him. He encouraged her attention, often smiling at her when she passed by. When she saw him bring some books one day and write some characters she stopped by.

"You write Chinese?"

"A little. I am trying."

"That character is wrong. Let me show you." She bent over and wrote the character he was writing, this time correctly.

"Just that little dot, small thing!" David exclaimed, smiling.

"Yes but in Chinese details matter. Otherwise the writing looks ugly!"

She suddenly realized she felt very comfortable around him. It was as though she was able to speak freely. That initial reserve and halting conversation of the first day had gone.

From that day on they talked more, first about Chinese, then about their lives. He learned more about her and she about him.

Her name was Fu Chun. In Chinese *Chun* means Spring. Chun Tian was a name her parents had chosen to evoke the freshness and beauty of spring. Her name had often provoked derision from older relatives and strangers. In Chinese mythology this season is the one in which the male and sexual overtones are ascendant. The word *Chun* is often used in connection with fertility. There were the *Chun Hua* books and pictures (such as those of the great Ming Painter Qui Ying) whose libidinous images taught young people the intricacies of sex. *Just one spring breeze* was often a metaphor for a one-night stand, and *Spring Palace* (*Chun Gong*) was a metaphor for blue movies. But she would bat these references aside. These were the thoughts of older generations. Younger people associated *Chun* with youth and hope, freshness and new ideas. She would also think of the great historical *Spring and Autumn Annals*, or the Spring Palace of ancient China situated outside the east gate of the capital. Nevertheless, as she was growing up she welcomed the use of the less embarrassing *Chun Zi*, or *Little Spring*, which was often used in reference to children. She had decided to use the English name for that season, and thus, unlike many English names adopted by Chinese, there was a close correlation between their actual and adopted names.

Spring was only 24, almost thirty years younger than David. She had a great imagination. She had been in Shenzhen for a little over a year.

"You like Spring don't you?" Laurie said to him one day. He had been going to the tea house more frequently and she had noticed. Everyone was talking about it.

"David is going to fall in love with a Chinese girl." Laurie had told her husband.

He had just shrugged,

"These foreign teachers, they all just want to sleep with Chinese girls, then they run away back to America."

Laurie playfully hit him with her pillow.

"*Huai Dan!* You rascal!"

David wondered how Laurie knew so much about Spring and him. It was as though in China details about one's private live spread faster than the internet.

"How did you know her name?"

"She told me when we met."

"She's beautiful isn't she? Too beautiful for a tea house I think." Laurie added.

David shrugged, irritated. From then on he tried to see less of Laurie.

He didn't care where Spring worked. He had seen all sorts of women in his long life; rich New York debutantes, struggling Hispanic students, bored housewives, Starbucks coffee girls. His mother had been a secretary, his father had once been a goat herder. What were these artificial social classes to him? If he cared for or liked someone that was most important. If she had a pretty face and a nice body that was icing on the cake. And anyway, he was lonely and didn't have time to be a picky elitist.

"Do you want to really speak Chinese well?" Spring asked him one day.

"Very much."

"If you give me an English lesson then I will teach you some Chinese." she said smiling. She showed him a green book titled 5 minutes of English a Day.

"I'm studying this book!" she laughed gaily.

They found time to meet during the lunch hour which in China lasts for over an hour and a half. She would come to the school where they would meet in the music room. The first time she brought a friend with her, another girl who had just arrived in Shenzhen and was looking for work.

"Why don't you get a higher paying job at a trading company or business?" he asked Spring's friend after she told him she had a university degree.

"Ha!", she laughed derisively, "You don't know anything about China. You have to have a Shenzhen hukou to get good jobs in Shenzhen. Spring knows."

David looked at Spring, who nodded.

In later meetings Spring would arrive alone.

One day she saw the radio cassette player and switched it on. She took a few pirouettes. She was in a happy mood. David was astonished.

"I didn't know you danced!"

Although Spring had not told David she had been a professional dancer before. She had worked for almost two years as a principal dancer for a troupe in Macao. She had left that job when the manager, a tall domineering man, had told her one night to work longer than she had initially agreed to. He was a balding man, with expensive eyeglasses he was quite proud of. He could often be seen polishing the large frames with an almost manic intensity. He had a great admiration for German opera, particularly Mahler, and when long ago a woman he adored once exclaimed, 'What a handsome man Mahler is, and what beautiful glasses!' he promptly dispatched an order at the local optician's. However, the glasses delivered to him differed in certain details. He complained but to no avail. When the optician asked him why he wanted a particular design and wasn't happy with this one he walked off in a huff after bargaining down the price. He was actually quite pleased with the spectacles, but he saw no reason why he had to explain to a stranger his admiration for a woman. On the frame was a large logo. It was a red circle with a sickle and two mysterious characters D Z within. The effect was that late at night, because he had bloodshot eyes, he seemed to have three eyes, each very red and baleful.

Ever the martinet, his habit was to supervise the dancers late into the night. Spring was his best dancer, but one night she was feeling unwell. There was an ache in her ear and her jumps were not as high or as strong as she wanted. In addition, the night intruded upon her consciousness. The sky over Macao was gloomy, and over the dirty, rugged skyline of buildings and the open-air stage the clouds shone like soft, nebulous cotton balls. There was an indescribable feeling in the air, and the moon lent the scene an invisible force. For a moment, just as she was trying a difficult twist the words of a great and famous poem that every Chinese child knows by heart ran through her mind:

Before my bed, the bright moonlight
Casts its frost onto the ground

It was for only an instant, but long enough that she lost her balance and careered into another girl. She recovered and continued but the words of the poem continued to drive into the perfect center of this woman so young and bright with life. It was as though something within her was beckoning and the silvery moon was singing to her the remaining words of the poem,

I raise my head to look at the bright moon,
And lower it as I remember my hometown

So when the director demanded to know what was wrong and insisted she remain until 3 in the morning, well past the normal 1 or 2 am, she looked at his three baleful eyes, at the bare wooden floor and the elaborate spectacle of Qing dynasty costumes around her and in that moment decided it was time to move on....

"Come on, you should try." Spring smiled, beckoning David.

"No, But I'll play piano!" he laughed. He stepped to the piano to accompany her.

"I didn't know you play piano." She stopped, astonished.

"Well I do, so keep dancing."

So that afternoon he played piano for her. He had wrong notes everywhere. There was a time when he would have regretted ever playing in such a way, without regard for the accuracy of the intonation and pitch, but this was a different time, a different place. Spring clapped and laughed gaily.

Partly in jest, exuberant after his performance, he exclaimed,

"Well, if you teach me dancing I may teach you a little piano too. But they must be modern dance steps."

She nodded seriously.

David was a little surprised she assented so readily.

They met every schoolday promptly at 1 o'clock, when the children and other teachers typically took an afternoon nap. As she sat beside him on the stool in the music room reading English phrases from the grammar book he noticed things he hadn't noticed before, like the inky quality of her hair that seemed to absorb all light like a black hole at the beginning of time. He saw the smooth curves of her face. It was an oval, egg-shaped face, with a very smooth skin and large doe-like eyes. But it was her hair that imprisoned him. Although it was held back in a tight bun, it was a repressed force. He imagined how it must look when unraveled into all its magnificent length, like black strands of energy reaching down for a reunion with the very depths of the earth. He noticed the hair around her ears, even the occasional strand that lusciously reached from her armpit. Hers was not so much a physical beauty, as an almost aesthetic one, characterized by the word for beauty *Piao Liang*, or better *Chun Mei*, the latter words evoking the sad and mournful quality of music.

Her beauty was also a barrier for he could not read her mind, however hard he tried. His knowledge of Chinese was still extremely limited, and he was too old to rely on the impulsiveness or charm of youth. His approach to learning about her had to be one of understatement, of respect and caution. She knew very little English, but she was a quick learner. As for his dancing, he was energetic, but clumsy. His allotted half hour was a mix of bumps, bungled twists, and attempts to reduce the sweat on his brow without appearing too self-conscious. Spring just gave her beautiful smile. As they got to know each other more it seemed that she said less and less. It was as though they did not need to speak what they already understood. She did not have to say much to communicate with him. As far as he was concerned her silence was a blessing. It finally gave him an excuse to be quiet and to just listen...and watch. With English speakers, David would talk too rapidly, barraging them with thoughts and ideas that were imaginative, but too eager, and lacking in subtlety.

She sensed the deep hunger within his soul, that of a man who resisted change, then welcomed but could never quite catch up to it. There seemed also within David a certain melancholy – perhaps because time was passing by so fast and he had not discovered an alternative to life's transience – his immortality confirmed. She was ultimately a visual person. She felt what she saw. But her view of him extended beyond his clothes and the creeping bitterness in the way he walked. She fell for his eyes. They were naked things, so innocent and frank that they almost embarrassed her. They were brown and deep, like an open book.

David was aware of this attraction of his. Long ago, (so many things seemed long ago), a woman had said to him,

"You have beautiful eyes, but they do not show any love for me."

Another told him,

"That's the first thing I noticed about you, how your eyes were so wide as you looked at everything around you."

To her it seemed they would shimmer or dilate in proportion to his wonderment or his many moods. When she saw him narrow his eyes it wasn't because he was angry or uneasy. She felt he was just seeking to cover his nakedness, like Adonis or Eve ashamed, to prevent revealing the curious and secretive soul within.

But she did not see all these things right away. She would discover them over time, day after day, month after month. It was almost by a sort of osmosis that the physical quirks of this man blended for her into an entity of interest, then tolerance, respect and more.

As for her own eyes, she felt they were too small. Chinese tend to admire large eyes as a sign of beauty and she was no different in this respect.

He sat back and observed what was around him with an uncharacteristic indifference. It was as though the world passed him by and he experienced phenomena like motes on the edge of his consciousness. He tasted, touched, listened and saw but in return also only tasted, touched listened and saw. The deeper understanding that comes with judgment was beyond his penumbra.

Like a true existentialist, he wanted to experience the moment, but also be free to divorce himself from it immediately afterwards. As he grew older he had slowly begun to realize that life requires commitment, even if commitment means having memories that refuse to disappear. So, in the twilight of his life, for he was now over fifty, there was the paradox of a man who was capable of deep feeling, but was tugged on one hand by a tendency to intellectually reject meaningful events with an abruptness that could be startling in its execution, and on the other hand be haunted by memories of what might have been.

When he saw her sitting on the bench next to him, it was the like the first time he was seeing her. For the first time it was as though he knew her and would know her deeply, but he did not exactly understand why. He sensed her to be a catalyst in his life but his intellect did not recognize how. In the great Chinese novel *Dream of Red Mansions* the main protagonists have an inkling they have met before even though they have not. It is as though in some alternative existence they are linked like glass beads rolling on a foggy mirror, never sure where the true reflection lies.

Afterwards he had retreated to the library. He found quiet places a necessity. Like most deep men, he treasured solitude, even in the midst of chaos. That morning, as David looked out the window. It had just rained. The green, wet vegetation seemed covered in a light transparent oil. Sunlight on the leaves sparkled like gold dust. Children were playing in the courtyard. He wondered why it was that on an earth so blessed with life and fullness, so rich with love and the sun that radiated the pulse of the earth itself, he was so alone.

Later that evening he read again the letter he had received from his mother.

Liebe David:

You know I just got a computer so I thought – after thinking many times, including reading letters from you – let me start writing my notes on my life – for whom? I'm telling you this so you have a little background about my life before I met your father. I don't know but perhaps just for fun and for posterity, and for you too it seems! Now you want to know more so I guess you are the right vessel with whom to share my thoughts.

There are so many answers. Where do I start? Well, when I left home to work in Boston, I had just graduated from Simmons College. My first 'digs' when I left college were with my friend Marylou – and another girl on Charles Street, a supposedly exclusive area at the foot of Beacon Hill in Boston. It was a very small apartment and while there I worked for a lawyer, Mr. Gordon, on State Street in the financial district of Boston.

He was surprised she had written so much. Normally her writing was spartan and her missives were short. David realized he was embarrassed by her effusiveness. He felt she was revealing too much. It seemed almost uncouth to be poring over these old skeletons. He went on.

It was 1958 and I lived there for two years. During this time I think I was still finding my way a lot — the other girls were only interested in finding a husband — which the other girl did, I can't remember her name right now — and Marylou had a loser boyfriend —i.e. he was very unschooled, and she was very keen on learning. In fact, when we all broke up after two years together she went off to France to really learn French! And the other girl married her MIT boyfriend and lived happily ever after.

I can't say things as beautifully as you but it's the best I can remember and is the only way I know how! After about one year in this flat I moved on to Park Street with two good friends. These were rather dramatic times for me because several events happened which moved my life in a completely different direction. Meanwhile I had left my job with Mr. Gordon and was floating around in temporary secretarial jobs. Finally a good friend suggested I take a summer course to qualify as a Primary School Teacher (how things turn around, now that you too are teaching!). I did and then got a job in the Hartmann Elementary School. Every morning from September to June we would trudge off to our jobs — I taught 10-11 year olds and though I basically like teaching, since I had no experience. I was thoroughly exhausted most days. At the end of the year I was anemic. My two friends were also all teachers, so we were all busy that year.

One day, during this time, I was coming back to my flat on a streetcar and a black man sat behind me. I guess he thought I was not too threatening so we started to talk. He was from Nigeria and lived almost across the street from my flat. He invited me to a party or perhaps it was just to come and talk, so I did…one thing led to another and soon we were going steady. A lot of things happened after that and I met your father. That meeting was my destiny but I'll tell you later. I didn't intend to write such a long email but I got carried away.

Anyway I can tell you more of what I've written later.

Love,
Mutter

He didn't respond right away. He did not want to. He secretly took a deep breath of relief that she was so far away. He was thankful that from this distance he could ruminate and control the maelstrom of his emotions.

✳✳

One day Mr Deng stopped David in the hallway. He introduced David to two young women standing meekly beside him.

"You need to know more about this country. My two friends are good teachers. They understand the importance of science and they want to learn English. I told them you could help. Maybe you can go to the ethnic minority village together and learn about China's peoples."

He jumped at the opportunity. That afternoon the two visited Splendid China ethnic theme park, Together they walked through scores of miniature villages representing each of China's fifty-six ethnic minorities, from the Russian and Mongols of the northwest to the Key Zhu and Bay Zhu of the south and southwest. Day by day David became aware of the vastness of China, and the variety of its people. Yet he didn't need a theme park to tell him of the marvelous diversity of China — it was displayed on the streets of Shenzhen. Each day he would see the broad cheek-boned Han people, the creamy skinned Sichuan ladies, and the darker, swarthy Ke Zhu of Guangdong. Occasionally he saw the Muslim vendors from Xinjiang leaning against their carts decked out with sweat meats and raisins, their characteristic Islamic *kofias* leaning precariously over their half shaven, weather beaten faces. Sometimes he would see bald monks in their flowing custard yellow robes swiftly and purposely strolling along million dollar malls and beside parked BMWs. Most of these people, including some of the monks, had come to Shenzhen for one purpose — to get rich or as close to rich as possible.

Amidst this urban conglomeration of flora and fauna, he was profoundly aware of his solitude and reminded of Kenya. When growing up in Nairobi he had always been reminded of his separateness, either by allusion or directly.

"You cannot trust the Luos. They have big mouths and are always boasting. They think they are smarter than everyone else."

He remembered the words of the Kikuyu night watchman from long ago.

"I swear to goodness, they are just lazy good for nothings!", the old man had told the young boy before the warm fire beside the gate to their home in Nairobi.

They had been sitting beside the glowing flames, talking about nothing in particular. The boy felt a curious kinship with the watchman and enjoyed these rare evening meetings. In the husky darkness the distant hills rolled humplike beneath the luminous moon. The sound of the crickets beat an almost deafening tattoo across the fabric of the night. *When was it? I think it was during the rainy season I had visited his fire,* David guessed. The downpour of the past few days had left puddles next to the old man and the boy. As he listened to the watchman's stories the licking flames and moon were reflected in the water. Every so often a hidden object, perhaps an insect or a falling leaf would send ripples across the smooth surface, forming what seemed like thousands of moons and suns. *Maybe we're like these reflections*, he thought, *We break up and come together again when everything is peaceful.* So he dreamed.

In Kenya everything is tribal. David never understood why everything had to have a social flavor, and refused to recognize this for a long time. Retiring by nature, he ate his school lunches alone in the music room with a beat up old upright piano for company. Others taunted him,

"Why don't you come and play with us instead of hiding here?"

Once he tried to join their soccer game.

"Go away, *chotara, half caste!*" rang in his ears.

Their black faces looked at him laughingly. He couldn't reply. Those hated words froze him up.

During adolescence boys who had been friends for years would split up into their own groupings. *Birds fly with their own kind*, goes the Chinese expression. Luos with Luos. Indians with Indians, Kikuyus with Kikuyus. All that were left were the mixed race boys and the occasional white alien. *Multiracial society* was a term commonly used to describe Kenya. While growing up he never examined the validity of these words. He was lazy and took refuge in glib generalizations. He hid behind generalities and it was easy – for he treasured his solitude. Solitude has the double blessing of giving oneself freedom to both choose one's habitat and be free of social rules, regulations, criticism and taboos.

"Don't worry. You are a citizen of both worlds.", his mother would tell him if he happened to hint at his discomfort in this variegated world. He instinctively knew what others only sensed, that they all were exiles. At his school tribal associations came to trump patriotic pride or even long held friendships: the Kambas stayed with the Kambas, the Luhya with the Luhya, the Kikuyu with the Kikuyu, the Luo with the Luo and so on. The mixed races and the few whites were forced to find common ground among themselves.

This supremely variegated version of racial divisions that plagued America for 400 years had in Kenya existed for much longer.

Spring too was something of an exile. Her fate was to be a dancer working in a tea house, in a nation that extolled businessmen and bureaucrats. Except for calligraphy and brush painting, art in China is a low key affair. The government promotes so called 'cultural fairs'. The items on display and the artists supported often have a strong folk component. This art, though genuine, often has the effect of portraying minorities as benign, perennially happy, colorfully clothed folk dancers with quaint traditions. The raw stuff of personal and social psychological conflict often seen in western art is here rarely on display. Part of the reason is a quiet censorship but it also has much to do with the diminution of the individual in Chinese society. *Society first, Individual second* goes a well known expression.

She was working in the tea house for the money, not for the passion. Although she was determined to eventually find a job that would include her dancing for now she was content. She was paid over 3000 Yuan a month, had lodging and meals and was sending some money back to Henan to support her family. She was also not Han but of Manchu ancestry. Later, after she got to know him better, she lent him a book about the legendary Manchu Empress Cixi.

"We were once kings." She would later say to him.

"A great woman. My family." and her bad English trailed off.

She meant to say that her lineage was linked with that of the imperial family. In the last fifty to sixty years the Manchu had faced persecution and ostracism from the ruling Han (who in large part controlled the Communist Party). In the sixteen and seventeen hundreds the Manchu spread out from Mongolia and captured Beijing, which they made the capital of the Qing dynasty. They were a harsh people and their feudal systems were reputedly more severe than their Han counterparts. In time they merged with the Han and are now virtually indistinguishable. Although early communist leaders such as Sun Yat Sen tarred them as colonizers from outside, they were largely assimilated. Many changed their names to Han variants so they would be smoothly integrated into the system. However, Spring's family had maintained their surname *Fu*. These days her ancestral surname meant nothing. A hundred years ago it meant privilege and an aristocratic pedigree. Spring herself told David of her family's history.

"Our name is special. I tell everybody. We were once kings and queens. Do you know what they say to me?"

"What?"

"They say I am a rebel, a *fen qing*."

David thought it was an appropriate term for Spring. He felt she had something of an aristocratic aura about her. *Fen qing* is used to refer to youth in their twenties and thirties, somewhat contemptuous of the status quo, typically university educated, often bloggers, and fiercely proud of China. Their attitude is encapsulated in the two letter alternative they use to address themselves, FQ. Like Spring many Chinese pay special attention to their names and the characters that represent them. Written Chinese has a history of over 4000 years. Almost 40,000 symbols represent various sounds. Yet even with so many characters several Chinese sounds (such as the character for thorn) are unpronounceable in English, and vice versa.

He thought she was deep, like himself. To him not only was her skin as smooth as warm velvet, her body lithe and voluptuous but her smile was also like the veils of Maya. Beneath the veil was always another. Charm lay in her mystery. If one merely sought a smile and friendship that too would be forthcoming. Yet there would always be another veil to lift.

Perhaps it was David and Spring's shared sense of exile and solitude that attracted them to each other. One marvels at the miracle of different races falling in love. It is as if they are in rebellion at the great social forces that strive to keep them apart. This love testifies to the power of love over division, of universality over locality, of brotherhood over enmity, of the world over the nation, of friendship over duty. Neither of them knew these things when they met (perhaps they never would). They may not have cared to know. To her, reality did not lie in psychological constructs but in sounds, sights, shapes and colors. She was Spring, a woman in the prime of life, and Shenzhen was a city whose air was full of love and energy.

Sometimes people thought she was superficial. She craved quick gratification and loved what others thought trivial, such as the flowering of a weed in a pot, a cherry on a banana split, even mobile messages.

Such as the one she had received over the New Year.

Like many Chinese text messages, these poems and stories were passed on from friend to friend, acquaintance to acquaintance, originating and vanishing in the digital ether. From where they came no one knew.

When one has no money, one raises pigs,
When one has money, one raises dogs
No money, eat vegetables at home
Have money, eat vegetables at hotels
No money, drive cars on the road

Have money, ride treadmills at home
No money, try to get married
Have money, try to get divorced
No money, one's wife is one's secretary
Have money, the secretary is one's wife
No money, pretend to have it
Have money, pretend not to have it

This message was unusually long, at least four pages on her mobile. She nevertheless had saved it and forward it to her friends.

In the country chickens wake people up
In the cities, late night revelers wake up the chickens
In olden days, performers sold art
These days, they sell their bodies.
Its all such a fucking waste of time.

David walked out into the streets of Shenzhen that evening, and came across a cripple squeezing melodies from a *Suo Na*, a trumpet like flute. He passed by the restaurants with the garish red signs and beautiful women hostesses luring guests into their lairs. He saw the men squatting like praying mantises while at rest and observing the world as he did, and yet not as he did.

Even modern Shenzhen could not suppress the inner China that burst through the cosmetic western façade. Red was everywhere. Red signs, red clothes, red tassels and lanterns. Like a smoldering fire in the Chinese breast red and all its dynastic and communist significance were burned into the body politic, never extinguished. These days the ruby red of automobile lights and neon building signs seem like the glowing breath of the modern Chinese dragon.

David saw the women clustered in groups in front of rows of shoes for sale laid out neatly on the sidewalks, all the time watching Chinese soap operas on the TVs above their little kiosks. In darkened streets people walked around peering down at ubiquitous cell phones whose light reflected in their youthful faces, forming a ghostly flock of floating bluish white heads. Next to the fruit vendors men were sitting down in little groups on cheap plastic chairs loudly chatting, smoking, drinking cheap beer and eating barbequed chicken, squash, shrimps and onions, casually exposing their glowing white bellies to the cool air. Shenzhen men often dress formally, in simple cotton shirts (or golf shirts) and trousers. Even construction workers wear suits at times. They rarely wear hats, and almost always smoke. Warnings about the dangers of smoking are a lost language, and the Marlboro man silently lets loose his sickle. Chinese men rarely smile. In fact they often seem so serious and deadpan they put Eastern Europeans to shame. This evening he saw many men surrounded by their children. They would hug and play with them, smiles showing from ear to ear. It was as though a hidden, warm side of them emerged when among family. He saw a little boy held upside down by his grandmother as she inspected the crack in his bum. Another child on the sidewalk squatted and had a good pee in full view as she coached him on with a cluck-cluck or two of approval. *Sometimes*, he thought, *Shenzhen is like a great and booming potty training school.*

Above them the air seemed to tremble from the heat and smoke of their steaming plates. Wives with husbands in tow rolled trolleys filled with sheets of glass, wickerwork and other bric-a-brac. High up on the buildings the laundry hung out to dry, as if to waft away the sights and occasionally fulsome smells that issued from the streets below. The occasional Mercedes whizzed by, like an anachronism, into the night. And through all of this the music of the cripple seemed to beckon to David and convey the stories of ancient China, of passions and regrets, of lands far away, of great romances. The melody surged into the very depths of his soul, like a dance of kindred spirits on the edge of his existence, but within it at the same time.

Before he knew it he had walked several blocks. Lost in his reverie he found himself in a section of the city he did not recognize. It was getting late and was starting to drizzle slightly. Wanting to quickly return to the school he found a bus stop and hopped on number 12, which always stops outside the school. The bus was mostly filled with people returning from late evening work.

At the next stop a man entered the bus. He was middle aged, wore gray slacks and shoes and a simple t-shirt. He clutched an umbrella in one hand and a newspaper in the other. Recognizing the driver he sidled up to a nearby seat.

"Hey mate, what's up?"

He spoke slowly enough in Mandarin for David to understand.

"Class over already?"

The driver was a younger man, he wore a blue shirt over his white t-shirt, loose fitting and revealing a bulging belly. Whenever the bus slowed down or stopped he would lean back in his large seat, drag the back of his hand across his forehead as though wiping away sweat, and lean back as though to display his protuberant midsection.

"No, but the teacher kept spouting so much I couldn't take it. Had to leave!"

"Ha! No kidding."

"These classes cost a lot you know. 300 Yuan this time. And after driving my shift, it's exhausting."

"That much. I know some places that charge up to 900. They're always increasing prices."

"It's nothing to joke about!"

"Too true."

"300 Yuan! I think they raised the price."

"You bet, before it was only 50. Takes my breath away!"

"Too true."

The older man neatly unfolded his newspaper and started reading. David recognized the print and headlines of the *Global Times*, a popular international news daily. He awkwardly grasped a huge blue and white umbrella with some Chinese company logo in large white characters and crossed his legs to reveal white socks and a flash of skin above the ankle. After a brief silence he moved closer to the driver, where the light was brighter. He squinted in the direction of the wet windscreen (it was slightly drizzling).

"Can't see the damn paper! Fuck! I didn't bring my glasses."

"You can't see eh? That's a bummer."

"I forgot them today. It's also too dark."

"Getting old, y'are, that's it."

And they kept up the conversation. David loved to listen to these buddy conversations about nothing in particular. They were always so fluid and the people just took speech for granted. Somewhat cordial, somewhat flippant, always obliging. Sometimes they spoke their hometown dialects, which he didn't fully understand. However he understood the basic gist of their mandarin. At such times he felt he was finally penetrating the culture, and the simple and banal became almost an art form.

Back in the apartment, the table lamp softly shone a bath of purple light over the room, The kitchen was swathed in darkness but through the open window sounds of music from a distant bar could be faintly heard. On the corridor outside the door some footsteps clattered by, followed by silence.

He added some notes to his diary.

Why I am a great musician *To learn Chinese one must have the voice of a flute, the cultural sensitivity of a diplomat, the memory of an encyclopedia and an ability to dance. Spoken Chinese is amazingly sensitive to dips in pitch and volume. A high or low pitch for the same syllable differentiates buy from sell. Also vocal clarity is essential for distinguishing such consonants as 's', 'x', 'z','c'. Add to this over 4000 years of etiquette and one's lesson is still incomplete. To write Chinese, the sequence of strokes clarifies meaning. In quickly written script, where every stroke is not clear, only the sequence and rhythmic succession of strokes identifies the character. Yet how marvelous is the feeling of dancing with the brush and feeling the lilt and tempo of black ink over light paper. I realized from the first that to learn the language one must first be an artist, then a dancer. Behold the Immigrant Muse!*

I spy with my eye *Blackness is reviled discretely (as in America). Yet black basketball heroes are in. Large noses and mouths are out. Red lips, white teeth are in. Then again, all are balanced by other attributes. Those attributes considered negative are often offset by positives, such as wealth or prestigious citizenship. The Black American becomes the American Black. "I spy with my little eye" is a poem changed by my English students to "I spy with my eye…" And the little boys and girls complain they have slits for eyes. Yet as China loses itself in aesthetic ambiguity, it will slowly return to the beginning, richer than when it started. Ying brightens into Yang, which in turn revolves into Ying. It is as the last Goldberg Variation - it has returned to the aria, or so it seems, but it is richer, wiser and more full of dreams than ever before.*

On Conservative Chinese Girls *"Mrs. Li is a good conservative girl" says a man over lunch. Mrs. Li says, "I prefer to think of myself as a modern woman" and laughs. Conservative means respecting and obeying one's parents, getting married and having children, having good manners while advancing one's interests. Rebellious means refusing to sing the company song, frequently talking back to one's parents, staying single well into one's thirties or forties, even having many lovers. The archetypal classical rebel is Lin DaiYu, the heroine of the great 17th century novel "Dream of Red Mansions"*

Why I am a multitude *I refuse to own land, to have a family and all its useless appendages. Thus I am a stranger living amongst the most extended family in the world.*

He checked his email and wrote a short note.

Liebe Mutter!

Met someone recently. What a wonderful girl! She is a dancer and works in a tea house! She is from Henan province in China, called the heartland of China. I have come to know her quite well, as she wants to learn English and shares many of my musical tastes.

I feel really strange sharing this with you, but I realize how I never communicate about the people I've met. So I'll make a little exception this time. However, I am a crusty old dodger. You have pressed me so long to get married but it probably won't happen. I'm too set in my ways and I prefer my solitude.

Nevertheless, for the first time in a long while I feel I have met a kindred spirit in this girl (although, she's just 24 years old)

He didn't know how to end the email. *Should I really tell her about my romantic interests? I feel I should. After all, she's telling me about hers.* He typed in a few more words.

Back to basics! Your last epistle was truly food for thought. Obviously the Nigerian wasn't my father so tell me more! How did you meet the Old Man? What was it that drew you to him? The more specifics you give me the better! You tell me, I tell you. OK?

I also remember you used to play piano quite well and even considered a concert career. I never told you this, but in some ways I feel great guilt that I cut short what might have been a promising career. Better that you had not married and had me. By now you would be sharing the gift of music with the world in a concert career. My father also mistreated us. I sometimes think that I inherited his bad traits. These relationships with parents are a complex thing. You mentioned your mother and you also had some difficulties. She died when I was a child and I don't remember much. Tell me a bit about her. I'd like to know.
D.

That's that, he thought. He felt a little dirty, as though he was prying too much. He was reminded of once when he had seen his mother naked – something he didn't want to repeat. He did not realize that it was too late. He had opened the box and the creeping revelations would begin, first hints here and there, in time a raging flood of data. He hesitated for a minute then hit the *send* button.

That night he thought of Spring. What was she doing? Was she thinking of him? But he was filled with many other impressions. He was absorbing this strange place day by day and women were just a part, though an important part, of this strange land.

"I had collected some old pieces of wire that had been lying by the roadside where the big cars and trucks used to drive past on official business. Twisting them together I had made a little wire grooved wheel that I could push along with a stick. The children of the village had never seen something like this before. "Let me try, let me try!" they cried out. But I kept away from them because my father hated to see me play with them. "They are dirty and filthy. They will make you dirty and filthy too."

- From David's father's journal

THE CHILDREN

David taught 8 hours a week. Each class was about 45 minutes. He taught second and third level students who were 7 and 12 years old respectively. Today he was teaching the 12 year olds. Walking to class he could hear the jet-plane-whizzing-down-a-tunnel din that always erupted during classes. He nimbly stepped into the cleanly lit classroom and stood before the thirty odd well-dressed scions of Shenzhen's middle class elite.

"Hello Mr. David!" they promptly stood up and shouted in unison.

"Good morning. Please sit down."

They scrambled into their seats. They wore blue and white tracksuits that gave their bodies the look of giant amorphous blueberries.

Together they dutifully read Chapter 2 of the standard English textbook. Giggles and whispers bubbled up from among the blue and white ranks. The sound seemed to ebb and flow like a universal hum that varied in proportion to his monotonous voice. He suddenly closed the book and looked up. The students were talking among themselves, doodling, few were attentively listening. He realized he had to get their attention.

"Let's name some countries. 1 gold star for each correct answer! OK!"

The jet plane din continued, though at a lower level.

"OK?" he said louder, eyes glaring madly.

"OK!" they roared like an express train.

"America!" One hand popped up.

"Italy!" Another waved.

"France!" someone roared.

He wrote each correct answer on the blackboard. Then there was a blank silence. The teacher volunteered.

"How about in Asia? There's Japan. Say JAPAN!"

"JAPAN!" The class roared.

"There's Taiwan! Say TAIWAN."

There was a confused murmur, which petered out into silence.

"But teacher…" a fat little boy who was always quick to answer shot his hand up.

"Yes?"

"Taiwan is not a country. It's part of China!"

"Really…" and he realized that this was a faux pas.

In 1949, after losing the Chinese civil war, the Taiwanese Kuomintang party led by Chiang Kai Shek set up an alternative government in Taiwan and declared itself independent of China. Ever since then the two countries have locked horns over who belongs to who. Although it has its own indigenous population, Taiwan has for much of its history been colonized by Western and Asian countries, including Holland, China, and Japan. The mainland Chinese believe Taiwan is part of the motherland. They will vociferously, even violently, react to any claims to the contrary. The Taiwanese, on their part, believe their little island is a sovereign nation, under no compulsion to merge with the adjoining mainland. Official (and many unofficial) mainland Chinese discussions of Taiwan uncritically reject this thinking, and dismiss critics as 'provocateurs, 'renegades' and 'unrepresentative of the true will of the people.' David now realized this belief was not just a theory propounded by the communists in Beijing. In fact it was fiercely defended by locals and their children.

He scratched out *Taiwan* from the board.

Later they talked about some of the favorite things people do in their free time.

"Reading!" said one little boy who wore oversized glasses. He always seemed to be pointing his small nose before him at forty-five degrees to the horizontal as though he were balancing his spectacles.

"Soccer!"

"Ping Pong!" Others shouted.

The class was raucous. Some students were chatting and others were shouting out answers all at once.

So he decided to focus their attention.

"What about this!" he shouted.

He swung his legs onto his desk, stood up on the frail wood, and started dancing the mambo. He slowly gyrated his hips and made a swooning outward motion with his feet. He looked at the ceiling as if in reverie. The sea of blue and white before him turned silent, so suddenly he thought they had gone into shock. There was complete silence while he gyrated on the desk feet above the floor.

"Dancing!" he laughed.

The children just looked at him mouths wide open. The smallest little boy suddenly came up to him in a jerking motion, almost as though pulled by an invisible and wanton hand, and tugged his trousers.

"No! No teacher David! Don't do that!"

It was as though their teacher had committed a mortal offence. He had once again broken an unsaid code. For some reason he thought at that moment of a scene from the *Bridge on the River Kwai* when the English Officer was talking to the Japanese prison camp commandant. It had been something about allowing officers to do manual labor with the enlisted men. *British officers don't so that sort of thing! It's just not done!* or something like that.

He was an officer in this Confucian system. The students were the enlisted men. They could do naughty, outlandish things. But he couldn't. This first day he had already learned that the teacher occupies a special, almost revered place, among the Chinese. They are the high priests, schools are their temples, and students are disciples.

He realized he had let his trousers down, metaphorically speaking, so he jumped back onto the floor. This time the students were quieter and more obedient. They did not know what to make of him.

After the bell rang a girl came up to him and started to feel his hand, massaging the long hair on his arm.

"You have so much hair!" she laughed.

Then another girl who had not said a world during the entire session showed him the crucifix dangling from her neck.

"You see, I believe in Jesus." and she smiled, her beautiful white teeth sullied only by one black gap.

She fiddled with the little gold cross, her small fingers caressing and running over the golden yellow object with a nervous love. He thought of the Chinese girls who always walked on the street, arms linked and heads bent gently inclined towards each other, speechlessly intimate, like spirits who find in each other their mutual benediction.

"Do you believe in Jesus?" she asked.

"No, not really!"

"Why?"

"I just don't. Some people are different."

"Are you American?"

"Yes."

"I want to learn break dancing too!" And she smiled anxiously, all the while rolling her fingers over the crucifix.

The boy with the awkward glasses said "Can you teach me to break dance?" Unconsciously he took David's hand in his own. David looked at the child's large owl-like eyes and was speechless for a moment.

David had little patience, particularly with children, and yet he was very popular. The children listened to him and confided in him. To them he was a strange concoction American clothing, chocolate skin, deep voice, gruff demeanor and omniscient knowledge. He liked children, but in an abstract sense. He felt they not only had energy, love, ideas but also had needs he alone could satisfy. A liberal thinker driven by a conservative heart, he was full of ideas to make the lives of children better.

Just not here.

Although he sometimes enjoyed teaching at the school, he had no strong desire to help these well off, a tad spoiled little kings and queens of Shenzhen. For that he was paid money.

He had the simple idea that the world in general had been kind to him and that he should do something, even small, to help the less fortunate. Parts of him told him he was being sentimental. But there was a core that said 'Behold the world and it is generally good. Help those who need you.' So he had already decided when he came to Shenzhen to give a little. These school children didn't really need him, he thought. Orphans and the destitute needed him more. He wanted to give them something unique, not the normal mathematics, English, science, physical education, food, drink and housing. He resolved that of all possible donations, the gift of art would be the most noble and rewarding for the children.

He decided to contact the local orphanage. Between Laurie and Spring and a lot of sign language he found a way to get in contact with the local social welfare government bureau. Late one afternoon before his lesson with Laurie rushed up to him. She was breathless, her face flushed and excited.

"David, good news! Spring and I managed to locate Mr. Liu who is in charge of the Welfare Bureau. He has agreed to let you visit the children!"

Laurie blurted out the words, happy and smiling. His face broke into a broad smile.

"That's great! Awesome? Can I just go there?"

"Yes, but you first must sign this." And she handed David a piece of paper that was written in freehand English. He looked at it closely.

This is to certify that _____, an English teacher at the foreign school on Cai Tan Road, wants to help teach the children music. He does not have any diseases such as tuberculosis and is in good standing in China and the United States. He promises to respect and obey all rules and regulations regarding the orphanage and the children.

[SIGNED]'

A copy in Chinese was attached. Laurie handed him a pen and he quickly signed his cryptic signature with the letters barely decipherable and slanted towards the right.

Laurie smiled happily and said,

"Good. Now I will send this to Mr. Li. And you can go there on Saturday. Spring has a car and she will pick you up and go with you."

Laurie looked at her watch, and turned with a worried face to Spring who also had to return to work.

"Class...class!" and she walked off without another word, waving back at him.

He was pleased that Spring wanted to go with him. But in his mind this was not a date. He really wanted to visit the children and if she wanted to help that was great, but he could do without her if necessary. The times he had discussed helping orphans he had also sensed something of a reluctance in her, as though this donation of their time was something of an extravagance, of a plunge into the darker side of Shenzhen.

That Saturday afternoon he waited for Spring outside the gate of the school. It was about 9 in the morning and the sky was clear and blue. In anticipation of the students who loved their wares, vendors crowded the sidewalk with smoked tofu and fruit. The pungent, almost foul odor of the popular tofu filled the air. Dragon eye nuts, cashew nuts, raisins from Xin Jiang, red eye beans from Shanxi and many other fruits were arranged neatly on the sidewalks. Cries of *Hello, hello...* followed him and when he ignored them, their attention turned to other fast walking pedestrians. Cars and trucks honked their horns with wild abandon. Uniformed guards stood ramrod straight outside the school and the neighboring government buildings. Her tiny white Honda pulled up on the other side of the street from him. He walked over. She was dressed in dark slacks and a white top. She had wrapped a brightly colored scarf about her head. She smiled at him,

"Wait here…"

And she quickly walked to the little kiosk a few yards away and bought some bottled water.

"Here." She handed him a bottle.

He noticed how white her hands were, how glowing was the skin. Her fingers were long and slender, lithe and flexible, of someone sensitive and perhaps used to an easy life. A hot flush rushed though his body for a moment as their hands touched. They set off.

The orphanage was located in one of the poorer working class districts of Shenzhen. A non-descript gray building, it sat like a huge gray cigarette box amid residential high rises, shops, a vocational school and the district police station. The high rises stretched seven or eight stories into the air like gray banshees with thousands of eyelike black holes for windows. From one of the windows he saw what seemed to be racks of hanging yellowed flesh. *Probably an illicit slaughterhouse*, he imagined. The branches of ancient fading magnolia trees seemed to stretch out towards the sullen sky as though grasping for forgiveness. The wide boulevard lined with pale yellow and gray granite sidewalks was strangely deserted, except for the occasional taxi that trolled vulture like in its search for customers. A four to five foot high concrete wall surrounded the social welfare center itself. Two entrances abruptly broke the wall's linear regularity. An electronic sliding railing with a broken strobe lamp dejectedly blocked half the main entrance. When staffed, the guardhouse occupant would slide open the railing a little, leaving just enough space for a car to enter. The other entrance further down the street on the same side led to the adjoining old person's retirement home.

Once inside the gates a ramp and stairway surged up to the main building entrance, a shining pair of huge open glass and steel doors fronted by a covered terrace. Frequently children and the building guards would lounge on the terrace, playing, discussing the day's events or watching the passersby as they waited for the next meal. High overhead, iron railings covered every single window like bulbous, netted eyelids that shielded the world from the dreams and nightmares within. Inside the main entrance was a large reception area. On the left was a huge rectangular table behind which was a plain metal chair. On the wall above the table the white brick was inscribed with hundreds of calligraphic Chinese characters, among which a few stood out in bolder relief.

Later someone explained to him that the quotation was from Confucius and pointed out a few characters translated as:

Study without thought is careless, thought without study is dangerous

He later thought hard about these words. He knew Confucius often invested simple phrases with multiple meanings. What was the meaning of *study* here? Was it intended to be something bookish, like theoretical mathematics, or was it even casual undisciplined reading? What was *thought?* Was it *reasoning?* Didn't mathematics always employ thought? Or was it *reflection?* Not to say that these meanings did not overlap, but perhaps Confucius meant to emphasize one meaning over another. And *careless?* What was this? Later he learned the character (*wang^*) could mean *deceptive*, or *crude*, or just *careless*. What was it? And why should there be a distinction between *study* and *thought?* Weren't the two naturally intertwined? And then he thought of the children. Do they really know what this means? Can they know? Children want love, safety and answers to life's questions. What love was there in learning? What safety was there in this building? And what answers could there be when questions abounded without end?

Straight ahead was the elevator and a recess where a guard in uniform dutifully passed the hours. On the right and straight ahead was a corridor leading to a covered playground from where the sounds of children laughing and singing could be heard. On the right wall was a pair of magnificent oak doors that led into a small auditorium for receiving and performing for guests. As the two of them walked in they saw it was partly open. Other than the guard the entrance was deserted. A young woman quickly strode through the wooden doors heading for them. She was in her twenties, plain looking but smiled warmly at the two of them. She smiled so brightly in fact, with her eyes narrowed in merriment, that she seemed to be laughing with joy.

Spring smiled too, but in a more serene way. It was as though she were somewhat aloof from the scene. The other woman laughed often, covering her mouth with her hands as though she were afraid to show her teeth. Spring saw at once that this woman was a little embarrassed, perhaps not entirely sure how to handle the foreigner. She thought to help her but did not.

"Hello, you must be David. I'm Miss Li, Thank you for coming today. Nice to meet you!"

David introduced Spring and after some pleasantries, Miss Li explained to the two her job was to assist visitors in meeting the children and taking part in volunteer activities. Many volunteers visited the orphanage, she said, but none taught piano. She led them to the elevator.

"Let's go and meet the children."

Spring was surprised at how cordial the reception was – just to greet the American. But she also knew foreigners were rarities in most of China. Despite Shenzhen's proximity to the international hub of Hong Kong, it was not unusual for local Chinese to stare open-mouthed at foreigners walking by. Then again, as in most developing countries, foreigners, particular Americans and Europeans, were regarded as representatives of a rich country, and afforded due courtesy, sometimes with an embarrassing alacrity.

On the third floor they stepped into a classroom filled with about 20 children, seated expectantly around an upright piano, aged from about 6 to 8 years of age and dressed in their Sunday best. Both girls and boys wore clean new parkas and sweaters, even though it was one of the hotter days of summer. A little girl wore a bright blue parka with a pink riff about the collar. The coat was the full length of her body and her pale face half peered out, wide eyed and smiling.

"Hello!" he said, smiling and waving his hands

"Hello!" they mechanically shouted in perfect unison, their eyes wandering around the room, hands twitching at their coats and skirts.

"How are you?"

"Fine thank you! And YOU?" and the YOU had such a lilt it sounded like a gigantic hiccup.

Two nannies dressed in blue tunics tended to them, gently coaching them on what to say or shushing them when they got too lively.

Miss Li explained to him that the orphanage was divided into two sections for children and elderly respectively. There were about 400 children and 100 elderly taken care of by about 60 teachers and staff. The first floor was the reception area. The second floor included a TV room and some living quarters for the older children. The third floor was a play area. They were now on the fourth floor, also a music and play area where most of the youngest children lived. The children ranged in age from newborns to about 12 years.

"Can I see the babies?" He said.

"Of course."

She led them to an adjoining room. It was behind a caged metal door on the open corridor, as were all the children's living quarters. He learned later that the children could still easily go in and out, but these doors helped keep in the smallest children. The room was large, about 15 by 3 square meters and completely bare except for scores of wooden cots, in each of which was a small baby. He sensed something unnatural about that room. His unease had nothing to do with the bare walls or even the concentration of lone children. He realized after a moment the remarkable thing was the silence. Not one child was crying out. One nanny was bustling from cot to cot, tending to them. Suddenly overcome, Spring picked up a child and hugged it. Its big brown eyes just looked at her as if both surprised and indignant. Its rubicund finger grasped hers tightly.

"How many children are in here?" He asked Miss Li.

"Oh, about 50!" And she smiled.

"That many!" He wondered abstractly if she ever stopped smiling.

"How did they get here?"

"Many were brought here by police after being abandoned from all over Shenzhen."

"Are there any other orphanages?"

"Just one, in Bao An. Bao An was one of the Shenzhen districts."

He looked at Spring, expecting her to say something but she was in her own world. As she held the child she remembered her own childhood, of her mother and father. She had grown up in a poor section of Zhengzhou, the capital of Henan. At that time, several years after the Cultural Revolution, her parents often told her of the privation of those and previous times, the beatings and humiliations of the intellectuals and above all...the great famine of 1956. Their own parents had seen neighbors eat the rotting bodies of strangers during the worst days of the terrible hunger. They had seen children without clothes and with distended bellies. Then during the Cultural Revolution, barely 10 years later, after Mao proudly proclaimed that this was the time for throwing out the old and bringing in the new, they had seen schoolchildren, like babes with sharp teeth, stone their teachers to death and force dunce caps onto the white whispery heads of elderly Zhengzhou doctors because they read and loved *Dream of Red Mansions*, perhaps the greatest novel in Chinese literature.

In 1985, when she was only about 5 and her mother was with child, she remembered how happy her mother was. She already had a girl and a son by her husband, a village doctor, but she wanted another.

"Why do you want a baby, mother?" the little girl had asked.

"Because I do not want you to be alone. I want you to have brothers and sisters that will love you like I do." She smiled, and her pale skin, normally as white as lamb's jade, was rosy as if with the blush of a second youth.

At that time the little girl did not know about the one-child policy. To curb China's spiraling population, the government had issued strict laws against having more than one child. While most obeyed, due to financial reasons, fear of heavy fines and punishment, or simply because they felt the policy was, in fact, reasonable, others protested. These protestors were often simple peasants. They had no money to pay off the corrupt government officials and so suffered the most. For thousands of years they had lived among extended families and had had many children. To them children were both a blessing and a sign of respect for their ancestors. Who were these upstarts from Beijing who wanted them to weaken their family line? How dare they issue *fiats* against having children who would love and nourish them in their old age! The girl's mother had already had a second child, a son, against the dictates of the Henan provincial authorities. They had levied heavy fines on the family, docked the father's pay and added a supplemental 'extra child' tax to their annual burden.

"They cannot control me. If I want a child I shall have one. These people have no right to decide for me!" her father had said.

One day the girl saw two men and a woman come to their little apartment. They walked in the open door (the summer heat was unbearable) as if they owned the place. Heated words were exchanged.

"You have a choice. It is you or your wife. Come to the hospital with us now!" a man smoking a cigarette pointed at her father, who averted his daughter's gaze and only looked at his young wife.

"I will go." he said, and the girl could not see his face but she knew he was very sad.

Later that evening when he came back from the hospital, he looked very weak. His face was as white as the paper from Xian that calligraphers call *Xuan Zhi*. He lay on his bed, his wife tending to him, for a whole day and a half – this man who had never gotten up past 5 in the morning! After that they had no more children. But she had two brothers who loved her and played with her.

Spring was very despondent after that. She wondered how her father had let those cruel people mistreat them so. Many times after that she stayed away from them, particularly her father. It was as though he had been weak and she wanted to think of him as strong and proud. On such days she would often go outside and play by herself in the street or behind the house in the vegetable garden.

One day she was playing outside and found a beautiful flower. It had somehow survived the boots and wheels of the hardscrabble villagers. Peeking out from behind some bricks in an alley, the chrysanthemum stretched out towards the light, its petals a brilliant gold, its leaves like slivers of emerald reaching for heaven.

"How pretty. How beautiful!", she thought.

Her father came up to the child and took her hand in his.

"What a pretty little flower."

He pulled it from the rich, loamy earth and placed it behind her ear. She burst out crying. She thought he had killed it. He tried to comfort her after that but she cried for the whole afternoon. Then he came up to her and said, wiping the tears from her eyes,

"Did you know the story of the little golden flower?"

"No. What story?" She mumbled and didn't look up.

"Well, a long time ago there was a little golden flower that grew in a little meadow in a big forest. It used to love to soak up the bright sunlight and drink the fresh water that fell from the sky. Each day was like the rest, and the she was very happy.

One day, many people came to the meadow. They built huts and leveled the trees to make paths and roads. The little golden flower was very afraid. The air was dirty and men with big boots threatened to stamp on her. But she couldn't move.

"Where can I go? What can I do?" She cried.

And then one day a little boy and girl were playing nearby and the boy saw the flower.

"Look, he said, what a beautiful flower."

And in an instant he plucked it and gave it to the girl. Now the most amazing thing happened after that. Did the flower die? No. It realized that it could still feel the sun and the air that blew over the grass. The little girl was so happy. She kissed the boy and ran away.

"Where are we going?" said the little flower to himself. "What a grand adventure."

He felt a lot of bumping and some of his petals fell off. To the boy and girl they had only gone a small distance. To the little flower it was as though they had traveled across the world. Eventually the little girl dropped the flower and the two ran off playing. The flower found itself in a beautiful meadow, even lovelier than the one before. It started to rain. The thick soil and water washed over the flower. It felt so good it fell asleep.

It slept for a long time. When it awoke it felt strange. It felt so alive. And then it saw that it had grown new leaves and roots had reached into the ground.

It was smaller than before but it was younger and stronger too. And when it looked around, there was not just one golden flower but many. When the girl had ran over the field many of its petals and pollen had fallen on the ground. The meadow was a carpet of gold. All because the little boy had showed the girl he loved her."

"What a silly story!" Spring muttered. Then more quietly, she looked up at her father and asked.

"So the flower didn't die?"

"No, it just changed – into something even prettier."

"Can you do that with my flower?"

"Sure."

The two of them placed the flower in some water. The next day they replanted it, this time in an area of their vegetable garden. Under the daily care of the man and his daughter the plant grew stronger. Soon it was thriving and other plants grew and bloomed beside it. Afterwards Spring loved her father as before.

Her father told her many stories. His stories were often light-hearted and sunny, but sometimes they were dark, like the Henan coal pits he used to work in. They always had a moral quality, something of the humanist. Sometimes he was deadly serious, as though he were reading from stone tablets inscribed with God's tears.

After their forced sterilization her parents seemed to grow apart. It was as though something dark and disruptive had penetrated the previously serene center of their lives. Spring's mother started to accuse him of sleeping with other women, charges he vigorously denied. He would then storm out to drink with his friends. Her mother would go into the bathroom and weep silently. At these times Spring retreated to her room.

After one of these arguments, Spring was in her room writing in her diary when her father walked in, his face somewhat despondent.

"Homework done yet?"

"Boring…can you tell me a story?"

He sat heavily on the bed, as if tired from his work.

"Oh all right…as long as you finish your homework, agreed?"

"Of course *Ba*!"

"It's about an earthquake…the one that happens only once in a thousand years."

The store about the flower had been a happy one. These days his stories were ever more morose. However they were always fascinating to her. She had heard this story before. The overall story line would be the same, but bits and pieces would change at each telling, as though he was obliged to protect himself from his own boredom.

"The great earthquake in 1976 (I call this *the year of curses*) killed 240,000 people at Tangshan City in Hebei province. Think of this, Spring, every day you see new faces, faces on the street or at the places you walk to and from. In a lifetime you cannot imagine so many faces as died that day. Their lives were forever crushed in an instant of bone-shattering terror. Every face you see is a life, a unique being. So many, so many."

"In the grim days after the first shock, amidst the stench of death and the rubble of destroyed homes and buildings, a couple had been found alive under the rubble. For five days they had lain one on the other, crushed together by a huge mass of concrete from the top of their one-story brick home.

"The woman had been wedged under her husband. They were crushed so tight they had to breathe one at a time. While he breathed, she couldn't and vice versa. In normal times they had seen very little of each other. He had often been far away on government business and spent very little time with his wife and daughter.

"On that hot summer night they had gone to bed early. Their daughter was sleeping with friends near the school. They had woken up when the ground began to roar and roll. Around them the sounds of metal screamed and groaned as it was rent apart. The slow rolling roar of the ground itself turned the serenity of night into chaos. In seconds, the massive block of the room fell onto their bodies in a cloud of dust that filled their eyes and clogged their noses.

"*Li Ting*, can you hear me," was the first sound the woman heard.

"She coughed, for the dust was deep in her throat."

"*Wang Shi*, what happened? I cannot move."

She tried to move, but the pressure increased. It was hard to breathe. She wanted to scream but could not.

"Is this how I will die?" she thought.

"Breathe slowly, do not rush. We have to pace ourselves, otherwise we will be unable to breathe." Said her husband.

His body lay on hers, both faced upwards, though crosswise, forming a rough T shape.

They survived by talking and comforting each other. They talked about many things to while away the time.

"Keep talking," he would urge her, "help will come shortly."

"After the second day when no help arrived he had despaired. He had wanted to kill himself under those huge impersonal boulders, as the water from lashing rain drip-dripped onto their bodies. He had tried to turn his head sharply to break his neck. He had given up any hope at being found alive. But his wife would not let him die."

"You were born in the year of the Monkey!" she said to him. "You were destined to live for 500 years. Don't give up! Don't leave me! Remember our child. She wants her father to support her for the rest of her life. Can you leave her without a father?"

"Like a small spark that is nourished by tender dry barks, the flame of life rose in him. A great feeling of love, duty and fiery acceptance of his partner burned into his core, and he knew he could never give up. Can you imagine, while they still breathed, what they must have thought? Who could not fear the prospect of dying inch by inch, breath by breath, minute by minute?"

He quickly went on, as though trying to forget that part.

"But as the two of them lay under the rocks, they spoke of their courtship 14 years before, of the first time she had cooked *zhong zhi* dumplings for him. They recounted their first visit to the movie house together. On the fourth day, they heard sounds from above. The man found energy where he thought he had none and yelled,

"Help us, help us!"

A man's voice shouted down. "Who are you? Is anyone down there?"

"I am Wang shi. I am trapped with my wife."

Six hours later rescuers had reached the couple. But only one could be removed.

"If we take one of you, the slab will fall on the other."

"Take her.", he said of his wife.

"But the rescuers dragged him out first. The slab wobbled terribly, but held. They pulled out his wife shortly afterwards. They were free."

Spring's father told her this story, and from time to time he would smile. The only time he didn't smile and looked sad was when he said

"They didn't realize until much later that their daughter had died not far away. The quake, said their rescuers, had leveled the school and nearby buildings instantly. Her death had been quick."

Her father smiled at her.

"Why did I tell you this story? There are bad things people do. There are good things people do. But we must care for another, love another, even sacrifice oneself for another."

Spring knew what her father meant.

The little girl remembered these things and she remembered the stories of the great famine and the hardships of her family and her fellow Chinese. When she was older, she once saw pictures of soldiers shooting women and children beside lime caked pits filled with dozens of bodies. The photos were grainy and she couldn't tell if the people were Asian or Western, but it didn't matter. She wondered how people could do such things to each other, and then she remembered her father's story and words.

"There are bad things people do. There are good things people do."

Over the years she had changed her father's words in her mind and she could easily imagine him saying:

"Many times you wonder how we can have such opposite feelings in each one of us. But we have to accept and work for the good and love each other – because only love keeps us going."

At first these were her father's words. Then they became her thoughts and her feelings and she did not remember whether it was her father or Spring herself who may have said something. But the message was the same: In the great rubric of life, evil and virtue, love and hate, pain and joy were all like parts of the *ying* and *yang* - complimentary, and eternal.

Now at the Shenzhen orphanage, Spring looked at the child in her arms and thought of one thing.

Family.

She knew what it was to be loved by family. In China there is nothing more important than family. So she understood the depth of loss suffered by these children at the orphanage. And yet, there was something uniquely underhanded in her appreciation. *For she also wanted to be away from them.* They were to a certain extent, an inconvenience, and although she too, like the foreigner, could be idealistic, she was also profoundly pragmatic in her approach to life. She saw that foreigners loved Chinese children but in her opinion they saw only the exterior parts. They valued the pretty, smooth shining faces and imagined the children were of the same stuff all the way though. How blind they were!

One day she would have her own children. Foreigners adopted. Chinese adopted too, but there was always the distance between such children and their foster families. Foreigners were always so trusting. They could give away their hearts so easily. But in China it was different. Chinese had lived among their own for so long, they could *smell* otherness. Even beating such adopted children was sinful – like hitting another's child. Giving away their heart and soul was impossible. *Otherness* was like an invisible repellant that made them cling to their own. In ancient days, people had lived and shared the same surname together. Kings and nobles had punished them not individually, but en masse. The crimes of the individual resulted in the suffering of the community. The great legalists of feudal times had brought discipline upon their warring kingdoms by executing whole generations for the crimes of individual family members. And yet these days, although the young men and women wore and lusted after *Guccis* and *Burberrys* in an unashamed race for materialistic glory, family always remained important. To be without it was not only shameful but, for many, impossible to imagine.

Also there was the matter of pride. Letting foreigners see shameful parts of China was– and here she was no different from others- embarrassing. But she rationalized this, and did not feel it as strongly as Miss Li, for example, might. So she looked with some disdain at the pretty clothes that the children were wearing for their foreign guests. She remembered how embarrassed she and her friends were whenever they spoke poor English in front of foreigners – therefore they avoided speaking English at all.

David also knew this was an official spectacle of sorts. The children would later sing songs for him. He would play some piano. It seemed to him as though they were performing for each other. He disliked this halo of officialdom. *In future I won't call in advance. That's how the real teaching will begin*, he thought.

David saw a photo of a young woman on a table. She was hugging a small boy and her brown eyes were smiling happily. The photo was the only colorful object on the drab paper cluttered table. It projected like a ray of light from the surrounding metal and concrete.

"Who is that?" he asked Miss Li.

"She's one of our teachers with one of the children who lives here."

"No, you cannot take photographs. I hope you understand." Miss Li said to David when he took out his digital camera. Still smiling, she nervously explained.

"In the past people have taken photos of the children and written or published embarrassing or inaccurate information."

David was a little surprised. Spring understood. In China distrust of foreigners runs deep. She looked at the children in the room and she saw

David looking at them. There was again that expression in his eyes that blended sadness with wonder and she felt drawn to him as she had that first day in the headmaster's office. He was vulnerable and incomplete. She tried to look at the children and feel as she imagined he felt, but there was no wonder, just sadness.

He leaned over one of the babies and saw a small white face. The tiny fingers and toes were curled up as if to scratch the cold air.

"Look, she is holding my finger!" And the baby looked up at him, strangely silent, as though in awe.

"He doesn't know what to make of me." the big American laughed.

"You Americans", Miss Li blurted out, "You are always so happy!" and she laughed with her hands over her teeth.

At that moment it was as though David saw the sincerity and dedication of the staff. These were not blind ideologues, he thought, they were just good people trying to make a living . Helping children was part of their lives. David would discover that far from being a monolithic and insensitive institution, the staff in this grimy building were true gems. Like Miss Li, the other teachers were serious about their work and truly served the children.

The little baby had that thunderstruck look that is poised somewhere between speech and bursting into tears. But she uttered not a sound. Her fingers grasped his and wouldn't let go. It was as though all the sounds in the world had been absorbed and transmuted into her tight fingers. Her big black eyes looked at him with great compassion.

They returned to the older children next door. They were so beautifully dressed for the occasion he was embarrassed.

Instinctively he moved towards the piano.

"Do you want to hear some music?" Without waiting for an answer he started the *Fantasie Impromptu* of Chopin. The children listened politely. When he finished they remained silent, as though waiting for direction, like young boys and girls looking expectantly at the magician's black hat. One of the assistants quickly clapped and then everybody clapped. He made a mock bow and smiled,

"Do you like music?"

"Do you like music?" the children repeated.

"This is a piano, PEE-AANN-OOO"

"PEE-AANN-OOO"

"Very good!"

David contrasted the attention he got here with an experience he had had back in Atlanta. Just before he had left for China he had tried to drum up some contributions to bring to the orphanage. He contacted a local newspaper reporter.

"What makes you think you can get your help the orphans project approved by the Chinese Government? You haven't contacted the Chinese consulate, have you?"

The reporter on the phone had a tough New Yorker or New Jersey accent.

She continued aiming staccato questions at David over the phone, as though he was preparing for a heist or a con job.

"You left your job. Why? That must have been quite a compensation package for you to retire on after only 7 months." To David she was like an armadillo digging for ants.

"Well only for a year or two, but it's not as though I'm retiring..." he stuttered, unsettled by the aggressive tone.

"About your orphan project, it's a good idea, but that's all it is. I'm afraid it doesn't warrant an article at this time, and I think my editor will back me up on this?" With that they had cordially ended the conversation.

He jumped up gave some of the children high fives. One of the girls, dressed in a plain blue skirt with a pink plastic rose in her hair came over to him. He sat her down on his lap. She placed a tiny hand on the keyboard. It barely touched 2 keys. Then with her hand on the keys, her eyes wide she just sat there and looked up at him, motionless. The other children came up, one by one, and they started to touch his hands, his jacket, the piano, moving close to him as though to replace the other girl. Into this silent procession of sorts another little girl in a parka shuffled up and said,

"Me! Me..."

From then on, he visited the orphanage once each week, every Saturday at 3 in the afternoon without fail. Spring accompanied him a few times at first. Then she abruptly started making excuses why she could not go, such as

"I have something I have to do on Saturday."

Or

"A friend is visiting me this weekend. Maybe some other time."

She did not want to be surrounded by hopelessness and poverty. Her life was about optimism and light, fulfillment and love, family and friends. For her the orphanage offered none of these things. In fact, it seemed degrading to her. She did not want David to see this part of China. Then she thought about her reasoning and felt guilty. When she realized she was thinking about it a lot, she decided it wasn't worth the time.

On the other hand, David was somewhat relieved. It was hard enough courting Spring. His charity was a part of him that he wasn't yet ready to reveal to her or anyone. It was as though he was a horse with blinders. He had a worthy goal and it was straight ahead of him. While he was at the orphanage everything else was a diversion, even the teachers and staff. David wanted a direct connection to the children. Thus to him the teachers and staff, even Spring, were secondary. Although he had to deal with adults he never forgot he was there for the children.

When Spring accompanied him she noticed that he behaved more circumspectly, with less confidence and authority. In fact, she thought, *he's boring*. Eventually, David made his own way there and it stayed that way. If the taxi got lost he would call her on his cell phone and she would unfailingly give the driver the correct directions. The classes started out with about 10 children and gradually were winnowed down, either because children lost interest or didn't have the time or talent. For many of these children piano was secondary to the novelty of the foreigner. For others, it was secondary to obtaining attention, affection and even love from a stranger. And for very few, the music itself was the draw.

At first David taught about nine to ten children each week, allotting each a few minutes. As if the result of some secret game of musical chairs, some would be out one week and back in the next. Others would leave permanently and new ones arrive, like autumn leaves gently dropping onto moving water. Then the total number of students started dropping. He noticed they also seemed less motivated.

"Why aren't the children playing piano as well as they did?" he asked Mr. Ma, one of the arts and crafts teachers.

"They have very little time to practice." he said forthrightly.

"How much time each day do they have?"

David had suggested at the beginning that the kids be free to play the piano each day. Mr Ma demurred and doesn't seem to want to tell why. Perhaps he doesn't know, David thought.

They decided to concentrate on just 5 children. Each would have a little more time and Mr Ma could help them practice when David was away. Week after week he would give them high fives, hugs and tell them how great their improvement was. However, he also told them areas they were lagging in. Some did not take it well. One child, a little girl, decided not to continue after he told her she needed to practice harder. Others attacked the music with dogged persistence. Each had their own way of learning. One boy, a very tiny lad of about 6, would sit straight up on his chair like a martinet, feet several inches off the ground. He would fiercely look at the book and keys, and play and sing with great resolve.

"One, two, three, one, two, three…"

He seemed to look straight past the book and keys as though looking into the piano innards with some sort of x-ray vision.

Another child, a girl called Luo Ling Hui, attended every class with her hair decorated in colorful flowers and jewelry and bright clothes that seem to repel the gloom of the green and gray walls. She was only seven or eight but listened with great attention. Her hands were small and pudgy but she played with simplicity and confidence. When sunlight flowed through the window it seemed to give her dark hair and smooth, glistening skin an almost otherworldly appearance. One day he gave the children McDonalds pies . Some ate. Some didn't. She didn't.

"Why aren't you eating, Luo Ling Hui?" David asked.

"I'll eat it later", she smiled bashfully, the light sparkling in her happy deep brown eyes.

She held onto the pretty red and gold package as though it were some rare, fragile and exotic jewel.

A few weeks later he noticed she wasn't there.

"Where is Lo Ling Hui?" he asked Mr Ma.

"She was adopted and now is living in America." Mr Ma said, smiling.

David was gloomy but happy she found a family. *She can forget me*, he thought, *but I hope she doesn't forget the music*.

David would bring his study materials with him. One day Miss Li was thumbing through his Chinese dictionary.

"Many of the characters are not used aren't they?" David commented.

Of the more than 40000 characters in Chinese many are rarely used. Mrs Li pointed to 2 particular characters and said,

"These are often used."

Each character had over 30 strokes.

In his notebook David carefully wrote down the names of some of his students with the help of Mr Ma.

Zhen- Rui which roughly translates as	DISTINGUISHED AND FARSIGHTED
Shen-Peng/ DEEP ROC	
Bao^ Xin- Lian/	PRECIOUS LOTUS FLOWER
Fu/ Pei/ Dong-	AUSPICIOUS LEADER
Fu/ Xiao/ Chun	AUSPICIOUS SPRING DAYBREAK
Luo/ Ling^ Hui-	SPLENDID MOUNTAINS
Long/ Si-Yang/	GREAT DRAGON THOUGHTS
Sha- Zi − Hui-	CLEVER AND SMART

Zhen Rui was a small shy boy with tousled shiny black hair, and a smiling face who always sat at the back of the music room, as though he wanted to fade into the wall. He would smile gently to himself as though trying to pacify ghosts within his bent body. He moved awkwardly, like a small, fleshy puppet. His large head was gingerly balanced on his skinny torso. He had a vivid red scar beneath one of his ears, the result of a beating long ago. He grew his hair deliberately long so as to cover it. Yet his real hearing was within. He was earnest and intelligent. Whenever David called on him he would smile gently, hesitantly come forward and play with effortless concentration. His hands were huge. He easily reached an octave in his right and about 10 fingers in his left. When he played he would pass his long slender fingers first over the keyboard as though he were an old blind man feeling a baby's skin for the first time. He was eight years old, but tall for his age, well over a meter. As though ashamed of his height he hunched slightly and seemed to shrink into his chair.

"His heart is very weak. One day someone will take him for an operation in America." Miss Li told David one day.

From the first day he had instinctively moved towards the piano. It was as though there was an invisible cord that bound him to its sound. What kindred spirits he saw or heard in the music remained a mystery, for all one could see was that bittersweet smile and tussled hair. In spite of his hardships, his smile was genuine and his dreamy eyes suffused the face with nobility. There are angry eyes and sad eyes, scornful eyes and fearful eyes. Most moving are bittersweet eyes, both laughing and sad, as if they know the world's darkest parts - those parts which blot out childhood and limit one's time on earth.

Zhen Rui knew a little English and from time to time he would walk with the teacher hand in hand to the gate of the school and they would talk a little. David would speak halting Chinese and the little boy some equally tentative English. He asked David many questions.

"Where are you from?"

"What is America like?"

"What countries have you been to?"

He has seen so much, said Zhen Rui to himself. In that nether fantasy world that children have, Zhen Rui thought of grand cities far away, of golden haired, blue eyed American children, of boats and palaces and of people who always had food, clothes and ice cream and were kind and good to each other.

"What is America like?" He once asked.

"It is a big country, with many people."

"Are they like China people?"

"Some of them."

"Are they like me?"

"No, no-one is like you, Zhen Rui!"

And the boy pondered further, and instinctively grasped the man's hand.

"Do they like Chinese people?"

"Some do, some do not!"

"I think they like China."

"Why?"

"Mrs Li says they have a lot of money!"

David was puzzled. He didn't see the connection.

"So what?"

"China is poor. They must like us. Otherwise they wouldn't come. You are here!"

He smiled happily. The teacher did not understand the logic, but the child was happy, and so was he.

Another time the wind was rustling through the trees and both teacher and pupil heard the wailing sound through the open window.

"The trees are singing." Zhen Rui said

"No its just the wind blowing through them."

"No the trees are singing and dancing!" the boy shouted and immediately looked down at his feet, as though embarrassed.

David didn't answer.

A letter was waiting for him that evening.

Dear David,

You don't need to tell me about this woman you met. That's your own business. However I do think you're robbing the cradle!

You asked me about my Mom. My mom, as I said, never really understood herself and as a result had many moods and would also be inconsistent with people. She would seem the epitome of hospitality to all and sundry and she did like people but once they were gone she would backbite them and undermine them. So I got mixed messages, which confused me too. Also several times in her life she needed to go to a rest home (once after a hysterectomy) she lost touch with reality — no doubt today they would give her a few pills — perhaps it was a chemical imbalance- but she hallucinated — perhaps a genetic propensity inherited from her mum — but she did comeback to normal after about 2-3 months in a rest home and we carried on.

She often taught piano during her life — she did love music and she liked teaching but by my estimation she was a lousy teacher. She had no patience. Still people came to her because she had a charming and a loving personality to them — and basically, to be fair, she was charming and loving, but I knew she had lots of moods and often slept to get away from reality, which was often too frustrating for her. Come to think of it, everyone needs to think of a way to deal with frustration — in fact I am writing this to you because I was frustrated to learn from my cousin Jenny that her ticket to come and visit me in Nairobi still isn't right — but it has taken me a long time to know how to deal with frustration and I am still not very good at it. I think I learned this lack from my mum. Mums do become scapegoats, don't they? But I did love her very much and she tried her best. She just didn't know any other way. I say a lot of this because it's easy to blame parents for one's problems. Regarding your father, he was often beaten as a child. Men in those days were often autocratic and dictatorial. His life growing up with a very hard father was difficult. His mother was often abused and eventually ran away and left him. Maybe your father didn't know any other way. Remember, your life is your own and whatever you do, I am proud of you.

Love,
Mutter

He quickly responded. Thoughts were flashing through his mind of children, of parents, of strange men and women in strange lands, of elopement, of unrequited love and harsh betrayal. The day's events with the children, particularly with Zhen Rui, crazily circulated in his mind like clothes in a washer, without form, with energy and without direction. He had known almost nothing about his father's father. That he was a hard man did not surprise him. Then again, he speculated, his mother could have been making it up so David would pity his father. He found his mother somewhat strange, somewhat a mystery. He resolved that one day he would get around to understanding her more. She would remain a mystery to him and that was just fine. For now he wanted to find out about his father. Focusing, he replied

> *Liebe Mutter!*
>
> *You made a great decision to leave America to go to Kenya. You were so young then, only in your twenties. I am much older now than you were then and yet this was a big decision for me too. I gave up a lot by coming here: high paying jobs, my piano LOL, but I knew I had to start fresh. I also wanted to find a partner, a kindred soul. Was it the same with you?*
>
> *Love,*
> *David*

Dreams don't die for me, he thought. *They just evolve or are put on hold.* He sighed. Outside the sky was uncharacteristically dark. His eyes were heavy. He realized his thoughts were all over the place, rambling and disconnected. He slept long and peacefully that night.

My earliest memory is of following my mother through a field of maize just after the harvest. She was walking very fast and I couldn't keep up with her. 'Wait! Wait for me!' I must have shouted though I do not remember the exact words. The sun was very bright and the maize was taller than me. I think I was about three or four years old at the time. I was frustrated trying to keep up with her. I only saw big and fat legs in front. No matter how hard I tried. I wanted to walk faster than her. Perhaps this is why I became competitive. I wanted to move faster than my mother in every way.

- From David's father's journal

THE ARRIVAL OF SPRING

"Where are you from?"

David didn't reply to the taxi driver's question.

He was thinking of other things…such as meeting Spring again.

Three months had passed since he arrived in Shenzhen. The United States was deeper in the quagmire of Iraq. Americans everywhere were cautious about their actions, as if afraid of some global retribution. There had been a time when America was the envy and love of the world. Where Gene Kelly had once charmed the residents of *La Seine*, now the French protested against McDonalds and globalization. The Muslims railed against Imperialism. The Russians revolted against their own diminution. All blamed the Americans.

For the Chinese respect was founded upon fame or wealth, what they termed *ming* or *li* respectively. One could be famous and poor, and this was worthy of respect. One could be wealthy and not well known, and this was something to be proud of too. The Americans had always had both, but now, with the debacle of Iraq and the decline of the American economy, together accounting for perhaps the greatest loss of wealth and treasure in centuries, some educated Chinese saw opportunity in America's apparent decline. These young, brash, smart Chinese were confident of their strategy, one based on years, even decades of incremental advancement. This strategy was one of quiet dominance, without overt aggression, but cold and remorseless like the python that curls delicately about one, then crushes its bones.

Americans had changed too. Where once they had been placid now they were anxious. Where once they had merely been irritated, now they were snappish. Where they had been confident, now they were more afraid to be away from home than ever before. Many Americans seemed unaware of the changed situation and were like floundering whales, unwilling to accept certain perceptions and adapt to other cultures.

David was determined to avoid these national flaws. He had never been particularly patriotic *a la Kipling*. He was proud to be American, but he did not flaunt it. He wanted to be known for who he was, not who he represented. Regardless, he quickly saw that Chinese always lumped foreigners into categories. French, Africans, Germans, British, Americans. All this multi-culturalism was summed up, in their view, into the *lao wai*, or foreigner.

To him being American was about absorption. Kenya, America, white, black, Luo, Judaism, even Lithuanian ancestry (though his maternal grandmother) were all parts of him. He sought to identify the deficiencies and strengths of different cultures. Categorization was useless to him, like endless surgery. Bones, sinews, hair, skin were stripped apart and left behind a lifeless body. David was attempting to navigate between cultures as an observer, without commitment to just one. He wanted to absorb the best and recognize the worst. *Isn't this the quintessence of being American?* he thought.

Confucius had long ago said,

My best teachers are among we three people working together

In this phrase Confucius had recognized that in a group, one often falls into the mistake of only recognizing others' faults and one's strengths, hardly ever noticing one's weaknesses and others' strengths. By understanding one's limitations and others' strengths, one can grow and achieve one's dreams.

David eventually realized that this sense of separateness was a natural first reaction to meetings between cultures. And he felt sanguine about the prospects for eventual acceptance and understanding – in particular acceptance of him as an individual. And even if that were not to happen, he really did not seem to care, so he told himself. I am an existentialist *par excellence. I am subsumed in the moment*, he thought, *As long as I can feel, see, touch, smell or taste, I don't give a damn about abstracts like the future or the past.* Like existentialists, David ignored the past, though at his peril, for it exerted a far larger influence on him than he imagined.

When he had returned to the school after a trip out of town with some friends he was shocked to discover that the once magnificent boulevard with the great trees was now a place of bones and tusks. Workers had uprooted the great mangroves whose arched roots weave like petrified eels over the ground. They had also slashed down the leafy cypress trees. Deep unkempt holes remained where trees once stroked the heavens. Like red mouths with torn lips they seemed to scream in execration at the bureaucrats, developers and master planners who had paved paradise and put up more subway stations, buildings and parking lots. The few remaining trees were surrounded by excavation drills and spades tossed randomly around their trunks. Sidewalks once shaded and cool were now bare brick stones that lay naked to the elements. Pedestrians who once lounged beneath the arbors as they took their meandering Chinese walks now seemed to rush past the graveyard of green bones and tusks, as if ashamed.

One of the school guards stood looking out at the scene. David walked up to him.

"What happened? Are they going to take all the trees down?"

The guard, a young man probably direct from the provinces, peered at him closely.

"Yes, they are taking away all the bushes."

He used the Chinese word for bushes (*cao*), not trees (*shu*).

"But the large trees, they are taking those down too?"

"Yes, those too."

"Why?"

"It's for the subway. They have to remove them."

He saw the pain in the foreigner's face and added,

"And place others there. It will be even better."

"How can it be better? The trees were beautiful!"

The guard wondered about these foreigners. They did not understand development. It was good for buildings to replace trees, to construct new subways to get people more quickly from place to place. What was wrong with taking out a few bushes?

"But those trees took years to grow!"

"They will grow quickly. Don't worry! They will be beautiful."

David shook his head and walked to the class corridor. A young girl who happened to be passing by opened the door for him. He felt embarrassed. She did not know him. People don't normally open doors for strangers. He insisted she go in first, so she did.

"Why did you open the door for me?" He asked her suddenly. She looked back,

"It is polite. Bye Bye!" She smiled and trotted away.

A colleague later told David the uprooted trees were taken to an area in Nan Shan prefecture several miles away and replanted. However, he still despaired, for the trees were no longer there to succor him. He believed that most would die. They were too old and the roots were so long and broad. Dying would take a long time.

"Where are you from - America?"

The Lunar New Year was fast approaching. He looked through the taxi window. He sensed something different about the way people walked. There was briskness in their steps, as if everyone had an appointment to go to. Even the famous slow Chinese walk, called *liu da*, a rambling thing that issues from the balls of one's feet, seemed to have a mysterious and sacrosanct purpose. It reminded him of the way some New Yorkers stroll through Central Park or down broad, tree-lined boulevards. He absorbed thousands of different faces and was suddenly filled with exhilaration. It was a sense of totally unfathomable happiness that pushes out one's chest and ebbs and flows with one's every thought.

A young girl, her head half wrapped in a plain scarf, walked hesitantly down the street, as if along a church pew on her way to communion. Her eyes looked down at the sidewalk before her as though meditating over secret and mysterious thoughts. Elsewhere two girlfriends walked in perfect unison, step by step, hand in hand, as though they were twins.

They passed a dirty blue truck parked on the sidewalk. The back and sidewalls had been hoisted up to reveal heaps of Xinjiang oranges, bananas, and pear leaved crabapples. Before the truck were neat rows of peaches, gold, red and blue plums and pears from Guangzhou, tubs of fat raisins and grapes, sweet yellow grapefruits from all over China. Huddled within the fruit truck, as though escaping the biting winds from the south, an old man with wizened eyes and coarse hair sold the fruit to passersby with a youthful alacrity. Two young migrant workers wrestled playfully, trying to knock each other off balance. In this young city young people were in the prime of their lives, and they wanted to flout their strength.

Paper cutouts were on windows and glass doors. Red lanterns hung above building entrances, proudly arrayed every few meters above busy streets. Scrolls of calligraphic writing hung on doorways and outdoor displays with such auspicious greetings as

Happy New Year
May You Grow Rich

In the evening, neighbors, family and friends would bustle about in preparation for the great mealtime gatherings when they would bring cash and gifts. The train stations of Shenzhen and Guangzhou would bulge with tens of thousands of passengers daily as the huddled, sweating migrant workers struggled through bulging lines to the waiting trains for home. This was their most significant vacation. They would temporarily leave work and return to their distant hometowns and villages. Back home they would kill a pig and make all sorts of delicious delicacies. Then they would spend the evenings feasting with their family, handing out gifts of money and making preparations for the coming year.

Keeping to tradition, flowers and plants were everywhere. Lotus, dahlias, lilies, yellow croakers, gay potted bouquets of tangerines and lemons, honeysuckle, marigolds, petunias, orchids, sunflowers, moon flowers, Chinese violets, lilacs, but mostly gold and red chrysanthemums abounded beside apartment doors, in public gardens, and at entrances to gas stations. David felt he was part of a huge family, a vast movement of kindred spirits that were at once separate from him and yet one with him. There was love and energy in the air, and he felt surrounded by this dazzling, mortal human world with all its myriad temptations and possibilities.

Spring had called him that morning.

"I want to talk to you. I need your help."

"What is it?" He said (his Chinese had improved)

"Let us talk at dinner. I will tell you later."

And they had left it at that.

"Where are you from - America?"

The taxi driver repeated the question, more insistently this time.

"China!" David answered without turning away from the window.

The taxi driver didn't reply. He had turned to curse at a bus driver in a dialect David didn't understand and didn't want to. He was absorbed in his own thoughts about the concert and about Zhen Rui.

Back at the school David had proposed an idea for a grand concert to the director of the orphanage, which had come to naught. One of his Chinese friends had offered to help and at first the director seemed keen on the idea. The concept was to pull together various foreigners from across Shenzhen to perform before a Chinese audience. The foreigners would be pretty much free to choose their own skit at the 'dog and pony' show, as a Russian friend indelicately termed it. Donations for the concert would go to the orphanage. Then it had all fallen apart. His Chinese friend called him one day to tell him a high ranking person at the orphanage had suggested delaying (a euphemism for cancelling) the concert because there was too much government paperwork involved.

"This is China," his friend explained , "If you try to do things from the bottom up, it can easily be stopped by someone at the top. They make decisions in secret and often from the top down. Smart people are often afraid to make decisions themselves. Why? because they are afraid of making a mistake. In China, you cannot make a mistake and advance in your career."

He angrily added,

"And the worst of them drink and go out for dinner with their powerful friends, spending our government money like crazy."

"But it is much better than America." He quickly went on, as if to correct any misperception.

"China is on the right path. Our leaders are strong and we will pass America one day!"

David accepted this news with the fatalism that seemed to run through him like an invisible ether. He also felt that there were perhaps more prosaic reasons. He realized the idea was perhaps too new. In China, where the government is everywhere and regulations are common as air, innovation is the bureaucrats' *bete-noire*. It produces complications and more paperwork. Therefore, the simplest and most perfect response is to use the dreaded phrase

"Something is missing. You must go elsewhere...or wait."

He felt sad, but casually so, as if he had all the time in the world. Regret was a burden he didn't want. Perhaps now was not the time to push the concert idea any further.

Much else had happened these past three months. A Chinese family had adopted one of his students. He missed the little girl with the funny hairdo and bright earrings but had resigned himself to the transience of these children.

Of course there is Zhen Rui, he thought, and he smiled to himself.

Zhen Rui had developed amazingly fast. The smiling boy with the spade-like hands had shown a natural gift for the instrument. In the first week of lessons he had mastered most of the major and minor scales – and had memorized them. Although his fingering was awkward he had progressed from easy kindergarten melodies to a simple Chopin nocturne within a month. And he seemed to be ever hungry for more music. So the teacher slowly (for he believed in patience and method) fed him more Chopin nocturnes, some Beethoven sonatas from Op. 1 and, recently even a Rachmaninoff prelude from the Op23 set – those glorious pieces that were composed in the Russian's youth – those years of unrequited love and passionate idealism.

The boy never seemed to realize he was special. On the contrary, he would just smile modestly when praised; perhaps mutter a word or two, bending his head down ever so slightly as though pushed down by an invisible weight.

"Thank you, I like too." he would say in his creaky English.

Sometimes in the passion of the moment he would lengthen the end of his words to change the meanings of his sentences, such as the time he wanted to say,

"I have a problem." which instead came out as "I have anal problem."

But David gently corrected him and they moved on.

He wondered where this child's destiny lay. The boy seemed to have a symbiotic relationship with the piano. He would lunge at the piano as though drawn by an invisible elastic rope, his hands raised before him like huge pink flippers. And then he would draw back, his face grimacing as if in pain. Although somewhat contorted, his motions made of the music a habitation of sorts, framed in a smooth and often technically flawless performance.

"When will you come back?" Zhen Rui would ask David after each lesson.

"Next week."

"*Zhen de*, Really?"

Zhen Rui didn't remember much about his parents. Most of those memories, if any, were foggy. He had faint memories of angry, discordant sounds. He remembered two old kindly faces, shriveled and tanned, beaten by the intense Asian sun into a leathery wrinkled contentment. These were the two old people who had rescued him from the latrine pit. Of the village in which he was found and the exact circumstances of his discovery – he had no clue. There were other faces too, of the policemen in blue and green clothes who had faded in and out of his life, and of the workers in the orphanages that had come and gone. His *yang mu* and *yang fu*, or foster parents, had in the end left him too. They were too poor to raise him. Afterwards they would visit the orphanage to see him from time to time. Then their visits ceased. He had never found out why.

From the beginning he had always had a special sensitivity to sound. Whereas others can remember faces, Zhen Rui always remembered sounds: the rooster's plaintive morning call, the pop tunes from the t-shirt bazaar down the road, the swish of calico dresses over wooden floors at night, the distant crackles of explosives at construction sites, the hushed whispers of lovers on park benches, even the sound of waves lapping up on the beach at *Da Mei Sha*. He would particularly remember the *jin ju*, or Chinese opera, his *yang fu* used to listen to on the radio every morning. Visibly relaxed, the seventy year old farmer would then head to the fields whistling and carrying his hoe over his head like a salute. Zhen Rui would not know the names of the music or any historical details, but he never forgot the sounds. In his life there had been few constants. Except for the sounds in his head, life was a shifting quicksand of broken commitments.

His one happy memory had revolved around music. He did not remember exactly when he first saw the *pi ying*, or shadow play. It is said that over a thousand years the shadow play was created to console an ancient Han King who had lost his beloved wife. Wandering minstrels and puppet actors would travel across China, performing for villagers and nobility alike. The exquisitely carved puppets made of leather, silk and wood would dance and cavort behind a white sheet, their grotesque shadows merging with the sounds of singers and musicians.

That night the shadow play was about the famous epic *Journey to the West*, or *Xi You Ji*. In this classic, the Buddhist monk *Tang Zan* travels to India to collect and bring the holy scriptures back to China. On his arduous journey though lands filled with ghosts and dragons, gods and demons, he is protected by the Monkey God, *Sun Wu Kong* and the two immortals, *Zhu Bai Jie* and *Sa He Shang*.

"That is Bai Jie!" he remembered his *yang fu* telling him.

The fat, half pig, half human immortal would lurch across the canvas, grasping after food and women, always outwitted by the crafty Monkey King. This was the first time the villagers had seen a *pi ying* performance. The county government, spurred on by some nebulous 'reforms', had sponsored the event for the first and last time. The Chinese music was high pitched, seemingly atonal and screeching to the ear, the words stretched in ways that seemed to distort their meaning. Zhen Rui, however, heard something else. It was a continuity of line, a fluidity of sound that entranced him and soothed his unsettled mind.

"I will be like Bai Zhu!" he said afterwards to his *yang fu* and *yang mu*.

"I will dance, fly and sing like him."

The old people had smiled and quickly forgotten. Their lives were too hard.

This was no time for beauty.

One day in late winter David and Zhen Rui were studying Beethoven's Op 1 piano sonata. This piece was written during the classical *Sturm und Drang* period of the turn of the 17th century, when Ludwig van Beethoven, the precocious *wunderkind* from Bonn was taking Germany's music world by storm. His works, though less elegant than those of Mozart and more impulsive than Haydn's, broke new ground. Next to them the conventions of Haydn and Mozart were polite, like afternoon Earl Gray tea and scones followed by an evening of absinthe. In the Opus 1 sonata, although his debt to Haydn is clear in the structure and phrasing, there are elements that elude easy categorization. Almost Dionysian in nature, a darker, brooding force seems to emerge from the rarefied air. In his work *The Art of Tragedy* the great sage Nietzsche contrasts the formal beauty of Apollo with the ecstatic, primordial urges of the wine god Dionysus. And so in early works, such as Opus 1, there are moments when, in one's imagination, the blue Danube morphs in to the Styx, and the Moldeau river pounds on the gates of Kiev with terrible abandon.

He remembered how the boy seemed to automatically understand these things. Of course, there were the inevitable wrong notes, but the impulse, the line, the phrasing had passion. He possessed that unteachable spark of line and purpose. Many have said of Artur Schnabel, the great Austrian pianist of yesteryear, that his ability to extend the line of a melody was unparalleled.

A Tang Dynasty poet once wrote, after listening to a harpist,

He waved his hand for me, and the sound seemed to flow over innumerable mountains and gulleys.

While this child was no Schnabel (or not yet) his passion reminded David of dreams that rise, sphinx like from the ashes, and of the audacity of one's hope.

David pushed Zhen Rui.

"No, you must drive towards the end of the phrase, like this."

He swept his arms up dramatically, as though reaching for a distant peak. The boy instinctively moved forwards into the music, making their dual movements blend into one.

Zhen Rui turned around and said,

"Beethoven is angry, but he makes me happy."

"Wow, you speak really good Chinese!"

David's attention snapped back to the taxi driver. *This guy is getting on my nerves*, he thought. He shook his head. He ignored the praise (which every Chinese person says to every foreigner who can say "hello" in Chinese) and reminded the taxi driver where to go.

In general he did not like taxis. He preferred buses although being in close proximity with the Chinese could be a strange experience. For example, one morning he had entered the no 21 bus at Jing Xing Hua Yuan bus stop on his way to a coffee house at Xiang Mi Hu Road. He headed to an empty seat at the back of the bus. The moment he had sat down, the lady next to him had stood up and moved to an adjacent seat. She was small and thin, probably in her thirties. Her tight, leathery face spoke of many years of hard toil in farms and paddies. Her long hair was drawn very tightly back into a bun that projected almost vertically from the back of her head like a half drawn stiletto or a platypus beak. She wore layers of thin polyester shirts and a jacket to shield her from the cold. Every so often she would turn back to glance at the foreigner with a gaze that was charmingly expressionless. David discretely sniffed the air. *Am I carrying an unpleasant odor?* He thought. He had showered and used 35$ an ounce cologne that morning. *My clothes?* He was wearing a checkered authentic wool sweater and new Calvin Klein pants. His shoes were fake Timberland, but new and thoroughly vetted. *You win some, you lose some. Some like you, some hate you*, he reasoned, and relegated it to the back of his memory.

By and large, he loved buses. They were economical - less than 20 cents a ride - clean, and sometimes even had little LED TVs with the local news. And there were tons of interesting people: gorgeous girls who looked at him with some interest; construction workers dressed in stained khaki trousers; cherub-faced kids heading home from school; old couples chatting and guffawing; young mothers closely shielding their infants from the crush; men hollering at or fiddling with their cell phones *ad infinitum.*

Ecce Homo! he would almost declare in a burst of Nietzschean merriment, marveling at the sounds, sights, shapes and colors of turn of the century Shenzhen and its people.

Shenzhen taxi cab drivers, however, were another story.

To David they were often short tempered, purposely delayed stopping the meter, sometimes would stop to pick up local Chinese and ignore foreigners, give back too little change, and above all, never stop asking invasive *where-are-you-from-where-do-you-live-do-you-rent-or-own-your-house* questions. They were, however, much better behaved than infamous New York cabbies. In David's opinion, cabbies around the world tended, like policemen, towards a general cynicism of the human condition, perhaps because their jobs every day forced them to see much of the worst in people. So in general he avoided cabs.

"Where are you from?"

The driver was insistent. He was a young man with a pockmarked face and bright eyes that nervously and energetically switched between the road ahead and the rearview mirror.

"China."

"Come on you expect me to believe that? Where are you from?" In the rear view mirror David could see his smiling eyes and imagined the driver's toothy grin.

"Where are *you* from?"

"Pakistan." The very un-Pakistani looking driver chortled.

"Really? What city in Pakistan?"

"What city in Pakistan are *you* from?"

The driver changed the subject.

"OK, you're from India?"

"No, America." David relented.

"Americans are terrible people. I hate Americans."

"Really. Why?"

"They are always fighting. Iraq, many places. Americans suck."

"Oh."

"Yes, and China has always been peaceful. We don't threaten other people..."

"Really, and Taiwan?"

"Taiwan is part of China and peaceful."

"But China has a history of more than 4000 years of war."

"Yeah, but those were internal wars."

"Internal wars are the worst. Look at the American Civil War. 500,000 Americans dead."

"I have nothing against the American people, just the government."

"American people also have lots of problems."

"I like Americans. Americans OK. Much money! What state in America are you from?"

"California (he lied). Where are you from?"

"Hunan"

"Great food! But quite spicy."

"Yes."

They made more small talk on the way to the restaurant, but his thoughts were still with Zhen Rui. His mind flashed back to that day.

"Beethoven is angry!"

The boy had laughed and started playing the first movement. David stood up, and as was his habit, meandered about the cavernous room, half listening, and half observing. The single upright piano stood in the corner like a lonely bar of chocolate. Bric a brac smothered the walls. Neat rows of pink and yellow baby strollers donated by the local Wal-Mart lay next to an entertainment center with two abandoned TVs. Papers and exam preparation books scattered over the smooth curving mahogany top of a huge conference table. Behind tattered cardboard boxes a once proud leather sofa crouched next to some metal desks. At the far end of the room the Chinese characters for *ice-cream* were scribbled on a green blackboard above a small stage. *Happy New Year*, *Love*, and various musical symbols were haphazardly added. Festive banners drooped forlornly from the ceiling above the stage. He absent-mindedly looked past the grimy windows into the damp air that hung like a grim yellow curtain over the enclosed quadrangle below.

"Keep going. That's good!" he encouraged the boy whenever he heard hesitation.

Outside the window the four orphanage walls peered into the boxlike space. The barred windows of the other rooms in the orphanage masked inhabitants whose dreams and hopes were the unbounded stuff of youth, ever straining to reach beyond limits set by health or wealth. Once in a while he would see a flash of bright linen or a flushed cheek, hear a laugh or see the back of a child's neck. The boy coughed, the music stopped for a moment, then resumed. The teacher continued his stroll, wondering what the other children were doing. *What was there to do in this drab place? How could they bear to survive here day by day?* He thought of his own youth, those long ago, poor, poor days when he too wore shabby clothes and torn sneakers and no one wiped away the dirt from his face. *Children are strong, they quickly recover*, he said to himself.

The taxi stopped outside the restaurant. The fare was 17 Yuan (about $2.50). David decided to break 100. The driver looked at the note as though it held a deadly bacterium. He held it up to the light, squinting as he carefully searched for the tell tale signs of a false banknote, a common phenomenon in Shenzhen.

"Haven't you anything smaller?"

"Sorry that's all I have."

The driver grumpily gave the American change from the 100. David checked and quickly discovered he only had 80 Yuan. He glowered at the driver who quickly handed over the remaining three.

Not far from the school, 'The Little Sheep' was perhaps one of the most popular restaurants in Shenzhen. Occupying 4 floors of a weathered brown building, every evening dozens of people would sit outside on plastic chairs waiting for tables within. From above the neon silhouette of a fat cartoon sheep peered out over the street like a garish pink, green and white carnival deity monitoring its parading minions.

"*Huan Yin Guang Lin!*" said women in red and gold *chi pao* dresses as he walked up to the door, cheerily greeting him with the words for *Welcome Honored Guest*.

"Hello, hello!" a women in a blue jacket hurried up to him, her eyes at once solicitous and anxious.

"I am here to meet someone.".

He spoke in Chinese. She spoke some English, which he didn't understand. He repeated himself in Chinese. Embarrassed, she gave him a puzzled look and giggled, although he was certain she understood him. He looked around the busy room but didn't spot Spring. The he remembered: she had told him she would be on the top floor.

"She's on the top floor."

He headed straight ahead towards the elevator. The hostess kept smiling, bustling to keep up. When they got off the fourth floor, he saw it was even more crowded than downstairs. Stepping out of the elevator he had to steer through a bunch of people. Some of the people stepped aside, giving him such a wide berth he felt there was something wrong with him. He was now a little nervous and hesitant. *This never happened with the men, just with the women*, he ruminated. *Is there something wrong with me? Did I brush my teeth? Enough under-arm deodorant? Don't they like me?*. That moment in time he *so* wanted to be liked, even by people he didn't know and would probably never see again.

"Oh, I see her over there."

He pointed to Spring, who was waving and smiling at him from a table next to a window overlooking the street. He headed over, the hostess leading the way through the roomful of wooden tables filled with steaming hot pots and plates of vegetables and meats. The clientele were mostly young but varied: businessmen in black jackets and white shirts holding court beneath fumes of cigarette smoke; young women dressed in tight shirts and tighter jeans sipping cokes and stealing glances around the large lofty room; families with children running back and forth beneath the tables like black and pink balls of energy.

Spring was dressed in a simple white blouse and caspian black slacks, her hair loose and free, curling about her alabaster neck like thousands of live tendrils. Seated next to her was her American friend Rebecca. Rebecca was Chinese American, also a teacher at a neighbouring school and had met Spring at the beauty parlor next to the tea house. The two had struck up a relationship. Rebecca doted on Spring with the tenderness of one who at once sees in her friend her future, her past, and all the beautiful things that she has been denied. Spring had, as the ancient Chinese opined, *a smooth brow and ivory teeth,* but Rebecca had a low brow often furrowed with worry lines. Cyclops has have one eye. Unicorns have a horn. Rebecca's large gums made her smile look like three lips. Rebecca spoke fluent Chinese, and, in Spring's opinion, spoke better than some natives.

Spring's ruby red lips, though thin, had the charm of reserved, deep, subtle amorousness. With Rebecca it seemed as though new pimples would appear about her cheeks and mouth every week, as though on a hidden schedule. As if to hide her discomfort she would talk a great deal. Her words bubbled over each other like frothy waves of sound, first hesitant, then ever more rapid, next exploding in a flurry of gestures. Finally they would recede like the sea tide, dazed and languorous or quick and brittle before the next onslaught. It was a circle of energy that was wondrous to behold and less wondrous to hear.

"Oh hi Mark. Spring asked me to come. You see she wants to explain something to you. So exciting, so exciting."

Her eyes went wide as though in shock. They waited for him to sit down. "Hi."

He warmly directed the greeting to Spring. He nodded curtly at Rebecca who averted his eyes and looked at the table napkin.

"David, you come here before? This is a famous restaurant. Very famous in Shenzhen!"

"No, first time."

And he continued to look directly at Spring who looked back at him just as directly with a smile on her face. He felt embarrassed for an instant and looked around.

"Very nice, so many people. What type of food?"

But he was really thinking of how happy he was to see her again. It had been *almost a month!*

Rebecca interrupted.

"Sichuan. The food is from Sichuan province. A very beautiful place. And they have delicious food. But David, you know we are so happy you came ..."

She looked with wide eyes at him, and giggled and continued

"For you maybe can help Spring dance!"

And she chuckled for no reason, and Spring also smiled happily. He laughed too, although he didn't know why.

"Sichuan food very spicy...very hot!"

Spring spoke her English carefully, but firmly. Around him people mostly spoke English. Those who spoke Chinese to him didn't know English well. Even then they would do so reluctantly, as though to speak Chinese with a foreigner was something far too intimate, like leading a stranger into one's bedroom. It was so hard sometimes to learn Chinese in Shenzhen.

He smiled warmly at Spring, completely ignoring Rebecca. Their eyes met and it was as though she had already said too much for she quickly smiled in an utterly false way and looked at Rebecca.

He had not seen her for almost a month. The last time was when they had their dance lesson at the school. She had then told him she had to go back home to visit her relatives because they had some money problems. He did not ask more but just felt sad she would be leaving him. At that time she explained everything matter of factly, as though she were talking to a friend, or even to a fellow workmate. He knew she didn't owe him anything. They had always been somewhat cordial to each other. She scared him in a way. It was as though he were afraid if he showed his feelings too openly or even touched her it would be a breach of some unwritten rule. He wanted so much to be a part of her life but did not know how, and he blundered from meaningless sentence to meaningless sentence without ever saying what was truly in his mind. He looked at all the red lanterns and gaudy paper cuttings, calligraphic scrolls and red and gold traditional clothes, the laughing adults and screaming children. All these young people...All these young people had things to do except himself.

Maybe I'll just play mahjong or something! But I can't play even that...maybe solitaire. I'll be all by myself. It's a real shame! he thought to himself.

He looked outside the window of the restaurant. Across the street a crowd was gathered. The focus of their rapt attention was someone sitting in what seemed like a stationary vehicle. A woman was sitting in a vehicle that looked like a golf cart without a canopy. Although her back was slightly towards them and they couldn't see her face, she was small and fiddling with controls within the vehicle. As she sang into the microphone a loudspeaker system carried the lyrics far across the busy streets. The music was sad and nostalgic. Her voice was at times weak, at times strong, but always plaintive.

"She cannot walk. She sings for money." Spring said, and looked at him closely. She had followed his gaze.

Rebecca interrupted, feeling as though the attention had shifted from her. She couldn't understand David. He was a mystery. When he looked at her she did not feel comfortable. It was as though he was like a father and a teacher together, a little like an old boyfriend.

"They want money. You know money is everything in Shenzhen. People are paid to beg in the streets. Then they go home to nice houses. You cannot trust them."

She continued talking about poor people and rich people in Shenzhen (but mostly about the rich).

"If you get all sad what's the point? David - Spring has good news"

"I'm not sad." he laughed again, somewhat hollowly.

He looked at Spring again and wondered why he had laughed.

"They're trying to survive. It's hard out there."

He looked more closely at Rebecca, who, sensing his attention, suddenly stopped in mid-sentence.

"Spring …Spring will…"

Spring continued David's thoughts.

"She is poor but she works hard. In China people work very hard…"

Spring touched his hand lightly as she reached over to the menu. He felt a shiver of excitement.

He handed her the menu. When she smiled he felt a tremendous sense of gratitude, as though she had done him a great favor with this small gesture.

The waiter came over and the two women spoke very fast Chinese. Rebecca's Chinese was very good, so fluent in fact that some locals called her a *zhong guo tong*, a word that roughly translates into *Chinese expert*.

"What are you guys saying?"

Rebecca promptly answered.

"This food is very famous. It is from Sichuan, a province in China. Have you been to Sichuan David?"

She had already told him the food was from Sichuan. Irritated he answered.

"No."

"Very wonderful. Sichuan food is very spicy, how do you say, hot. This restaurant makes hot pot. We'll order many vegetables and meats and cook them here at the table."

Spring then said something to Rebecca, her eyes serious and concerned. Rebecca started and turned to David.

"Oh, yes, you don't eat meat, yes?"

"No meat, fish or chicken.", he said in slow Chinese.

The two women at once raised their hands to beckon the waiters, who always were hovering behind David, quietly monitoring him. A young waitress hurried over and the three had a spirited conversation. Finally, Rebecca sat back against her chair with a smile of triumph.

"OK. We will have vegetarian food as well. You know we have to be careful about the soup. They use a special boiling soup. Many herbs, and certain fish and meat flavors. We told them to use a special soup with no meat or fish. It was hard. Spring is very persuasive!"

"What delightful girls you are!"

"Yes, we are!"

Rebecca giggled and looked adoringly at Spring, who smiled angelically. Then she turned to him.

"Spring needs your help. She has been asked to organize a special performance for the New Year celebration. She wants you to play piano and she will dance!"

"But I do not know any Chinese music!"

"Oh do not worry, it is a very famous song, called the *Butterfly Lovers*"

David did not see how its being famous made the music any easier.

"Do you have the piano music?"

"Yes, and Spring's friend can play the violin."

"You know the story of the Butterfly Lovers?" Rebecca continued.

"No."

"Along time ago a young man and a young woman fell in love. Because the families opposed it, they couldn't get married. The girl's father forced her to marry another man. Her lover, very sad, went far away. Lonely and sad, he fell ill and died. The woman went to his grave and threw herself inside. Afterwards people saw two butterflies come out. Because they loved each other so deeply gods turned them into butterflies that would always be together."

"Why were they turned into butterflies?"

"I do not remember. Do you know?" She asked Spring, her eyes wide open.

"It's just a story, don't take it too seriously. It's a fairy tale, Like *Romeo and Juliet*.", Spring smiled.

"I'll take a look at the music."

"Oh David, you are so good!" Rebecca coyly smiled at him.

"No problem." and he raised his cup of tea jovially and clinked it against theirs.

Spring and Rebecca were careful to keep the rim of their cup below his when they clinked together. In China, this is a sign of respect for the other party, and indicates *bon ton*. Spring suddenly laughed nervously.

"I miss home. We used to make all sorts of *Zhong Zi* during the Spring festival time. Making the dumplings took a long time, sometimes the whole afternoon!"

No one said anything. David and Rebecca were wrapped in their own thoughts. Then Rebecca looked at Spring sympathetically,

"Better to just buy them at the supermarket!"

"Today I did that too. But when you make them, Rebecca, and everybody in the family helps wrap the leaves, it is such fun!"

She thought often of her family around holiday times. There is a famous poem in China, known and memorized by all Chinese children:

Alone in a strange land as one's guest
During festive seasons I think much of my family

She felt a pang of homesickness and thought: *I'm not even a guest in Shenzhen. I'm just another migrant employee. I miss Henan so much!* She missed her mother and father terribly.

At the spring festival family and friends would gather around a big table before a smorgasbord of colorful and tastefully arranged dishes. New Year cake, pork chops, water noodles, *the ant running up the tree* dish, braised fish and dumplings galore. In front of the table would be their Panda brand television set with grainy pictures of the Spring Festival Community Festivity Program broadcast from Beijing. Not far from the round table filled with food there would be two small tables.

On one was a small bust of Chairman Mao or *Mao Zhu Xi*, as he was respectfully called by the villagers. The somber white porcelain face would look over the small warm circle of friends like a white guardian angel.

As was tradition in many households the bust was hollow with a hole in the base in which family members put their most precious belongings, such as the household contract or *hu ben* and money. These two items represented survival in China: the *hu ben* allowed them to live in a particular locality, and money paid their bills. One afternoon hen Spring was cleaning the table she had discovered money inside. From then on, from time to time, she would quietly take small amounts such as 5 mao or even 1 Yuan to buy her favorite things. For one Yuan she could buy a *Suan Da Fen* package. This package of sweet and sour candy would always conceal a tiny spoon exquisitely carved with the features of famous characters in Chinese history, such as *Sun Wu Kong* (The Monkey King) and *Si Da Mei Nu* (the Four Beautiful Maidens). She would collect these spoons and keep them in her cabinet beside her bed. Her mother knew that Spring took the money, but she said to herself *Children will be children, trying to control them is like herding monkeys!*

Next to *Mao Zhu Xi's* bust was a small altar. In a large metal pan placed in the center would be a pig's head. Fruits and delicacies surrounded it. A symbol of good luck and wealth, this ostensibly macabre object symbolized respect for one's ancestors. She had at first been afraid of the vast bloated, pink head with the baleful eyes. Year after year it would appear for a few days in Spring. To her its eyes became softer, weaker, until she ignored it altogether. Spring remembered how on the festival evening the children would run and tumble around the tables, almost as loud as the drumbeat of firecrackers outside. Once, when the neighbor's two year old, Little Wu, toddled up to it and started to cry, she took his hand in hers and said,

"Don't be afraid, Little Wu, its just *Bai Zhu*. He's fat and funny and won't hurt you."

Then if the boy wouldn't stop bawling, she went on, gently patting his hand,

"I used to be afraid of him too, but he won't hurt you. He's your friend."

And to emphasize the point she touched *Bai Zhu* gently on the snout.

"Don't Spring! No one touches the altar except your dear blessed grandfather in heaven!" her grandma would scold the little girl.

"Your dear grandfather... such a great man. You know he died trying to save our village from the Great Flood. Son, (and she pointed to Spring's father, who just harrumphed) don't forget to go to his grave tomorrow and bring him some of the *chou do fu*. Stinking tofu was his favorite food!"

Even though she was just a little girl, Spring remembered these stories of when she was growing up like it was yesterday. There would be lots of beer and white wine to wash down the food, many jokes and stories of one's adventures in the previous year. Eyes and ears would be rapt with attention.

Spring looked out the window. The sky had turned into an angry, smoking gray mass across which the clouds, still visible in the twilight, swept with a vengeance. It is about to rain, she thought. *It's like my hometown just before the rain comes.* The clapboards on the unfinished buildings beat an arrhythmic tattoo over the din of the vehicles that snaked along the streets like shining dragons with monstrous orbs for eyes. She was half listening to the conversation between Rebecca and David. *Americans, they are always so happy.* She thought to herself, and sighed. The musician had left long ago and now the street seemed lifeless except for the wind that ruffled the hair of pedestrians and heralded the coming of the rain.

David paid for the dinner. A few seconds later the server came back with a smile on her face,

"Sir, that 50 is fake."

She dangled the note in front of them almost accusingly. David couldn't see any problem. It was crisp, colorful and looked just like any other 50 Yuan bill.

"Here, let me see." He reached out his hand.

Instead Spring grabbed the bill and gingerly examined it.

"This isn't fake. No way!"

Rebecca grabbed it and with one hand folded it in half and with her thumb and forefinger rubbed the two halves together. The sound was loud and raspy.

"Definitely fake."

She looked smug. At that moment David decided he didn't like Rebecca.

Another customer, a young man, peered over from the next table, his face squinting at the dangling bill.

"No, surely it isn't. It looks good to me."

"Sorry sir, it's definitely fake."

The server smiled again.

Ignoring the discussion, David swallowed his embarrassment. He fished in his wallet and handed over some 20 Yuan bills.

The waiter came back a short while later, this time not smiling.

"This bill is also fake."

She showed them the 20-Yuan bill. David realized these were the bills he had received from the taxi driver. He cursed himself for not being more cautious with his change. *I got my 3 Yuan, but lost 70.* he thought, smoldering with rage.

"Oh this is ridiculous. Can't you see he is a foreigner and doesn't understand?"

But the server just smiled icily and retorted.

"We can call the police! We should report these things!"

Spring was furious. She paid the bill herself, over David's protestations.

"I'll never come to this restaurant again. They don't know how to treat you!"

And she stalked out, with David and Rebecca following her sheepishly.

As they walked back to the car, David looked at her proud, straight back and a warm sense of kinship swept over him. If it hadn't been for Spring, his attitude towards Shenzhen might have changed that night, but she had defended him.

"It's not a big deal...if you stay angry I won't play the piano for you."

She stopped in mid walk and turned her head. Her eyes were flashing like hot coals, her hair blew across her face. She swept away a few strands of the black fleece from her partly open mouth.

"What?"

He walked up to her.

"You were so hard to the restaurant workers..."

"*Ta Niang De!*" She cursed

He repeated what she said,

"*Ta Niang De!*"

"No, no, you cannot say that David, that's a dirty word. It means something you should not say."

"I know exactly what it means."

But Spring just smiled at David, quietly, mischievously. He realized she was no longer angry.

The three stood hesitantly beside Spring's little car. Across the street a small wiry man was trying to load a huge bundle of cardboard onto his bicycle. But it was too heavy to lift onto the bike. Seeing the foreigner looking at him, he stopped, looked around as though he were waiting for someone. Then realizing he had no choice - that he and his cardboard were fated to be together - he went back to wrestling with his load. David suddenly said,

"Well...when do we start to practice piano...and learn more polite Chinese?"

Spring laughed. It was a tinkly laugh, like the sound of carillon bells on a mountaintop in spring. But she still didn't say anything. Her hand rested on the open door, calmly, deliberately, gently kneading the rubber seam, looking at him with a strange expression.

David glanced at Rebecca, who smiled half anxiously, half relieved that Spring was no longer angry.

"Just the two of us...practicing requires concentration."

Spring opened the door to get into the car. Just as she entered, she turned her head around, smiling at him.

"I'll call you."

And with a growl and puff of exhaust smoke the little car sped off into the crush of ruby lights and honking horns. He looked in his wallet. He had about ten Yuan, excluding the fakes. He would take the bus back home. The American was soon lost in the swirl of Shenzhenites celebrating the coming Year of the Rooster.

He hadn't thought much of his father recently. Other than those first few nights in Shenzhen, he had approached something of a peaceful state. Recently he and his mother had shared letters and emails. While David enjoyed re-reading the correspondence with her, it was also with a sense of dread that he continued dredging up the past.

He scanned the first letter from his mother.

Liebe David!

You've asked me so many questions over the past few months. I have also been waiting for your reply to my last email but I wanted to tell you a few more things about your father and how I met him

About the time I had just graduated from college in Boston, I was floating around between various secretarial jobs. I finally took a summer course to qualify as a Primary School Teacher. I got a job at the Brockton Elementary School.

One day, (I think I told you this) during this time, I was coming back to my flat on a streetcar and a black man sat behind me. I guess he thought I was not too threatening so we started to talk. He invited me to a party or perhaps it was just to come and talk, so I did. There were very few Africans in the Boston area at that time, the late fifties. Being raised in a Jewish community what did I know of black and white and all that? But at that time I was very lonely and insecure. Any friendly face was OK with me. Within a short time I was having an affair with him, and felt I loved him, but after only one fairly turbulent week he flew back to Nigeria. I was devastated, but a friend of his befriended me and told me he was married anyway. Boy — my eyes were really opening.

Anyway there was to be another party on the following Sunday and this new friend said he would like to take me. It was at that party I was to meet my fate — i.e. your father. He was attracted to me and within a few days he came to my flat with an American friend (older) and asked to take me out. I was on my way to a completely new life.

He had a flat in Cambridge with some other African students and I was there almost every day from then on. I felt I loved him very much — he was very charming and there never was a dull moment — but he was not faithful to me although he told me he loved me too. I am still grateful it was before the days of AIDs or I would definitely have been a dead duck. He was very promiscuous and would have killed me! I of course was totally innocent and thought I was in love.

After two months of steady romance and fun, he said he had to return to Kenya. He said I should come there and if I liked the country we could marry. I took him at his word. Now I realize this was a line he gave to every woman/girl he met, but I didn't know that then. So I planned to fly to Kenya that year.

Naturally my parents were devastated and after I flew off my dad had to take my mother on an extended trip so that she could get over her deep depression. After all I was her only child and I didn't realize how this would affect her — I was too young and inexperienced to understand what I was doing. I only knew I was in love and wanted and needed a new life. So I flew off.

Well, that's how I met your father. And the rest is history...so they say.

Mutter

The letter was cryptic, without similes, euphemisms, analogies and images. The ending was abrupt. It was as though she had reached into a deep part of her soul and had been forced to spit things out.

He had replied as follows (he copied all his letters to her):

Liebe Mutter!

Your epistle touched me deeply. It made me think of new questions and explained a few. Do you know that this is the first time I heard of how you met my father? Before it had always been in bits and pieces. I also remember grandma and grandpa very well. Why do I think of them? Perhaps because you once told me how your mother broke down when she heard you intended to marry an African. You were her princess? Was your marriage to my father a form of rebellion against her? They are long gone now but they are like ghosts in my mind. Whenever I have reason to think of them, they appear very clearly, as if it were yesterday.

All these faces from long ago... I loved grandma. She always treated me well, and she loved you very, very much. Do you still have that short description of her I wrote and sent you a long time ago? I've looked and haven't found it. Maybe you can send it if you have time.

Things are quiet here. I am still learning new things about China. But there are irritations too. One thing hard to get used to is the noise. Chinese people like sound, lots of it. People shout on cell phones, turn the TV volumes full on in the gyms, and carouse on streets until late at night. I think the communal nature of society has so long been averse to privacy that silence is a middle and upper class privilege. We take it for granted but for hundreds of millions here who are moving slowly and inexorably up the ladder into the middle class, it's a strange delicacy. Then again, being a musician, perhaps I am too sensitive. So I love it when I can retreat into my silent apartment and control the sound, such as through my piano. Ecce homo!

Love,

David.

He was tired or writing and even more tired of reading. Now that he had initiated this trans-Atlantic conversation, the subject bored and exhausted him. Except for the occasional dream he did not think about his father.

Had David applied himself he could have switched off these fleeting ghostlike images. But the artist in him took an almost narcissistic delight in these surreal vignettes. It was as though they urged him to explore himself, to examine himself, his mind, his feelings, all in an inexhaustible stream of revelations. Through his father he understood more of his mother. Through her he understood more of himself. It was as though David was in an ecosphere where the flutter of an Indonesian butterfly's wings would cause ripples across the Alaskan tundra.

He was strong, granted. Bad sleep wasn't a curse. Nor was it unexpected in the course of one's life. It was a starting bell. It prompted actions. It could be treated like a bad stomach ache or a morning hangover, but it impelled David to dissect and explore himself and all his contradictions.

There was a time, long ago, when he had felt that these contradictions refused analysis. He would then think of the story of the millipede. Its 100 legs always worked instinctually, unthinkingly, in concert with each other. Once the millipede tried to reason just how they worked, it couldn't walk anymore and subsequently collapsed.

Then was then, now was now. Today David was in new territory. His life had already reached a nadir of sorts... financially, artistically, socially. So he felt he could risk understanding himself. Nietzsche once said of self-discovery, *beware of looking into the abyss lest it look into you.* David had always sensed the abyss but shirked peeking into it. He could now *take a bath*, as stock brokers and analysts say when they lump all their bad news into one report so that the only direction remaining is up. Furthermore there was an almost scientific, objective curiosity within him that seduced him into these ruminations. For example, he absolutely did not, as his mother had started out to do, dwell much on miscegenation, and racial relations. To him they were important issues, but by no means the most significant. As his mother had written in her letter *Any friendly face was OK*. David was thus almost post-racial in his thinking. His issue with the world, as he saw it, was simply that of a guy who happened to have a poor, failing father. The problem of race, he had always reasoned, was fundamentally an issue of being an exile. For one who had always been an exile, by temperament, by religion (his Jewish mother), only partially by race, how could he, as some might expect, lump issues into a racial vat? It would be like adding another stripe to a zebra - it hardly made a difference. *Any friendly face was OK.* To him, love had drawn his parents together and skin color was incidental. When he looked close enough at his mother he saw spots of brown on her splotchy pink skin. When he looked at his father's picture he saw blackness, but it seemed to him a symbolic blackness, a superficial veneer that masked a more real pain of abandoned love and willful violence. Though strong, their passion had quickly faded. David would discover that at the end of the day, jaded libidos and idealism had wreaked havoc on their marriage and his story, his travails, were ultimately a product of this unrequited love, not of race.

He went on.

Liebe David!

When I landed at Nairobi airport he wasn't even there! But I looked and asked around and met an Airport Supervisor, who knew him (he was well known) and said I should go to her home where she would then get in touch with him. After some hours he appeared and we went off together and started living together. Of course right from the beginning he was drinking heavily, staying out to all hours of the night, abusing me (sometimes hitting me and often verbally insulting me) but I was in love and very, very insecure so somehow I hung on. I had come in August and in December we married at the Civil Office with two witnesses. We were then living in Rosslyn Estate in a big house which was quite lonely and every night I cried for my parents; I also spoke often with an acquaintance, Audrey, who was suffering similarly. She also had a Luo husband who was not the greatest. Incidentally, some

years later she died a premature death. A death that was always something of a
mystery, but was probably precipitated by the very unhappy marriage she chose to
stay in.
      And then I had you!
      Are you still seeing Spring?
Love,
Mutter

The letters had been received weeks ago. He read them again with some
sadness. Ever since he could remember he had believed his parents eloped to
Kenya. Whenever asked how his parents had met he had said,
      "My father was a brilliant student who met my mother in Boston. They
met at a party and fell in love. Their families did not want them to marry.
However, they eloped to Kenya where they married."
      The reaction was almost always, "Wow. How romantic!". David had been
mislead or had deluded himself. *He hadn't even met her at the airport! What type*
of love was that! He thought his mother's love had been strong and genuine,
though perhaps a little over the top. His father's feelings, on the other hand,
had been grudging, even hostile. David sighed.
      He hadn't replied directly. He had changed the subject in his emailed
reply. He preferred to hear *her* stories, about *her* experiences.

      Got your epistle. As you know I was back in the States for a few months tending
to some things. I'm back in Shenzhen. Spring had a hard time recently with an old
boyfriend (he was cheating on her). We're good friends and share things. Maybe.
      Tell me more about you and my father. What was your daily life like?
D.

He read her answer. The letter had arrived in less than a week, unusual
for China.

Liebe David!
      I'm glad you are happy with your girlfriend. Maybe we will meet some day.
But that's another story, yes!!
      Well my life was not happy. Except for you, I was very unhappy. I had had
heavy menstrual bleeding for some time and had started to take contraceptive pills
to curb the bleeding – which they did. However, very soon after our marriage in
December I got pregnant. I also, as you know don't talk much about my possible

concert career, but at the time I knew that if I had a child I would probably have to give it up for many years. I thought of an abortion but really didn't know how to go about it, and so just continued with the pregnancy and luckily felt OK. During this pregnancy I worked for the Nation Newspapers, but I lost this job as I was not concentrating and the boss was too harsh for my taste. However soon after I lucked out and got a job as secretary to the General Manager of Nestle, Mr. Francis Dumas, who was to prove a very good friend to me for some years. Through the most difficult years of my life he was a great support and this job kept me going psychologically and physically.

So I started working for Mr. Dumas and gave birth to you on a December morning. What euphoria! I had no idea having a baby would turn my world around as it did. I loved loved loved you and because of you survived and grew. Your father was happy to have a son but of course really couldn't love anyone but himself, which indeed I don't know if he did. Come to think of it, he probably didn't love himself at all. For after all, why would he mistreat himself so if he did?'

Anyway I went home with you (your Luo name means born while it was raining) and very luckily had an excellent ayah, Esther, a young girl from Kiambu who was brought to us by a good friend of your father's, and you were a healthy, VERY intelligent baby. But I continued to be quite lonely because "my husband" was never there and when he was he was not pleasant. I stuck this out for one year when a friend told me he would help me get away. I decided to go back to the USA.
More later,
Liebe Mutter!

Quickly, impatiently, he put away the letters and let his fingers swept across the keyboard as though waving away invisible layers of dust. He emailed a reply.

Liebe Mutter!
Don't remember the states when I was a kid... faint memories of playing on a swing in a foreign place, could be anywhere.
Your letters about my are good and direct...no bullshit and romanticizing... appreciate that.
Gotta run. I have a class with hungry seven year olds.
Love,
M

He had lied. It was too late for class.

Roquentin in Sartre's *La Nausea* declared *Three o'clock is always too late or too early for anything you want to do. [...] Today it is intolerable.* It was as though, in this afternoon of his life, intolerable thoughts forced David to grasp for any available time killers.

As if on cue, his mind now returned to Zhen Rui.

✳✳

The boy had coughed again, this time more emphatically...

"Go on, go on."

David couldn't help barking it out somewhat irritably. Perhaps the boy wasn't being alert enough, he thought. Yet the music was fine. He turned from the window. The boy faced towards the keyboard, his back to the teacher. His body was shaking. At first David thought he was just expressing himself emotionally, but the movements were jerky and abrupt, without rhythm.

"I don't feel well" the boy said.

Zhen Rui stopped in mid phrase and turned around to face him. David didn't reply. He looked in disbelief at the boys face. It was chalk white. The lips had a faint bluish tinge. And a racking cough issued from his exhausted body without cease, in a staccato of what seemed retching pain. Almost absurdly, he said,

"Stand up, stand up."

He had no clue why he had asked the boy to stand up. In any case, Zhen Rui was too weak to do anything, let alone stand. The older man moved closer.

"What's wrong...?"

But the boy just continued his racking cough. He didn't know why the teacher was now standing above him. *He's started to fly*, he thought. *I'm flying too.* Then he felt something cold against his cheek. He wondered what it was. He looked past the teacher and saw that the sky was blue and without a single cloud. Most days it was gray. He wanted to say something like *I'm sorry I can't play piano today* but no sounds came out. He was happy that the sky was blue. He looked at his feet and they seemed to be something foreign and very far away from him. *Whose feet are those?* He said. Then everything turned black.

Luckily, a teacher passing along the corridor saw the situation, rushed in and tended to the child while David called for help. Other teachers rushed in and before long the boy was on his way to hospital. David stood helplessly by,

his hand resting on the piano as if for support. It was then that he realized what
no ambulance or doctor needed to tell him. Many times we do not believe the
things we see or what experts tell us. It wasn't so much a deduction that had
enlightened David, as it was an innate, infallible sense of certitude.
He realized Zhen Rui was terminally ill.

One evening a few days after the restaurant dinner Spring found herself
looking down from the roof of a friend's apartment. Her friend was a doctor,
a short dapper young woman whose little girl went to Spring's school. She
owned her own apartment in a fashionable section of the city. She also had a
car and therefore, by Shenzhen standards, all these things made her a member
of the *bai ling*, or white collar middle class. She stood beside Spring on the
balcony. Her baseball New York Mets baseball cap discreetly hid her bad hair
day. She wore jeans that were a little too tight for her somewhat short, fleshly
frame. Her pink T shirt flimsily covered her white plastic bra. On it were the
words *FUCK ME* emblazoned in cherry pink.

Spring's friend lived in one of the many gated apartment communities
that have become ever more popular in Shenzhen. These clusters of apartment
buildings are like little cities, their concrete cocoons insulated from busy streets
by high walls and automatic gates. Security staff, domestic workers, small
parks and courtyards, swimming pools and hundreds of families composed of
grannies, grandpas, uncles, aunts, nannies, white collar couples and their little
princes and princesses form these latter day Chinese villages. In the center of
the courtyard below, the large communal pool spread out like an emerald tear.
It was surrounded by an attractively tended garden through which walkways
weaved like random strands of fettuccini on salad. A broad walkway wrapped
around the garden. Children were everywhere. Surrounded by anxious old
ladies and young nannies, they screamed, laughed and shouted, urinated,
collided, stumbled and crawled. Couples walked leisurely hand in hand, as
though they had all the time in the world. In Chinese fashion, a few elderly
men and women briskly walked backwards, or lounged on wooden benches,
shirts pulled up slightly as they gently rubbed their exposed fat bellies in the
cool air, a leg or two casually curled up onto the bench.

"You like the balcony? I had it refurbished from scratch. It cost me 50,000
Yuan. But it will add about 30% to the value of the home when I resell!"

Spring's friend proudly adjusted her Jessica Simpson sunglasses and followed the other's gaze. They were about twenty floors above the sidewalk. It was dusk and in the distance it seemed as though God's lingering kiss had smeared a faint pink blush over the horizon.

"I like looking at the birds and the city. It's so beautiful" said Spring as she touched her left ear as if it would reassure her of something. And she looked at a flock of birds swooping and diving beneath the granite sky. She had to leave soon to go and meet David but she liked it here and didn't want to go right away. To her left the brilliant night lights of Shenzhen looked like hundreds of necklaces of light flung randomly over the cityscape. To her right, only forty yards or so away, was an equally tall building. In the gap between and above, birds of all shapes and sizes were swooping and hovering in a frenzied rush of jagged acrobatics. As they danced in a paroxysm of motion hundreds of yards above the ground and beneath the indifferent gray sky, she thought they were performing a beautiful mythic dance, in rhythm with the earth itself. She wondered why they were all congregating in such a small space. Then she noticed that some of the 'birds' were in fact large insects. They were like huge wasps or grasshoppers and the birds were feeding on them. The insects made impossible motions as they attempted to evade the birds, and she felt an almost horrid exhilaration when she saw one insect jerk away from a wall and, in a fraction of a second, careen directly into a bird's red gullet. Slightly sick, she turned away. Her friend looked at her closely and said,

"What's wrong?"

"It's the birds, and the bugs they're feeding on. I will have horrible dreams tonight."

And it was true. Her mind was a vast receptacle into which impressions, trivial or profound, like flecks of color in a kaleidoscope, gathered, scattered, danced, flourished, congealed and finally formed. When she wanted to express herself, she found words wanting. When it came to revealing herself to others, it was through a face and a body that danced with her emotions. It was only natural, therefore, that dancing was her passion. She was like a trembling drop of water in a boundless ocean, through which the rhythms of dance were vigorous, alive and in sympathetic motion with the fluid world around her.

Like most performers, she was acutely superstitious. Dreams, in particular, influenced her deeply. Having seen sadness and poverty up close and finding it depressing and unseemly, she strived to see the good and happy in those around her. She wanted her mind to be full of happy thoughts and pleasant feelings. Anger was abrasive. Depressing talk was an affront.

Yet Spring was not a superficial person. When it was necessary, she could roll up her sleeves and wallow in the dirt like the best of them When she saw a particularly sad scene, such as that first time at the orphanage, her eyes would mist for a few seconds, and a few hours later it was as though it had been reborn. Once, in her childhood, her grandfather had held her close and said, "Little friend, dream and strive. Always think of the good things in life. You may be still unhappy when they do not happen as you expected, but your dreams will remain strong..."

At the time she was only six years old and did not fully understand. As memories fade we remember not the emotions so much as the import of the moment. Spring remembered the tone in which he said it but the actual words were vague and foggy in her mind. So she made them up. A force and significance emerged that evolved with time. He might have actually said something like, 'Doesn't this flower smell wonderful! 'These may have been the actual words, but the flotsam and jetsam of her experiences in life had changed the original sentences into something almost religious. Now *flowers* may have become *dreams*. The *smell wonderful* may have become *beautiful*. In her opinion, the conclusion was the same: Life was good, but one had to surround oneself with beauty. Truth was sometimes difficult to manage, and should sometimes be avoided. 'Truth is Beauty, and beauty is truth' were inverted in Spring's universe. Now if it was beautiful it was the truth, and therefore the truth was beautiful.

"Are you OK?" her friend repeated.

"Yes..." and as if a gear had shifted, she immediately started to gossip about what happened in school that morning.

"It was so funny..."

Spring launched into a story of one of the children in her class. The birds and their dinner banquet faded from her thoughts.

"...even at that young age, living in a white man's world, in the shadow of colonialism, I always felt trapped. It was as if there was a place high on a mountaintop, and I would never climb up to it. Magazines, books, the easy lyrics on the radio, all these things were stamped with pigmentation..."

- From David's father's journal

RECONCILIATION

There had been the sweet scent of freedom in his decision to leave for China. It had something to do with the *ubermensch* within him-that Nietzschean over-man that seeks transcendence through solitude and isolation. What could have been more solitary, more alone, more free than to be in the east, in what the Chinese had for four thousand years called *Zhong Guo*, the fabled middle kingdom and center of the world? And yet, paradoxically, this rarefied air had turned into a place that was almost like family, like community. In the extended Chinese family of his friends and particularly of his loves, he had somehow started to forgive his debts to himself. Like a chimney cleared of smoke and fumes, he was slowly liberating himself from the urges and circumstances that had long pressed him to be this or that, to be up or down, right or left. While this eastern existence had its blessings he knew that it was only the first step in a thousand mile long journey, a magic kiss that might open his eyes. He felt he was linked to this land in some way. If it prospered so would he. Conversely, its faults had the potential to corrupt him, so he reasoned.

At times David thought China would never escape the yolk of its history. Five thousand years of endless wars, suppression, emasculation, and invasion had taken its toll, a toll that was ground into the bones of its people.

"Five thousand years of history!" he proudly heard it said again and again.

And everyone he met in China seemed to have a version of the phrase or would repeat to foreigners verbatim, 'Five thousand years of history!', as though it were a golden emblem, a sign of nationalistic superiority, of a mother race.

In the school such references were inevitable. Textbooks referred to China's history as a seamless chain of linked and glorious accomplishments. Once he asked the children the question:

"What country would you most like to visit in the world?"

"Egypt!"

"Greece!"

"America!"

Another said,

"Egypt!"

Another chimed in,

"The Pyramids!"

David interjected,

"Why Egypt?"

A little boy with a mop of hair that swept over his oversize glasses eagerly poked up his hand.

"Because Egypt has many thousand years of history, like China!"

But to David China's was a minimalist history. To him it was a little like Wagner's music: it stretched for ages upon boring ages, only punctuated by brief moments of unforgettable brilliance and genius. Thus, to him, ever since Master Kong, known to the West as Confucius, with his students created, implemented and destroyed all other thought structures after him, there had been nothing at all remarkable about those five thousand years, except for the Spring and Autumn period, and the few hundred years of the Tang (600-900AD) and Qing (18th Century) dynasties.

David was learning that Confucianism had been China's religion of sorts, and schools were its churches. The young had been schooled to follow, not to lead. The Confucian school pursued the dictum

If the benefit is not perfect, change no laws

In essence unless the outcome was guaranteed to be perfect, change was discouraged.

Confucius had taught

Even the most beautiful shade of blue starts from the roughest hues

Which signifies that even rough material, when polished can become an object of beauty and praise. One's student, if diligent, could and should surpass his or her teacher. However in the years following the Spring Autumn period the Empire became ever more conservative. Under the influence of the Confucians, the emperors passed draconian laws limiting intellectual freedom.

The infamous Teacher Covenant or *Shi Cheng* stipulated that the scope of a student's writings, judgments and speech could never exceed that of the teacher or master. What the Taiwanese intellectual Bo Yang termed China's *bitter jug of cultural vinegar* retained its stench for thousands of years.

Faced with such contradictions, society tends to move towards the easier route, one of stability and ossification. The Confucian schools had long taught *Ren* which signified benevolence. But this benevolence was rooted in filial piety and submission to aristocrats and oligarchs. It was a grudging benevolence. Proffered to the weak and less fortunate, it always signified a master-servant or father-son relationship. In return it required a virtue – that of submission. It was particularly grating for a woman whose task was to,

Serve her father until he died
Then serve her husband until he died
Finally serve their sons until they died.

David had come to China to escape his own demons but he sometimes wondered if he had escaped from one abyss only to jump into another. There were dark moments when he wondered if China would corrupt him, would spit out his foreignness and make him something less than he was. And even though he fought against this leveling of himself it sometimes overcame him. He wanted to understand China, but he did not want to be Chinese.

In particular he did not want to be one of the crowd.
The crowd was rapacious.
The crowd was unfeeling.
The crowd was unthinking.
The crowd was vulgar and beneath him.

He remembered how one afternoon he had gone to the bus stop on Hong Li Road to take the 213 to the supermarket. An open market had sprung up in the past few days, and everywhere he walked vendors had laid out their wares on the busy sidewalk. Migrant workers crowded on the sidewalk close by. Pink, brown and red trolley suitcases lay on the short grass and reddish concrete. Piles of plastic buckets, rolls of straw bedding, plastic bags surrounded these migrant workers who, bird-like, squatted on the sidewalk. Some chatted to their comrades, but most just peered at the construction activity across the street, their mouths slightly agape and eyes wide open, as though waiting for someone to beckon them, welcome them to the jobs and livelihood that would support them and their families in Guanxi, Henan, Shaanxi and other distant places.

Two dogs, one large and black, the other small and white were dashing between the street vendors and workers like lizards around rocks. A young vendor sitting on a small wooden stool and dragging on his cigarette got annoyed. He grabbed a stone that was next to his neatly arranged Mao era collectibles (magazines, leaflets, copies of the little red book) and let fly at the animals. His aim was true. The fist sized stone struck the large black dog on the side of its head, just below the ear. With a huge yelp the large dog collapsed, bleeding profusely from a head wound. The little dog ran in circles around him, every so often whining and licking him on the face.

Meanwhile, oblivious to the drama, sandals and shoes clattered by. The workers continued to peer across the street and chat among themselves, although a few turned to stare at the spectacle. The tall buildings loomed overhead like big cigarette boxes. White air conditioners and laundry stuck out from their orifices like tattered ribbons. Just feet away BMWs and Jettas honked and maneuvered for space like angry metal steeds jostling for a meal. The vendors calmly laughed at the two dogs and chatted among themselves, their foreheads lined with wrinkles of poverty and calculation. A worker who was chatting to his friends suddenly stood up and came close to the dogs, curious at the hubbub. The little dog gave a loud yelp of anger and trotted directly towards the newcomer, head held high, short legs jerkily dancing and white teeth bared and snarling.

"Shit, you fucking animal!"

He backed away, fear in his eyes. The little dog then patrolled in a semi circle around the black dog, his eyes glaring at all and sundry. Its companion now lay motionless, its eyes turned up towards the harsh noon day sun, breathing heavily, tongue hanging out of its half open mouth. Anyone who came close got the same treatment.

A crowd slowly gathered. It was like a flaccid ball, void of elasticity. If pushed or poked it ceded grudgingly, with little resistance. If holes or gaps appeared among the spectators in such a crowd, people would quickly fill them in. This slow motion ball of people was strangely dead, never intervening in the event observed. He had seen this before on Chinese streets. It could be a father whipping his child into a cowering form on the sidewalk, or a woman lambasting and abusing her husband in the middle of the street, or a dispute between thugs and homeowners on Youtube. In America, people would feel obliged, out of impulses raging from crass egotism to noble civic mindedness to intervene or, if the situation was dangerous, pretend it wasn't there.

"Here, let me help."

One might say. Or

"How can you let that SON OF A BITCH do that to you?" another might yell out.

David, for his part, never once thought of helping the animals. That they were dirty or covered with blood never entered his mind. He could have called the police and pressed them, but his mind was strangely dead. "What can the police do?" he remembered someone saying to him. "My cell phone was stolen the other day. I went to file a report and they just ignored me. Shenzhen is like that." Today he was like those standing around him. He looked on with a morbid curiosity. Minutes later his bus arrived and he left.

An hour later when he alighted hauling his bag of groceries, the crowd was even larger. Faced with the spectacle of savagery, there was just a mute, wide-eyed silence. It was as though intervention was too taxing a thing. It was selfish perhaps, but it was deeply ingrained in China's history. For so long emperors and kings, despots and megalomaniacs, foreigners and ideologues had brutalized, humiliated, whipped, cajoled, divided, and bled the common man. Language, thought and action were like three great rivers traveling roughly parallel across the bloody welts of China's back, always in sight but rarely crossing. *No* was a word reserved only for the very powerful, and often used with extreme care. To criticize the emperor was to touch the tiger's tail. In the presence of the emperor, even masculinity was eviscerated. Young men, to curtail their potentially lascivious and independent thoughts and actions, were castrated. In Europe the castrati ruled the opera houses. In China, the eunuchs ruled the palaces. Particularly among the poor, one was always the observer, reactive, hardly ever proactive.

The tiny dog, barely a foot tall, stood vigil next to the now dead body. Next to this rock of luxuriant black moss like hair, the little dog held his head high like a gendarme, as though reaching for heaven but with toes stuck in hell. No matter how big and tall, any intruder who came to close was menaced. He fearlessly skirted out his territory, occasionally dashing to his buddy's cadaver with a quick and gentle lick and whine, as though his tenderness was a benediction from a priest. His wet licks were like tears that would raise him from the hot concrete, but it was not to be.

It must have been over two hours since the stone was thrown, David reasoned. And he wondered why he hadn't helped sooner. Why had he walked away when the dog could have been helped? Why had he been apathetic to the misery in front of him?

"You're like those guys in Seinfeld who were arrested for not being good Samaritans!" an old friend later told him when she heard the tale.

David looked at the crowd surrounding him. Like a confused man in a hall of mirrors he saw himself. He felt their peculiar fascination. As events were developing, tragedy and pain, like a sinuous thread, were connecting and proceeding one to the other. The fascination was not, like it was in Americans, mixed with judgment and resolution, but had a calm detachment, a non-partial, almost sage and clinical sense of observation. *I have become like them…*, and a horror and shame stole over him.

Then he remembered how on the crowded bus two large, swarthy men had instinctively stood up from their seats and given them to an old woman and a young schoolboy. *How rare to see such a thing in the United States*, he pondered. Of course, he recalled, he had rarely used buses in the States. But he had often used subways. Within those rattling metal tubes that snaked artery-like through the dark bellies of the cities to him there was always a common element in the faces of their human cargo, something combining fear, suspicion and indifference. He asked himself many questions. *Where in China did this instinctual courtesy come from? Was it kindness? Was it grace? Was it even tenderness and compassion? Was it the rote product of the only true church in China, that temple of Confucianism – the public school? Where did courtesy leave and kindness begin?* And it was at moments like this that he felt there was hope. Hope not only for them. But for him as well. Particularly for him. *Ecce homo!*

Things were slowly changing. Since the revolution a sense of obligation between citizens was developing. At times it erupted in a fierce nationalism, but since Deng Xiao Ping's Reform movement started in the 80s perspectives were changing more quickly. Even though many of the poor and under-educated (over 800 million of them) were caught in a time warp, trapped by older customs and attitudes, the young, like the orphanage's Zhen Rui and Teacher Li, were beginning to understand and value life's priceless intangibles. Although many were as if in a dream, unaware of or unable to control their selfishness, more and more were waking up, discovering art, service and, in particular, civic duty and thereby changing the Middle Kingdom.

One day he was sharing lunch with another teacher. Mr Zhou, an elderly man approaching retirement, had managed to hold onto his job despite the influx of younger teachers from the new universities. David had had a trying day with the children. Seeing the foreigner's worn face he said,

"You seem a little sad today, my friend. What is it?"

"Sometimes I don't know why I am here. This morning I couldn't control the kids. I'm exhausted."

"Maybe you will go back to America soon, yes?"

"No, I don't think so."

"I remember when I was a student in America. I like the American people you know."

"How long were you there for?"

"Just a few months. It was part of a government program. It helped me get a good job when I came back."

"What did you like?"

"I'll tell you a story. You know there is a saying here in China. It goes

In the home trust the family
Outdoors, rely on your friends.

I was living in Boston one winter. It was so cold. And I had a very old car. It broke down in the street. I had no friends, no money."

"You could have called the police for a tow truck."

"You don't understand. We Chinese would do anything rather than call the police or government. Too much trouble. So I just sat in my cold car. Then a pickup truck drove by and stopped. A white man got out. He was a poor man. I could see it from his clothes and his car. He said to me

"Need some help? Need a lift or a jump start?"

Well, I needed a jump start. He got the cables and started my car. No problem! I wanted to pay him but he refused. He waved his hand and said: " I'm just helping a guy in trouble"."

And then he left. I was astonished. This man wasn't my friend. I would never see him again. Such a thing is very rare in China. Most people who don't know you have no *guanxi*. They do not care. Or they want money.'

A teacher at the next table who had been listening laughed.

"I want to go to America too! I will test them and see if they treat me that way. A good test!"

Mr Zhou smiled and quickly changed the subject.

Another time Mr Zhou was in the teachers' lounge. It was a quiet hour and except for the two and a few children watching the TV the lounge was deserted. The two got into a discussion of the Cultural Revolution of the sixties. During that time Mao had railed against traditional ways of thinking, and had given unprecedented power and authority to the youth, including schoolchildren. For over ten years the country went through an orgy of self flagellation, destroying books, art works, and symbols of tradition and punishing the intelligentsia in the name of the communist state.

"How old were you?" David asked.

"I was in my twenties. My father was a professor at the University."

The old man talked without hesitation, his eyes fixed on the TV that was broadcasting children's cartoons.

"They made my father wear the big hat, the *Da Mao Zi* and the board. You know, it is like a fool's cap. And people would write words of abuse on the board. He had to carry them everyday no matter where he was."

"How long for? A few days?"

"Ha! A few days!" Mr Zhou laughed scornfully.

"What do you mean! A month perhaps?"

He smiled bitterly, still looking at the cartoons,

" About 7 or 8 months."

"I suppose many of his friends got the same treatment."

"Some! All of them! Whoever they knew came in for the big hat and the self-criticism classes. They would say "I know you. Then you must wear the big hat". Every one who is over 40 remembers,"

He went on,

"Those under 40 have no history of that time."

"Did you go up to the mountains and down to the villages?" David asked.

He was referring to the Mao initiative in the 1960s that made city children go to live in the villages and farms, ostensibly to force them to understand the way of life of the peasants.

"Yes."

"Did you like it?"

He shook his head.

The next time David saw Mr Zhou he was no longer his gregarious self. He puttered around his desk, as though he was avoiding him. It seemed to David that memories of that time had saddened him. David understood: there is nothing more bitter than remembrances of wasted youth and missed opportunities.

✳✳

He was lying on his bed the afternoon before the concert. It was one of those brilliantly impassive days when the earth below and the lofty kael above dance to the exclusion of humankind. It was the twelve to two lunch hour and most people were indoors eating or resting at their desks during the two hour long break. Outside the streets were deserted and the sky looked washed out. The few trees, stripped of their leaves, made him think of souls imprisoned in bony carcasses, or left free to roam as ghosts over the land. He remembered passages in *L'Etranger* by Camus; Meersault pursued by the Arabs; the opening line *My Mother died today. Or maybe yesterday, I don't know*; the screams of execration. And he had thought these things as he had looked out over the tessellated strips of cold, white concrete, in places draped like frozen, broken ice floes along the streets. He could hear the rustle of the sidewalk skipping flotsam and the cries of distant birds. He looked up from his bed and outside the window saw the silent and hungry mouth of a looming pale sky. Like a disembodied kite, a plastic bag wafted high, jerkily, between the buildings. Without perturbation, the great river of life flowed over and around him, with no beginning and no end, neither welcoming him nor discarding him. He just did not matter.

On the cluttered desk before David were the scattered pages of a letter he was writing and a framed photo. Other than that of his father it was the only photograph of Kenya he had brought with him.

The tree stood alone in the middle of a barren landscape, shrouded with clouds. The black and white photo had been shot on a safari long, long ago at the Mara in Kenya. It had been early in the morning. He had rented a guide and driver who had driven him across the savanna just as dawn was breaking. The leafless tree had been blasted by lightning or fire. From the straight blackened stump a few shattered, jagged branches reached outwards like fingers calling out to the heavens. In the far distance there was the pale dark blot of an acacia tree and, even further away the hills that undulate like a woman's belly. And above it all there was the unblinking, indifferent sky.

A wave of nostalgia swept over him every time he looked at this photo. He thought of friends long gone, places that had changed forever, loves that might have been, and missions that could have been accomplished. With some sadness he remembered unrequited love and his unfulfilled promise. He would see the dust on the glass (it seeped from the city into every apartment, no matter how airtight) and the scratches on the cheap wooden frame and realized with a little shock that the photo was over thirty years old. It had all gone by like a dream.

The phone rang harshly. It was Rebecca.

"So how are you doing David?",

She had made it a habit to ring him up every so often, ostensibly to check up on him. She spoke with her habitual breathlessness, sometimes punctuating the middle of her rapidly spoken sentences with little nervous laughs or giggles.

"Just observing. I'm postponing judgment for the moment."

"Good, because a lot happens around here for new-comers."

He had been in China over three months. *What was she talking about?* he wondered. *Was he still a new-comer?* He heard sounds of hammering and men's voices in the background as he listened to her.

"Having a party there? What's the noise?"

"Oh, I'm having somebody in to fix my toilet. I've tried to get the landlord to fix it for the past 2 weeks. It doesn't flush properly. No luck getting them to come. So just when I give up this guy knocks on the door, and he's here to fix it. Hold on."

She said something to someone else in the room. Then she returned to the phone.

"Man, these people. Now he says he cannot fix it because it is taking too long and he has another appointment!"

"You should lock him in the toilet and tell him you won't let him out until he fixes it!"

"You're bad," she giggled. "But this is the reality." she sighed. "This is how things work in China. Everything is slow and, oh, there's also no privacy. Word gets around fast."

"What do you mean?"

"Shenzhen has 4 million people, and yet they all seem to know each other. If you say something private to one person before you know it a hundred others know about it."

She put him on hold and some more hurried conversation took place. She returned to the phone.

"OK. he'll stay to fix it. Don't know why he suddenly agreed. Anyway, about privacy…the other day I was about to go to bed and the headmaster just walked right into my bedroom and started to discuss some business matters with me. I was dressed in a nightgown, for god's sake. And he didn't just come into the living room; he came right into my bedroom as if he owned it, which he does by the way…"

"That doesn't happen to me." There was an awkward silence, and he continued, "although I'm stared at a lot."

She ignored him.

"And that's another thing. Be careful how you project yourself. We're a novelty here. You may feel people stare at you like your skin is green and you have antennae sticking from your head and blood dripping from your ears. It takes one bad apple of a foreigner in Shenzhen to spoil things for the rest of us believe me. But you haven't told me…"

"Told you what?"

"Why did you come to China?"

"Many reasons. I wanted to live in another country. Maybe do a little work promoting my business skills…"

"But why China? There are many other countries."

He could not tell her why it was China. *How do I explain instinct?* He thought. China held secrets that fascinated him and it nourished his solitude. For some men, solitude is a sickness and they nourish it with an almost fanatical devotion, going to the very ends of the earth to be both torn from and wallow in it. He had lived in many countries and had many jobs. Like most wanderers he had a horror of aimlessness. To empty his mind of this aimlessness he had filled his mind with many books and ideas - even if they were boring and unfruitful, illogical and beyond purpose.

Now he was in his fifties and he felt all that he had between his ears was a lot of gray rubbish. So, not understanding himself, David told Rebecca what she could understand, *I'm here to do business, to learn the language, to help children in orphanages, to experience a foreign life* and all that. This was true, but they were fragments that dotted David's personal landscape, like shards of pottery across a blasted volcanic scene, lacking only the glue that binds and provides meaning.

"This place will redeem me." he wanted to tell her but remained silent.

"Anyway, some of the teachers are going out this evening for a short dinner. Thought you might like to join them. You up for it?"

"Sure, count me in."

They would meet in a few hours.

He read his mother's last email again:

Liebe David!

As I said I decided to go back to the US with you. My parents found a house for us to stay in. I couldn't stay with them as I had a black baby! Nevertheless they loved me but didn't know what to do with me and my baby. However, within a few weeks your father came after me! I had never expected this and I returned to Africa with him as I still loved him. But of course – after moving into a City Council House where we were to stay for about 4 years – he didn't change in fact was probably even worse.

I can remember running out into the night several times when he was after me to beat me and screaming for help which I never got. These memories are very painful for me to write about but I think I might as well once and for all. I can remember a neighbor coming out of his house trying to help me as I went screaming down the street. I think I eventually stayed in a friend's home and then begged your father to let me come back because I couldn't be away from you. EVER!

After many years I still have some of these memories but I don't hate him. I think perhaps he was the only man I ever loved. Funny how such contradictory emotions can stay with one for a long time. But you were the reason I stuck though it all- and why I decided to leave him too.
Mutter

The scent of cooked rice or the broken strains of an old song can reel out long forgotten memories from the deep pool of one's mind. This letter, in such a way, became David's cooked rice and snatches of once forgotten melodies. This letter startled him and dredged out things he had wanted to forget. He tried to imagine his mother running down a Nairobi street at night. Had there been people around? His reason told him there must have been - Kenya had too many people. But in his mind he only imagined her alone on the median, stumbling and crying, her once auburn hair pre-naturally white in the shock of the overhead street lamps. His reason told him that the Kenyans around her must have been startled at the sight. They would have thought she was crazy, a wild woman, no doubt. White women married to Kenyans were very rare at that time. Eyes would have peered from behind every curtained window. A baby might have been woken up in the cramped neighborhood. A small crowd might have gathered. They would have stood aloof, maybe even laughed.

The shame burned inside him. His eyes welled up. A solitary tear ran down his cheek. He remembered how he and his mother had lived with his father until he was about ten. Then he had left and they saw him less and less. He vanished into the hinterland of Kenya, back into the teeming masses of grungy apartment blocks, absorbed back into the semi-literate masses of Kisumu. He remembered few good things about that very black skinned man who shouted a lot and made his mother cry.

He remembered one night in particular. There must have many such nights, but it was this one that had stuck in his memory. Like a shard of shrapnel, it couldn't be jogged loose and it took random, undefined, unpredictable events, or certain recollections – like in her letter - for it to be jogged back into his consciousness.

He was about six or seven then. He was sleeping in his bedroom and suddenly there was a tremendous commotion. He looked out from the blackness towards the open door of the living room across the hallway. A bright orange glow from within showered the hallway with light. His mother's voice was screaming as if terrified. The child almost didn't recognize it. And then there were some thumps as of someone falling. His father's angry voice raised itself as if in a duet with the unrecognizable voice. He didn't remember what they were fighting about, but his stomach felt sick and empty. His mother was being attacked and he couldn't protect her.

"You bastard!" he remembered her screaming out.

And that was just one such night. There were many more. And yet, she would still be strangely forgiving of his father. She would criticize him and then in the same breath say 'but...' And David later realized that she still loved, maybe had loved only him. Only in his adulthood did he understand how it was possible for one to see beauty in a mirror that had been shattered in two. But his mother was immensely practical. Early on she had realized how naïve she had been, and how damaging domestic abuse was.

"I could take him beating me, but when he started beating you, my little boy... how could he do that to my little baby?"

At that point her eyes would well up and she could not go on. Only two things made his mother cry: the sight of a wedding and the memories of her son being hurt. Then, she would wipe her tears away and say,

"But I had you and that was his gift!"

She would grab his hand so tight that it hurt and put her face close to his,

"He had a brilliant mind. He gave you that and for that I am grateful. He was a brilliant man but a social failure." She would sometimes say.

For many years David had never forgiven him. On the few occasions he spoke of him it was with difficulty he used the term "father".

He had already started to write a reply. He used his fountain pen this time. He wanted to hold something solid to balance the heaviness in his heart. He slowly reviewed his scratchy rightward leaning ink marks.

Liebe Mutter!

I am doing well in Shenzhen. The teaching job is supporting me financially. I also get to meet new faces each day. Above all, the people and the culture constantly amaze me. Every day I discover something new. For example, men and women pedestrians constantly use umbrellas — even in the sun. 'It protects our skin and keeps it as white as possible' someone said without a trace of embarrassment. It is hard for most foreigners to understand China without personally coming here. And that visit should not be a shepherded, hotel tour group but a roll-up-your- sleeves-smell-the-dirt exploration of everyday life. In some ways I am also discovering parts of me that I did not know about, or couldn't articulate. But more of this later.

As I live in China I have come to discover more and more who I am, and what I am not. I have come to the realization that black, white, yellow are constructs that people use to distinguish themselves when it becomes hard to be singular. I was born black, grew white, absorbed yellow, and now I am a citizen of the world.

You always said that I never told you about my feelings, that I was so 'self-sufficient.' In fact, it was something of a mask and some of the things I'm saying now are probably a surprise to you.

For example I don't think I ever told you the first time I became aware of the power of skin color. I was about ten or eleven years old and watching a TV program. It was one of those imported American shows that are about kids growing up in comfortable white neighborhoods among doting, slightly amusing parents like 'The Partridge Family' fare. One of the daughters, a beautiful girl, was dating someone and the parents objected. At that moment I suddenly realized that a beautiful white girl somewhere would not like me because I had dark skin. This was a shock! That day I was sort of low on energy and just sunk into this morose feeling that I was a reject. That afternoon my natural optimism foundered and the negativity had time to seep into me like a poisonous ether, I remember it well.

I wanted to be accepted by the white world. I also wanted to be accepted by the black world, but less so — most of my world view and status symbols were western. Most Africans would have none of me — I was too 'white'. Just a ' half-caste' It hurt.

I retreated into my solitude. And in that solitude I discovered more of myself. By the time I was in my teens the 'individual' had become more fully formed and I would never again be only black or white. While I welcomed their artistic and uplifting components, I rejected racial categorizations. I have become a varied, diaphanous thing, part of it all and nevertheless tracing across it my solitary, inimitable path.

Although I am happy to be in China I miss Kenya at times.

Our Kenya is a quiet land. In spite of rickety structures perpetually on the point of collapse, Kenya and its people continue their deliberate, traditional ways. I remember the Nairobi streets where brightly colored carvings and cloths are on sale next to tattered out of date magazines and books. At our home, you entertain friends who, in spite of seeming impressed by my moderate success abroad, are mostly indifferent to the hurly burly of western culture. They are decent people. They speak straightforwardly. They hold their hands to their sides, without jitter or nervous energy and calmly listen to each idea. And the day trots along at a steady pace too. I can imagine myself there now. Sometimes I go nearly mad with the lugubrious tempo, and I wait impatiently for something, even if I don't know what. At other moments, I look at the flowers of paradise in the garden that poise for flight like bright yellow and orange wave banners and feel the quiet sense of time passing like a quiet angel bearing secret gifts, inevitable, inexorable, and, for those with a sense of unfulfilled destiny, like myself, with savage indifference.

But the race thing always intercedes. At the party you held for me once I still see how Natasha, your trusted friend, bubbled around the festivities, helping prepare and serve drinks and food. Her white face was lined with creases of merriment beneath a shock of white hair. Yet, underneath the pleasant smile, she was quietly skeptical of me. Not overtly, for she is probably unaware of this. Yet when I asked to take out her beautiful teenage daughter, some excuse about exams was hurriedly cooked up. 'You can trust Gina with David, can't you?' you urged Natasha with a smile. But the die was cast. A lurking suspicion of the black guy quietly spread across Natasha's mind, like the spread of ink through cream

Your last epistle deeply moved me. For weeks I did not reply. I was wondering what to say! On this birthday of yours I want you to know that I love you. I remember long ago, when I was barely four or five feet high, you sang 'For nine months I carried you, loved, you, nurtured you...no charge.'., And hearing that song I giggled or dismissed it. Dear mother, you weren't jesting, but it seemed weird to me. I realize that my life has certainly diverged from what we both expected. While I believe the grand finale is yet to come, for you it may seem I have crossed the high mountain. God forbid that you think that! Forbid that it be true! You have been the single source of stability and strength in my life. From time to time I felt as though the ground was shifting beneath me, threatening to suck me up into some nameless pit. A pit that was worse than hostile - it simply didn't care. And many of those times I thought of you. I imagined how you would react. Sometimes you would be happy and pleased. At others you would be sad. Yet always there was love and hope. I wish I could repay you in some way. I have been a difficult son, perhaps more so now than I was in divine and distant days. Perhaps even the thought of *paying you back makes no sense. I owe you my life. I owe you everything I know and a lot of what I don't. Mom, as you read this please do not think I've been attacked by schizophrenia or some mind softening disease. I feel perfectly sensible. In fact, I'm hungry and look forward to dinner. So please be assured that my head is firmly planted on my shoulders. I just feel a little sad. Life is so short. Mortality is an old friend of mine. As an artist, I have always felt obliged to at least be aware of it, and in moments of extremity, though rarely, I have come close to embracing it. Your divine epistle has brought me to a state where this sense of my mortality and yours is almost overwhelming. The clearest vision I have of you, above all, is of a kindred spirit that lights my life and to whom I owe the world.*

With eternal love, your son

David

Too little about Shenzhen, he thought. *Why did I write this?* He realized the letter was not yet complete. There was something missing. The last part needed something else - something to do with his father, he was certain. In time, he said, he would find out what it was. *There is a time for everything. There is a time for everyone* ran like a mantra though his mind.

That evening he joined Rebecca, two other women and one man at the gates of the school. The five teachers walked a few blocks. It was about seven thirty and the city's nightlife was beginning to hum. Flashing neon fitfully illuminated every dark corner and the brake lights of coughing metal beasts spun a ruby red web across the thoroughfares. On the sidewalks food vendors with their friends, family and customers happily squatted down around little charcoal braziers smoking with roasted eggplant. Old and young couples and friends took their slow walks in the gated compounds and parks while outside pedestrians deftly navigated their way home through Shenzhen's many obstacles: the occasional construction bricks scattered on the sidewalk, the DVD hawkers and their small trays of pirated movies, the lonely yellow striped metal pole jutting out of the sidewalk like some giant excavated forefinger.

The "restaurant" was really an outdoor kiosk adjoining a large dining room, one of the many local eating places that lined the streets of working class neighborhoods and served the less educated, less affluent workers of Shenzhen. Everything was plastic: pink and white tablecloths, dark tarpaulins draped over some of the tables to shield customers from rain, cheap disposable chopsticks, some shrink wrapped plates, and the occasional flimsy plastic bags that skimmed over the ground with the wafts of night air. Many customers chatted loudly and drank their beer with gusto. Oily food remnants and cigarette stubs remained on some tables. David hesitated. Seeing the look in his eye the other man grinned amiably,

"Don't worry, mate, the grub's good."

"Come, welcome, welcome!" a smiling middle aged lady in a faded red *chi pao* top worn over blue jeans led them to a table right between the door and the sidewalk where all the passersby could see them. It was good business to seat foreigners in conspicuous places as some Chinese would sometimes buy drinks and food just to sit close and observe them. Also, having foreigners seated at one's restaurant was a sign of status and gave the proprietor face, or *mian zi*.

The table was quickly cleaned and covered with a cream colored plastic tablecloth. A pot of hot flower tea and cups were served and someone placed a small glass filled with plastic roses on the table top. All of a sudden the arrangement looked quite cozy. As was the custom, the pot of tea was served with a round ceramic cup, saucer and small bowl for each guest. Rebecca placed the cup upside down in the bowl and poured hot tea over it to wash it. Then delicately, with her thumb, second and index fingers, twirled and rinsed the cup, finally removing it and placing it on the saucer. Holding the chopsticks in one hand directly over the bowl she rinsed them, letting the hot tea wash over them and into the bowl. In a final flourish she emptied the waste water into a large glass bowl in the center of the table. This process was repeated by each of the guests. The lady bustled around them, cluck clucking with concern and shooting orders in a soft but shrill voice to the fresh-faced waitresses milling around.

"You-Me."

"What?" Emily, the new recruit from Memphis said to Rebecca,

"Corn. In Chinese it's like saying 'you' and 'me'. Pronounce it like that and you'll never get it wrong."

"Don't confuse her," David said, twirling his chopsticks nonchalantly.

"He has to teach her to eat!" Ted, the Australian teacher laughed.

Emily smiled. She liked Ted but was a little embarrassed. Her huge glasses perched on her small bright red nose seemed to quiver.

"We'll try this," Rebecca told the hostess. They rapidly exchanged more Chinese until they were both satisfied. Rebecca had ordered for Emily *Song Ren Yu Mi* which roughly translates as "loose kernels of corn", a delicious dish of crisp fried corn kernels and green beans.

"So how are you fitting in so far?" David asked Emily.

"OK, but it's a lot to take in."

"Damn straight."Ted chimed in, winking at Emily.

"All Ted thinks about is DJing and getting into bed with Emily.". Rose, the other female teacher, smirked.

Everyone liked Ted, David thought to himself. Rose mostly kept her own company, already had been in China a year and had her own boyfriend. Rebecca changed the subject,

"What do you mean? DJing is important around here. It's part of life too."

"Have you got a gig?" David asked

"Yeah, got a gig this evening. I'm pretty excited about it."

"How did you get it?"

"Some friends I know. They said I'd be perfect for the part because I'm white!"

"What?"

"I tell you mate, they already have a black DJ and they want someone to balance it out."

"That's pretty strange."

"And that's not all you have to deal with,"Ted continued, his eyes sparkling and waving his big beefy hands, "they stare at you like you're an alien. Privacy doesn't exist man. My students don't give it to me. They cluster fuck right around me when I'm reading or doing something else. I mean even when I go to my dorm room, my neighbor leaves his fucking door wide open twenty four hours a day. I can see their dirty shoes, their bloody laundry. Fucking A! Don't they realize people don't want to see inside their freaking apartments? I can't stand that shit. But my major beef is about these kids. I used to tell them to go and leave me alone but they never listened. You know what I do now?"

Everyone listened.

"What do you do?"

"I just tell them "No money, no time." And, fucking A, it always works. If the Chinese understand something, it's just that. No money, no time."

A boy and girl came up to them as they were seated. The boy held a small blue guitar with decals of yellow sunflowers. The boy, about ten or twelve, was dressed in a blue dress and he had excessive mascara and makeup on his face. The young girl - likely his sister - shyly tagged along behind him. She had a red carnation stuck in her hair. She held a small bowl in which were some scattered bills and coins. Despite their poverty their youth gave them a sheen of beauty, as it always seems to those who are older. David reached into his pocket for a coin or two. The boy smiled. His teeth were black and rotting. David instinctively looked away, ashamed.

"Go away, don't bother us!" Emily said to the children.

Her face was suddenly turgid and livid with a mild rage. She spoke in Chinese but to everyone the meaning was obvious. The children just looked on blankly through their almond eyes. They probably didn't understand Emily's Chinese. The girl put out her hand to the newcomers and said something pleadingly. The others just looked at her with an almost benign indifference or just looked at their food or each other or anything else.

For a few seconds a strange feeling washed over David. To his surprise he was both repulsed by the children and attracted to them. He wanted to hold and even caress them, like a girl playing with her Barbie dolls. Ted's voice snapped him back to attention.

"These fucking beggars. Jesus, they're everywhere."

Emily spat out something again, this time leaning across the table toward the children, her face so low she seemed to lick the table top. The children backed away slowly and finally turned and walked away, seeking new opportunities. He expected some sort of reproof from the others for her behavior but they were calmly chatting in small groups as though nothing had happened. Ted was discussing with Rebecca how he was looking forward to the DJ tryout that evening, and she was talking to him about Asian boyfriends and business in China. Rose was trying to read the menu.

Emily was once again involved in asking the server for some more food.

"What is that sign up there? I think it's the God of Business." Ted pointed at a paper plaque of Chinese character mounted above the main door of the restaurant. Below the character itself was a picture of a jolly fat man with a long black beard.

"What are you talking about?" Rebecca interjected.

"The God of Business. A friend told me that Chinese people worship the God of Business. He's about as important and revered as Confucius or Buddha."

Rebecca looked at him in astonishment. She was an American-Asian, and were it not for her Minnesota English, she looked like an ordinary Chinese woman walking down the street. She giggled in half-admiration, half-perplexity at Ted on whom she had a crush.

Ted, impressed with himself, continued.

"In the classic "The Three Kingdoms" he is a great noble called Guan Gong. And he loves to drink lots of beer!"

"Really?"

"You betcha. At 23 he kills a nasty guy who threatens his family and runs away. Then he joins up with three other guys and they go around the country battling the bad generals and kings and saving the peasants. Worshipped ever since."

"I can't believe how cheap the food is here." Emily tried to change the subject, not liking what she was seeing between Ted and Rebecca.

"Not just the food, but even apartments. Someone I know is living with his Asian boyfriend..." said Ted, ignoring Emily.

"Do people often date the locals?" Emily asked during a moment of silence.

"I don't," said Rebecca. She shrugged nervously.

"Why not?"

"I don't. They are greasy and somewhat thin. They just don't seem right."

Looking at her Asian features, David wondered if she was sincere. He remembered what a mainland Chinese man had said to him about the Overseas Chinese, 'Yellow on the outside, White on the inside, like a banana.'

Rebecca felt uncomfortable.

"Hong Kong Asian men are another matter entirely." She spoke defensively to no one in particular. "They speak English and treat women with respect. Shenzhen Chinese are too rough. And they're often already married"

Her father and mother were first generation Americans. While the work ethic and attention to traditional values were strong, they had had strong disagreements with the older generation. She remembered how her mother had been kicked out of her grandfather's home in Taiwan during a visit many years ago.

Why? Because of the pumpkin cakes.

Rebecca had been around twelve when she and her parents visited her father's parents in Taiwan, where he had been born.

Her grandmother, a stout old lady with a bun of very black hair tightly wrapped around a decorated bamboo hair pin, had taken great pains to prepare a delicious dinner for her son's family and some of her good friends whom she had invited over for the affair. The dinner was held at a large restaurant in downtown Taipei. In traditional Chinese fashion the table was stocked with dishes, much more than could possibly be consumed. In Chinese culture such lavish spending on dishes gives one face or *mian zi*. Egg soup, meat noodles, mushrooms flavored with garlic, fried corn kernels, vegetable shoots braised in soy sauce, egg dumplings, oily crispy thick Chinese pancakes, fried chicken legs, Chinese cabbages in Guangdong sauce. All were represented, but it was the pumpkin cakes that were the mother lode. Ever since she remembered the Rebecca had loved the golden crusted disks of sticky pumpkin cake. In less than a minute she had waffled down half of the plate in full view of the guests. She took not one piece at each pass of the revolving table (as was customary) but two, even three, two, three times. And she kept eating more and more. Finally, when her mother joined the girl in her eating frenzy and made a clumsy attempt to get the remaining food put into a take-away bag, the old dame exploded.

"These American women," she said in a curt and audible aside to her neighbor, a plump jowly faced man, "cannot save money, but they are just too eager to make money, spend money and steal other people's pumpkin cakes. One should not pick up other people's money. *Shi jian bu mei!*"

She spoke in rapid Mandarin, not the Guangdong dialect that Rebecca's mother was used to. How was grandmother to know that 2 months before the visit Rebecca's mother had taken 2 months of Mandarin classes from the immigrant hairdresser who lived down the street. Rebecca's father, slightly irritated at his wife's anxiety, had snapped,

"Why bother? We're only going to visit for a few days, and you want to give good money to a hairdresser from Henan!"

But men didn't understand these things. His wife had always felt her husband's family looked down on her for being a crass mainlander. She was determined to prove that she was much more than that. He was ignored and every Friday evening was Mandarin day. He eventually shrugged and got back to doing things that Asian American husbands should do, like attending Republican business meetings and taking the kids to swimming classes.

Rebecca's mother cheeks blushed a bright red. Things are hardly ever stated so directly in Chinese society, for that is just not the Chinese way, so the outburst was all the more surprising and indicated a high level of disapproval. She said nothing, and hid her shame. The insult seemed forgotten in the chatter of conversation that continued.

On Thanksgiving Day, many years after that incident, five people were seated before generous helpings of Russian goulash, Thanksgiving Pie and crisp, succulent turkey whose rich filling spilled onto the silver serving plate. A voluptuous scarlet cranberry sauce lay on the Wilson Sonoma porcelain like a cold lava of melted rubies. Ripe cherries swam in snow-white cream. Fresh fruits abounded. Among the smorgasbord lay 10 year old cabernet bottles and the *piece de la resistance* - Lombardy Gorgonzola specially ordered directly from Italy. It had been aged six months to perfection and its greenish blue flecks and veins made it look like a block of pristine polished marble.

Rebecca, her parents, her little brother, her grandmother and grandfather were seated at the family table back in Minnesota. The two elderly relatives had moved in just months before. Suffering from the reverberations of the Asian financial crisis Taiwan's economy had tanked and their small electronics business had collapsed. The old woman had had a stroke and was recovering slowly. As was customary in many Chinese families, parents would often move in with their children. Physically weak and increasingly senile, Grandma often lashed out at her daughter in law. Accustomed to being in charge and acutely aware of her decline, she linked the country and her family with her woes. Her daughter in law, in her opinion, was *yellow outside, white inside*. She found fault with many things American. She would hold her anger for days and then let loose a flood of rapid Chinese invective:

"These Americans eat bad bread, disgusting cheese and too much salt. How they manage is beyond me. Too much! *Tai Guo Fen le!*"

And she would fling away the food they brought her. But if her daughter in law felt anger or resentment she did not show it. She would nod her head quickly, say nothing and leave the room. It was as though they lived in two different worlds.

That is, until that Thanksgiving dinner.

Rebecca's mother knew that the grandmother hated two types of food: cheese and pretzels. Too weak to feed herself, she often needed to be spoon-fed. When she tried to talk, the stroke made her produce a stream of bubbling, mumbling, incoherent sounds. The men feared her too much to feed her. The little girl was just that – too little.

Sensing her moment had arrived the younger woman attacked. When no one was looking she duly put out bits of pretzels and a dollop of fragrant cheese in every dish headed for grandmother's mouth. That night the old lady was off kilter and just too feeble to protest. The mother fed her, spoonful by dripping spoonful. And since Rebecca was entertaining everybody with stories of her new grammar teacher from Narragansett no one noticed the push and pull between grandma and daughter in law. In any case, interrupting would have been too impolite, like a stranger asking someone if they had dutifully burnt paper money at their ancestor's grave– not proper at all! In any case, the mother was discreet and delivered the pretzels and cheese as carefully as a secret agent might handle live bullets and C4. A piece in the turkey sauce, a few extra salty crusts in the noodle soup, and even some cheese in the wine. This slow poisoning developed its own rhythm and was at sync with the sounds of eating and conversation. Her spoons and forks danced like a Latin mamba – they caressed, fornicated, voluptuously swooned, tightly snapped back, and then struck at the jugular. Finally, when grandpa identified telltale pieces sticking out from the repast the game was up. By then grandma's face was like a cross between a prune and a sun dried tomato and from her pursed lips wafted a strong odor of gorgonzola. From the wrinkled center of her face fierce black eyes stared out in a speechless rage.

Afterwards, in the privacy of their bedroom. the husband exploded. It took marriage counseling and tearful midnight discussions between family members before the fray was finally settled. Rebecca, and eventually her father, took the side of the mother. Her little baby brother finally settled matters when he said one evening,

"*Mama he nai nai chao jia!* Mummy and Granny are fighting!"

After that relative quiet descended upon the family. One day at dinner mother raised her glass to the old lady's and tipped the other's glass just below the rim as a sign of respect. For in Chinese society great disputes emerge and are settled over the dining table. As Rebecca's grandfather used to say,

" A man's character is revealed not by the deals he makes, or even by the music he plays, or how he fights, but by the manner in which he uses his chopsticks!"

He then quickly added

"But making money is *still* important!"

David had had his own experiences with food in China. For example although he enjoyed Chinese food he loved cheese. The smell of cheese to most Chinese was like kryptonite to Superman; to be ignored or repelled. Similarly, even handling cheese seemed like rocket science to some. At the grocery store one day he came across some Gouda and happily requested half a pound sliced.

"I can't do it." said the assistant, her eyes peering widely over the face mask.

"Why not?"

"We don't cut cheese."

Behind her were two huge state of the art electrical slicers.

"What about those?" David pointed them out.

"No, no, they're only for meat!" she protested.

Suddenly from his left came a huge roar,

"No, No, No, that's not true! Over there, cut, cut, cut."

The bad Chinese came from an unshaven foreigner with broken teeth, a huge boil beneath his very red right ear and decked in gray and green sweaters and pants.

"No, I cannot," the lady protested.

"YES YOU CAN I WANT TO SPEAK TO MANAGER NOW YOU USE MACHINE OK OK

OK NOT NO NO NO!"

His stentorian voice could be heard clear across 50 feet of prime ultra modern rented floor space.

"It's OK," David said, in a subdued voice, slightly embarrassed as everyone in earshot was looking at them.

"I can persuade her to do it." David smiled timidly at him.

As if a button had been pushed, the other man switched to English, lowered his voice dramatically and said in relaxed, casual English,

"I tell you mate *they* never know how to deal with cheese."

Nodding his head, he smiled and walked off, leaving David to the confused assistant. She had removed her face mask and was giving him a slight, though nervous, smile.

David wasn't sure the woman felt miffed. *It's hard knowing what they are really thinking,* he thought to himself. When westerners speak of Chinese inscrutability and expressionless faces (save the stereotypical smile) they misunderstand the Chinese. Chinese language expression is modified by gestures and very fine voice inflexions. To most Chinese, therefore, the relatively large gestures and loud expressions of jittery and angry Westerners are puzzling or amusing, and not always recognized as angry outbursts. This is because English often admits differences in pitch to convey expression more than meaning. Conversely, in Chinese, pitch primarily conveys meaning over expression. Thus one rages at a waiter for misunderstanding an order, and the waiter only slowly realizes the foreign customer is displeased, the loudness being virtually meaningless to him.

Therefore

"What the HELL do you think you ordered for me?" might just as well be the question

"What order did you bring me please?"

Thus even the typical uplift in accent at the end of English questions has to be taught to Chinese if they want to learn to ask English questions. Putonghua, for example, simply adds the sound *ma* with a neutral pitch to the end of a question to form a question.

David looked at his companions and the Chinese children who were reluctantly moving away, and in his heart, he moved with the children. He saw foreigners as part of what he wanted to leave behind him. Sometimes he had the urge to just strip, shave his head and travel as a monk across China. He shook his head. *I'm dreaming.* Then he thought of the yellow dirt on the ground, the wrinkles on children's faces, his diminishing bank account, and that persistent canto within him: *I want, I want...*'

⁑

Spring had asked David and her violinist friend Zhu Zhu to perform *The Butterfly Lovers Concerto*, to which she would dance her own arrangement. Written by Chen Gang and He Zhan Hao in 1959, the *Butterfly Lovers Concerto* is based on a classical Chinese legend dating back to the feudal Tang dynasty (Ca. 800 AD). The violin music recalls that of the traditional plucked string instrument called the *Er Hu* As the ancient story goes, *Zhu Ying Tai*, an ambitious young woman, disguised herself as a man in order to achieve an education. Valued as workhorses, concubines, mothers or walking ornaments, women rarely were granted a serious education. Her true face hidden behind the lean, spartan mien of a scholar, she spent her days trolling through dusty scrolls and ink brushes preparing for the imperial exams, the then six hundred year old rite of passage to wealth and fame. Characters in their millions of permutations would emerge like furies from the dusty Confucian texts and swarm across the minds and dreams of young feudal Chinese from the provinces, binding them in a compact that rewarded meritocracy with prestige and privilege.

The young Ying Tai, her rosy face unmarked with the lines of experience and wrinkles of age, toiled and sweated in the murky innards of libraries and dormitories. In time she met a young scholar *Liang Shan Bo*. Unaware of her secret he visited her at her home after they had finished their three years of studies together. That summer when youth met youth and the blasts of winter had just fled the burgeoning flowers on meadows and hills, they fell in love and he proposed. Since her father had already promised her to another man he left, despondent. He accepted a job nearby as a county magistrate, pined away and died from his heartbreak. Shortly afterwards, Ying Tai, unaware of his death, made arrangements to travel to her future husband's home to be officially married. Beset by strong gales and winds, their boat was forced ashore near Shan Bo's gravesite. Recognizing where she was, she landed and cried. The ground opened up and, distraught and beset by remorse, she flung herself into its depths. Before the astonished party, two butterflies emerged from the horrid blackness of the tomb and flew away. Their bodies were never found.

In time history became stories, and stories turned into fables that symbolized the immortal nature of their love. Composed just years before Mao's Cultural Revolution, the musical drama of Chen Gang and He Zhan Hao fuses western and eastern tonalities and structures. Finding disfavor years later, its authors were convicted of backward thinking and sentenced to years in communist concentration camps. Eventually, like the Tchaikovsky violin concerto, it clawed its way up from initial disfavor to become one of the world's most popular musical works.

During the rehearsals Spring had just looked on while the other two played. She would stand beside the keyboard close to his hands, her face almost serene. She would look at his face from time to time. Sometimes their eyes met. His expression would be just so slightly quizzical, as though he were asking her

"Who are you? Why are you here? *What* are you?"

The rush she felt maddened her but it also made him supremely happy. This curiosity (if that is what it was) drew him closer to her, so much so, he almost lost track of the passages he was playing.

Most of the time she would gently incline her head as though she were examining his hands. Sometimes she would wear some loose slacks and an oversize t-shirt that made her look like some exotic sailboat tipped on its edge. Her hair would be tied back in a small bun. Large dark eyes would peer limpet-like from her moon shaped face. Occasionally a gentle furrow would ripple across her broad forehead, such as when she heard a wrong note or a voice was raised in passion or frustration.

"It needs to be faster." She would speak almost inaudibly.

Her voice would project as though from a distant place, at once commanding, at once cloaked in its own inscrutable logic. The softer the sound, the greater the authority.

"I can try. Zhu Zhu let's try again"

And he never felt his playing was good enough for Spring, who just maintained her sphinx like observation.

Spring would sometimes dance while they played. He noticed how intricate were the movements of her hands and fingers and he realized he was being slowly smothered by her beauty. It was a slow sensuousness that dulled his senses and stole upon him like a subtle wraith. He had memorized the music. To Spring this was amazing since she had given him just 2 days.

"How did you memorize so quickly!" She looked at him wide-eyed.

"Because you asked me to."

"I didn't ask you."

"Well, I guess I had a reason" He winked at her.

"Do that again!" she laughed.

So he winked again. She broke out in peals of laughter.

"I've never seen anyone do that before. It's so funny!" Like her friends she covered her hands with her mouth.

"Hey can you help me with something?" Her face suddenly turned serious.

He stopped playing.

"Sure, what's up?"

"I want you to meet someone. I am thinking of getting a new job. More money!"

She smiled. He felt a slight shock. He said nothing. She went on, oblivious to his glassy smile.

"I hate the boss at the tea house. She wants to control everything. I must leave. I've been offered a job as a dancing instructor. Perhaps you can meet my future boss. He really wants to meet a foreigner."

And without waiting for an answer (for she knew what he would say) she casually threw her right leg up against a wall to limber up. She effortlessly pulled her head down against her knees. Zhu Zhu, who had been calmly listening and watching Spring, smiled.

"Isn't she great! Look how hard that must be, even though it is a simple loosening up exercise!"

He nodded but inside he was in turmoil. *Why did she want to leave? Were things so bad? Why change?*

Would she leave him? How would they stay in touch? What of their lunch time dance lessons? And how could she - for he felt Zhu Zhu was also part of the conspiracy *- act so calmly?* He hated them for their seeming indifference. And he mostly hated himself for allowing himself to fall for this wisp of a girl, this jejune creature with the big eyes and lithesome figure. He looked at her. Her face was hidden but her hands were stretched and grasping her knee. The ring on her finger sparkled under the soft but bright lights of the ballroom. As he saw the gold and scarlet hues dance off the ring he suddenly felt very lonely. *Maybe it has to do with a boyfriend?* Even after all these months he wasn't sure. He had heard stories of Chinese women who have Chinese and foreign boyfriends at the same time, one for understanding, the other for money and status. He shut this thought out of his mind. His inability to accurately communicate (or even nurture) the inflexions of love and was not only a curse, but also a blessing. *This siren's past boyfriends, seductions and passions are her business. What do I care? What she loves and hates will be discovered in due time.* For now he was the ultimate existentialist. He wanted to live for the moment, to be with her and enjoy her company, without considering either the past or the future. Like all existentialists, David was too smart not to realize that the hours wait for no philosophy, and that life would eventually demand planning and foresight. But at this moment he paid little attention to these matters and being prudent. Therefore, from this curious mix of fatalism, resignation and optimism he recovered himself back to a state approaching happiness.

After one of the rehearsals she introduced him to her boss. Mr Li was a short man with a dark, swarthy complexion, who constantly said "Isn't it so, isn't it so?" at the end of every second sentence.

Like most Chinese middle class office workers he wore a simple short sleeved white polyester shirt tie-less and open at the top. His left elbow squeezed a small leather portfolio against his waist. A cigarette stub hung languidly from his right hand. His fingernails (particularly the little fingers) were long and uneven, yellowed from nicotine and neglect. How was David to know that in Guangdong and in certain other provinces, long nails were a sign of good fortune and the pinky's had to be extra long to compensate for their shortness? A stab of jealousy ran through David when he looked at this man who would be with Spring every day. After some small talk he tried to beg off to head home.

"No, no. Let me treat you to dinner. Please." Mr Li smiled and wouldn't take no for an answer.

Spring looked at David pleadingly and he relented.

"Sure, that's not a problem."

He could have said, 'I'd love to.' Or 'That's very kind of you.' But he was still ambivalent about this man. And there was something about the way he held that cigarette and smiled that reminded him of sharks and piranha.

"Your Chinese is very good." Mr Li smiled and offhandedly glanced at Spring.

"So's yours." David warily replied, also smiling.

"Of course, I'm Chinese!"

"Of course."

Changing the subject, David asked

"Where are you from? Beijing?"

"No, Anhui province. Why do you think Beijing?"

"Well you slur some of your words like Beijing folks. They don't say "a little" – they say "a lirrrrelll""

They laughed. Spring laughed for the first time. It was as though the ice was broken. David realized then that she desperately wanted to please this man. Her manner towards Mr Li was respectful, almost guarded, like a courtier next to a noble. It seemed strange to him, for he had always though of her as somewhat haughty and even standoffish towards strangers. His heart softened and he felt more at ease with the other man. He learned he was married and had a six year old son. He had previously been a colonel in the army and had met his wife there. They had married in his hometown in Anhui and come to Shenzhen when an old buddy offered him a job.

Although David was relieved Mr Li was already married he was still somewhat wary. Many Chinese men, if wealthy, take mistresses. Ronald had told him,

"One of my work mates is a married guy. He told me he's slept with 5 different women in half a year. When I tell him I don't believe it he says "I know I'm married but this is normal in China.""

When the drinks arrived, they made several toasts. Mr Li would raise his glass of beer, lead everyone to stand up and clink glasses shouting 'Gang Bei!' Then they would sit down, talk and eat, and as soon as glasses were empty make another toast.

They started talking about the Iraq War and disagreed over whether it could be won. Mr Li leaned forward, so close David could see the bristles on his chin. His dark eyes gleamed confidentially.

"The Americans will win. How could they not? The have the most powerful army in the world."

"But what use is it if the Americans are divided. Some hate Bush. Others like him."

"Yes, but they are too proud to admit defeat. Like the Russians in Afghanistan."

"They should listen to the Chinese strategist Sun Bin. What did he say? I forgot."

"You know *The 36 Strategies?* That is very famous."

"The last strategy he wrote. I remember. *"Zou Wei Shang."* The best policy is to go away."

"Americans will never go away." said Spring, who had been half listening, half chatting with Zhu Zhu.

"Maybe you're right" Mr Li pulled a long smoke. "They want the oil."

David interjected.

"Not all of them. But maybe you are right. America is like an empire. They need their soldiers around the world and they want oil for their cars."

Having agreed on the basics they fell into an uncomfortable silence. David suddenly said,

"Sun Bin wrote so many strategies. I am trying to understand them but sometimes the differences are subtle."

"You know, my friend, Sun Bin was a great general. He wrote the 36 strategies over 2000 years ago and people still read it. It is a great classic. I'm impressed by you." And he raised his glass up before his ever redder face and grinned,

"Gang Bei!"

Before the concert later that week Spring passed on to David an email from Mr Li:

Dear David:

It was a pleasure meeting you. I remember you like Sun Bin. I found the English for the translation. It is very simplified but here you are. Maybe some time you can teach me more English!
Stuart Li

Included were translations of all 36 strategies. David resolved to include them in his journal. David briefly replied, thanking Mr Li for the dinner and the translation. He suggested that one day they might get together for tea at the local tea house.

David had replied to Mr Li in written Chinese. His Chinese studies had quickly advanced. To the astonishment of many friends he had passed the advanced oral Chinese exam after barely three months study. He was now examining the Chinese language, particularly its etymology, in depth. His relationships with words had became more than an intellectual curiosity. He, at times, felt emotionally connected with some words more than others. One of his favorites was *Jia*, the word for family. To him this word exemplified the richness and subtlety of meaning of the Chinese language. The character itself, as are all Chinese characters, is pictographic in origin. The upper shape, rather like a flat table with a dot on top, signifies a roof or dwelling. Underneath it is a stylized drawing of a pig. The shape of the character evolved through at least 3 permutations to that of the present, which is a highly stylized but still recognizable picture. The archetypal pig character placed under the roof character became the character for home. The origins lie in ancient pastoral China. Animals such as pigs played a critical role in social customs and supported a subsistence lifestyle.

He would ruminate on such words as these. *Jia* to him had the warmth of a family. It seemed that China, in its blending of cordiality with real friendship and love was his family now. He respected the ambiguity of the Chinese language because this ambiguity reflected the complexity of life. He embraced it as wonderful, pervasive, subtle and always capable of expression.

The Chinese language and music have deep connections. Both are enigmas that are felt more than understood. Meanings are often in flux depending upon one's perspective, such as social status, personal mood, pitch of one's voice, the social context and so forth. In the music of Johann Sebastian Bach, the greatest apotheosis of fugal wizardry in the history of Western classical music, fugal melodies can be heard vertically (through harmonies) or linearly (through melodies). Impressions change as the rhythm or starting points vary. In the last page of his final work, *The Art of Fugue*, Bach, half-blind and dying, introduces a melody to the letters of his name B-A-C-H (where H represents B flat). The arrival of this melody is something of a shock, a vague shiver, a sweet infinity of expectation. Bach repeats the melody in the left hand, then in the right, always recognizable, overlapping and simultaneous, constantly changing the sounds that reach our ears. In his journey through China, David would see the Chinese language and music come together in many ways, and from many perspectives, as if characters and words, minims and rests were in a profound dance with themselves and the rhythms of the earth itself.

After he replied to Mr Li he started thinking about Spring. *What is she doing now? Am I just a headhunter to her, someone to help her get a job?* He didn't think so. Then again, he didn't really care. *As long as she needs me*, he thought, *that's enough.*

As for her, she was practical in the way of smart women who ignore their beauty or use it as a tool to dull men's minds. Often she wished she was ugly, for beauty was a distracting encumbrance. Like most Asian women she was conservative and valued serenity. She enjoyed the novelty of an older man's attention, but there was a part of her that held back. Some say that for young, beautiful women there is no difference between honey and money. Yet for her, even absent money, she valued taste and grace. Her friends would often say to her

"Don't worry, one day you will have a beautiful house of your own with many rooms and many children."

She truly wanted children. She loved children. Like many beautiful women who seem destined for a glamorous life by virtue of their grace and looks her goals were rather simple. To her children were fulfilling. They were somewhat difficult to manage but she was practical and firm enough to handle them well. She wanted to get married. She would work not on the stage, but at home, for her husband and her children.

She was young and had had many suitors. All had been found wanting. At first she hadn't been aware she attracted him. But during the rehearsals when he looked at her in his kind way, particularly when she saw his (initial) reaction to Mr Li, she immediately recognized attraction and jealousy. She saw him with clearer eyes now. He was well off, but he was too old for her, an object of pity, and without clear prospects for the future. She didn't know if he was even married. She felt nervous about building a relationship with him. But she also felt, although it was not yet clear in her mind, that he needed her. To her this made her feel important. He raised her self esteem. *But what did he want from her? Was it something only she could provide?* She thought these things and flattered herself, as most women do, that her affection, like fingerprints or DNA, were uniquely hers to give. He was in need of affection (she dared not to call it love), and only she, were she disposed to do so, could provide.

The day after their last rehearsal, they had their dance lesson. She thanked him. She had gotten the job. She said it offhandedly and her eyes avoided his. It was as though she did not want to see the expression in his eyes.

Puzzled, he shrugged his shoulders.

"You're welcome."

They continued their lesson as though nothing special had happened. The tape recorder belted out a catchy Russian two step that was taking Shenzhen by storm.

"People should never show their weakness. If you vanquish your enemy, do it completely. Mercy is for fools."To my father love was a weakness.

- From David's father's journal

WEAKNESS

Zhen Rui was confused and had a headache. When the teacher didn't visit him the first few days he was in the hospital, he hadn't understood. Then his confusion turned into a slow burning anger as the days passed by. He hated this hospital. He wanted to play piano. And he wanted David to be there. For the older man had been more than a teacher to him. He had been in some ways like a big brother – even a father. The anger percolated and turned into something between bitterness and resignation. But children are easily distracted and they heal quickly from emotional as well as physical hurt. So he just forgot about the old foreigner. But his feelings hadn't vanished. They had simply reverted to a darker place.

When David finally turned up, it was as though all the emotions the boy had experienced suddenly returned, shaken out of their torpor. They emerged in reverse order. First he was bitter and angry and didn't want to say anything. Then the anger turned into something softer and gentler. He saw that the older man was uncomfortable. With the wisdom of those who have lived on the edge of life the child felt and understood the older man's hesitation. He forgave him but didn't know it.

"*Ni hao lao shi?*" he greeted his teacher.

And with these words it was as though sunlight had washed away the darkness. The man smiled shyly.

"Hi Zhen Rui."

David's eyes seemed to shift from one side of the room to the other, as though he was afraid to meet the boy's direct, unflinching gaze. He saw his smooth skin, his bright eyes and thought *He looks just like a healthy poster boy*. But the sight of the bluish lips quickly banished that thought.

"I'm sorry." David said.

"It's OK *lao shi*. I'm sorry we didn't finish the lesson."

David was relieved. He looked at Zhen Rui directly. He spoke firmly.

"No, I should have come earlier, but I do not like hospitals."

The boy was in a small ward with a few other cots lined up military style against the pockmarked green and white wall. Catheters and tubes led from his body to equipment stacked by the wall. There were other children in beds, some with ventilating machines hooked into their bodies, others with blindfolds over their eyes to calm them. The boy lay cocoon like in white bedding, his shock of black hair splayed like a dark moonlike aura over the pillow.

"I want to play Beethoven." the child whispered, eager to change the subject.

"I can hear him in my head but it hurts sometimes. Most of the time it makes me feel better."

"That's great. You'll be out of here in no time."

But David was remembering what Teacher Li had told him .

"Zhen Rui has a rare blood and heart disease. He early developed pneumonia. Early medical care could have helped. The old couple who found him looked after him until he was about three. Although he got better, they could not keep him, because he was always sickly and they were very poor. They then brought him to the orphanage. Timing is everything ..."

She had lowered her head.

"The doctors long ago said that he probably would not live past 8. He may get better in a few days or a few weeks, but it will be on borrowed time. The doctors don't think he has much of a chance of living through the winter..."

She then laughed ruefully. David asked why she was laughing.

"I was thinking of my mother. I told her about Zhen Rui and she said he should see a Chinese doctor for traditional Chinese treatment. I said, "Ma, that is not enough for such a sick boy.". She just said, "Give him ginseng and hot water and the pain will go away. You remember how my arthritis went away after I used *zhong yi*.""

David remembered how back in Kenya he had once visited his old grand aunt in Alego. He had had a cold at the time and felt very uncomfortable sitting before her in the simple old house, virtually a one room shack with some old photos on the wall and a few stools next to an old bed.

"Try this, they will work for you."

She pressed into his hand some powder that smelled like ash and cinnamon mixed together. He didn't understand what she was saying until someone translated the Luo.

"Grandmother is saying you can use this for anything. Sniff it like this."

The translator made a motion with his nose as though he was snorting coke. David tried the medicine. He felt a burning sensation in his nose and coughed violently. The cold went away after a few days. David didn't know if it was due to grandmother's medicine but he remembered her kind smile and the absolute trust she had in her herbs.

"You can use it to treat everything, everything..." she had smiled.

David snapped back to the present and hurriedly continued.

"I have a present for you. It's a bracelet from a tribe called the Maasai. They live in Kenya where I grew up. The bracelet is made of colored beads and means good luck."

He took the bracelet out of his pocket and handed it to the boy who eagerly put it on his bony hand. It was too large and hung awkwardly. To keep it on he repeatedly splayed open his fingers, catching it on his tiny, fragile, bony wrist. The motion became instinctive after a while, making it look as though he was exercising his fingers the way an athlete flexes his hand to keep it limber in the cold.

"Did I ever tell you about the Maasai?"

"Are they good people?"

"Yes, I think most people are good, but the Maasai are also very brave. They wander about the country with only their cattle, which they adore and worship. They are very proud. Each Maasai boy is tested for courage when young by being sent out with just one spear and a shield to kill a lion! Once he has killed a lion he is considered a man! The Maasai rarely eat meat and mostly drink cow's milk and blood mixed together."

"That's horrible." The boy laughed.

It was the first time in a long while he had laughed. His eyes were bright and his body shook.

"I guess so, but they were so brave that even the British with all their fancy machines and guns didn't dare get into their lands."

Although the British eventually colonized Maasai territory after a hard struggle, to this day many remember the stories of their bravery. David remembered the few times he had seen the Maasaai warriors in their *bomas* of scraggly huts and fences. They wore red and white cloth draped around their slender bodies and the men decorated their hair with red ochre. At celebrations they would leap into the air emitting guttural roars. The highest jumpers were highly respected. To this day the Maasai keep to their old ways. They forbid taking photos of their cattle or themselves, believing cameras will imprison their souls. Some do it for a fee but others will violently attack photographers, such as overly persistent tourists.

David told Zhen Rui more about the Maasai. The boy was fascinated. He held the bracelet tightly. He would not let it fall.

All of a sudden Zhen Rui had a wonderful picture in his mind. He could see a lone Maasai warrior standing in his traditional pose on top of a hill overlooking the Mara. His body was bolt upright and he was standing on one leg like a crane, the other leg hidden beneath flowing scarlet robes. Both hands firmly clutched his long spear for support. Limned against the crimson and gold canopy of the African sunset it seemed to rip a long thin black slit into the horizon. In his mind's eye Zhen Rui saw the Maasai warrior's slightly cocked head looking at him. He shouted,

"Maybe one day I will go to Kenya!"

David smiled.

"Maybe, one day, if you study hard, we will go to Kenya, OK?"

"OK!" Zhen Rui shouted.

"Oh I have something else for you." David pulled out a small book from his backpack. He handed it to the boy.

"It's a book about a great man. It's about Beethoven. He was an amazing man. He had a hard life, was once also very sick like you, but he kept on. The English is very simple so you can practice easily."

"I love Beethoven's music. Can you tell me a little about him?"

"Well, I can tell you a story if you'd like."

"Yes, yes, please."

David paused, and then took a deep breath.

"Let me see… It was about some time ago when I heard about it."

"Heard about what?"

"Why, it wasn't very clear at first. The new Shenzhen concert hall had just been built. You know the one. Right next to Book Center and the new library. Big and shiny. Cost millions of Yuan to build."

"Yes, I went to the library there with some teachers a few times."

"Right, well just when it had opened, people told their friends about a strange foreigner who had been at every major concert featuring at least one work by Beethoven. He always sat in the same seat, right in front with the local government dignitaries."

"So what?"

"I'm getting there. Hold your horses!", and David took a sip of water.

"What was most interesting about him, these people said, was not his wild head of hair or old-fashioned clothing. It wasn't even that he picked his nose and snorted *ad lib* next to the Mayor and his wife. After all, Shenzhen has been known as the spitting capital of China, so even puking and snorting in the open is nothing to write home about. No, what most alerted them to this celebrity was how every ten minutes or so he would bellow across the hall in very, very bad Chinese "Louder, louder, what's wrong with you nincompoops! Let's hear more power!" Scowling, he would then fall backwards in his chair, eyebrows arched, perpetually critical of each performance."

"Sounds like an interesting man. It took a lot of courage to do that in front of everyone."

"He was a foreigner so everybody just shrugged. According to many Chinese, foreigners have crazy customs and are mad anyway so best just to look politely on or ignore them."

David laughed. So did the boy, whose headache had vanished.

The teacher went on, warming up to the story.

"I happened to be visiting some friends at the *Di Wang* building (you know it is the tallest skyscraper in Shenzhen) and I met an old friend of mine, a teacher I had worked with a long time ago back in America. Chinese guy who has lived in America, *hua qiao*. "David, you sexy dog you, where have you been?" He said to me, "I've been trying to find you ever since we got a hold of him."".

"Why did he call you a sexy dog? What does that mean? How can a dog be ...sexy?"

"I'll explain some other time. For now forget it, just a way of speaking. Well I then asked my friend," "What's up, who are you talking about?" He said "Who am I talking about? Why, Beethoven, of course. He popped by to see us. You mean... you didn't know?""

Zhen Rui was now sitting up in his bed. David continued.

"Well, I heard rumors, but I thought it impossible. Wait a minute, it *is* impossible. Are you out of your mind?' I said."

"Yes, how can that be?" Zhen Rui blurted out.

My friend said, "Listen, he's here, don't question it. Take my word for it. Would you like to meet him?"

"All my life I had worshipped this man. Ludwig Van Beethoven was the greatest musician who ever lived. So OF COURSE I wanted to meet him. Would I have the courage? Would you?"

"Of course I'm brave enough." the boy said. His face remained quite serious but he was wondering if he could really face a ghost or demon such as this Beethoven.

"Furthermore, who cared if it was impossible? Stranger things have happened."

David's eye's twinkled.

"After all, sometimes impossible things happen, right!"

"Right!"

"Peter M., my friend, and who worked at one of the biggest music recording companies in China, led me up to the eleventh floor, through a line of people, and into a big office overlooking the Public Security Bureau. Inside were about five people who surrounded a diminutive figure reclining on a settee. Among them were people I remembered from previous days when I had worked in the American music industry. There were American and Chinese recording executives."

"What is a recording executive?"

"These are people who pay other people to write and perform music, are very good at telling lies and hiring lawyers and in the end keeping most of the money. Anyway, let's continue. Beethoven looked very smart in his *Tan Shan* shirt, made of white silk with embroidered dragon shapes. He could have been from old Beijing. But of course he was a foreigner. He had tried to tie his hair in a pigtail Chinese style but it had come free and seemed to explode over his head like a white cloud. His face was unshaven and very red. His big bushy eyebrows were twitching. But his eyes…what eyes…so shrewd…so wise."

"That's funny he was wearing Beijing clothing! Why do foreigners want to wear such clothing, *Lao shi?*"

"Because China's ancient culture fascinates many foreigners. They want to learn about China. And they want to show their respect for the Chinese people. Shall I go on…?"

"Yes please!"

"But some of the buttons were undone and there was a brown splotch or two of some hastily sipped noodle soup near the collar. His face was red. His eyebrows were twitching in rage and his fists were clenched. He seemed to be upset over what a very tall thin man had said to him."

"No. I cannot have it!" Beethoven shouted.

"Mr. van Beethoven, you don't understand how sudden this all has been. We need time to prepare."

"Absolutely not!"

"Sir, it is absolutely impossible that we cede you the copyrights to our recordings. We assumed you were quite dead, *bu hao yi si*, pardon my frankness, when you made them. And anyway in China everyone copies everything so it doesn't help much to have a copyright!' He sat down, wiping his forehead with a handkerchief."

The teacher turned to the boy,

"Zhen Rui, do you know what a copyright is?"

"No."

"Well, when someone writes a new book or some new music many people want to make copies of it. But the person who created it wants to make sure that he is paid a little because he or she created it. Do you understand?"

"I think so."

"So when they create the work, the government gives them a certificate called a copyright. It tells everyone that if they copy this work or sell it they should first ask the creator for permission and maybe pay a little money."

"So Beethoven wanted money for his music?"

"Exactly."

"So do I have to pay him for playing his piano music?" He looked worried. Except for ten Yuan a month in pocket money from the orphanage, Zhen Rui was quite poor.

"No, not you. Just the people who make a lot of money from his recordings. CDs, DVDs and so forth."

"I see." Satisfied, the boy rested his chin on his cupped palms and looked philosophic.

"But in China people copy things all the time so I think he is going to have a hard time getting money here."

"Probably. But he tried. Anyway Beethoven said, "Ha. Look, young man, I have had to scrape away all my life to make a decent living. I now have the opportunity to make millions. No, I must have my way. Fifty percent royalties on all recordings of my music! Furthermore, I will have to show you people a few things about interpreting it correctly." "But Mr Beethoven," said a Chinese businessman whose face smiled even as he sweated, "you should go to America. That's where our headquarters are. We really don't have much power here.""Rubbish, YOU can tell your bosses in America. And right now China owns much of America. Hell they're always borrowing money from China. Capitalists. Communists. They all want to make money — off MY music. And this is the biggest market of the future. So it's only natural that I talk to you people first!""

"I think he was joking!" Zhen Rui laughed.

"Calm down. Let me finish!" The boy quickly became mum.

"All this time Beethoven was yelling at full voice at the people present, and I assumed his deafness was not total. At this latest outburst the executives withdrew to a corner of the room and nervously conferred. They looked like a bunch of cowering penguins in their deep blue suits. Beethoven, meanwhile, on seeing me, beckoned me over. I introduced myself as just an admirer of his music. To this he muttered something in reply, and grimaced. "Look, young man.", he said, "you look reasonably intelligent. Let me tell you something." And he leaned over to me as though he had a secret to tell."

"What did he say?"

"That's enough for today. I'll continue next time I come."

"But I want to hear more."

"First read the book I gave you. Next time I come I'll continue. OK?"

"OK. So when are you going to come again?"

"Soon."

"Really?" Zhen Rui looked at him anxiously.

"Really. Right, that's settled." And he gave the boy a high five. Seeing that the boy was now tired, he quickly left.

Outside the room he bumped into Mr Ma, one of the orphanage music teachers. Mr Ma had been at the orphanage many years and was only in his late twenties. His lean, long jawed face was almost always serious, and he worked with great dedication. When happy or laughing, his eyes would light up and twinkle. At such times there would be a dash of puzzlement in his eyes, as though he would never have guessed something could be so humorous or startling but was glad it was so.

From the beginning Mr Ma and David had been close. There was the shared dedication to the students that bonded them in spite of their many differences in class, stature, jobs and culture. Mr Ma had a beautiful girlfriend whose picture he kept on his small wooden table next to the bed. She also was a teacher and they planned to get married the following year. Mr Ma, like Spring, was from Henan province, often referred to as the *mother of China* for being the cradle of Chinese civilization. His family, like many peasants, was very poor and he scraped by from month to month on just over one thousand Yuan. The typical salary in Shenzhen is two to three thousand Yuan per month, or about 300 to 400 dollars. This often includes include rudimentary boarding, some meals and basic health insurance. Yet, although Mr Ma was poor and was acutely aware how little separated him from the homeless and abandoned, and that his pay was lower than normal, he had an abiding belief in the goodness of others. In a more affluent life he may have been a rich congregation's preacher or the office workaholic who trusts the goodness of others just too much to get the next promotion. Perhaps because David saw some of these things in himself they had bonded well. He smiled when he saw the younger man.

"Mr Ma, good to see you!"

Mr Ma smiled and carefully and stiltedly spoke virtually the only English words he knew.

"Good to see you TOO!"

He was dressed in basketball clothes and his face was gleaming with rivulets of sweat.

"How was basketball?"

"No, today was football, not basketball."

"With some of your friends?"

"Yes, every week we play football and basketball."

"Are you here to see Zhen Rui?"

"Yes." And immediately a pallor drifted over his face, as though a dark cloud had descended to shut out the light overhead. His voice was deep and somber.

"I came to see the little one. How is he doing?"

"He seems a little weak but he is in good spirits."

Mr Ma nodded his head, was silent for a moment, and then asked

"What do the doctors say?"

"It's very serious. They think he will need to go to America for an operation. Even if he goes they think he will not live very long…maybe a year."

Mr Ma looked at the big lanky foreigner and saw the pain in his face. David's eyes avoided his. They were red from lack of sleep and the lines beneath his eyes were deeper and darker than Mr Ma remembered. His simple white polyester shirt was rumpled but clean. His normally short and dark hair had been uncut for days and white strands gleamed under the bright hospital lights like bleached silk. But it was his hands that grabbed Mr Ma's attention. They were large and spatulate and seemed to tremble slightly, as if with emotion. When he gestured they had immense confidence and authority. The teacher tended to cover one hand in another as though for protection, so he often looked as though he was wringing his hands in anguish. Today they quivered at his side, pulsing with an irrepressible energy, as if they sought and were denied speech. Dumb and mute, they seemed to offer no prospect except exchanging dumb motion for emotion.

When Mr Ma saw those sad hands he had an epiphany. In that moment he saw him not as a foreigner but a man who had worries and hopes, dreams and aspirations, and who, like Mr Ma, had struggled to lift himself after being dashed onto the hard and bitter tarmac of life. He touched the big man lightly on his shoulder.

"Don't worry. Maybe he will be OK. He's a good lad."

Mr Ma briefly went in to visit the boy and give him some books he had brought from the orphanage. David waited. As they were leaving the hospital, they passed by the local supermarket. Over the last ten years Jusco, the Japanese grocery chain, had set up scores of stores in mainland China.

About 50 people were gathered outside. They had hoisted large red banners with slogans such as:

Chinese People Don't Support CNN
Don't Buy Japanese Goods
Let Foreigners Beware Our Patriotism

Recently the Japanese government had issued schoolbooks that glossed over the Nanjing massacre. In 1936 Japanese troops had invaded the Chinese city of Nanjing. According to most historical accounts, over 300,000 Chinese were murdered in the orgy of rape and pillage that followed. The Japanese government had refused to withdraw or amend the schoolbooks. Following the schoolbook publication many Chinese were furious at foreigners, in particular the Japanese. Protests were launched in several cities, including Shenzhen. At about the same time a CNN reporter had criticized the Chinese as 'barbarians.'

Many of the protesters wore red volunteer jackets and milled around trying to prevent people from entering the store. Jusco employees stood uncertainly at the lofty door looking out from empty neon-lit interiors. The once bustling hallways and entranceways were empty and forlorn.

A young woman with a bullhorn was shouting commands to the others, mostly young men in their twenties. Her high pitched voice drummed a staccato of angry words that could be heard blocks away.

"We are all sons and daughters of China! Listen to me! The Japanese government is preparing 20 million dollars of advertising. The Jusco supermarket chain alone is preparing 5 million, to give us discounts on items during the May 1st holiday. But they're crazy if they think the Chinese people will pack Jusco during the holidays. They're crazy if they think we will walk over the dead bodies of our kinsmen in Nanjing!"

The crowd roared. They struck up the national anthem and waved their flags. Then the lady resumed.

"Japanese TV is hard at work preparing to film Chinese people flocking to Jusco, to show that the Chinese people are just words and no action. If you love China tell your friends and family to not buy at Jusco. If you love China you will not sell your soul and lose face for orders and luxury goods! If you lose face, you dishonor your country. You will then let the foreigners sneer at us. Maybe we are not as strong as them but when we unite let them beware!"

"Come together and protect your China. Show you love China!"

Then suddenly from the street behind her there was a scuffling sound and the wail of sirens punctured the speaker's shrill voice. Men and women in smart blue and white uniforms were pouring out of vehicles on the street. The police bounded up the steps and shouted at the crowd, firmly but politely,

"Citizens, please leave now. This is an unauthorized gathering. Please go home."

The sullen crowd reluctantly folded up their banners and signs and melted back into the crowds of onlookers. But the young woman shouted

"What are you doing? We are fighting for our country. This is a peaceful demonstration!"

A young police captain came up to her, his face grim.

"Don't give the government trouble, young lady. Please leave."

"Sir, we cannot let these foreigners abuse China."

"Trust the government to do the right thing. Now is not the time to create trouble. You must leave now."

She angrily put her megaphone in her bag and left. Then she saw David standing looking at them. She laughed.

"Hey, you see, Chinese policemen are polite. They do not beat us up like in your country. You too should trust them or you can go back to your country!"

David didn't know if she was joking. He just stared blankly at her. Mr Ma gently elbowed him,

"Let's go, David. We should not stay around here." Many in the crowd were staring at the two of them, their voice grim and serious. They left quickly.

"Will they boycott the store?"

"For a few days. The May First Holiday will be here soon. There will be lots of price discounts and Chinese will buy again." Mr Ma laconically replied.

"Let's get something to eat, Mr Ma." The other man protested slightly but gave in. They headed to a nearby restaurant.

As they walked to the restaurant they passed by a young girl in a schoolgirl track suit silently kneeling on the sidewalk, her head bent down. They stopped to look. White chalk characters on the gray, square tiles before her uttered a plaintive message.

I am a poor student from Jiangxi, my mother is very ill and my father has no money. My uncle was very cruel and my sister died...I wish you a merry new year and best wishes!

They both dropped a few Yuan into her bowl. Some other people huddled closely and silently over the beautiful chalk calligraphy. Like stone sentinels they just looked on with cold fixed gazes.

When David asked why they were not giving money and just standing there Mr Ma said,

"Chinese people are like that. They like to watch but do not do anything."

"I don't think so. I think they respect and appreciation her *shu fa*. I think many Chinese, even the less educated, love beautiful calligraphy! It's in your bones!"

Mr. Ma shrugged and didn't say anything.

The restaurant was busy. They seated themselves in the atrium as they waited for a table. From their seats they could see across the bustling room.

Some tables nearby were being prepared for new guests. One of the waitresses, a woman in her forties, had removed the table cloth to expose the messy soy sauce underneath. Instead of cleaning away the sauce, she had just placed a fresh table cloth over it, and then put another red one on top, obscuring the mess. Mr Ma suddenly said

"You see...you see..!"

"See what?"

Mr Ma's faced looked irritated. David didn't know what had upset him.

"You remember long ago you had asked me about saving face. When you saw the girl defending the police you saw a little. That I can understand."

"So?"

"But just know when that waitress cleaned the table. That was the same... but worse!"

"What?"

"That's what saving face in China is about. Do not try to fix the underlying problem, instead just cover it up. Chinese have two concepts, courtesy and understanding. They have the same pronunciation, *Li*, but the characters are different. In China, *face* is everything. People are courteous because they have to be. In Western societies it is different."

"How's that?"

"In Western societies I think people are compelled by an inner sense of duty, often a moral imperative, to respect their neighbor. In China respect is forced down people's throats, the reasons vaguely understood."

"I see...I remember Bo Yang the writer wrote something similar..."

"Who? It's all about saving face..."

Mr Ma's face clouded over. In a more muted tone, he continued,

"And that's why we have been such bad musicians..."

"What do you mean?" David remembered Mr Ma's love of music. He played the *Er Hu*, a traditional Chinese stringed instrument.

"In China it is always for show, outside the individual. The greatest expression of the individual soul, music, or even of society, the historical epic, like your what do you call it... the Greek ancient story book..."

"Homer's *The Odyssey*." David interrupted.

"Yes, that book. Such a book cannot be found in five thousand years of Chinese history. So, David, what you are doing is new for us Chinese."

"Meaning...?" David smiled, bemused.

"Your gift of music is opening up the orphans to their own souls, to their inner selves. It will free them to be themselves."

"Now, *that's* an original idea of yours, Bo Yang did *not* say that..." David said.

There was a moment of stunned silence from Mr Ma. Then they both laughed. Mr Ma and he had both read Taiwanese author Bo Yang's most famous book, *The Ugly Chinese*. In it was a similar story about a waitress. David was amazed Mr Ma knew about *The Odyssey*. The serious events of the past few hours seemed to dissipate for a precious few moments. He would later learn that in China many children in middle school are taught to read (in Chinese) Western classics such as *The Red and the Black, The Human Comedy, Pride and Prejudice* and *Jane Eyre*. Western schoolbook syllabuses, on the other hand, rarely include Chinese classics.

He remembered how not long ago he had gone to a local Starbucks. Popular cafés were now popping up more frequently in Shenzhen, and the green Sun

Queen was ubiquitous in many districts. He had brought his computer. He found a comfortable seat but couldn't locate a power outlet. He walked up to the counter.

"Is there a power outlet anywhere near my seat?"

The three workers, two women and one man, looked bemused, as though they were searching for elusive words and phrases. One of the women pointed to the opposite end of the room,

"Just over there. That's where they are."

"But I cannot move there. It's too busy. Are you sure there are no outlets in this area?"

"No. That's it. Over here." She said, tossing her hair, eyes bright with certainty.

Despondent, he returned to his seat. A nearby couple stood up to leave and he noticed a power socket within plain sight. Later he discussed the incident with Mr Ma.

"Why did she say that? She was an employee. If she knew she would have told me, right?"

"Yeah, maybe she didn't like you."

"I don't think so. She always greets me when I go there."

"Then she didn't know the right answer."

"Then why didn't she just say, "I don't know…""?

"No way, she would have lost face. Better to do wrong than lose face."

David thought Mr Ma was joking. Wasn't this the new, bold, young China? Wasn't it surely shorn of Confucian inhibitions? Yet he had seen this phenomenon many times. When he asked questions, it was difficult for people, particularly in social settings, to simply say,

"I don't know."

A few days later he received an SMS message from the Shenzhen security bureau. It read:

Dear Fellow citizens:

At this time some of us have been very patriotic and great citizens. As we defend our motherland against attacks from others we must be dignified and proud. We must not be unwelcoming. We must show the world we have great civility and hospitality to all foreigners and foreign businesses. Let us show the world the new China!

Shenzhen Public Security Bureau

He smiled at the note on his cellphone as he remembered the supermarket incident. Eyes were everywhere. Later that day he saw some images of the protests on Pearl TV. This Hong Kong station daily broadcasts its English news service to the mainland. Offending snippets are routinely censored. Such topics include the big three: Taiwan, Tibet and Falun Gong. However, sometimes bits and pieces get through. He saw a crowd of people storming an upper scale department store in Shenzhen. The sea of people waving red banners turned violent and a nondescript man suddenly leaped from the crowd and smashed an outdoor glass sculpture with his fist. His face hardly grimaced, but glass shards fell to the ground. The tsunami-like crowd then swallowed him back into to the seething red and yellow throng.

Later that day he added some new entries to his diary.

The Policeman. *The average Chinese policeman is good natured, diligent and ready to share some tea with a stranger. He is concerned with his or her image and does everything he can to avoid paperwork. Thus he will sweat, huff and puff, and even take a bribe to resolve situations before they go to court or the administration. But it is also done with a true sense of community and even magnanimity. This man too has a limit, and will explode into foul-mouthed curses if an uncultured ruffian spits onto his clean waiting room floor.*

The Shenzhen Businessman. *Certain parts of the country are said to produce outstanding businessman (people from Hubei province, for example). A Shenzhen acquaintance from Hubei province has a canny ability to understand people's needs. He does business in a candid and honest fashion, works hard through long hours and with his beaming smile and big heart lavishes attention and support on his friends.*

The Bitter Foreigner *There is a tendency among foreigners who have lived in China for a long time to belittle its political and social systems with great passion. Freedoms such as political criticism that they take for granted in their home countries (and rarely exercise) develop an allure that torments them. Indifference to politics turns from contempt to bitterness, until they privately rail against the political repression and the social backwardness of China with all the charm of a rank sore. 'You teach English here?' says one portly Australian to me in a confiding tone,' Of course you do, they won't let us do anything else!' 'I can't stand these students.' says a young American teacher,' they are all over me. 'Do this, do that, what is this, what is that! I never have any time or any privacy!' 'What unlimited cheap labor?' says another,'All this economic miracle stuff is a dream, based on piracy and intellectual theft. That's the China miracle!' This bitterness* *is particularly pronounced among Americans and Australians, less so among the Africans, Asians and those from the Middle East, perhaps because the former think have lost too much, and the latter believe they will gain much more.*

The Spiritual Materialist *I sometimes feel America has spiritual poverty and material excess in abundance. China, on the other hand, has material poverty and spiritual richness. Is it possible for one country to have an abundance of both at the same time?*

✶✶

"Shut up!"

The word blasted through the classroom.

That day his class ended in chaos.

It had begun normally. He had walked in. The students stood at attention,

"Good morning Teacher David!" They bellowed out their greeting in unison and then sat down.

He had been temperamental, randomly switching moods between sternness and playfulness. At first the children were in tune with his moods and shifted as he shifted. Then, minute-by-minute, they moved away from him, as children tend to do when they instinctually seek an authority figure, gravitating away from drama and instability.

By the middle of the class they were ignoring him, as though they realized his powerlessness. He relied on a stern stare to keep some, like the boy who was playing with his PSP, in check, but it was no good. Like the proverbial leaking levee, each hole he plugged led to water being released somewhere else. His circle of comfort was no longer secure. Dings, vibrations, rattles, bumps, shouts, murmurs, bells clashed against the outer wall of the circle he had dug around himself. Unsettled, his ordered universe was breaking apart. A dash of rage and a rush of fear came upon him in tide after tide. His fists clenched, it was as though he were on the periphery of a vast whirlpool.

As he was drawn deeper and deeper into the maelstrom, his insecurities, like a ghastly procession of wraiths, emerged. Rejection, failure, inadequacy, uselessness. *Why do these kids ignore me? Why don't they respect me?* David's head ached.

"Shut up!"

Again. The roar was a primeval thing. Guttural, filled with anger and frustration, it was probably heard clear across the school.

For a moment there was stupefied silence. The children looked up at David, just like he had seen the workers that day look across the street at the construction site. But the silence lasted just for a moment. The small boy clutching the half hidden PSP like a forbidden jewel glanced at the flashing screen, oblivious to the teacher's rage.

"Ha!"

From the eye of the storm, where silence and stillness reign, all once again succumbed to the great disorder of the periphery. The boy's 'Ha!' was both a sound of triumph and a signal to others that a joust had been won. The class burst back into the symphony of chaos, and the teacher's bellow was forgotten. He clenched his fist and before he knew it, lunged for the PSP. He grabbed it. Things might have ended there in more normal circumstances. But that had not been a normal week. The anger within him was like a raging torrent. Like a vacuum sucks the air, it sucked his reason from him and substituted dumb emotion for temperance and caution. He raised his other hand in a fist.

Had things been different the bell might have rung at that moment.

Had things been different perhaps a deep breath and a cooler head might have pulled David back from the abyss.

Had the world been different, perhaps his rage might have been lost in this spinning ball that whirls about the sun.

To the class it looked like he was reaching for a fly near the ceiling although some students, the quieter ones, looked at him strangely, as though they were indeed wondering who this man really was.

His fist came down directly on the boy's face. The child seemed to crumple in his seat. A shocked silence overwhelmed the class. David lurched back in horror at what he had done. The boy cowered before him, whimpering. A small stream of blood was trickling from his nose. The PSP lay on the ground, blaring out techno music. *What have I done?* David thought. One of the students ran out of the classroom. His chair fell down. It sounded like a bomb in the silence.

"Teacher David hit Bao Jin!"

His high pitched clear voice could be heard clear across the school. Other students also jumped up and left, some shouting, some crying. Amidst the hubbub, teachers rushed into his classroom, at first one, then many.

David reached out his hand to comfort the boy, who violently turned away.

"Don't do that. Leave him alone." A teacher brushed David's hand aside.

Fortunately, the headmistress calmed down the parents. No bones had been broken and the child was prone to nose bleeds, it was learned – a sufficient excuse for bureaucrats. Mr Deng stepped in to mediate matters with the school administration and education bureau, who both wanted to fire David.

"It will be embarrassing for the school and the department." He advised them, "Let him finish his term and he can go back to America. Do you want the whole world to know you made a mistake choosing this man? I don't!"

His argument worked.

Later he talked to David.

"You gave the kid a little pat on the head. He's a troublemaker anyway. Don't worry. This whole thing will blow over in a few weeks but you cannot go around hitting children. We Chinese do not beat other people's children. Of course, beating our own children is OK. For you it's different. It's very serious because you are a foreigner. If you do something like this again it will be very bad. They may confiscate your passport and do other things to you."

Mr Deng delivered his comments without pause. When David tried to answer he was curtly dismissed with a wave of Mr Deng's hand. For days afterwards no-one came near him, let alone talked to him.

Only Spring tried to understand.

"Why did you do it?" she asked him during their class.

"I couldn't control myself."

"You're a man. Of course you can control yourself."

"Sometimes I get so angry I can't hold back."

"Why?"

David paused, then slowly said.

"My father used to beat me. I promised myself I would never do it. I feel so ashamed."

To his surprise he started to cry.

She held his hand. She pitied him. She forgave him even as she wondered.

Where had it come from? That towering flash of rage and energy had erupted from what inner volcano?

David pondered what he had done for several days. He remembered the old sayings

The sins of the fathers are visited upon the children

In ancient China, the sins of one man were reason to banish or execute three generations of his family. He wondered if he would suffer for the sins of his father. He wondered if he would in turn inflict the violence that had once been wrought on him. Unlike his father, he was usually even tempered. David's eruption of rage was the result of an extended process. For too long he had maintained his own counsel and tended to his own wounds. As a result he denied himself much of life's spontaneity. The ability to give of himself unreservedly was stunted, like arms with stubs for fingers. Love's path was, for him, a confusing, multi-lane highway with too many exits. His caution and temperance were a direct result of his self-imposed solitude.

Although David's rages and ecstasies were few and far between, they were a force of nature. When they erupted there were severe consequences, such as with Bao Jin. He wondered why he had hit the boy. *Was it my fist, or my father's?* he asked himself again and again. He also knew that memories of children are fickle things that inflate over time. He remembered how his father had beaten him. He remembered the big dark, calloused hands - and the sticks, but he didn't remember the pain. He mostly remembered his mother's anguish, the tears in her eyes and the wrinkles on her face that increased year after year. Their bond had been so close; it was as though he had suffered her every blow. Every tear that had fallen from her eyes had splashed on his face. Every humiliation she had felt had been his. So there was a crude and inescapable vengeance in the way he portrayed his father to himself.

When he talked to Spring he so much wanted her to love him. He despised himself for telling her about his weaknesses. *Why am I telling her these things?* he asked himself. In the great English classic *Jude the Obscure*, the English novelist Thomas Hardy wrote of how a mayor is revisited by the family he abandoned long ago, and how he must confront the demons of his past. He remembered a particular passage in which Hardy explains that sometimes a woman's love of being loved gets the better of her conscience. Though she is agonized at the thought of treating him cruelly she encourages her man to love her while she doesn't love him at all. Seeing him suffering, remorse sets in and she tried to repair the wrong. Perhaps he was this woman, he thought. I want so much to be loved and I don't, or can't love.

He saw this flaw in himself, and he saw his father as the cause. He wondered if either of them truly loved (or could love) anybody, and whether there was a cure for this sickness.

His father had been a brilliant man. He had succeeded beyond the wildest dreams of many Kenyans. He had had a sterling education and a career that made him rich before the age of thirty. But he had failed to bring that brilliance into his home. Some men are born wolves. They feed on love as they feed on women. Their lives become strategies rooted in lust and its concomitant, ambition.

In the end his father became a husk of what he once was. He fizzled out, drowned himself in liquor and burned. Once a decent man, unquestionably brilliant, he had been a victim of his own father and a brutal, patriarchal culture. Wracked by the inner welts of failure, his wounds took ever-clearer form in drinking, insouciance, violence and womanizing. Now, a grown man, David saw his father for what he was – an angry, unfinished vessel. For all his brilliance, his father had been blind to his excesses and lacked the wisdom of a third eye to guide him. In happier times, or more fortunate places, this third eye could have been a kind mother, a stern but fair father, even a good wife. David's mother could not fit this role. She had been just a child herself. She had been naïve and lacked the wisdom of experience. Memories of his father, sometimes vague, other times clear, tumbled in his mind like clothes in a dishwasher. Next to images of his father drinking in Alego and lying in a hospital bed were the shifting fuzzy, nighttime shapes that carried sticks and bottles of Tusker beer. He didn't remember pain. He just remembered sadness.

David realized that he had a problem with empathy. He could understand what others felt, but it was often their *physical*, not *emotional* pain. In this manner he understood Bao Qing's pain at being hit. He also disliked the boy for having what he felt was weakness. David failed to see how he had broken the trust between teacher and pupil. He could understand a broken leg, yes. Shattered loyalty or a broken heart, that was much harder for him to understand. Also he could, like his father, switch off empathy that comes so naturally to most of us. It had been easier that way – to switch it off. No pain, no worry. Yet, he was discovering that this power had a Janus effect. Although it insulated him, it also deadened him, dehumanized him. In return he would compensate by seeking extreme excitement. 'Why do you go sky-diving?' an old girlfriend had berated him when he spent weekends falling ten thousand feet from icy clouds to terra firma. 'You'll just kill yourself, you madman you. Aren't you comfortable with your life?' But he had needed the thrill because it made him feel alive.

He strained to think of good things his father had done, but remembered only one. That day they had gone to a hotel and his father had given him two shillings to ride the rocking horse on the veranda. He wanted to discover something good and redeeming about his father, but he couldn't. *My father wasn't evil*, he sometimes thought, almost with desperation. But although he racked his mind for memories of love and compassion, he found none. It was like he was foraging in a Dali-esque wasteland populated with melting clocks and broken dreams, desiccated phalluses and unrequited love. It seemed that he was rummaging through a mountain of brightly colored trash only to find that the doll that looked pretty from a distance was actually a corroded, bent piece of metal with a dirty ribbon attached. It was as though the dirty flotsam and jetsam of life had sunk to the bottom of a tub of sour vinegar and was now floating back up.

Was there a gap in his memory? Did his mother blind him? Did he really want to see the truth? When the mind becomes overwhelmed by thoughts and passions, one develops a headache and eventually shuts off. For many years he had shut off memories of his father and how they related to him. Now, as he saw what happened that day at school, he saw himself in a different light.

I will not be that type of man, he told himself.

About the same time that David was battling his own demons Zhen Rui woke up in his hospital bed. Outside it was very dark but one could hear the patter of rain. There was a strong wind and clapboards and loose objects could be heard clashing in the distance. He couldn't sleep. He was thinking of his music. He wanted so much to touch the piano, to feel the keys spring to life beneath his fingers. He wanted to see and hear the black and white machine that sang the songs of the earth. But he was weak and could barely move his hands. Then his fingers brushed up against the book the teacher had left. It was lying on his bed next to his waist. He picked it up slowly. It was an old brown hardback, written in English. While his English reading was very good he still had difficulty reading all the words. Embossed on the cover in golden letters were the words.

Beethoven

Inside the cover were some words written in pencil. The letters were jerky and uneven, like a chicken had walked across the page. He realized this book had some personal meaning for his teacher. Perhaps it had been a present. He opened the first page and with difficulty scanned the first line:

He was born in Bonn on a wet morning in 1770.

For the next few hours he struggled through the English but eagerly absorbed the content.

Ludwig was born in Bonn on a wet morning in 1770. 'Perhaps we should name him after the rain, or the morning,' his father pondered. But after exhausting a limited repertoire of names (he was only a musician after all) he settled on Ludwig. 'A nice solid sound to it,' he muttered. His wife almost died during the birth and the father tore his hair and protested something about the injustice of it all yet, in spite of the bloody garments and the air of frenzy about the midwife and her spectators, the child survived and the mother managed a weak smile.

It took Zhen Rui two hours to read this far. Over the next several days he read more.

The child didn't cry. He looked around and absorbed.. He was unruly. That he ran away four times when he was six years old was no surprise to those who knew him. He refused to take orders from anyone, even his father. He had an abnormal sensitivity to sound.

Zhen Rui thought, *I don't cry either, and I remember all the sounds I hear.*

He contended with a home in which wine flowed like a scarlet torrent into the worst places. After fighting with the constables to prevent his father's arrest for drunken brawls Ludwig was obliged again and again to carry the alcoholic Anton home.

Beethoven was like me. He did not have a real family, the boy thought.

The boy did not understand many of the words but he knew that Beethoven was a man of immense drive and will power. He saw in his struggles something of his own and wanted to learn about his music even more than before.

David returned to the hospital more frequently to visit the boy. He wouldn't continue the story. He would make excuses like he did not remember what happened next. Or he had to be somewhere and only had time to talk about other things. The boy did not understand but eventually gave up asking and learned about his musical idol through the book. Occasionally he would think about David's story and how it would end but then he would see a spider on the window, or a friend from the orphanage would pop in, or perhaps the nurse would come in cluck clucking as she changed the sheets. In time he totally forgot the story of Beethoven in Shenzhen.

"In my home and among my people it was common for men to drink late into the night. My father was an exception. He kept tight control over everything in his life, including drink. 'Clean this, clean that.' He would demand his wives and children maintain order in the house and in their lives. He would drink much but he never let it affect his kazi (work). He used to say 'Drink lets loose my demons. It is hard not to drink when you swim among fish.'"

- From David's father's journal

THE RECEPTION

Imagine a huge ballroom, scores of meters across, five or six meters tall. Bright red and gold banners printed with traditional Chinese characters are everywhere. They festoon the tall walls in long horizontal strips or dangle suspended like huge ruby lips from a Man Ray like installation. Pretty hostesses in green suits stand attentively by the large oak doors leading from the hall and elevators. They smile sweetly, demurely folding their hands before them. About 30 large circular tables neatly covered with white tablecloths, napkins, flowers, chopsticks, knives, forks, glasses and paper decorations stand grandly over every inch of the plush yellow-carpeted floor. Serving girls dash between obstacles like quicksilver on a metal tray. One feels one is in a magical field of giant white mushrooms. On the opposite side of the broad doorway is an elegant wood proscenium with crimson velvet curtains. How grand it is! How thoroughly has this scene been prepared for people and events! How synchronized! *How Chinese!*

When Spring and David entered this grand room they were a bit at a loss where to go.

"Come here. Eat something."

The friendly voice came from one of the stewards who was frantically directing the servers.

The young man led them to a side room to eat some snacks and meet other organizers and performers. Meantime the ballroom slowly filled up. Servers bustled between the huge tables with renewed energy. Spring left to get dressed up. David fumbled with the chopsticks and the food on the small table. Two young women sat across from him, peering curiously at him from timeto time.

"Do you have wooden chopsticks? Any dishes without meat?" David asked. He preferred wooden chopsticks to the common re-usable plastic ones.

"Here. Also try some *Bao Zi*." said one of the young woman. Her slim brown dress and short silky hair gave her diminutive frame a very youthful appearance. She pushed chopsticks and a plate of the white Chinese dumplings before him. Seeing his hesitation, she quickly added

"There's no meat in them."

"Thanks. I guess you can tell I'm a vegetarian!" He gingerly reached for one of the boiled dumplings and munched it slowly. He smiled.

"No problem!"

She smiled in relief.

"You must be the pianist." She said suddenly, her eyes wide open. She spoke excellent, if slightly over articulated, English.

"Yes, how did you know?"

"They said we'd have a foreigner and you're the only foreigner here! My name is Swan and this woman is the TV broadcaster."

They shook hands. Eager to continue her English conversation, she went on.

"We work at the TV cable station and are hosting the event."

Her friend nodded her head silently. David figured she didn't speak English or was shy. she sat attentively, unsmiling, like a good student in the front row of a classroom. Occasionally her body would slightly arch upwards and a slight furrow would darken her forehead as she tried to understand what they were saying. Failing even that, she finally rested her chin in her hands and looked bored. Clearly she was eager to finish the job and go home.

Spring returned to the table. She was dressed in a splendid diaphanous cream gown. David took several photos of her, and even asked Swan to take a few of the two of them. In one she posed playfully – offering him her outstretched hand as a graceful princess might. Her gown sparkled with numerous little glass stones and delicately embroidered flowers and trees. Her moonlike face glowed. David wouldn't look directly at her. He was an open book and his admiration embarrassed him.

But she knew. She was like Tolstoy's debutante at the ball, flushed with her beauty and conscious that the universe was in her pocket. She felt heady and afraid all at once. Stage fright was natural, and even a good thing, for it helped one focus on the performance at hand. She looked around at all the well-dressed people. They had come to see her, she marveled. The fact that two dozen performances were planned was unimportant. This evening, she believed, would begin and end with her. She had experience performing for even larger audiences. This would not be difficult, she convinced herself.

David spoke nonchalantly to Swan. He spoke of his plans to travel to other parts of China.

"If you ever need some help I can help you. I would suggest you visit Xian and Guilin. They are beautiful and have lots of culture."

Spring looked on, not understanding everything. When she saw him talking with Swan she at first didn't think much of it. Then like a small run in one's stocking that grows longer with the passage of time, or a burr in one's shoe that jabs without reason, or even like a mosquito that dives into one's ear as one is about to all asleep, it became more irritating. Their conversation continued and the light in her eyes grew dimmer. She never said a word.

"Spring, someday we must go to Xian and Guilin." He blurted out, his eyes shining. But she just looked on stonily with her half quizzical, unconcerned look. He wondered if she didn't like the gracious Swan. After a short silence he quickly said,

"Someone told me before I came to China that Chinese people are only interested in taking my money. But I haven't seen that at all!"

There was a short embarrassing silence. Swan looked at her plate of dumplings. Her companion looked at her watch. And Spring looked bored. At that moment the lights dimmed. At once the hubbub in the room ceased. Spring silently stole away. David headed for a seat near the piano. After a few words by the presenter, the woman who had been sitting beside Swan, the performances began. First a female army troop sang, danced, sweated and posed stiff-necked in their green khaki hats. Then, like a disembodied dragon of gold and scarlet parts, acrobatic dancers cavorted across the stage with powerful leaps and twists. A group of local Shenzhen students presented a skit that drew peals of laughter from the audience but which he didn't understand.

When their turn came the lights dimmed to a soft orange hue that turned the blue proscenium a deep green. A hush stole over the auditorium as the curtains pulled apart to reveal Spring curled up on the stage like a small pearly ball. He softly started to play the piano. She unwound from her pose. Like a moon rising from behind the sea she lifted herself up. Before the rapt eyes of the audience she began her dance. Although the stage was small she made it large by using every inch of space to arabesque, promenade and pirouette. Combining ballet and modern dance, her gestures were evolving and fluid. It was as though this gentle and lithe beauty was in a duet with an inner spirit. Sometimes she seemed to be battling unseen forces that threatened to topple and destroy her. At other moments she was like a butterfly roaming high across the heavens in rhythm with the cosmos. In the final moments, confronted by her lover's grave, it was as though the earth conspired to suck her down, down, down into its dark maw.

As he played the piano he could see her out of the corner of his eye. He saw her art and how it stilled even the most raucous in the audience. How true it was, he thought when the great Hungarian pianist Liszt had declared: *Music soothes the savage breast.*

Towards the end of her performance a man sitting across from him retched loudly. All eyes in the vicinity turned accusingly at the culprit, a short, stocky man dressed in a very expensive Western suit and brand new Gucci boots. Pudgy fingers projected beyond ill-fitting cuffs like desiccated pink tentacles. His eyes squinted nervously while his adams apple bobbed like a submerged marble above his tightly buttoned collar. He mouthed an apology and abstractly reached down to scratch his calf.

The final piano passage was quite difficult. Big chords required all ten fingers and unrelenting power. From the man's direction came another retch, shorter but still quite audible. David let loose a huge volume of triple fortissimo chords on the keyboard, simultaneously turning to glare at the culprit who seemed to shrink baack into the white table cloth. The violinist almost lost her rhythm and glanced nervously at him from the corner of her eyes.

Spring, unperturbed, serenely danced on. She was in the middle of a sequence of delicate movements, almost Indian in their juxtaposition of neck and fingers, arms and elbows, toes and heels. It was as though she was in tune with the rhythm of the earth itself, and nothing could dislodge her. The sounds from the man's table had ceased and the performance wound to a powerful climax.

After the performance she came over to the large table where the musicians had been seated with some other guests. Her face was flushed and radiant. She was shining with an inner glow that seemed to touch everyone close by. People showered congratulations on her. Like a child at her birthday party she posed for photographs and smiled happily. Finally she sat down and with him watched the rest of the performances.

"Very good playing. Where are you from?"

Looking up David saw it was the man who had almost interrupted Spring's performance. Realizing the question was addressed to him, not to the dancer. David quietly and coldly said,

"Spring was great. Thank you."

The man continued unperturbed. He stood close to David, who could smell the cologne and see the Gucci portfolio. *Does he have to be so close?* he said to himself with irritation.

"I see you are an American. Let me tell you about the Butterfly story. May I sit down?" He fidgeted his fingers as he looked at them both.

Spring, finally understanding, graciously smiled and offered him a seat. Nothing could dim her happiness. This was a time to be gracious, to treasure the lightness in the air and the tulips in the valley. David stiffly moved aside. The man sat down, nervously looking at the foreigner while pulling it close to Spring, who pretended not to notice.

" Every Chinese knows the legend. Hundreds of years ago, young people were not allowed to choose their lovers. Today it is different. A woman can be with another man, even a foreigner."

He smiled at them paternalistically. Spring blushed slightly.

"In this feudal society, two young people fell in love, but their family did not approve. The man was not rich enough and the father had already arranged the girl to be married to another. Her parents forced her to leave to marry another man. The lover, left in despair, pined away his life as a lowly beaurocrat and died. Like Romeo and Juliet, yes?"

Without waiting for an answer he went on.

"By chance she came by his grave on a stormy night. In despair she threw herself into the tomb. Then, magically, the people saw two butterflies emerge from the mouth of the tomb and escape into the air."

And he looked pleased as punch, his chin jutted out and he clutched his beer glass so tightly his red hands were white from the pressure.

"Yes, China has wonderful stories and things to teach foreigners."

He laughed and offered his glass.

"Gang Bei! Bottoms up! Do you like basketball?"

"Yes I do, but let us congratulate Spring." David raised a toast to her, which several other people at the table joined in. A woman shouted out to him:

"Spring is very charming, don't you think? She makes us proud!"

He had heard someone else say that to him but couldn't remember, but then someone interrupted, laughing,

"You know what they say in China about people's achievements,"

"No. What?"

"Spring knows. First thank the Communist Party, then thank the leaders, next thank your teachers and finally thank your family and your wife!"

People smiled and some laughed. Others didn't. He did not know if this was a joke at the expense of the CPPC or one's wife, but he laughed anyway.

Not far from them a group of people were standing and laughing. Since most in the ballroom were sitting they attracted attention and whispers.

"Some important government people, aren't they?" somebody whispered to David.

Like a flock of birds alighting on a field of corn the government officials were soon doing their own thing. Someone raised his tumbler, and everyone followed suit,

"*Gang Bei!* Bottoms Up!"

All dutifully, laughingly, downed the liquor. A rosy-cheeked spectacled woman from the group smiled at him. She toasted Sping, who beamed. Then she turned to David.

"Your piano playing was wonderful. Thank you!"

"You're welcome."

He toasted her. Unconsciously the whole table followed suit. He realized she must be someone important.

"She's the party secretary for the district." someone whispered.

The party secretary quickly turned again to everyone, jubilantly said some words in Chinese. She swept back her graying hair with a proud flick of the hand, took a final swig, toasted the group one last time and, with her flock in tow, swooped over to the next table.

He was standing up, but felt a little dizzy and sat down. Mr Bin, the Gucci man, looking at him, laughed.

"Don't drink too much. But drink enough."

"What do you mean?"

"I will teach you a little more about China. In Henan province there is a saying

Casual friends sip beer, Lifelong friends gulp it down!

Here many people consider the amount of beer one drinks as a reliable measure of their friendship."

"I guess that takes me off the short list. I cannot have many friends. I don't drink."

"Maybe, but consider that drinking a little is still OK. The great poet *Li Bai* used to spend the whole night drinking with his friends. According to him, he had to drink to write his great poems."

David just smiled. He didn't know why, but Mr Bin was becoming an increasingly interesting person. Mr Bin, on the other hand, instinctively understood that the foreigner wanted to understand Chinese culture more than he wanted to make money. Although he was loutish in some respects, he was a good teacher. Swan sidled up to David. She had also been making rounds of the tables. She whispered to him confidentially.

"You said you wanted to see some interesting Shenzhen sights. Maybe one day my friend and I can take you to the beach to have lunch at a fishing village. Or to one of our famous tea houses where we can discuss many things."

He leaped at the invitations. Spring passed (she didn't like Swan) but Mr Bin counted himself in. Swan laughed merrily.

"Good. I will call you soon to arrange the details."

✳✳

After the reception Spring invited him back to her apartment. Recently they had spent time there watching TV or cooking small meals. He loved these moments with her. All her friends and family were far away and it seemed she was completely his but that wasn't really true. She was often on the phone while he watched TV, munching sunflower seeds, and she was never physically close. Even when he touched her hand lightly as a gesture of friendship, although with a feeling of intimidation or even fear, she didn't respond in kind. He respected her too much to make the first move.

Her apartment was in a cul de sac off busy Shennan Boulevard. Quiet and lined with trees, it had its share of small shops and sidewalk vendors, but they seemed a notch above vendors on other streets. It was as though their clothes were a little cleaner, their shirts were a little whiter, their cut pineapples and lettuce a little more colorful, and their wares even a little more cultured (a book seller was there at least two or three times a week). That night the street bustled with people. A man in a blue tunic sat scratching his ear next to a small table. On the table was a big jar of water and carved pineapples that sat neatly like magical and luscious golden eggs. A little girl with hair cut short like a boy's stood beside him, slicing rinds from pineapples.

"Hello-o-o." she said, lilting the o-o-o-o-o in a slightly insouciant *chinglish*, that combination of bad English and worse Chinese that has spread like a virus across China.

Squatting on his heels, a chicken vendor squinted at passersby with a slightly bemused expression on his face. A shock of uncombed hair sprang out in four directions at once from his grizzled head. Two equally bemused brown chickens stood as if frozen before him, like oversized fried doughnuts. Further down the road, bunches of meter long celery, short lettuce heads, cucumbers, eggplant, artichokes, cabbage and cashew nuts were laid out in neat rows on white plastic sheets. On the opposite side of the small street a balding man in a white polyester dress shirt stood with his arms folded before a table draped with orange cloth. On it were curios and amulets of blue, green and white jade. A white sign propped in the center said

Jade products, factory direct
Artifacts and antiques for sale
We buy lucky charms

Others meandered slowly around the peddlers as they took their evening walks.

To the first time observer this strange Chinese walk, called *liu da*, is a curious thing - slow paced by western standards, feet splayed outwards, its character at once both naive and somewhat intellectual.

"Walk slower!" Chinese often criticize their foreign friends.

One looks around and sees couples, hand in hand, moving at a glacial pace. Older men and women treat the outdoors as their living room, even wearing their pajamas. In China, whose culture involves intense attention to detail, the slow walk is a mechanism for observation. When one switches from using cars to bicycles and from bicycles to a walk along the street, one can sees the colors of the window frames and the small statues in the yard. David observed these walks and wondered if his life would ever slow down enough so he could value this unique walk.

Her one bedroom apartment was small but clean. The living room space abutted an open kitchen on the right as one entered. The room smelled of jasmine and looked out over a small terrace of potted flowers and a rock garden. In the living room next to the sofa and TV was a brown upright piano. On the wall opposite the kitchen hung four traditional Sichuan opera masks. Like fiendish devils they glared and grimaced in thespian splendor. In Chinese theatre, as actors sing and gesture these masks are whipped on and off their faces with a sleight of hand too quick and deft for the normal eye to follow. An actor spends years of training to master this secret, thousand year old technique. Like Japanese Kabuki, the masks reflect exaggerated expressions. But unlike the grim, washed out colors of Kabuki, palettes of corn yellow, ruby red, apple green and other hues make the multicolored masks pulse with life. Above the piano was a huge poster of a kabuki actor. The room was elegant, tasteful and cultured, but untidy. Esoteric slippers and sandals were scattered in front of the door. A half empty bottle of Gatorade stood on the coffee table, surrounded by some scattered sunflower seeds. Beside a huge pink teddy bear, music books and children's drawings lay in untidy bunches on the piano and sofa. But even the flotsam and jetsam of her home seemed strategically placed to provide balance and rhythm. Thus the Gatorade bottle was neatly closed, not open. The sheets of drawings were laid out in a neat criss-cross pattern. The shoes and sandals had a *boutique* look, as though they had been discovered in exotic ethnic villages from different parts of this vast country.

She skipped into the apartment with him in tow close behind her. She was gay and happy, flushed with the evening's success:

"I feel so good!" she cried, and twirled around.

"Bravo!" he clapped.

She grabbed the juice bottle, took a swig and turned to him, her voice suddenly low and confidential,

"Really? Did you like it?"

"It was great. Everybody couldn't keep their eyes off you!"

"Yes, that's true. I think he liked it too."

"Who?" He felt a stab of jealousy. He wondered why she always injected information about men she knew just when he was alone with her. He didn't want to know about these people. They were like hostile ghosts that hovered above, threatening to destroy his happiness.

"Mr Li. I think he will definitely be pleased. He said I should start work next week."

"Your place is such a mess you silly girl." He pointed at nothing in particular, eager to change the subject.

"Yes, I should tidy it up."

They were silent for a moment. It was as though they suddenly realized they were alone together. Silence was unwelcome. It also seemed like their words were always imprecise and lurked about the edges of the truth. It was as though they just had to turn their heads to see the resplendent reality behind them but all they could see were two separate shadows cast against the wall.

"Would you like something to drink?" She absent mindedly asked.

"Yes, that would be great!" He answered without conviction.

"I have some *long jing* tea. It's very good tea. A friend brought it for me."

"I hope it wasn't Mr Gucci." He said, and regretted it.

"Who? What do you mean?"

"Nothing."

"What, you mean Mr Bin!"

"He was disgusting."

"Yes, very, but…"

"But what? He threw up while you were dancing. I almost clobbered him. He's a jerk!"

She smiled. It was as though she could not exactly say what she was thinking. She was like the camel's hair brush of a Chinese calligrapher, soft and malleable, by nature always on the edge of a thought. Like most Chinese, she was a creature of the heart, of emotions. To crystallize her thoughts and feelings was alien, almost obscene. But her softness and casual manner was also her strength, and nourished her talent at gauging the thoughts and feelings of others. Her genius was a Chinese genius. It was the gift of empathy. It wasn't stylized (like the Japanese) into a frigid politeness akin to a scentless flower. Like the black ink that flowed from the brush her empathy soaked into the dry paper of David's off-kilter soul. In the whorls and marks of his soul it defined edges and curves that stroked and massaged him like a balm.

"Maybe but…."

To David, Spring often seemed incapable of directly saying what was on her mind but, although he often preferred exactness to ambiguity, this time it was welcome.

"What! You don't believe me!"

"I also hate it when people spit or make those sounds." she conceded.

"Yeah like this."

And he imitated Mr Bin. She laughed.

"Why don't we just put him in prison?"

"That's silly."

"Why not? I'll have no competition."

"You small nothing. You're joking. He wasn't attractive."

"You know, just a polite, well behaved Chinese lady like you and a handsome foreign devil like me."

They were sitting side by side on the sofa, she leaning slightly on the teddy bear, while he pushed the books and children's drawings into an even more unmanageable mess. He touched her hand gently. She drew it away.

"Let's watch some TV."

"OK!"

But she had already jumped up and found the remote control.

"Oh it's *Ugly Betty*! My favorite!"

He didn't understand why so many young women loved this American soap about narcissist fashion executives. Many of his women friends at the school had said they loved it. Last week a teacher had rushed out of class early excusing herself profusely to the substitute teacher she had cajoled: 'I have so much to do, and then I have to catch *Ugly Betty*. I missed it last week!' Pressed for an explanation, one of his male friends had dryly said:

"Look, TV is mostly cheap shit from Rupert Murdoch and the Beijing communists. And 90% of airtime is ads for hair shampoo, skin whiteners and face lift clinics. What do you expect?"

He groaned inside.

"I'll get something from the kitchen."

She jumped up.

"No let me. I'll get you the tea I promised. She quickly returned with some sweet uncut oranges."

"These are from Jiang Xi province."

"Really?"

"Many people there plant oranges. They are famous all over China."

"Here let me cut them for us." And he took the knife from her hand.

She stared at him while he cut the fruit.

"What are you looking at?"

She didn't answer. She was a little miffed because she didn't know what to do. She grabbed her big teddy bear and was quiet for a second. Then she went to the kitchen and absent-mindedly started to wash the dishes. Suddenly *Ugly Betty* was no longer on her mind. She looked at the man across the room with a strange expression on her face, one that would have surprised him had he seen it.

David continued watching the TV. He suddenly stood up and walked over to her.

"Here, let me help."

"No, I can do it myself." Flustered, she picked up the bottled water instead of the Ajax.

"Sorry, Teddy bear inspired me!"

She laughed.

"OK, here." And she handed him a grimy plate. He poured a generous amount of dish cleaner and scrubbed with the green brillo pad. She did the same. He looked closely at her dish.

"It's not clean enough."

"Yes it is."

He rubbed his forefinger on the plate.

"Do you hear the squeak?"

"What do you mean?"

He made a small squeaking sound with his mouth. She smiled.

"You're strange. Chinese men don't wash dishes."

"Really?"

He was very close to her. He saw how wide, deep and black were her eyes. They were honest, open and very, very beautiful. He cleared his throat.

"I guess I'm not a Chinese man."

"You have a strange way of cutting oranges."

"Yeah, but it's the best way."

She was right. When he cut oranges he always made the second slice slightly off axis. Most people make the second cut at right angles to the first. His method left more of the sweet pulp exposed.

"You're strange." She laughed.

As she spoke she gripped her hands together, one in the other. Every so often she would squeeze her fingers, which, like putty that refused to mold, kept bouncing back. She was very close to him, and she was looking up at him. He felt uncomfortable. The air-conditioning in the room didn't seem to be working. The shirt seemed to stick to his back in places. He imagined patches of dark silk etched against his body for her to see.

He didn't say anything.

"Are you waiting for something?" She asked him, laughingly.

He liked the sound of her voice. It had that sweet shivery quality that describes softness, indeterminacy. It was a generic thing. He told himself any woman's voice would have had the same effect. In his admiration for the other sex, points of attraction were often broad characteristics of the species. She could have screamed obscenities, and still the high, soft sound would have seduced him. He mentally shook his head and brought himself back to the present. She was still so close.

It was a curious thing. This sensualism. It colored much of his world. It galled him to abstractions and hyperbole. And yet so much about him was precise. The time he woke up in the morning. Always late yet always exactly twenty-five minutes after the alarm rang. When he had worked back in America he would have arguments with colleagues at work, as his obsession with results and goals could be alarming.

"When will this be ready? What date can you commit to?"

Very pleasant, even charming, he would speak in sooth, mellow tones, yet insist that the deadline be met.

Here in China there was a lessening of urgency. From time to time, he would break out of this shell. Like a phoenix rising, he would disperse the ashes with great bellows of laughter or a genuine smile. His teeth would shine; eyes would glimmer between sad merriment and a dreamy happiness. A true Dionysian, in another life he may have craved raw meat, melted cheese, bachanalic orgies, and romped happily across smooth hills in a loincloth. In this life David could settle for vegetarianism, high cholesterol counts, the intellectual thrill of a strange language and people, and a woman who entranced him. Even as he saw and remembered all these things he was looking at her skin and the lobe of her ear. He wanted to touch it. He saw her lips and he wanted to kiss them. And without direction, with out another thought he did just that, impulsively, like a butterfly opening its wings beneath the sunlight. She seemed to become limp, almost like a rag doll. She was so light.

"Get down here." he said roughly. And he turned and grabbed her shoulders and gently threw her down on the soft carpet, her face to the pillow that had toppled from the sofa. She didn't say a word. He very deliberately and gently kissed her bare shoulder. It was ever so smooth and even salty to the taste. She was quiet and once again her face was inscrutable. Her body, perfectly still, seemed like a strung bow in the arrow, powerful and arresting in its latent force. He continued to kiss her neck and rubbed her shoulders firmly. Still he didn't dare to think that that night would be consummated.

"Let me take this off. Just the back."

He slowly unzipped her blouse. It was a discovery to see her broad brown back exposed to him. The pink lamp above them gave the room a fleshly and carnal air. And still she was quiet. Her bra formed a broad white stripe across her back, thick and challenging across the brown field. He now lay beside her, still kissing, ever so gently, as though she were a butterfly that would spread its wings and flee at the slightest sign of aggression. Images of her at the concert next to the musicians came to him. He saw her brush her hair back and in this fragment of memory awakened in him what seemed an almost sacred intimacy. He reached for the broad white strap and fumbled on the catch. His fingers seemed not to obey him and yet he wanted to give in to the moment, to fall into the awkwardness of his own impulses. And still the sight of her smile and her thick ebony eyebrows, arched and quizzical, flashed across his mind's eye.

She moaned slightly. It was a low, almost Zen like sound, like the *aoumm* of the Tibetan monks. It rose not just from the body and the soul but also from the ineluctable force that plays a vast and coded music to life's enveloping rhythms. She moaned again, this time more deeply. He turned her over to him. Her face was suddenly flush against his. He almost lost his breath against the sheer rush of her closeness. Her lips were next to his. Her cheek was so close he could see the pores. Her eyes, though closed, were open to his maleness. So he kissed her on the lips for the first time. It was more than a kiss. It was an elimination of space. Space that lies between the traveler and his destination, between the beads of water on blades of grass that reach out to suck each other into themselves, between the outstretched fingers of God and Adam. They must have lain like this for at least twenty or thirty minutes, because the movie became silent somewhere in between. In the perverse and banal way that trivial things obtrude onto matters of great import, the TV had switched from *Ugly Betty* to a hair infomercial, as if to interrupt the holy force that swamped the room. He reached for the remote and switched it off. The silence of the night was suddenly full upon them. The air was full of love. And in this strange city, foreign and distant, their closeness made him them love the city. The distance that keeps us apart slowly dissolved against the force of their union. Love makes optimists of us all.

She had insisted upon a condom. As he entered her he was almost disappointed by the lack of physical sensation and yet overwhelmed by a sense of triumph. It was as all their interactions in the past several days, even several months had led up to this moment. The truth is that penetration was the end of it all...almost. She breathed heavily, in deep inhalations, as though she were gasping for air. Her breasts were full and rotund, tipped with a faint pinkness that dissolved beneath the carnal glare of the lamp. And for a moment their bodies limned and joined against the sheets and they knew that they would remember this moment as long as they were capable of remembering anything. She pushed against him and he against her. No longer did her smile flash through his thoughts. No longer were images projected against her, obtruding into her space. Just a quiet, steady and wonderful rhythm. An all-enveloping warmth. Her hot breath against his cheeks. Her wonderful black hair, loose and like a hydra sucking the whiteness from the sheets into smooth mellifluous ebony oil. And from time to time she would open her eyes with a bitter merriment almost. When he came inside her he almost wept for joy. She grasped him and shuddered. In his selfishness he did not know whether she was satisfied too. But she sank back into the whiteness and they lay against each other, sweating skin against sweating skin as the cool air from the sea caressed their heaving chests.

"I remember that song because it sang about dreams. My father once told me, "Without dreams you are like a bird with a broken wing. You cannot fly. I want you to dream, as I dream for you." My father had many evil thoughts and did many cruel things, but he said many truths."

- From David's father's journal

BEETHOVEN AND CHINESE TEA

In Shenzhen almost everyone has a certain look. The look is like that of a searcher, and it has an air of bewilderment about it. It is a look that appears only at certain times. One is perhaps standing nonchalantly by the open window and spots it almost by chance. One sees this look in residents of the city who have come from all over China to look for wives, husbands, money and the freedom to be themselves. There are the tall shrewd girls from Sichuan, the swarthy men from the South, the grandstanding and arrogant businessmen from Hong Kong. There are the aunties, uncles and grandparents who react in various shell shocked ways to the newness of this boomtown. Even the orphans have something of this look. Like Zhen Rui, they are like flotsam tumbling on the edge of a magical whirlpool, struggling to keep afloat and at a distance, yet bewitched by the rush of water.

After 6 weeks in the hospital Zhen Rui returned to the orphanage. The immediate danger to his heart had passed. Weaker, paler than before, he found reserves of energy to laugh and play and continue the study of music. That one so ostensibly weak could in fact be so strong took everyone by surprise.

"Where does the lad get such energy? Heavens!", one of the old nannies smiled, as she lugged a tub of laundry into the creaking elevator.

She turned to him, her face wreathed with joy, "I think it's the music, Teacher David!"

Indeed David noticed that when the boy started to play piano, the wrinkles would seem to lift from his face, as though the pain had vanished. At times his ever-present bittersweet smile would morph into something almost beatific. Mr. Ma and David were his most frequent adult companions. Music linked the three of them like an invisible but powerful strand of energy, and turned their contradictions into synergies and their ennui into vigor. Every Saturday David would take the No 320 to *Che Guan Suo* and walk the two blocks past the hawkers and mom and pop shops to the Social Centre.

"I see that Beethoven is so different from Chopin in a number of ways, such as the loudness and softness." said Zhen Rui.

The boy excitedly leafed through the Beethoven Sonatas and the second movement of the Chopin E minor concerto. He had gained confidence in his English and together with David's rapid improvement in mandarin they could discuss reasonably advanced topics without difficulty.

"What do you mean?"

"Well, look at this part from Beethoven's sonata. You see how he quickly becomes very loud. His loudness is..."

He struggled with the right English word. He would often flip between English and Chinese.

"...sp...special."

He used the Chinese word *te bie*.

"OK, I'm following."

"Chopin is different. He makes me think of pretty things, like flowers and ice-cream. He is also loud but it's...not the same."

"Yes, that's true."

"So how can I learn this?"

"What do you mean?"

"With Chopin I sometimes want that loudness I hear in Beethoven. Can I do that?"

"I think it depends where you start learning. The first thing is to listen to the book. Chopin tells you in many places how he wants the music performed. Listen to the music and his directions and you will find the direction and integration you need. And it will be different, of course, from Beethoven, but it will have its own uniqueness and power."

"If I don't...who cares?"

"Who cares? Well if that's the case, it is no longer Chopin. It becomes you and not Chopin. You *must* care. This is not where you want to be. Listen to the book and you will still be yourself. You will become part of the music. Rachmaninoff, another great composer, once said, to perform music well one must work within its boxes. The smaller the box the greater one's power. Think about it."

Zhen Rui nodded his head slowly, and didn't say anything for a long time. Then he looked up and said,

"I guess that's true, because even when I play by rules I start to like the piece more and more."

"That's it. With music one grows to love the piece. It becomes part of you and as you learn more you love it more. And yet it still is Chopin and still is Beethoven. That's the secret. Love."

Every so often Zhen Rui would show David a new piece of music he had discovered. In his free time from classes he found the time and energy to go to with Teacher Li or Mr Ma to the newly opened city library. He would borrow volumes of sheet music and books, mostly Chopin, Beethoven and Rachmaninoff. These books were often new and barely used. Seeing the shiny tomes his eyes would flit from measure to measure like a humming bird darts from one sweet flower to another. Seeing his young, excited face David would imagine a new China a place of youth, fearless learning and assimilating of western culture. Here was optimism and passion and the rejection of boundaries. Then, when the boy coughed, a cloud seemed to pass over his face as he remembered.

"Look, I found this last week. I love this melody."

He played a few passages from the second movement of Chopin's E minor concerto.

"That's a great piece! Do you like the melodies?"

"Yes, very much. And it should go like this right?"

He started to sing. David had always told him that melodies should be played as they are sung, with high points and low points, focal points and parts that are secondary. Zhen Rui had absorbed this lesson well. So he sang out aloud what he felt the melody should be.

Zhen Rui was no singer. His singing hurt one's ears. The sound was loud, brassy, with no tonal fluctuations, as though he were tone deaf. Zhen Rui had a long, pink tongue. When he sang it would sometimes flick in and out of his mouth. The sounds would be interspersed with moans and whistles.

"Mmm, mmm, mmm....sss...sss....sss"

David once dreamed he had recorded Zhen Rui singing. In his dream he played it back to Spring, who said,

"It sounds like a devil...how can a person sing like that?"

People passing by in the corridor outside looked curiously in their direction and picked up their pace to wherever they were going. Some of the younger children would poke their bemused heads from the railed corridors on the opposite side of the quadrangle, looking into the windows of the music room, as though a fierce monster dwelled within. But Zhen Rui would continue his wolf like howling with such sincerity and passion no one could or wanted to stop him. As far as he was concerned, the orphanage did not exist. The sounds in his head were now, during these precious hours, his home. He was like a bird flying high over the city, basking in the golden glow of the sun dancing with the gusts of wind and the pounding of his beating heart.

Fortunately for David, his vocalizations were short. Afterwards Zhen Rui would look eagerly at the teacher and cough slightly and nervously.

"It's like that right?"

David would nod and say

"Just like that."

The boy would then start playing the melody without fuss, a gentle smile on his face. The pieces he selected were often far beyond his level of playing, even given his precociousness. David, however, would not dissuade him but instead emphasize the pieces they had already started to learn. In time, the newer books would be quietly returned back to their gleaming shelves in the city library, others selected, and the cycle would repeat itself.

During one weekend lesson, Zhen Rui was deep in thought over something. He seemed distracted at the keyboard and when the teacher talked to him he would look down at his hands and grasp the middle finger of his left hand with his right, stroking and squeezing it slowly and deliberately. Finally David walked to the side of the piano and dropped a huge book on the keys. The boy jumped out of his seat in astonishment.

"Do you know why I did that?" David said sternly.

"No. Why?"

"All musicians should keep playing. Their concentration should be so deep that nothing, NOTHING can disturb them."

The boy sat down slowly, his brow furrowed, and resumed playing.

The next lesson David repeated the same trick. This time the boy kept on playing, as if the sounds of the crashing books and jarring sounds from the keyboard were detritus, to be ignored and forgotten.

"Very good, Zhen Rui. You are learning bit by bit."

"I have a secret." The boy almost whispered to the teacher.

"What is it?"

"I think of Beethoven. You know?"

"Yes?"

"I remember the story you started to tell me. He always focused on his music. Nothing distracted him."

"True."

There was a moment of silence.

"Teacher?"

"Yes."

"Why didn't you finish the story?"

"I wasn't sure you understood. Also I thought you were not that interested."

"No, no, no. I liked it! Can you tell me the ending?"

"Are you sure?"

"Yes. Yes!" His eyes sparkled. They had been in class for over an hour and the boy welcomed the diversion. His eyes were tired but so plaintive the teacher could not refuse him.

"OK. So where did I leave off. Let me see..?" David sat down and scratched his head slowly.

"He had just met some businessmen."

"That's right. He had met some executives who wanted to make money from his music. He said to no one in particular. "I'm surrounded by idiots who don't want to listen to what I have to say. They're only worried that I will sue them and take their money. I have watched the state of my music in your century, and, quite frankly, it is slowly being drained of blood. I gave it the power to make man reach into himself and confront his destiny. Instead, every man hums a brief motif from the Fifth Symphony or the *Appassionata* after a concert, and then promptly forgets what it all means, once they start to eat their noodles.""

"I don't understand all that but I think he's saying that music is more important than money."

"Got it. So Beethoven looked at the group in the corner, focusing particularly on the tall one with the glasses and nose like a beak. Suddenly he broke out into a huge bellow of laughter. He laughed so hard that tears streamed down his cheeks, and he clutched his belly with his thick, padded hands."

"Why did he laugh?"

"He was laughing at the businessmen. He said, "Look how seriously they take me! And I was only speaking tongue in cheek about the royalties. That's all they care about. The money, I mean (and he winked at me). They are simply terrified I'll take their money." And he howled with great yelps of laughter."

David was silent for a minute, laughed and said.

"One has to laugh in life. The way a man laughs tells a lot about his character. Always laugh fully, Zhen Rui!"

The boy nodded eagerly.

"What happened then?"

"Well the lanky businessman came over. "Really, Mr. van Beethoven," he ventured to say, timidly coming out of his corner, "You should know that we really respect your mon…you. In fact, last year your works netted us over thirty million…We Chinese even learned how to market it like the Americans."

Beethoven wanted to say something but the executive went on.

"You know my English name yes? It's Ronco. After the great American businessman. He sold people junky inventions such as the Pocket Fisherman and beef jerky dehydrators. He taught me a lot. Of course your music is grades above…even for stupid Americans. Unfortunately these bastard Chinese copycat thieves love it. We produced a hit CD called *Feng De Beethoven* (Crazy Beethoven). The children love it. Everyone loves your music even though there are lots of bootlegged copies on the Internet!"

He mentioned the last phrase in a tone of gloom.

At this point, the Maestro jumped up, grabbed me by the hand and pulled me to a door in the rear that I hadn't noticed. Before I knew it I was rushing down the rear stairs after him, noticing only the shock of dark gray hair that quivered in the wake of his resolute motion.

Before I knew it we were on the street and heading towards Shennan Boulevard. He walked so rapidly, almost falling over every step, that it took me a considerable degree of effort just to keep up with him. His eyes were narrowed and peered ahead with steely intensity. As if by instinct the people in his way moved aside to let him through. As for me, I was constantly bumping into people and excusing myself for shoving little old ladies aside.

Soon we were seated at a busy noodle shop, a plate of *mian tiao* and hot dumplings lying between the two of us. The Maestro hadn't said a word up until now, and peered at his *oolong* tea as if it held an unfathomable harmony. While he sat in disconsolate gloom, I had a chance to take a closer look at him. He leaned his left ear against his palm, almost as though hearing an inner voice, and his eyes fastened onto the teacup below him. Deep lines and wrinkles mapped his rugged face, and his mouth, tightly shut, betrayed an almost ineffable sense of purpose and determination. His furrowed brow shone from a thin film of perspiration, and his hair, wild, unkempt and massive, gave his body an almost comical sense of top-heavy disproportion. Without a word he stood up, excused himself and headed to the bathroom. While he was gone, a thin Chinese man of medium height in a worn leather jacket and sporting a crew cut reached over from the next booth,

"Hey, man, spare a light?"

He reached over a long, pale and bony group of fingers that clutched a flaccid cigarette. He spat on the floor and picked some food from his teeth with a toothpick with his other hand. I lighted the cigarette for him quickly, and tried to ignore him.

"I dig your pal's threads, man. His hair however, is, man, totally, you know, totally disgusting. No style. What's his problem?"

"He's Beethoven." I wearily said, using the Chinese pronunciation for *Beethoven*.

"Say what? With a name like that I can't blame him for being down. Has he got a Chinese name?" and he blew smoke rings about his head.

"No, no Chinese name. His name is unique. Beethoven, Ludwig van Beethoven, B-E-E-T-H-O-V-E-N, Beethoven!" I said in exasperation, spelling it out in English letters.

"Yeah, right." Suddenly uninterested he looked at his watch.

"Anyway I have this date, you know, and I gotta go, as they say. Give your pal some *shampoo*, you know, S-H-A-M-P-O-O (he used English letters). I'm from Hong Kong and I can't wait to get back there away from these primitives and their strange foreign friends. You know my wife won't come here – she's afraid she'll get stabbed and her organs sold to some hospital." and he got up and stalked out, his mouth lifted in a half suppressed smirk.

"What happened then?" Zhen Rui interrupted.

"I'm getting there. Hold your horses. After Beethoven returned from the washroom, we walked to Lian Hua Park. I remembered his love of nature and hoped he would like the kites and the trees. In fact, once there, a weight seemed to lift from him, for he seemed taller, and wrinkles lifted from off his face. He talked a great deal, and occasionally would whistle very badly and very loudly. We always talked very loudly on account of his hearing disability. Hardened migrants and even city people turned their heads to wonder at our high decibel discussions. From the little I recall, his thoughts were deep and far-ranging."

"He must have said many important things."

"Yes. He asked me, 'Where is music today? I no longer see anyone learning from it. It has become incomprehensible to the ordinary man. In my day, though I was not as popular as my students Moscheles or Spohr, I could hold my own with them. Throngs would turn out to hear my latest work. I was well known even among the *potato eaters* from the farms. Many people have written that I was uncultured and knew only music. I admit I was no man of letters, and wrote clumsy prose, but I tried to be true to myself!'"

At this point David stopped and looked at Zhen Rui.

"You see, Zhen Rui, that's the point of the story."

Seeing the boy's puzzled face, he continued.

"You know you are very ill and had to go to the hospital, right?"

Zhen Rui nodded slowly.

"Well, you came back to the orphanage. You didn't give up. And you continued to play piano. Even though you are still weak, why did you continue to study?"

"Because I felt I must. Music makes me..." And he didn't know what to say.

"Beethoven also, he didn't understand why but he too didn't give up. He lost his hearing. He even wanted to kill himself, but music kept him going. You too must keep going."

He went on.

"Beethoven told me: Young people too willingly skirt over bumps in the road, and dash for the easy life. While some of you young people truly love classical art, and here I not only mean Western music but even Chinese calligraphy, there are too few of you. And many young people are spoiled. In fact, you ought to *limp* after your goals. Respect music. Respect artists and *ubermenschen* (supermen) and the society cannot go wrong. We are brothers in this cold and hostile world and with each other we may travel far or not, but we must love each other in the time we have, so we may live with dignity and freedom to create.'"

David realized he had gotten carried away. He had offered a lot of concepts that no eight year old could understand. He quickly added,

"Beethoven finally said to me, "As for your young friend Zhen Rui. Tell him to keep going, keep charging ahead, keep learning music and he will get better.'".

Zhen Rui's eyes were wide open. Although he didn't understand all those strange people's names and ideas, he loved to see the passion in the teacher's eyes. Surrounded by the gloom and sameness of the orphanage, he instinctively bonded with his charismatic teacher. David cleared his throat and went on.

""China has its musical culture too." Beethoven declared, tossing back his mane of rumpled hair.

"Like what?" I said, curious about his opinion.

"Look at that beautiful simple song *The Jasmine Flower.*" And he proceeded to half hum half sing the following phrases. He waved his hands in the air as though he was conducting an orchestra. The sounds were all out of tune, and he sounded like he was snorting, whistling, and roaring all at once. But one couldn't deny the passion. His whole body was at one with his mind.

Flower of jasmine, oh so fair!
Flower of jasmine, oh so fair!
Budding and blooming here and there
Pure and fragrant all declare
Let me take you with tender care,
Your sweetness for all to share.
Jasmine fair, oh jasmine fair.

"This beautiful song came from the fields of China, just like my tunes came from the sweat and brows of simple people who worked in the fields. The Italian Giacomo Puccini took this tune of love from *Jiang Su* province, added a few variations and created something for the ages. The man was on his deathbed for God's sake! Turandot! Turandot! What a marvelous opera."

He lapsed into silence for a minute, as though meditating, then continued.

"This is what music is about, beyond borders, weaving cultures. You must absorb and live this lesson. Behold!"

"At this point a fat pink woman (probably an English teacher hired by a local school) with a huge black afro and darkened eyebrows, purple lips and a huge white paper flower in her hair dashed up to us, eyes bulging. Behind her trotted a small group of young Chinese schoolgirls, likely her English students."

"My God! You...you're Beethoven!"

"She immediately fell on her knees and started kissing his expensive crocodile leather boots. All the little girls looked at her as though she was crazy, then giggled and laughed at the crazy foreigners."

David got down on his knees before Zhen Rui, imitating a groveling motion. The boy laughed.

"The Maestro looked at me in perplexity, frowned and said, "And above all, remember me only as a man who looked a little deeper. Not a deity. For goodness sake, don't look upon me as a deity. All of us can look within.""

And he pulled away from her, winked at me, and gave an enormous roar of laughter that must have been heard clear across the park. I knew then that I had met a God."

Zhen Rui clapped his hands, laughing and coughing, coughing and laughing.

"Thank you teacher! What a wonderful story!"

David bowed and the two high fived.

✳✳

A few days later he went out for dinner with Swan, her boyfriend Alfred and Mr Bin. Mr Bin had been determined to follow up on his invitation to the American and wouldn't take no for an answer. Spring was busy anyway with her new job and he felt somewhat neglected. David at first feebly protested he was busy, but then caved in. He was also curious to see Swan again.

The dinner was non-descript, mostly bland food served in a cavernous restaurant with scores of waiters and waitresses darting among the loquacious patrons. They made small talk while he ate some simple vegetables and noodles. The others smoked, swapping bits of conversation in both Mandarin and English.

After dinner they went to a famous Shenzhen teahouse, a short walk away. He had been to this area in Futian district a few months back but now it was different. In Shenzhen the streets may stay the same, but the shops change frequently. Every few months a few go out of business and new ones arrive. In America bigger ships swallow up small shops. In China, small shops eat other small shops, like swarms of cannibalistic piranhas. Like an immutable core, one travels at the center of this vortex. *My gift is that I can mutate enough to make the world my home*, David thought to himself.

The tea house was located on a quiet tree lined residential street. A few steps away was a barber shop where kids in punk hairdos, tight jeans and toothpick shoes would lounge outside chatting on slow nights as they waited for customers. Across from the entrance was a half built park with cobblestone walkways and scraggly young trees held up by tripods of bamboo. Beneath the tall eucalyptus, Mercedes and BMWs surrounded the main door like modern day wagons circled around for protection. On a quiet corner a woman grilled green onions and beef on a rosy charcoal brazier as a few customers squatted on tiny plastic stools, heads lost in their bowls. Other than the hum of cicadas from the small park it was a place where repose seemed to drip from the languid branches overhead. Red lanterns hung above the shrouded windows, behind which figures moved like characters in an oversized Balinese shadow play. A pair of stone dragons about waist high stood sentinel on either side of the solid oak doorway. Occasionally a customer would furtively stash a slow burning cigarette stub on a paw or in a stony maw. And just as discreetly, the young hostess dressed in her blood red Manchurian *Chi Pao* would sweep away the mess. Sometimes, when she would be otherwise engaged, the faint wisps of pinkish smoke would magically linger above these chimeras and startle passing strangers or innocent children.

Inside the door was a small table on which was perched a blue and white ceramic status of a smiling god in flowing robes. To the side was a poster that said:

We pay up to 100 Yuan of free parking for our dear customers.

It was crowded inside. Mostly men, some women, and even a few children were huddled over tables, playing cards or Chinese checkers, or just chatting and drinking tea and beer. From the private rooms further within floated a symphony of voices - gruff, shrill, plaintive, ecstatic, alarmed, and delighted —and always the sound of mahjong blocks that rattled like marbles falling onto a stone floor. A faint scent of cigarette smoke hung in the air.

The large room was roughly divided into two areas separated by a low lattice of carved wood. Glass jars filled with tea leaves and dried flowers, polished marble stones, earthen teapots and urns, and small wicker baskets filled exquisitely carved wooden cupboards and shelves. On the walls were works of brush calligraphy in the cursive *Cao Shu* style.

One was a brush painting of a single character. What a marvelous, magnificent character! To this day how few foreigners realize the significance of this most basic of characters, a square with a single vertical line running through its middle. It is *zhong,* the word for middle, or more importantly, when by itself or followed by the *guo* character is the character for China itself, the Middle Kingdom. So the square represents the world and right in the center of it, as though straddling the very universe itself, is China. While Copernicus and Galileo ultimately disabused the Western Popes and Kings of the belief that the earth was the center of the universe, China long held fast (and to an extent still does) that *Zhong Guo* was the very font of stability and the center of the universe. When David looked at the calligraphy he marveled not at the word but at the fluidity of the brush strokes, those graceful forms whose bold black strokes seemed to rip open the walls of a parallel universe, leaving behind black scars of terrible beauty and the artist's own experience of the human condition. Freely formed and rhapsodic, they contrasted with the almost Mondrian like square lattice wall decorations.

David had long known about Chinese calligraphy. Museums and galleries in the West occasionally displayed works from China, but they always seemed to be in a section of the museum that no one visited. When he discovered calligraphy in Shenzhen, it was from a completely fresh angle. Now he could hold the soft brush, dip it in the ink, smell its rich odor, and feel the thrill as the rich black ink swept across the white *Xuan* paper like the moon's shadow steals across the earth, in an ineluctable, graceful and remorseless wave. And when he channeled himself into the ink and paper a stillness would sometimes envelop him. It was a sense of contentment that banished daily pressures and headaches into some other region. The wet brush hairs would align into a perfect sharpness that dipped and leaped like a swallow between eaves of pagodas and tall blades of grass. The point would dance and race with the spreading blackness like a surfer challenges the wave. Unlike the surfer's dance, this motion would be forever captured in a sequence of characters that were a profound synthesis of meaning and form. Terse characters alluded to abstract meanings. Their significance skirted on the edge of definitions. Form lay in the dancing, skipping, leaping, weaving, lightness, pressure, speed, willfulness and deliberateness of the line.

For over two thousand years great men had perfected the art of calligraphy. Acknowledged by many as the greatest calligrapher of them all, *Wang Shi Zhi* turned his childhood pond black with his incessant practicing. Too poor to afford ink, he had practiced with spring water. At the height of his fame, admiration for his work was such that the great Tang emperor decreed that his masterwork be entombed with him, so that he would enjoy it in the afterlife.

Then there was *Huang Ting Jian*, the eccentric *wunderkind* of the Tang Dynasty, whose elongated jagged strokes slashed across the paper in an El Greco like rush of ecstasy. His great masterwork *Luo Yang Yu Qi Shi* (The rain over Luo Yang City) would boldly herald a new direction for calligraphers with its vivid strokes that seemed to link the characters in one bold cursive spurt of inspiration. David loved this man's work. His passion and unorthodox styles recalled Beethoven and Rodin, men whose goal was, as William Shakespeare had mentioned in *Midsummer Night's Dream*, to give *to airy nothingness a local habitation and a name.*

When one hears Beethoven or sees Rodin for the first time, one wants to touch and feel their work, even to dance. So it was with Huang Ting Jian. David wanted to ride the wave of his brush strokes from line to glorious line, like a driver tests his new car on valley curves or a child floats and dips on a roller coaster. It was a thrill. The calligraphy in the tea house was no masterwork, but it was another sign of the long, long cultural road that seemed to make everything in China, no matter how outwardly insignificant, a sensual pleasure and an object of study. In America there was a pervasive sameness in the buildings and the cities. Chain stores and mega-corporations provided clean but sterile interiors and soulless facades. Here in China, things could be dirty but they were always rich. Walking into a street could be like walking into an open mouth. Here even beggars wrote beautiful characters on sidewalks and dinner was a festival of kindred souls. Globalization had already invaded the cities, and Shenzhen was an avatar of the coming days. Yet Shenzhen still retained an ineffable something that made it first and foremost a Chinese city. And this was perhaps why, modernization notwithstanding, he still enjoyed the place.

To the left of the entrance was a long corridor leading to the private ante-rooms and rest-rooms. The layout of the room, in spite of the expensive furniture, had a topsy turvy quality. Large clumsy looking Haier fridges and air conditioners were casually situated next to exquisitely carved shelves and cabinets. A pink and green transformer from one of the air conditioners partly hung off a beautiful wooden shelf. The Chinese are people who live by the heart, not the mind. Formal on the outside, passionate and impulsive within, their architecture and dwellings reflect this almost Apollonian and Dionysian contrast. Chiseled and immaculately balanced on the outside, the interiors are like their character, full of impermanence and disproportion, places of the heart.

The waitress led them to a corner table away from the door. They sat back in the elegant old wooden chairs covered with plush pillows and started to talk. Mr Bin, who Spring and he had privately labeled the *Gucci man* for his penchant for expensive western brands, clutched his *DuPont* portfolio closely as though it held all his worldly treasures. Some sweat had formed a t-shaped patch on the back of his short sleeved polyester shirt. A black leather Mont Blanc belt barely held his nascent pot belly in check. With relish and much relief he sat back and crossed his legs, one hand rubbing the back of his crew cut, and the other scratching the exposed skin above his expensive socks and shoes.

"Maybe we should take a private room?"

He wanted to show everybody how generous he could be, for he had the money to afford it.

"This is fine." said Alfred, and Swan nodded her head slightly in agreement. If Mr Bin was disappointed he didn't show it. Barely nodding his head he jumped out of his chair, clutching his cell phone to his ear, and moved out of ear shot.

David scanned the menu.

"What's this?" he said, pointing to some characters he didn't recognize.

The hostess who stood smiling over him, hands folded, nodded.

"Yellow mountain tea."

"What type of tea is it?"

"It's a special herbal tea, not sweet or bitter, but very fragrant."

When the glass of tea came it emitted a sweet fragrant odor that reminded him of the pleasant smell of the frangipani that floated over the eucalyptus trees on hot Shenzhen nights.

Alfred, who had been interested in David from the beginning, as he had had few dealings with foreigners, noticed how he was fascinated by the décor.

"Those wooden furnishings are very expensive."

"They're very beautiful."

"About twenty to fifty thousand Yuan just for a few. I know the factory outside of Shenzhen that makes them."

He said it casually but felt obliged, because in China, everything valuable has to have a price.

Mr Bin had come back. He leaned towards David.

"What type of car do you have in America?"

"I don't have a car. I sold it a while back."

He whipped out a bunch of keys and placed them on the table.

"Look at these. They have a remote sensor."

And he went into a description of how his car openly sensed when he was coming and could start remotely.

David and the others just nodded and allowed Mr Bin to lead the conversation.

As for Mr Bin, he knew that the others were sort of condescending to him, particularly the American. But he didn't care. Ever since he had been a child, he had seen how the Chinese were intimidated by foreigners. He remembered the words of his family and school mates as though they were uttered yesterday.

"They look down on us."

"They think Chinese are dirty."

"They only want our goods and want to steal our country."

"They have no respect for their parents."

"They make love with anyone."

They would criticize the *Lao Wai*, and on streets even shout at the rare white face (for they were all white back in those days) the pejorative terms *Gui Lo* (White ghost) or the sing song *Hellooooo, How areYOUUUU*.

But they all loved the foreigners' goods: TVs, cars, boats, planes, even books and TV programs (like old *I Love Lucy* and the *Jetsons* reruns). Foreign brands, even bicycles from next door Taiwan were luxuries to die for. Now there was McDonalds, Starbucks and Kentucky Fried Chicken to slaver over.

But Mr Bin was different – and he knew it.

He loved foreign products but distinguished the people from the things. He was proud of China. He was 100 percent Chinese born and bred. In his view, he had 5000 years of glorious history behind him and the current direction of China was a splendid, incomparable and glorious thing. He also knew the old saying

If someone gives you some respect, give it back a thousand fold

Every native Chinese knew that this had two meanings. If someone helped one in a predicament, one must repay that person back not by an equal amount but by much more. Conversely, if someone were hostile, one must be supremely gracious to that person, making them seem like the mannerless idiot, compelling them through shame to assume some grace and respect. In the West, the bastardized (and inaccurate) translation had become:

Do unto others as you would have them do unto you

Though the meaning was profound it missed the essence of the ancient master's true meaning. Mr Bin was actually well read. He knew he was a bit of a buffoon but like many buffoons, his foolishness and arrogance at times bordered on wisdom.

There was a time when he had disliked foreigners. When he first came to Shenzhen he had had a low paying job as an assistant manager at a Christmas tree factory. He had never been in social situations with foreigners and at first didn't know what to make of them. He remembered once when a foreign customer visited and they went out for drinks. The boss invited him along because they were from the same village in *Jiang Xi* province.

Most foreigners then living in Shenzhen frequented the Shekou district. A hub for the oil industry with many multinational employees, every weekend Shekou's bars and streets would be thronged with Australians, Germans, Americans and other foreigners seeking sex, drinks, parties and fun. At times it was hard to find the local Chinese, except for the shopkeepers and prostitutes. It was as though there was something in the air that was too rough, too undisciplined, and too free for the locals to feel comfortable. The three of them went to a popular bar. The moment he saw it Mr Bin didn't like it. There were no Chinese inside. No private rooms for people to drink. Everything was very loud and women were scantily dressed. Worst of all everyone was speaking English. An Australian lady bustled back and forth helping the waiters carry drinks, smiling and making people feel welcome. Their customer, a chain smoking German with graying hair and a cynical, jaded look ordered a beer. The Australian woman came over to greet them .

"Welcome mates. Where you from dearie?" She was a tall buxom woman with a very red, freckled face. Her long auburn hair spilled over her shoulders like a mass of smoky cotton. Her tight blue jeans revealed an ample posterior that she was clearly proud of, for she wiggled it whenever she walked. Her blue eyes shrewdly scanned the room even as she was talking to them, always looking for signs of discontent.

"Hamburg."

"Lovely place, went there long ago with my hubbie? How long you here for love?"

"A few days. Some business to take care of."

The two continued to make small talk. Then Mr Bin noticed that the Australian woman was totally ignoring he and his boss, talking only to the German.

Flustered, Mr Bin tried to order a drink by himself. He raised his hand. When no one came over, he shouted out loud.

"*Ta ma de*!" he cursed, "a fucking drink here. About time!" he said in Chinese.

Although the room was very loud everyone could hear him. The Australian continued chatting, as if unaware. If her intense blue eyes revealed anything, it was almost impossible to notice. A Chinese waiter came over.

"Yes sir, what can I get you?" He spoke in English. Mr Bin realized he was a *hua qiao*, someone of Chinese ancestry but born elsewhere, probably the Philippines. He didn't know what to say and the waiter didn't know Chinese. The Australian quickly interrupted.

"Get the man a Pilsner Joseph."

Mr Bin was too humiliated to say anything. Later he exploded when chatting with his boss.

"I hate these foreigners. They all look down on us. That man was Chinese and yet he can't even remember Chinese. Fucking *wang ben*."

He used the pejorative *wang ben* which means someone who has lost his roots.

"Think of the money. .. and learn English." his boss said sternly. Then they went out and got drunk together.

That was the best advice anyone had given him since he arrived in Shenzhen. Afterwards he signed up for the government English course, took evening classes at Book City and studied 3 hours a day for 2 years straight. As he started to work with more foreigners he gradually became more comfortable expressing his opinion. The dislike slowly evaporated, like the water rises into summer mist over the mountains of Lian Hua Shan.

"Bloody fucker! Don't be an idiot. That's a dumb move."

The loud voice came from close by. They looked over. At the table a few feet away were four twenty-somethings, three young men and a woman. The man who had shouted was berating another man sitting across from him. Playing cards were splayed across the table. David's attention was drawn to the lone woman. She was a knockout. She was drinking a glass of tea and was leaning over the board, passionately interested. Her hair was tied haphazardly in a bow and was so long parts covered her face, exposing only part of her neck. Her eyes flashed with anger when she lost money, and sparkled with merriment when she had a good hand. It was her lithe grace and energy that enchanted him. Easily the most beautiful woman in the room, she seemed supremely oblivious of her attraction. Perhaps because she tended to look at the quiet man beside her more often, with a special tenderness, David realized they likely were lovers.

This man, her boyfriend, dressed in a golf shirt and expensive slacks, was somber and quiet, ignoring the man who had shouted at him. He was peering closely at the cards, quietly bobbing his knees. Every so often he would interrupt his perusal to take a slow careful drag on his cigarette or scratch the back of his head. When he was doing well he would lean back in his chair with a slight smile, the light shining from his oily forehead or the bridge of his aquiline nose. There was something dangerous about the economy and deliberateness of his motions, as though he were conserving a ferial, violent energy.

"Give him a break." The woman said, snapping at the man who had shouted, who nervously dragged on his cigarette, his eyes warily flickering above his rosy round face.

Every so often his spectacles would slip down his nose and he would prop them up quickly, as one would try to flick away a gnat. He wore a New York Mets baseball cap, beneath which strands of thick oily hair tumbled over his neck.

"Fucking cards, fucking people." He said and whipped out his cellphone.

"Don't worry about him." She said to her boyfriend, who shrugged.

Meanwhile the other man chatted loudly into the cell phone, his eyes all the while nervously focused on the cards. The third man was leafing through a magazine, from time to time giving strangers who passed by suspicious looks. From the look of his well built body and disinterest in the game, David imagined he was a bodyguard. There was something sinister, crude, and even gangsterish about the four. David thought he saw a bulge in the bodyguard's jacket but thought *Only police are allowed to carry guns here. I must be imagining things.*

"*Xiao Huang Di!*" said Alfred quietly, as though he didn't want the other table to hear him.

"What?"

"Little Emperors." He said to David, "That's what we call the Chinese youth. Families in China are allowed to have only one child. Since they are only children, they are so spoiled."

"It's true. What do you think, Mr Bin? Do you think I'm spoiled?" Swan laughed.

Then she stopped, and sipping her tea looked quietly at Mr Bin, who had been playing on his PDA.

"What? What?" He looked up, eyes bright.

She repeated the question.

"I don't know." he said, and turned his attention back to his PDA. Alfred continued.

"For many years now China has had a one child policy. Families can only have one child. This will create many problems."

"Why?"

"Other than human rights issues, many of these kids are damned spoiled. They are treated like kings and queens. They are the apple of their parent's eyes. Is that what you say?"

Mr Bin looked up.

"It's good. Because China has too many people. We have to control the population. Also it's only for the Han people. The minorities still can have more than one child."

Mr Bin did not like the way Alfred kept criticizing China in front of David.

Alfred ignored him.

"In about twenty to thirty years many older people will have no one to support them. In Chinese tradition children always supported their parents. The more children one had the more support. Now one child will have to support maybe four old people. A big burden."

David nodded.

"And it's not just the children are rude. People in Shenzhen have no manners, even when driving." Alfred continued.

Everyone nodded.

"They throw their garbage on the street. They block the roads. They think because they have money they can do anything. *I hate it*. There is no culture. Just yesterday I was driving on Shennan road and this guy with a big Ferrari pulled right in front of me. Then he threw a coke from his window. I got that shit all over my windshield. And if that wasn't enough, this morning some guy in a Mercedes stopped at the traffic light beside me. Rolled down his window and threw a huge spitball in my direction. I have to clean the car at least once a week because of these uneducated people."

"In some ways it was better when I was growing up. We were taught to respect people. *Kongzi*, you call him Confucius, killed a lot of good things but he taught us to get along."

Everyone understood. The West has its churches and synagogues. The East has its mosques. In China, the school is the church, and Confucianism is the unspoken religion. Chinese do not like to say no. Schools are where they learn how to say it. While this modern Confucianism is not fundamentalist, it retains its broad principles - the goodness of civility and humility, the denial of self and the supremacy of community and government.

There was silence. Everyone, even Mr Bin was looking at Alfred. It seemed quite unusual for mild-mannered, good natured Alfred to vent his spleen.

He went on,

"And all people think about here is money." He threw an accusing glance at Mr Bin, "China will never change."

He seemed exhausted after saying so much. He passed his hand over his brow and finally declared.

"I want to make money and live in another country."

Mr Bin laughed. Looking at nobody in particular, but speaking in English he said,

"You foreigners don't understand some things. Here we now have strong leaders. They are taking us in the right direction. In twenty years we will be stronger than America."

"He's nuts." Alfred joked, "He doesn't understand."

"Understand what?" Mr Bin said, half smiling, half irritated. It was clear he hadn't impressed Alfred.

Mr Bin understood more than he let on.

In China the thirst for knowledge is great, and respect for the teaching profession and the well schooled is huge. Mr Bin's parents had long saved money for him to go to school. Since he was the oldest his parents helped pay for his studies. Since there was no money left, his sister, a very smart student, never got beyond middle school, Although people speak of the abundance of learning institutions in China, except for the first few grades, getting a good education in China is an expensive and difficult challenge. He had gone to university, but since he didn't have a Shenzhen *Hu Kou* he had to work at a series of menial jobs when he arrived. The *Hu Kou* system (national registration system) was developed to control movement of the population, particularly from the villages to the cities.

"We have too many people. We had to find a way to control or people would overwhelm our cities." he once overheard someone explain to a curious foreigner.

The *Hu Kou* system restricts many smart students and graduates from working in certain cities from going to the schools of their choice. In China university expenses are almost always out of the parent's pocket. National Education subsidies (like the American Pell Grant) don't exist. Everything must come out of a household's savings, and even then there are so many

Chinese who want the same thing, a good education, that getting into good schools is very difficult. Mr Bin had seen all this firsthand but sometimes he enjoyed playing the dolt.

Suddenly conciliatory he cooed "Here, have some tea, have some tea, *he yi bei.*"

But Alfred wasn't finished.

"*Pigu zhi hui naozi!* This, David, is what rules in China!"

"What does that mean?" David interjected.

"It means one's ass directs one's head." Said Mr Bin, now quite calm, a buddha like repose seeped over his fleshy, well nourished features.

Mr Bin knew that if living well were only about etiquette, life would be easy to master. A crash course in placing forks and chopsticks on the table, and deciding the best cloths to wear would serve a big purpose. However, his understanding was deeper. He saw, in his simple way, that civility, though related to etiquette, was different. It was the art of absorbing the strange into one's periphery without denying oneself. Perhaps he did not know much about etiquette, but he made pains, at least with regard to other men, to be civil. As for women, *that* was a different story.

"*Pigu zhi hui naizi!*" David repeated, fascinated.

Everyone laughed, Swan blushed.

"Not *naizi*. *Naozi*. *Naizi* means a woman's breasts! You're saying an ass directs one's breasts!"

Swan broke the ensuing silence with a short laugh, and then laughed again for no reason. She was actually feeling quite merry. She chalked it up to the green tea. But she was nervous. She thought she had seen one of the card playing men before, perhaps on TV or the internet. She laughed so loud the man in the baseball cap looked at her briefly. Seeing him looking at her she quickly looked away, slightly alarmed.

Mr Bin continued to ignore her so she joined in the conversation between Alfred and David. She turned to Alfred, casting a glance at the foreigner.

"What! Culture! Of course there's no culture. The city is only thirty years old, you know, Deng Xiao Ping created this city. He was on a boat next to the old fishing village when he said, 'Let's build a brand new city here.'"

Mr Bin perked up.

"Deng Xiao Ping. A great Chinese leader. Smart man. Because of him, now I'm making lots of money. Five years ago I was an outdoor security guard and selling Christmas trees. Then I worked hard. Now I am making over 200,000 Yuan a month."

She ignored Mr Bin and continued, looking at Alfred quizzically.

"I *hate* going out with him, because everybody thinks he's my boyfriend!"

Alfred laughed. He enjoyed it when Swan talked about him. It was as though she was paying him the attention he deserved. After all, he was paying for this expensive evening.

"You see how nasty she is! I toast you David. It is my sign of respect for you."

She turned to the American, a serious look on her face.

And they clinked tea cups.

"I so admire you, because you really have a deep knowledge of China's culture. It's very good."

"Yes, now you are half Chinese!" Mr Bin interjected laughingly, not wanting to be left out of the conversation since the American was now involved.

"No, I am a complete Chinaman!" David smiled quietly.

"You foreigners are so interesting. Chinese men are so boring!" And she stood up abruptly, looked at the other two men and said something in Chinese that made them laugh.

"Sorry, but I was being truthful…" She sat down and half apologetically looked at him.

"I'm sure you were…"

"Yes you're interesting. I tell you honestly. I like your eyes…You have nice eyes, but everything else…" she drew the back of her hand across her face in a swift motion as though wiping something away, "…is CRAP!"

"Well, thanks, I appreciate having something you like. I'm sure there are some other things you might like too…."

She looked at him mischievously. He was surprised to find himself flirting so openly with Swan. She was clearly highly educated, spoke excellent English, and the attraction was mutual. He was flattered by her attention but she was too headstrong, almost intimidating. Sometimes, as with the joke about his eyes, he couldn't tell if she was for real. It was as though she had a beautiful mask on her face. It laughed, joked, and flirted but was also the inscrutable repository of a thousand secret thoughts and passions.

"Don't forget me!" Alfred interjected. He felt a little lonely at being left out of the banter.

"Who's forgetting you dude?" David laughed.

"You're interested in China and you like it I think but let me tell you something. I admire two things about the west. Just two things. The rest is worthless. Listen carefully, because these are things we Chinese do not have."

He leaned forward in his chair, putting his face within inches of David's.

"First there is duty. Western people have a sense of duty. It's like we Chinese need to be *forced* to do anything. Westerners aren't like that. Here it's *you must do this, you must do that*. The westerners love their mothers and fathers and they keep their homes clean. Have you seen the Chinese home? It's a mess."

David nodded. He felt slightly uncomfortable, like a guest made to help wash his host's laundry. But he also felt a slight sense of relief, for he agreed with Alfred. David couldn't stand the sense of chaos in the houses he had visited: clothes strung randomly across railings, sofas arranged like office furniture in the living rooms, sandals piled in smelly random heaps beside the door, harsh neon lamps in living rooms shining through the bodies of trapped bugs, illuminating a potpourri of jarring colors and clashing shapes.

"Yes, yes I suppose so."

"Westerners love their mothers and clean their houses because they feel obliged to do so, whether or not they must do it. They have the freedom of duty. China is not free this way."

He paused and took a sip of his tea. His ruddy face beamed as he continued.

"And the second is romance. Westerners are romantic. They love women and care about them and know how to charm them. Roses, flowers, champagne at sunset. They can have *fun* with their women. Chinese are not free to love. They are serious, they are *forced*, they do not have the luxury to enjoy life, to what do you say *let loose*."

"Hear, hear. David you are so lucky. You will have many women and have lots of fun." Swan laughed.

Alfred sat back, proudly, as though he had stared down an opponent, or had beaten the odds at a game of poker. *Where is his opponent?* David wondered.

For some reason Alfred had removed a jade ring he like wearing and placed it on the table close to him. He tended to hold his possessions, such as his portfolio, very close to him, almost as though they were glued to his body. The ring was peculiar to David. It was quite large and the figure of a lizard was sculpted out of the green jade. He noticed David looking at it.

"What do you think of my ring?"

"It's interesting. Can I take a look?"

The other man smiled and picked it up, moving closer so he could see it.

"You know it's very traditional to have such a ring. You know why?"

David grasped the ring and tried it on his own finger. It looked awkward and he quickly removed it.

"No. I know that jade had a rich tradition in China. What's special about it?"

"The animal is a mystical lizard with three legs and no ass. *Pi Qiu*. It doesn't shit. It just eats and nothing comes out."

Swan giggled. Alfred ignored her and went on.

"You see, it is a symbol of luck, particularly of wealth. It helps the owner accumulate money, and he never loses it. It's a very old tradition."

Swan giggled.

"Well you just lost it. You gave it to David!"

Alfred looked startled and quickly took the ring back. He laughed nervously.

"She's right. If someone else touches it the luck transfers to that person."

He quickly put it back on his finger. David wondered how it was that Alfred, with his two degrees (Swan had told him), including a PhD, could be so superstitious. He had come to realize that many Chinese, no matter how 'scientific' their background, tend to be deeply superstitious.

David learned that jade, which occurs in several shades ranging from white to dark green, occupies a special place in Chinese mythology. Mined in Henan, Shanxi, and Xinjiang provinces, it has been imported for thousands of years from neighboring lands such as Burma. In ancient times, it was the custom to place a piece of jade in a dead person's mouth in the belief that it prevented decomposition. Coolness and purity are its hallmarks, and as such, jade is often linked in the popular imagination with beautiful women. He later discovered: *nong yu* , literally *playing for jade*, means sexual intercourse; *pin yu*, or *handling jade*, means cunnilingus; *yu jiang, or jade sap*, is a woman's saliva. And it goes on. *Jade-fluid* is semen or vaginal fluid, the vulva is the *jade-wall*, and the penis is the *jade-stem*. A girl has *jade legs* and a *jade bearing*. In popular religion the supreme deity is the *Jade Emperor*. Connotations are uniformly positive and auspicious.

"No sweat. I won't be getting rich soon." He laughed quickly.

Alfred laughed.

"You think we don't trust science? I can see it in your eyes."

David shrugged.

"What do you mean?"

"Many foreigners think we are a superstitious people. And yes we are. But some of us take your science seriously. We have Nobel Prize winners."

"He should talk to Gao Fei." Swan airily chimed in.

"Who's Gao Fei?" David looked at Swan but Alfred interjected.

"He's one of Mr Bin's friend's"

"Was a friend. Now an idiot." Mr Bin sat up in his chair, his round face suddenly alert. Alfred explained, placidly as though enjoying a good cigar.

"He was a brilliant businessman. Started in Shenzhen as a window cleaner. In three years he formed a consulting company that now earns millions of dollars each year. Last year he had a nervous breakdown."

"Breakdown! Hah, he just didn't work hard enough. This is a man I have known since we were children. He and I did a lot of business together. We worked together all day, drank beers, traveled together."

"Then what?"

"One day his wife calls me and tells me he doesn't want to go to work. I go over and he's in his bed. It's 11 in the morning! He says: " I can't do it anymore. The sky is falling on me. I just want to sleep."His wife and I try to convince him to go to work. We can't. "Give him a few days. He'll get better." I tell his wife. But no way. He gets worse. He stops drinking. He doesn't want to be seen with me. He starts apologizing to everybody, even his children, for being a bad father."

"Sounds reasonable to me. What's so scary about that?"

"That wasn't so bad, but then he started seeing a …what do you call the…psy…psy…"

"Psychiatrist." Alfred volunteered, looking quizzically at David. David nodded. Mr Bin continued.

"That's right. Only mad people, sick people see psychiatrists. He loses a lot of face. And because he's my friend, I lose face as well. I tell him cool down on the doctor. "You're fine. Come with me to Dongguan and we can get some beauties for a few nights!" He laughs at me and tells me. "You're part of the problem. You have no life, no balance. Like everyone else in this damned country." Now I can take a lot, but no friend of mine is going to tell me that. We had a big argument. He's no longer my friend."

"So is he better? What's with him now?"

"One day his wife called me in a panic. She was at the hospital. The previous night he had stayed out all night playing mahjong with his friends. When he returned they had a huge argument. She told him she would leave him that morning. As she began to walk out he punched the wall in frustration. He fell to the ground in terrible pain. She returned to look after him. She didn't know what to do. I went to the hospital and he said to me in private,

"The doctors tell me it is a severe fracture. It will take months to heal." He was smiling from ear to ear. I asked him why he was smiling. "Now she won't leave me. I broke my own hand to keep my wife!" Anyway, that convinced me he's nuts. You should see his wife. She is a real dog. Bad teeth, two throats, sweats all the time. Yells at him all the time." Mr Bin grimaced.

"He's still seeing the shrink. That's the point." Swan said, smiling sweetly at nothing in particular.

"Yes. Now Gao Fei uses skype to call his New York psychiatrist every week. He lies on a couch and talks about anything, no matter what comes into his mind, for hours to this stranger. And he pays him good money to do it. He still doesn't work – just his wife. There, that's science for you."

No one said anything for a few moments. David took a sip of the tea.

"Great tea. Good green tea!"

Their attention was distracted by a commotion at the next table.

The voices were louder than before. They saw the quiet man was in a heated conversation with the guy in the baseball cap.

"What the fuck did you say?" He took a drag on the cigarette very slowly; his eyes cool and steady as they gazed at the other man. He didn't raise his voice but the menace was obvious.

"Did you insult my girl?"

"What are you talking about?"

"Did you insult my girl, you cock-sucker!"

The quiet man didn't move an inch, but the man in the baseball cap twiddled his PDA phone nervously and adjusted his glasses. He jutted his chin forward, half defiantly.

"Of course I didn't'. I just told her to speed up a bit, ok?"

"That's not what you said, you chicken shit," the girl interjected, her eyes blazing.

"You looked at my tits. You said they were as flat as an airplane runway and told me to bump it up!"

"Look, Feng Dao, I didn't mean anything. Don't believe her."

"There was a loud bang. It was like a single firecracker. Everyone in the vast room looked stunned. From a distant corner someone shouted

"No firecrackers, that was three months ago!"

What holiday is it today?' Someone else yelled.

Another woman berated a child, thinking he was up to mischief.

The scream was a silent drawn out sound. It had apparently been in full volume for at least a few seconds, but in the shock of the moment no one seemed to notice, least of all David, who looked at the woman and absentmindedly wondered why her mouth was so wide open. He followed her eyes to the baseball hat that was now on the floor, its owner's bald pate exposed like a shiny boiled egg within a halo of black wiry hair.

He didn't move. He was sitting in the same posture, his mouth open but no sound was coming out. His eyes were fixed dazedly on the quiet man, who was holding a small snub black metallic automatic on his lap. Then a small streak of blood trickled from the corner of his mouth and the PDA phone man slumped forward. At this point the woman's voice broke through his consciousness like a foghorn from a passing ship. Simultaneously, pandemonium ensued. The tea house seemed to become a blur of moving polyester, shawls, linens, children's' dolls, fleshy hands and faces. People leapt over overturned tables and chairs and rushed to exits. The three others stood up, the quiet man first. He leaned over, picked up the wounded man's PDA phone, threw a bundle of one hundred Yuan notes on the table and walked out with the others in tow, calmly but quickly. Other women screamed and the blood flowed on the floor.

Although he had been seriously wounded, they later learned, the man would live.

"Shenzhen is like the Wild West. You don't insult a mobster's girl." Alfred explained.

He said it somewhat laconically, as an old hand who has seen it all before. The man refused to press charges and the police weren't inclined to do so anyway. No one had been killed, they had enough on their plate and, as Alfred explained, "They're not paid to go after rich people." Swan also remembered where she had seen the shooter before. He had been involved in some Hong Kong smuggling activity a few years back. She had reported on the story herself.

"I can't believe I forgot about it. But the guy looked a little different this time."

Soon after he wrote the following to his mother. It was a long email and recounted the teahouse incident. At the end he added the following:

> ....Although Shenzhen is like the Wild West sometimes, it is quite safe so don't worry about me. What sometimes such events do is make us think of how life is so unpredictable. Yet in spite of this unpredictability we move ahead.
>
> I also thought of a young student of mine at the orphanage who is very sick and may not live very long. I sometimes wonder how it is that people struggle and persist when the odds are so overwhelming. We musicians, writers, artists can't compare to people like him, who make the struggle something beautiful and profound.

The greatest art comes from he who turned the pain into something beautiful, like Beethoven did with his Eroica symphony when he was coming to terms with his deafness. The Chinese calligrapher Huang Ting Jian of the Song dynasty lived through great social turbulence. His jagged, sharp calligraphic strokes would be a boon for any handwriting expert. On an artistic level, the results are superb, deeply moving.

Rilke wrote a great poem. He describes an ancient sculpture of the Greek god Apollo in which the head is missing but one must imagine how its beauty

... burst forth from all its contours

like a star: for there is no place

that does not see you. You must change your life.

To this day I do not fully understand this poem, but it makes me think of how beauty and sadness co-exist and how passion impels one to action. Keats once said that truth is beauty, and beauty is truth. Socrates said that one must know oneself. And in China Confucius used to say that the thousands of different things in life all are intermingled and flow from each other.

So even my sick student is part of this great river of life. I also think of what you experienced. There must be a purpose to it all. At the very least we must be truthful about things that have happened — right? And the truth impels us to act, hence change our lives, as you changed yours again and again. Such is life!

More (or less) next time!

Love

David

"I suddenly realized there was a big difference between me and them. I wanted to be friends with this girl. But something had come in front of me and said 'No way!' It had nothing to do with intelligence or character. It had to do with my skin. From that day I took comfort knowing that my father, my uncle, our women and families were the same blood and culture."

- From David's father's journal

LOVE

Love has the wonderful quality of banishing from one's mind the malevolent energy of nightmares and catastrophes, failures and sadness. Like the first bracing flakes of snow it drops gently upon one's cheeks. As tender green leaves reach up from the dark loam towards the golden sun above, a vernal freshness alights upon one's world. Spring and David saw things with a greater optimism than before. Life was happier and many things that had once seemed important now seemed less so. For him the irritation of a dirty apartment, the snorts and grunts of Shenzhen citizens without tissue paper, the endless ennui of hair commercials on television, the stares of others, now all seemed petty and not worth noticing. For her the frustration at children who couldn't remember their dance steps, the beggars who shoved their bowls up inches from her face, Rebecca's endless gossip - all these were subsumed by a great and luminous glow that emanated from within. For both of them the world was now a place of light and rebirth.

After that night spent with Spring David forgot the incident at the school. In particular he no longer thought of his father. It was as though he had been liberated of a memory, freed from a bad dream that was rooted in anger, violence and unrequited love. The anger was that of a son who craves the attention of an emotionally distant father. The craving was so deep that the child hadn't seen the hole in his heart until many years had passed him by. Then, in random moments of reflection, he would realize that his inability to be a team player, to return love, to be terrified of penury, all these were symptoms of unfulfilled love. In most respects the lives of father and son had been like clouds drifting apart, tethered only by the powerful emotional memory of domestic violence.

In the beginning there had been moments of mutual tenderness, such as when his father told his stories of the old Luo village. However even these memories provoked a dull pain when remembered. In time the pain receded but the *memory* of pain, though weak, was always on call. For him, his self-denial and the painful childhood memories linked the boy with his father.

David was now a man in love. He didn't know how long this catharsis of new love would last. Years had rushed by as fast as river water over stones in a gully - ten, twenty, thirty years had already passed. He wanted to seize the moment. Like the true existentialist he was, he had automatically resolved to explore the unknown path with Spring. The success or failure of his seeking her love would depend on something he had rarely experienced - the mutual trust that lies in normal loving relationships. Lacking this, his courage and willingness to step into the unknown might be for naught.

As for her, giving herself to him had been a spontaneous thing. She had been surprised at herself. It was as though she had let go of a very important part of herself, something tied up with her sense of dignity and propriety. Perhaps it was that she felt safe with him. With him there would be consequences, but those consequences would not involve retribution or shame.

No one had to know about them, she thought.

In a country where the exchange of intimate glances between a man and a woman is seen by society as proof of intimacy, a part of herself believed that they were seen as just teacher or friend. Another part of Spring knew that there was more to this than meets the eye, and it would be obvious to others. She also liked the status of having a man, a rich (so she supposed) foreigner doting over her (which was undoubtedly true). Like most young woman, it flattered her to have such attention. The result was that she was confused about her feelings and did not know it. She felt she liked him but could not love him. She might love him in the future but was irritated by him. She wanted him and yet was repulsed by him. She admired his mind and yet looked down on him. Slowly, like a snake sheds its skin or a flower's petals drop off, her excuses not to be with him fell away. They began to see more of each other. She would find time to see him after work, while he often skipped classes just to be with her. They would go to fine restaurants, take trips to the nearby beach at Xiamesha, and at the end of the day, watch Korean TV soaps, and make love.

The suggestion that they visit Lijiang in Yunnan province came unexpectedly. Whether it was David who mentioned that he wanted to visit the most beautiful part of China and Spring taking that as a request for help (for she had relatives who lived there) or whether Spring had first mentioned neither knew. David wanted to be with her and also see the older China (or a representative part of it). Spring considered him something more than a friend and yet less than her lover, but wanted to do something to reach out to him. He was not a man accustomed to subtleties. Even if she had provided him a window into her soul, he would have responded to her allusions directly and bluntly, for he had little skill at divining others' intentions. So on a bright afternoon when she suggested that she could make some arrangements for the trip he immediately assumed it was an invitation. The sunlight bounced off her dark hair, which, tied in a bun, still released a few strands that hung over her cream cheeks like threads of black gold. Delighted, he said,

"I'd love to go. When?"

And she of course, had to provide a date. They settled on the third week in April, when it was still somewhat cool in Southern China and the rains had not yet begun.

Email, text messages, messaging services such as QQ and skype, cell phones and computers were as typical of Shenzhen as the innumerable high rise complexes, beauty salons and shampoo commercials. Every day, from alleys, buses, offices, gyms and bathroom stalls ring tones would dissipate and congeal in an ever-dissonant chorus. Friends and associates would often call or text him for help in correcting spoken and written English. Although their queries were casual and limited to the occasional elusive phrase or word, sometimes they revealed more. So he was always on the lookout for such SMS and email messages.

One day, on a whim, Spring came across a poem a friend had texted to her. Not understanding all of it she texted David.

Bao Jian, what does this mean?
Marlow says:

Had joys no date, nor age no need
Then these delights my mind might move
To live with thee and be thy love.

))*)

David replied

It means you're in love baby

She didn't reply at first. Then about an hour later Spring sent him another.

Who is Marlowe says

*)

David replied

An english poet. Christopher Marlowe.

))*)

Later he told her
"It's great you're improving your writing. You should also speak more. Practice makes perfect."

Spring laughed with embarrassment.
"But it is so hard. What if I say something wrong? My English is so bad."
On the contrary, Spring's English was now quite good. Whether it was innate or nurtured, this lack of confidence when it came to speaking English was widespread in China. In a language where the slightest tone can spell the difference between uttering a word of praise or a curse, and where saving face is the primal social urge, this hypersensitivity to learning a foreign language wasn't surprising. Over time she had grown more confident and her aural English had improved. Yet it was with a small shock and much delight that he had received her text about Marlowe.

David asked her to send him the complete poem for context. However, he really wanted to read more of this beautiful English poem of Christopher Marlow's. He had forgotten the sweet shiver of great poetry, how great English is a dance between the earth and one's soul. He felt a tinge of regret. Once taken for granted, time that he might have spent learning about the great English classics had been put on hold, to resume in future years. And he realized that there was a hidden cost to living in China and learning its language and culture.

He marveled that Spring was not only learning basic English but was also interested in the ancient classics. What was next on her list? Marlowe, even Shakespeare? The thirst for knowledge ran deep in China. He remembered something the great Canadian pianist Glenn Gould used to say: something about how musicians bored him because they could only talk about music. Glenn Gould, perhaps the greatest Bach interpreter of the twentieth century, was an eclectic who lived like a hermit, insisted on popping precise quantities and types of pills before performing, had a manic horror of germs, tilted his piano bench at an angle and depth such that the keyboard was almost level with his nose, sang while recording and planned to spend his last years in an igloo in the tundra. It was Gould who had wrenched David out of his deep depressions during adolescence, those barren years when time flies by too fast, just when one needs time to make sense of it all. He had not known what Bach's music could sound like until he heard Gould. Gould had been to his traditional piano repertoire as cabernet to coke, richer and less frothy, a pianistic *tour de force*. Spring was moving beyond Henan into an exciting new world. It was as though both of them were moving from the village into more complex and exciting worlds.

In China, people were slowly but surely moving broadly and deeply across Western culture. Over the past thirty years foreigners had been entering the east in a marvelous dance of mutual re-discovery. This opening up that had started thirty years before with Deng Xiao Ping had seeped like rich honey into the glassy cracks of the Middle Kingdom, filling the holes with something at once sweet, delicious, profane, materialistic and profoundly refreshing. Eastern musicians were conversing with the western painters, taxi drivers were listening to Bon Jovi, and dancers were studying Marlowe.

"We do not want to close China!" A businessman had once said to David, commenting on talk of punitive trade sanctions against China.

"China was for a long time very closed. It could be easy for the leaders in Beijing to just close the doors again." His voice quavered slightly. Whether it was a hint of fear or due to the slight chill from the cool breeze, David didn't know.

He read the poem again. This time the regret had disappeared. There are some things in one's mother tongue that are instinctively felt and perhaps beyond the power of translation. He was a traveler. The bond between his mother tongue and himself was strong and passionate, amplified by his exile from English. Ironically, he would never appreciate the iambic pentameter more than now.

One night, after they had had a long sumptuous dinner at one of the best hotels in the city, they headed back to her car.

"Do you want to come and pick up my father from the airport?"

She mentioned it casually, as though she wanted to go to the supermarket to pick up some brown sugar. She wanted him to meet David but had kept it a secret from both men.

"What? Your father? Right now? With me?"

She nodded her head, unperturbed and started driving.

"But I haven't prepared!"

"Prepare what?"

She looked at him, puzzled.

"Nothing."

He wouldn't betray any weakness. She smiled and continued driving.

"How do I say hello to him, or welcome him to Shenzhen… using respectful Chinese?"

She pretended not to notice his suppressed panic.

"Shu Shu, Huan Ying Lai Shen Zhen!"

"That's all. It sounds too simple!"

"Shu Shu, Huan Ying Lai Shen Zhen!"

He rehearsed the line in his mind again and again. All the time he was wondering what her father would think of her riding with a man almost twice her age at this time of night. They soon pulled up on the side of the street beneath a large bridge. Large and nondescript, the bridge overhead sliced across the sky like a massive broken gantry. Around it the neon lamps of streets and bypasses flickered and hummed in a chaotic web of spidery tendrils.

"Here? Not the airport?"

But she had already opened the door. Her father was standing beside the road. Despite the glow of the lights above and slightly behind him it was dark on this side of the road and his figure was indistinct. He stood very straight and was dressed in a dark suit, a small trolley suitcase on the ground next to him. The bright light behind shone a halo about his head, giving him an almost phantom-like appearance. A burst of light from a passing car illuminated his face for an instant. David saw a craggy, dark complexioned face. A few wrinkles almost as deep as knife wounds framed his intense brown eyes. A swath of black hair, a bulbous nose and thick, dark eyebrows gave his face a rakish, virile appearance. His lips were full and fleshy and in particular revealed him as a man of earthy likes and dislikes, one who loves to touch, taste, hear and see the world around him, even when it would be improper to do so. There was a hardness about the eyes and chin that also indicated a man who has touched the edge of infinity and flinched back, steeling himself through discipline and self-denial. Even though there was a cool breeze from the sea, the doctor looked slightly uncomfortable in his wool jacket.

The other man looked at him with interest, though not with hostility. He moved to take the bag himself but David had already placed it in the back seat. Although David demurred, the doctor and his daughter insisted he remain in the front seat. In the small car there was the faint but unmistakable odor of bad breath and perspiration.

David's shock at unexpectedly being introduced to a parent of the girl he loved slowly faded away but he still felt the father's eyes drilling into the back of his head. Father and daughter chatted in an almost formal manner. Occasionally, when he happened to glance back and see that craggy, almost Dionysian face, he felt a small shiver of terror. He didn't know why, but even that feeling faded away with the buildings and night lights that they passed on their way to their homes.

On the straight and broad Shennan Boulevard people were milling around everywhere. Men. Women. Short. Tall. Many young, slender and dressed attractively. All were relaxed and enjoying the cool bright night. The women were relaxed and confident. They stood as if at attention, their faces and high cheekbones clearly profiled in the yellow glow of the street lamps. Young children tenderly held their parents' and grandparents' hands. People walked slowly along the road, savoring the air that was thick and sweet with the scents of magnolia and eucalyptus, warmed by the low branches whose fragrant leaves brushed one's cheek like an angel's kiss. It was as if they had all the time in the world.

China was flowing around and through observer and observed, like a great celestial river touching heaven and earth. It was as though they were both wave and boat, riding on and supporting each other. Like y*ing* and y*ang*, sun and moon, raging fire and cooling water, passion and stillness, China was both inside and outside of them. Never boring, it could at times overwhelm one with its passion, at other times, be as light as a drop of sweat on hot skin. One could only marvel at the sheer power and beauty of this river of life. The bright silver disc hung in the black ceiling of God's cathedral. Its silver glow shined down benevolently on the tides of passion and the rhythms of life of the streets below. For the briefest instant, they were as one, in harmony with the world, seeing and seen, touching and touched, hearing and heard. In that halcyon moment it was as though all these people whose senses brimmed with life were equally unique and special.

"Here, this is for you."

Spring's father handed her a ragged piece of paper. She couldn't see clearly in the dark. She looked closer and saw it was a photograph. She snapped her eyes back to the road.

"Thanks *Baba*!"

"Something for your home. To remember your mother and I."

He talked to her but all the while was peering at the American. The father looked upon the foreigner with some distrust but was too polite to show it. He was courteous, almost coldly so. He didn't see why she had to fraternize with this man. Not only was he a foreigner, but also was about his own age! Yet there was something else that repelled him, a more unconscious than conscious feeling. He saw in this man something of his own darker side. Perhaps it was the way his eyes' shifted nervously when in unfamiliar situations, or the way his hands fidgeted when things were still.

Spring's father was a smart man, one of the smartest around. He had become a doctor at an early age, had achieved promotions faster and higher than many others, but because he was so smart, he only trusted himself. Unable to use his brilliance in teamwork he had been limited in his professional life. Essentially a wolf at heart, he was, like a wolf, rapacious and alone, self-sufficient in love and cautious in his calculations. He loved his daughter, but he loved her mostly for what she gave him. His was not a selfless love. Now that he saw her giving to this man, no matter how little, he felt rejected. He was like the single child who punches the newborn sibling just arrived from the hospital. But he kept his counsel. He licked his wounds. His large brown eyes were placid and inquiring. He smiled politely, and observed.

They returned to the apartment after dropping David off. He had bid farewell in overly formal Chinese to her father, who just nodded seriously. On the drive back he was silent. Finally as they entered her apartment he looked directly at her.

"Who is that man?"

"*Ba*, he's just a friend. Don't worry."

"Who is he? Why is he here?"

"He's my English teacher."

Spring didn't want to discuss David with her father. She wanted to skirt the already nebulous boundaries of her relationship. It was as though there was comfort in the ambiguity of their relationship, peace in this city's relative freedom from strictures.

"Have something to drink. It's late."

"Some *pu er cha*. You know. That's my favorite tea."

He felt his pants were loose. He forced a hand between his belt. It was the right number of notches. He wondered if he had lost weight.

"Yes some tea would be nice. I'm also a little hungry. Maybe some pork."

He slowly walked towards the room. Then he suddenly turned to her.

"It doesn't seem right. He's not the same. You should have a young Chinese man. What happened to that …what was his name?"

"Yang Lao."

"Yang Lao was a good kid. These foreigners. If you get married you will leave us alone here in China. And if this man hits or hurts you you'll be too far away for me to help you."

"Never. As for Yang Lao, he was OK until I found him kissing other girls. *Ba* let's not discuss David or my boyfriends now. OK?"

"Did you…"

Spring didn't understand. She stared blankly at her father.

He cleared his throat.

"Have you…with the American?"

He grasped his belt with both hands and nervously tugged at it, avoiding Spring's eyes.

"What?"

"That is my business, *Ba*! Are you…How could you!"

"I'm sorry. I was just …"

Please just rest. You've had a long trip, she said coldly

He lowered his head.

"I worry about you here in Shenzhen, that's all."

Spring was already headed back to the kitchen but father hadn't finished.
"Don't walk away when I'm talking to you."

Spring froze. Her father made her feel like a little girl. She loved him and
sometimes could not say no or defy him. He was her father. The old man went
on.

"Is he rich? How old is he?"

"I don't know. I think so."

"Why are you with such an old man?"

"He's interesting and teaches me good English."

"Men like that always want something in return." Her father shrugged.

Spring tried to change the topic.

"*Ba*, when you're here I want you to cook some of your *hula tang*."

Her father and mother always loved to make this delicious soup.

"He and other foreigners come here and use us. They use women. They
use them and throw them away, like old paper."

Spring felt very uncomfortable. Her father's questions were like lances
that forced her to coldly assess her situation. They were without sympathy,
like those of an anonymous clerk from behind a government office window.
The soft penumbra that enveloped her Shenzhen life seemed to shiver and
implode under the assault. Her parents had never really welcomed her move
to Shenzhen. It was too far and in their eyes it wasn't even a real city.

"How can it be a city if it's only been around thirty years. Better you stay
here and marry a doctor, a banker. There are many men with government jobs
too! " Her mother had said. But Spring wanted the freedom of Shenzhen, and
she knew that her parent's still loved her, in spite of what they said.

Her eyes welled with tears.

"Why are you so cruel? He's not like that."

There was something in her voice that touched her father. He realized he
may have gone too far. A softness tinged his reply.

"*Xiao Chun*, Little Spring, don't cry. Your father loves you. Your mother
and I just want to protect you, that's all."

Spring didn't say anything. Her father gently went on.

"Tomorrow I'll prepare some *hula tang* for you."

The discord rankled even after the old man went to bed. She felt something
in her pocket and pulled out the photo her father had given her. It was a black
and white photo of her parents at their home back in Henan. They were sitting
on their old sofa. Her mother had a serious look but her mouth was smiling.

Her father was serene and had one arm around her shoulder and the other hanging from the armrest, a cigarette dangling from outstretched fingers.

It was the sofa that caught her attention.

Whenever she thought of that sofa she thought of her mother. It had been in their home for as long as she could remember. It was one of the wooden sofas that are popular in many Chinese homes. About one and a half meters long and about three feet high at the back, it's heavy rosewood was carved into gentle curved shapes at the armrests and other edges. In the Ming and Qing dynasty fashion it was simple and graceful. According to traditional Chinese furniture making of that period it did not use any type of varnish, thus exposing the natural grain of the wood. Also according to tradition it used mortise and tenon joints instead of nails and glue, which gave it a strength and simplicity prized by Chinese. It was a beautiful but nevertheless very uncomfortable sofa. Besides having no pillows to cushion against the hard wood it had no support for the neck. As a result, her mother's tired head often leaned to the side or flopped back in a dead man's pose.

It seemed to Spring that her mother had sat on that sofa every day. It was as powerful a memory of her mother as her scent or her smile, her frown or the way her hair refused to stay down, or the twinkle of love in her eyes when she was happy. This photo brought back many memories.

The sofa was strategically placed in the three-bedroom apartment. It faced the three rooms directly, with the window to the left where visitors coming to the front door could easily be seen (they were on the first floor of the apartment block). On the right was the kitchen entrance. Also on the right was the bathroom. From the junction sometimes the smell of food and latrine joined forces, but even then her mother didn't seem to mind. Since the apartment was next to the street it was also quite noisy. On the left was the parent's bedroom and the center room was Spring's. The apartment block had been made in the fifties with Russian construction material. At the time the Russians had foisted much of their cheap and sub-standard goods onto the gullible Chinese. As a result after heavy rains sometimes water seeped into the living room or moisture dampened the open surfaces. To protect the sofa, her father had two marble bricks placed under the four wooden legs. Since her mother was very short, her legs would not reach the floor. So when she sat she would look very stiff with head straight up and legs dangling. But no matter whether the location was uncomfortable or comfortable, noisy or quiet, smelly or fragrant, hard or soft, the sofa was her mother's eternal habitat.

Strategically placed, it was the ultimate vantage point. Like the rocking chair of Whistler's *Mother*, this wooden furniture was this woman's *terra firma*.

When Spring had been born it had always been the warm light coming from the sofa's location that comforted her. And when she could barely walk, she would see her mother always where she could reach her, smiling, eyes serious but strangely mirthful, looking on with the love only a mother possesses.

Often when she would wake up and leave the bedroom or take a break from doing homework in her bedroom, the first thing she would see was her mother knitting. She would look up, her reading glasses half perched on her nose.

"Hi treasure!"

Her face would light up while her eyes remained narrowed and serious, and the child would always respond to that warm, welcoming, proud voice.

When she was in high school she would sometimes return late from the library. Her mother would be sitting knitting with her eternal smile and say something like

"Hello my love, would you like something to eat?"

At other times they would tell stories to each other about work and school, about boyfriends and love. Every time her mother would give her advice and encourage her.

While she was in college she would often return home for the New Year or the May holiday. Her mother would still spend hours seated on that old sofa, whose edges were now a little faded, dented and scratched in places from the innumerable dings and knocks of a household blessed with the antics of children. At these times of reunion she would leap up and reach for the calendar on the wall to mark out the remaining days her daughter would be with them.

When she had graduated and was working in Shenzhen, she would less frequently return to visit her parents. Each time, the scene would be the same, her mother calmly knitting, eyes serious, and mouth gently smiling.

But now her hair was whiter and wrinkles had appeared on her mother's once silken face. Her legs still dangled off the sofa.

Spring remembered how they had talked of love. In one such conversation they were discussing boyfriends and love and the conversation shifted to cars and bicycles. Then, quietly, as though she were trying to hear a hummingbird's wings, her mother said

"You know how I met your father?"

Spring had heard this story many times, but always from others, never from her mother's lips. In the years after the Great Famine and Cultural Revolution that followed, their story of love had become famous in their small village community. It was as though people needed a reason to live again. Perhaps it was because of the contrast between love and hate, pain and pleasure, sin and redemption, decline and rejuvenation, that her parent's love seemed so glowing with hope and promise. She shook her head

"I've heard pieces. You never told me." Spring sounded reproachful.

"It was his bicycle."

She said it softly, the word for bicycle, *zi xing chi*, sounded like the whistling of wind through trees, for the mother spoke the word with great tenderness. She put down her knitting on her lap and looked out the window as though she were remembering something. Perhaps it was because of the sudden softening of the wrinkles around her eyes or the extra whiteness about her eyes as they opened up, Spring sensed the happiness that flashed like a lucent spark across her mother's face. At first she spoke slowly as she parsed every word. Then her tempo became more rapid. As she spoke her face lighted up, as though from an inner fire. The sounds from her mouth seemed almost emotionless in pitch next to the force of her shining eyes and smiling face. It was as though an inner force had seized control and a wound up energy was now being released through her clipped, fluent phrases.

"I remember how he loved his bicycle. It was a red bicycle. It was his sister's. He once said to me, 'It's embarrassing. It's bright red. A girl's bicycle. The other kids made fun of me. Now I'm used to it and I love my bicycle."

He had a special trick. He was the only kid in school who could do it. One hand would hold the seat. Then he would gently push. The bicycle would travel by itself in a straight line. Farther. Farther than anyone else. I was so impressed. He was a superman. I used to stand behind him. When I stood behind him I saw how straight his back was. He was so confident. He pushed the bicycle so gracefully. I first fell in love with his back. And then the rest of him! I knew he would one day be my husband. After school I punctured my tires. He would come and try to fix them When he couldn't he would take me home. I would sit on the back of the bicycle. He would steer with one hand and hold my bike with the other. I would sit behind him and look at nature. These moments made me very happy. These bicycles were part of our lives. In those days they were very expensive. Only people with special permits got bikes. If you donated blood they would give you a permit. When I was in middle school I got my first bike. My father went to the hospital two times. It cost almost 100 Yuan. He made only 40 Yuan a month. It was a big investment. "We live far from the school. My daughter must have a good education. She should not be tired from walking." My father told the government official. I was so happy to get my bicycle. "

She stopped, wiped her eyes and didn't say anything for a long while. Then she went on.

"With cars your living space gets larger. You can go more places. With bicycles you see nature. You fall in love."

The daughter wanted to hear more, but the old lady was tired now. It was as though she had spent herself in releasing her soul. Her tiredness was a wholesome, healthy thing, not the desperate, wracked and cramped tiredness of people whose actions are in perpetual opposition to their feelings. She was at peace. She could sleep now. She looked around and saw the calendar on the wall. It was crooked. She reached up. She was old, and she reached up slowly, as if in pain. As she was reaching over part of her shirt got caught on a knitting needle and tore. Meanwhile the daughter had gone to the kitchen to prepare some tea for her mother. Looking back she saw her mother's predicament. Not knowing her daughter was looking the old lady took off her shirt to look and perhaps mend it. When Spring saw her mother's bare wrinkled back tears suddenly ran down her face. She couldn't stop crying. In that moment she was filled with an awesome, overwhelming love.

Spring waited for a long time to hear more of the story but never did. It was as though she had already heard too much. Her mother never brought it up again. The younger woman, from an innate sense of respect and understanding, didn't ask. Everything had its time. If the story continued, it would be at her mother's time, at her own pace. If not, then she respected her mother's space.

Afterwards they would still talk and share private moments together, her mother always encouraging her and taking great delight in her stories and experiences. She never told her how she had cried.

When she saw the photo he had brought she realized at last that the sofa itself had became part of her childhood and her growth into womanhood. And the sinews of that old, tattered and bulky piece of uncomfortable wood were now forever fused with her mother's love.

But she also knew her mother would disapprove of her relationship with David. She remembered a conversation they had had long ago. On one of her visits home she had accompanied her mother to the nearby park. Every evening elderly couples and a few younger ones would converge on the square for free dance lessons. This evening it they were learning the foxtrot. A few feet away some residents were practicing *Tai Chi*, the ancient martial art which combines graceful motions with inner serenity. A few feet away an old man sitting on a bench was humming to the tune of the Beijing Opera music he was listening to on the radio. As they sat on a bench looking at the activities and families walking by with young children, her mother suddenly clutched Spring's hands in her own.

"One day I will play with my grandchildren."

"I do not intend to get married right away, Ma, so stop thinking of that." Spring laughed.

"No. I want to play with them on my knees. Just as I did with you."

"I may live far away, but I'll find a way." She gently answered.

"Promise me one thing." Her mother turned her head from the *tai chi* to look directly at her daughter.

"What?"

"Promise me you will never leave China…to live I mean. You will never leave your parents."

"Ma, how can you ask me that?"

"Don't marry a foreigner. I've seen it in your eyes. Perhaps you will one day leave us and go far away." Her eyes moistened with tears."

Spring didn't say anything. She just bent her head. A cat jumped up on the bench and was a welcome distraction. The man who had been listening to the radio came over to take it back. He recognized Spring's mother who recognized him and the two started to chat. She had forgotten about her mother's entreaties until now, when she grasped the photo in her hand. She put it away and sighed.

Outside it was a quiet night. Rain was imminent. There was a pregnant stillness in the air. Only the muted whistling of the wind could be heard. Otherwise, even the crickets and birds were silent. It was as though everything was waiting for a proclamation from above.

That night after he left Spring and her father, David's mind was roiled by thoughts of his own father and mother. He had a sudden impulse to write to his mother. It had been a long time since he had done so.

Liebe Mutter!
You finally left him. How did that occur? What made you take the final step?
D.

After David wrote the email he went to sleep. He dreamed he was in a hotel room in some strange Chinese city. From the lofty window he would see dozens of construction cranes looming over the city like pale white insects sheathed in moonlight. He was suddenly seized by an overwhelming urge to relieve himself. His member was red and swollen and as thick as his leg. Instead of going to the bathroom he decided to open the window and spray his package over the city. He slid apart the screens and stood on a bench so his middle was at window height. Just as he was about to let loose a searchlight from below flashed its beam onto his startled face and a booming voice roared:

'Ey! ta ma de! What the fuck! What the fuck are you doing!'

He tumbled back into the room and the bright beam careened crazily over the window and onto the ceiling. Mortified, he slammed shut the window drew the curtains. For the rest of the night he couldn't sleep, terrified someone from the public security bureau would break down his door and frog march him to the police station. Then he turned his head and saw Spring staring at him, her eyes wide open. Furious, she yelled at him in English,

"You're a very *BAD* man. You are such an ICEhole!"

At this point he woke up from his dream He was in a sweat and didn't realize he had been dreaming until he saw that he was home, not in a strange hotel room. He staggered to the bathroom, and with great relief did his business in comfortable surroundings.

Outside a peal of thunder exploded across the city, shattering the stillness. In seconds the rain was falling in torrents, its sounds drowning out a chorus of car alarms.

"She needed me to escape the drabness of her own life.
'I'll just get married to a nice Jewish boy and spend the rest of my life in Brookline.'
She once said, half joking
'And I'll get married to a beautiful Jewish girl and we'll spend the rest of our life in Nairobi.' I smiled."

- From David's father's journal

LIJIANG

2000-year-old Kunming, is the capital of the western province of Yunnan. Yunnan borders Vietnam, Laos and Myanmar and lies at an altitude of 1800 meters above sea level. Established in 279 B.C by the soldiers of the Chu kingdom it grew from the 'five foot path' *Wu Chi Da* of legend into the Southern Silk Road that linked the great Asian trading routes with the Chinese interior. Snow capped mountains on all sides have long looked down upon a lengthy procession of historical figures, from the Kunming Man of the Stone Age to the rail magnates of the Burma Road that reached to leafy Haiphong in Vietnam, and even the ragged denizens of Mao's Long March. Today, amidst modern skyscrapers and the concrete flotsam and jetsam of the industrial age one can still find ancient, crooked and winding lanes and cul-de-sacs. They meander like dirty threads through sun-baked clusters of one and two story wood and mud buildings stuck into the ground like mud-soiled boxes. Before the reforms of the 1980s Kunming was a *hardship post* or *Bian Jiang*, where errant government officials were banished. Just as the Romans had long ago banished their black sheep to Hadrian's Wall, disgraced officials were left here to stew in their impotence and bitterness. Now over two million live in the bustling city. The vast majority of the population, as in much of China, lives in the rural areas. Over half of the Yunnan's population of forty million people encompasses twenty-two ethnic minorities. These include the Naxi, Yi, Lisu, Bai, Pumi, Dai, Miao, Tibetan, Hui and Zhuang.

At the airport, Spring's aunt and two family friends greeted them. The aunt was a diminutive woman who took great care of her clothes and appearance. Exquisite patterns of curls, almost architectural in their symmetry and spacing, overwhelmed her face. Seeing her for the first time David was reminded of the discombobulated bangs of an old librarian he had met long ago. She had fled the monotony of the Narragansett Public Library to live in Mombasa, Kenya's ancient and romantic port city, where she spent her savings on the local gigolos and her beauty salon.

It was a hot and humid afternoon. Gray clouds hung over the city. They drove to her aunt's house, where they would be staying before proceeding to the folk villages of Lijiang and Dali – their central destinations. Above pristine and carefully tended farmers' fields birds flocked and creened in the air like ash blown over hot coals. Warm, energizing and welcoming air ruffled their hair and caressed their skin. As they moved away from the airport and closer to the city, they passed hundreds of the non-descript gray and white buildings that have begun to characterize suburban China. Kunming itself, the capital of Yunnan province was a nexus of untended, gritty thoroughfares bounded by sickly trees. The highway was lined with auto shops, markets selling vegetables and small mom and pop stores.

David was struck by how miles of roadside shops displayed nothing but life size busts of dead mid-eighteenth century European men. Seeing David looking curiously at them, Spring's uncle said,

"In China, you find whole streets, whole towns even, that produce only one item. The other day on a business trip in Shanxi province, I drove through a town that produces just toilet seats. Everywhere you look you see toilet seats. On the streets, in the shops, on the signs. All kinds. It is known as the toilet seat capital of China. In America you have a place in California, or is it Nevada, that's like this. It's called Garlic City. Yes?"

The man driving the car was her father's good friend, an old army doctor, now retired. His face was thin, almost ascetic. Deep bushy eyebrows overlooked a narrow pasty white face. Like Spring's father he had an almost martial discipline about him. He sat very upright, as though there was a steel rod in his back, and never took his eyes off the road. Even when he laughed (for everyone was happy to see Spring again) it was accompanied with a crease of his brow. His was a short laugh, almost like a cough, that of someone who had seen a bit of horror, even terror, in his life and forever after decided to ratchet down his humor. His wife sat in the back with the two other women. Her hair was cut short to her neck. Her body was stocky but not fat and she wore sunglasses that hid her eyes.

Spring was talkative and excited. She spoke quickly and seemed wired. Throughout the trip she had been thinking about David. The spectacle of her bringing a strange man from so far away to see her relatives unnerved her, filling her with a mixture of dread and anxiety, and she giggled constantly.

While her parents lived in Henan, not Yunnan, these people in the car were close to her, like family, and she asked herself why she had taken this step of bringing him here. Family ties in China are very strong, often including extended families. In new, young cities like Shenzhen women have more control over their lives. In the hinterland, on the other hand, it is often different. More conservative, Chinese society has different expectations. Spring knew that many people thought of a woman as a child until she was married. The ancient saying went,

At home obey the father
When married obey the husband
When he dies obey the son

While things were not that rigid and traditional anymore, there was much truth to this Chinese saying. She was glad he was charming and was wearing conservative, expensive clothes. Her aunt took notice of such things, particularly clothes. She had told her family he was just a good friend and her fellow English teacher. She had promised to show him some parts of China, she had added.

"He is too old for me, anyway." She would laughingly say to her mother and aunt over the phone during their frequent calls.

"But he is not married and he is over 50. What can you want from such a man?" Her aunt would say.

And she could imagine her uncle sternly talking to her aunt and quoting from tradition:

By 15 one must excel in studies
By 30 one must know one's career
By 40 one must know one's purpose in life
By 50 one must be famous
By 70 one cannot be surprised by anything!

"Has he any money?" her aunt would press on.

"He has enough, and is very smart. He is a Harvard graduate." And she said that not only because it was true but also because Chinese have great respect for the big American universities like Stanford and Harvard.

About a week before they had left her mother called her.

"Why do you want to go to Yunnan. Don't you have work to do?"

"My new boss doesn't mind. He's a nice guy. How's the weather back home?"

"Hotter. It rained yesterday."

"Make sure you keep the house dry. When *Ba* gets back from business in Shenzhen he'll make sure, I guarantee it!"

"*Bao Bei*, who is this man you are going with? Is it safe?"

"Ma, you're just like Baba. David is just a foreigner friend. He teaches me good English and wants to know more about China.".

"*Bao Bei*, yesterday Li Hong told me about her daughter."

"Yes, what was that old *pa lao poer*, up to?" She used the Chinese for *sourpuss*.

Spring did not like their neighbor Li Hong. The village gossip, she was always spilling secrets and boasting how much money her son was making as a tour operator in Shanghai. Li Hong had early taught Spring that in small towns and villages, just like in small companies, there are no secrets. This was one reason she liked Shenzhen, for here there was relative anonymity, the ability to start one's life without the pressure of history and the constant onus of family. According to Li Hong, her son had countless foreign friends, often traveled abroad, had his own car and apartment, sent money back home every month without fail. To all this Spring just shrugged. Her mother, on the other hand, admired Li Hong and the two were always chatting about this and that. Sometimes Spring wondered what her mother saw in the other woman.

"Li Hong is a good woman. You just don't like her because she didn't like your dancing.. She said Mr Huang's daughter came back from Shenzhen yesterday. She had had three abortions and her last boyfriend left her for a woman from Sichuan. She wanted to kill herself, but her parents persuaded her to come back. You should not be with these strange men."

"Ma, David is not like that. How is Xiao Hui?" Her younger brother was preparing for the middle school exams. Her mother sighed.

"He doesn't study as hard as you. We are praying for him to do well. Bao Bei you listen to me. Some men should be avoided. They wander the world with no attachments. They have no sense of responsibility and cannot protect a woman."

"Yes Ma."

"I have a feeling about this man. He isn't Chinese. That's not good."

Spring wanted to talk about anything but David. Finally she found an excuse to end the call.

They had lunch at her aunt's home. Her aunt's mother lived there too. *Nai Nai*, as Spring called her, was glad to see Spring. She had always encouraged Spring's dancing, even when others in the family had been skeptical. Spring felt protective towards Nai Nai and always asked after her when she talked to her Sichuan relatives.

Once, long ago, Spring had invited Nai Nai to visit Shenzhen but the old woman had declined since she disliked flying. She remembered how long ago, she had been detained for spitting in the plane. It had been her first time. Spitting wasn't the problem. The cabin crew understood that and would have provided her with some toiletries. Instead, ill at ease and fidgety, she had innocently tried to open the cabin door to release her package, not aware that they were about to take off.

"What's wrong? Everyone does this!" The old lady protested.

Meanwhile passengers and crew scrambled around, seizing her hand, which was already on the door lever. One of the crew was from Tibet (*I could tell from his features*, she said later) and that explained his ignorance.

"Rude, lazy man, he just couldn't understand." She thought to herself.

"I didn't know where to go." She said to the stewardess meekly.

The stewardess wasn't amused. When the plane landed in Shenzhen a few hours later she was promptly detained and questioned. She looked too old for a terrorist and too young to be senile, and the police released her about thirty minutes later. The story was written up in the *Shenzhen Times*. She insisted on taking the ten-hour bus ride back home the following morning. The words of the Chief Security Officer rang in her head for days afterwards.

"Dear Auntie, next time please listen to the stewardess and read the information provided in your seat pocket, OK?" *What a piggy man*, she muttered to herself.

Now she was much older and sitting next to the American. She reminded David of his own grandmother, who had died many years ago. She would have been in her late nineties now. Jewish, born in Lithuania during the pogroms she had fled with her family to America. There she grew up, dutifully married a man named Joe Baker (Also a Lithuanian immigrant who had changed his name) and lived a conventional life – until two things happened: her daughter married a black man, and her husband's death granted her the freedom to roam.

Like Spring's granny, the men in her life had dominated David's grandmother. Her father refused to let her go to college (for which she never forgave him) and it was only after her husband died that she felt free again. In her autumn years it was as if she had been born again. She traveled the world with abandon, teaching piano and making friends easily. In time she reconciled with her daughter and even grew to love her black grandson.

David looked closely at the little old Chinese lady. In the quiet tranquility of the afternoon, as Spring chatted gaily with the other relatives, it was as though time was flowing by like a stream of honey dripping from above, spinning its seemingly motionless golden thread before his eyes. As a clock quietly ticked somewhere in the room his mind wandered back to the other old lady, the one who had lived across the sea in America.

"When I was young," Ida once said (for David called his grandmother Ida, as did her daughter) " I won my high school music talent competition. I wanted to win the victrola so much but because I was Jewish, they gave me a book instead."

Ida was forever seeking the victrola. She clung to life not out of love but out of fear that it would engulf and snuff her into anonymity. The result was a breathless *allegro con brio*. After she had fled with her family to the *land of the free* she found herself still shackled by tradition and chauvinism. Her father refused to let her go to college and compelled her to earn wages at a young age. She was musical and loved learning. Her pianism became her frenetic differentiator. Through music she stood apart.

"The night of the prize giving I cried so hard. That was one of the saddest nights in my life".

She would say this with nonchalance, while she scooped out borscht from the fridge.

She had many faces, each forming filters, like colored planes of glass, through which her inner sun shone. In the darkness of the night, such masks sometimes appeared, like a schizophrenic Janus face or a rose whose blush dances in tempo with the moonlight. Once, in the dead of night, as David sat reading in her living room, she suddenly appeared in the kitchen. She was like a pale ethereal ghost with ashen skin, something wafted through the windows by the cool Boston air.

" I hate washing dishes, but someone has to," she said absent-mindedly to no-one in particular, " and the washer just runs up the electricity bill".

So in this wee hour she floated into the kitchen to do her duty. Her gray wisps of hair (hidden daily under an ill-fitting wig) floated about her face like fragile tendrils of ashen seaweed in an ocean current. As if in a ritual of great solemnity and dignity she cleansed the dirty plates of the day's detritus.

The kitchen could be seen from the dining room table where he sat, book in hand.

"How can she do this? But look at her, look at her. She looks like Einstein!" David said to himself.

He imagined how many millions across America wake up day after day to scrub their dishes in such a swishing mantra.

Since she started washing the dishes she hadn't said a word. The water passed over the steel and porcelain, the sounds erasing the silence of the night. She was oblivious to him and all else.

"Grandma, how can you wash dishes so late? It's almost two in the morning." he asked her, wondering if even he could break the calm that settled over her face like an invisible ether.

"If I don't do it, who will?" she would mutter, as though to herself.

As she said this, her body remained poised over the sink and her face was immobile with a preternatural calm.

"Oy Vey! Playing piano and dishwashing - these I must do." she added.

Nothing else calmed her so much.

That was a long time ago. Even now, as he vacationed in Lijiang, David remembered some of their conversations and the occasional reflections she shared with him during the years he knew her and lived with her. These words from his early college years, aphorisms of banality and genius, like dust trapped in the web of youthful memories, emerged again and again in his mind.

When David arrived in America in 1975, life was easy for him and grandmother was part of the reason. Although her house was simple and lacked opulence, he had been content.

It was an ordinary dwelling. The brick tan yellow building with the brown roof was single level but because it was constructed on a small hill the basement floor jutted out from one side, making it look taller than it really was. The lawn was flat and plain. In the eyes of a stranger its beauty lay in everything that was around it and not in itself. The trees were lovely and with the seasons their moods would change. These tall colored presences would drop their foliage onto the grass like a gentle stream of holy water anoints the yielding flesh of an outstretched palm. The path to the front door was clean and well kept. Ida made it a solemn responsibility of hers to daily sweep the leaves away. Since the front lawn was modest in size and flush with the road it offered little privacy. For solitude he would slip away to the back porch. Only neighbors could disturb him there. Largely Jewish but with a fair share of WASPs this Newton neighborhood had few dark skinned residents. Most residents were families and elder folk. The atmosphere was sedate. The wind calmly rustled the leaves, cars rolled quietly up the shallow hills, and old men bearing canes and school children strolled by without haste. David had avoided the front yard. In it he was different and vulnerable. To him being on the front lawn was as conspicuous as a penny black stamp on white bonded paper envelopes. Privacy is commensurate with wealth. The more one has of one, the more of the other. Since Ida was not wealthy, merely well off, he hadn't enough privacy and for a long time wished they were rich. But within the house and on the back porch the solitude was sufficient.

Furthermore, the kitchen was full of food, and grandma provided a welcome running commentary.

"David, have some clam chowder. What about me you say, dear? Oh, I'll have some left over borscht I have in the fridge… Give me that apple core. Yes, it's a good thing to save food. After all, food is food. That is what money is for - to buy good food with."

And to his dismay and partial fascination she would pop the little pieces of the apple core into her mouth, even after he had eaten most of the fruit. She was like a very old mother with a very young child. She was also a matchmaker, teacher, companion, and dancer. In short, she was a jack of all social trades.

But everything was so easy…so soft. The chicken tasted like butter. The car was always in the garage waiting for him to take it out. The weather was always perfect. The neighbors buzzed back and forth, issuing welcomes and greetings like ritual proclamations of bourgeois solidarity. The only hard things about his courtship of this new land were the chairs in Ida's living room. Everything about Ida's home was either hard or soft. The green chair was soft. The sofa was hard. The edges of the bathtub were sharp and unyielding. The patio bench was firm and stiff. The architecture of the house was angular and brusque. Yellow leaves that dropped in the fall formed soft cushions might have soothed him if Ida hadn't felt compelled to sweep them away. Her daily attitude to David was ambivalent. Hard and soft. Soft and hard. One day critical and bitchy, the next gentle and magnanimous. Her piano playing was always clinical and exact. It was the wrong way to play, according to connoisseurs of classical music, but it fitted a precise plan. What that plan was, he was unsure. But the rhythms were pointed, the accents were abrupt, and the notes were correct. She *believed* in her performance and that made it appear right. And she believed in *him*.

"David, one day you will be the president of Africa. And you will marry a beautiful blond who will do anything for you. She will fall madly in love with you."

"I m not going to marry a beautiful blond. In fact I probably will never marry. Did you buy some apples today?" he would retort.

"Of course, the big golden type. The type you love."

"What about you, Grandma? What will you eat?"

"Oh, I have some borscht left over. And some delicious lox. Do you like lox? It's the food of the rich. That's all they eat in Marblehead."

Ida always admired the Boston suburb of Marblehead for its beautiful houses and millionaires.

Glad to have shifted the topic from marriage to borscht, David would mumble a vague reply and lurch towards the fridge.

"You know the world will be brown one day. When your mother married a colored man, I realized that we're all going to be the same. There is no point worrying about it. When I meet people, I tell them that my African son is so smart."

"I'm not colored, Grandma. I'm mixed. No one says colored anymore. And why do you have to say African. We're just your grandchildren. That's all."

Yet again he had been reminded of his blackness.

Ida was a great dreamer. She spoke well of almost everyone she met, too often to the point of obsequiousness. Her thoughts and comments, however, were often so prescient he marveled at the quickness of her mind. In a supermarket she would see a pretty twenty something walk by and quickly accost her. Her bright smile and baby blue eyes, most of all her sweet, melodious, voice had the power to stop a rampaging elephant in its tracks.

"Excuse me darling. But are you a dancer? You've got beautiful, strong legs..." She would purr, her silken voice evoking calm, happiness, apple pie and cream, molasses and vacations at Disneyland.

"Actually...Thank you. Yes, I dance..."

Ida would by now have seized the hands of the astonished woman, and proceeded to examine them. She held each one like a scientist would hold a rare dinosaur egg, salivating over each nail, wrinkle, knot and fold.

"And your hands, such smooth skin. Have you ever thought of playing piano?"

"Well actually, I have..."

"Meet my African grandson David. He is going to be President of Kenya one day. He is a brilliant student at Brown..."

David squirmed inside and flashed a quick nervous smile.

"But he is looking for some company. You two should get together and visit the museum sometime."

David's brown face would grow a shade darker.

"Grandma, really, you don't..."

"Yes, he is so smart. What are you doing next weekend? Do you have any plans?"

As far as Ida was concerned, David was not going to lounge around her house eating and watching TV when he could be working or dating a future wife.

"Actually no..." the girl would say, smiling at David.

Sometimes Ida wasn't so bad, he thought.

In spite of her geniality, her constant praise could turn venomous.

"David, you're driving me out of house and home. Oy , I was a rich woman before you came, and now what do I have? I have nothing. I'll lose the house. I'll be driven into the nursing home down the road. When are you going to get a job?"

"Grandma, you're the one that keeps spending money on me. You bought me the coat. I didn't ask for it. You are too good. It's your fault."

"Get a job! When are you going to find work?"

"I don't want to work. I come here to relax." David often returned from the university during holidays.

"Oy, this worry is too much for me. Maybe you're right, I shouldn't worry." and she would look at David with the red returning into her face, sighing.

"We are lucky, you and I. We have our health. What is the use of money if we have no health? Here, take twenty dollars. I feel good now. Go and buy some food. Get some apples. Buy yourself some ice cream. The deli down the store has delicious Reuben's. Shall we go together?"

She accused the boy of waste, and it was true. He looked upon her largesse as a right, without seeing the years of backbreaking work that had enabled her husband to buy Ida a house and provide her a comfortable retirement. His youth was indulged and remorse came much, much later.

His mother once said. "We Jews are never satisfied with our achievements. A great children's storywriter said that he wanted to be a 'serious writer'. We always want to be more."

Ida wanted achievements first, fame later. But, missing the excellence she sought in her life, she compensated with an almost gnawing lust for fame. And when she couldn't achieve fame, she settled for simple recognition.

To fill the hole in a life marked by a rambling inability to state clear goals, she sought to learn and absorb everything about her. Her capacity for absorption was limitless. Like a desert parched by the stinging heat of the sun, she sucked in the water and still ached. Ida was a *dithyramb par excellence.* She was a free spirit. She darted from interest to interest without dedication to one alone. In a world saturated with information and lack of time, Ida could be counted upon as the community savant, the matchmaker *terrible*, the Renaissance Woman *non plus ultra*, and, above all, the High Priestess of the Children's Musical Academy. She would fish for students and offer guitar lessons to young bait after only a few months of self-tutorship. Free fish dinners were an added bonus for lessons well done (even when not so well done). From time to time she would persuade some charmed family to invite her abroad. How? Through giving free lessons to the youngsters. In turn she would receive free room and board. In her estimation this was an insuperable bargain.

"Oy, what a deal. Meals paid for. A roof over my head. The one bad effect was when I ate pizza in Puerto Rico. When I came back I was so sick. The first time in my life I realized that a country is only as good as it's food! How I love America!" She roundly concluded, and still continued to travel the world.

When David was growing up in Kenya, he looked forward to her visits. She would bring chocolates and gifts. She and he hit it off rather early. He kept to himself and devoured his books and music. She taught him the rudiments of Hebrew. Since Ida had no knowledge of Hebrew grammar, she would coach him in the phonetic structure alone. As he sat on his cot next to her and they read aloud the bizarre sounds without meaning he would suppress his frustration and hang on. There was a point when he gave up because he felt he was learning nothing. Nevertheless, her eagerness was infectious, and her generosity overwhelming. Even now he could remember the whiff of her perfume and hear the sounds of the servant women washing their clothes and plates outside in the garden. Even then she would spend money liberally. He supposed it was his own thriftiness that made what was normal generosity on her part appears as an act of monstrous magnanimity.

Ida discarded bad memories. There was room in her mind only for those happy reminiscences. In that respect she reflected something he saw often in China. She found it almost impossible to admit her errors and mistakes. Thus so much of what she said sometimes seemed like exaggeration. For when one omits discussion of one's errors all that's left can seem like exaggeration and sarcasm. Her house was Spartan in its simplicity, and shorn of photos. David once asked her why she never kept photographs. "Why keep those things?", she replied. "Everyone in them is dead. We should look to the future alone." She never volunteered to speak of her demanding upbringing, and when prompted, would speak factually and with no trace of emotion. Yet, David thought, some of the events she mentioned must have evoked bitter feelings. Her father, as she and his mother described him, was a rough, course man, impatient and driven to succeed. He operated a junkyard which, single-handedly, he built up into a profitable machine of Boston industry.

"He was a scary man. He used to shout at my mother all the time. She ended up in an insane asylum. When he came home from work, I used to hide under the table. I was so afraid of him."

Ida had golden hair and blue eyes as a girl. She always said this with pride, for to her it had been a sign of status, of belonging to her new homeland. Perhaps that is why she always wanted David to marry a blonde Aryan Swede. In any case, ethnicity was a factor in many of her relationships with people. Like most elderly white people in the United States, she often referred to African American's as *colored*. He had resented the term. She never realized his resentment. With respect to his family, she repeated again and again her theory that rationalized her daughter's interracial marriage.

"Lets face it. As people marry people of other cultures, eventually everyone will be mixed. There will be no Jews, No white, No blacks, only brown people".

On account of his own insecurity David never understood how deeply Ida valued him as a person. There was the bitterness of regret about her own daughter. He remembered how his mother once described Ida's reaction to her elopement.

"When I decided to marry your father one of my friends who was there told me that Ida was tearing her hair out at the discovery of my engagement. She couldn't stand the thought of a black man marrying her Ruthie. For many years she wouldn't even talk to me."

In fact Ida had a nervous breakdown. Her husband took her out of the country on a three month trip to help cure her and revive her spirits – she was so depressed. What surprised him also in hearing these recollections was how often his mother other referred to grandmother as *Ida* and not as *Mummy* or some other familiar term. As the years passed by with no possibility of starting again, the two grew closer and there was a stronger bonding. In her last years Ida was never called as such but became *Mummy* and was treated by her daughter not with caution but with growing tenderness and respect.

Without Ida, Boston would have been like the North Pole, cold, bitter and unwelcoming. In her absence, fresh from the plane at Logan, surrounded on all sides by young people who had a hard enough time understanding homegrown Americans, let alone a transplant from Kenya, he would have been hard put. With her it was easier. Although he had little money, Ida would send him the occasional $25 check and shelter him on weekends and the odd holiday. It was a relief to escape to Boston on weekends. He had few friends at the university. Riotous on weekends, it was the most provincial of Ivy League universities and clannish in its smallness. Retiring and aloof, he was rarely invited to parties, even when the air was filled with the scent of bacchanals. Friday night would find popular Thayer Street a virtual catwalk, saturated with lesbians and skinheads in chains and nose rings, white bread refugees in plaid shirts and Gap jeans from Nebraska and Kansas, the loners, the misfits, the intellectuals, the nerds, the oversexed and undersexed, the lovers, the dreamers, and the victims of unrequited love, all spinning and whirling in a traffic jam of draped flesh and unstroked libidos. To him every weekend seemed a Valentine's holiday from which his species of single – that is black, aloof, arrogant, reticent and bookish - were excluded and only tolerated from a distance. Hence 16 Hartman Rd, Newton Mass became his place of self-exile. With Ida he could eat, talk and make music. Those days were special. Although the odd fights occurred, by and large things were fine.

David thought he had forgotten those special moments. Now, as he held the warm cup of green tea in a house in Asia, seeing the old ladies, memories arose in his mind like butterflies swept up in a gale. He compared *Nai Nai* and Ida's faces. Over time old people have the amazing property of becoming indistinct in appearance. Their shrunken, sagging faces and stooping walks all seem to blend into a universal image. Like babies faces that are uniformly unmarked with the frowns and wrinkles of character, they seem like a marvelous breed of global citizens in the autumn of their life. A bittersweet feeling coursed through him. He was reminded of lazy afternoons long ago when schoolboys scratched their names on old water towers pursuing their deathless dreams. These thoughts were fleeting, like the damp smell of grass after the rain and the warmth of the sun overhead. Unlike Ida who would not look back, he now welcomed these transient thoughts.

One weekend when he was visiting Boston Ida and her friends dragged him to the Museum of Fine arts. This small group of elderly friends enjoyed being together and although Ida often criticized some of them for not inviting her to their houses or offering her little gifts when they visited she couldn't do without them. Mary O'Brian was a tall Irish American woman who lived with her son's family and was a good friend to Ida. She, alone among Ida's close associates, treated the old lady fondly and with a special sweetness, almost as If Ida were Mary's own beloved mother. As for Mary she was an attractive woman for her age. Slightly younger, her posture was firm and upright and her makeup was unfailingly spotless. It made her look younger and next to her, Ida's attempts at makeup reminded one of an aged clown dabbling in paints. David often wondered how many hours each morning Mary carefully moistened her dewy morning cheeks with fresh scent and Clinique. She provided Ida with pleasant company and occasionally treated her to free meals at a kosher deli in the neighborhood. Ida reciprocated by driving Mary to free events at which the two would sit side by side, talking and looking like the oddest pair of friends. Mary would sit straight up, attentive and on display. Ida would crouch in her seat, slightly hunched forward as though to launch an attack. Her red rouge would be clumsily smeared across her face and her wig hidden under a colored kerchief. She would tightly hold her little green pocketbook on her lap and interrupt her concentrated look with an interested glance at passers by. Very often she would accost some hapless child who wandered by.

"Hello, dear, and what is your name?", she would say in the sweetest of voices.

"Umm, Jimmy."

"Jimmy, do you play piano? Does your Mother give you lessons? Huh dear?"

"Umm, no..."

"Here give me your hands, honey, let me show you something," and Ida would take the child's hand and start stretch exercises with his fingers.

"Do you know how to play a scale? Here, let me show you how it works.", she would continue.

Before long the bemused parents would be standing closely by and join in the conversation. Often Ida would meet people (and future piano pupils) this way, by grabbing the children and snaring their parents. She had a genius for extemporaneous conversation. She would make her presence known in the oddest places and introduce herself to anyone who listened. Her gregariousness also helped her make easy friendships with those in her own age group. Instead of sitting at home and watching cable TV, these folks would join Ida in her odd activities, thereby adding spice to their later years.

Mary, Ida, and David entered the famous museum and, in the rush of people, got separated. He made his own way through the Renoirs and

Cézannes. He was admiring an impressionist still life when the sound of Joplin started up from the other end of the museum. He immediately knew it was Ida. Somewhere within this grand building his granny's fingers were producing those sounds. When Ida played piano, she never performed a piece in its entirety. Instead she would segue various portions of *The Entertainer*, *The Minute Waltz*, *Kitten on the Keys*, a very allegro Beethoven sonata adagio *et al* in one never ending stream of harmonies. The little that she played she played very well, and the many that heard her loved it, while a few disliked her music as a plebian abomination. In any case, Ida would dream away, and to hell with the critics. *On with the show, folks! Hats off to the elderly lady! A genius is born in Boston!* Recalling her independence he was reminded of an old Chinese saying:

Walk your own road, and let others say what they will!

When he rejoined Ida, she was in a gallery thumping on a grand piano in the center of a circle of people. Children were clustered around and everyone was facing her. Even the paintings seemed to stare wide-eyed at the scene, as if overcome. As Mary told him later, a museum guard had first warned Ida not to play as *unauthorized sound* was prohibited. Needless to say, he was ignored, and, reluctant to disturb a popular event or seem impolite to a senior citizen, retired into an obscure corner of the museum.

Recalling this, David realized how absolutely impossible it would have been for such a thing to happen in China. Were someone to walk into the famous *Forest of Stones* museum in Xi An or the Forbidden City in Beijing and start an impromptu concert on their pianos, the security guards would never have allowed it. They might even have arrested the miscreant for disturbing state secrets. But here in Boston, in one of the world's great museums, Ida blithely carried on with her music. For about an hour and a half she played and taught, giving piano lessons to the little children that clustered around her. As David saw her that day in a grand old Boston Museum in the bleak cold air of winter, he realized at last that Ida was a person in firm grasp of her destiny.

Ida gave and gave. She was good to him. Although a crusty bitterness and acidity always remained, it was in small portions. Her excess of praise was sometimes false but always was uplifting to those who needed a crutch. And there were many. Ida brooked no diminution of magnanimity. From time to time when it was not reciprocated or treated selfishly, she would open wide her blue eyes, like a puzzled baby might. Taking comfort in the next day, she left behind the past. Without fear she greeted strangers like friends and offered them whatever she had to give.

All David had of Ida now was memories. To conceal them would be wrong. The creature that woke at night to scrape the dishes and become one with the night breeze, was now a part of him, full of the scent of love. *People as special as Ida make us wonder where they could possibly go*, he thought. *Energy like hers cannot, must not vanish. Surely nature cannot be so unjust?*

"What do you want to see when you are here?" Spring's aunt asked him. Her voice came as though out of the mist, distant and far away, almost disembodied, he had been so caught up in his thoughts. He absentmindedly replied.

"Playing piano in the museum..."

Spring flashed him an angry look. The aunt looked confused. He wondered why her eyes were so small and her eyebrows so very thin. She was sitting so primly on the chair, her knees together, one hand holding the cup of tea and the other on her lap. He just smiled and looked at Nai Nai, who was sitting on the other side of the sofa, closest to him. She had a beatific smile on her face. She reminded him of his mother, who also had the gift of a serene smile, the one professional photographers love to include in family group photos. Her smile was as calm as it was mysterious, simple enough to be complicated.

"*Nai Nai*, I think you have seen much in your life. Have things changed much since you were a young woman?"

The others looked at him as though they didn't understand the question. Spring's aunt moved protectively a little closer to the old lady.

"I just cook and help around the house." The little lady finally said, not looking at him but peering somewhere between the old TV and the wall.

And with that, she relapsed into silence looking at him with her beatific smile. For several seconds no one said anything. Spring scratched her leg nervously. Then everyone in the room laughed. It was a good natured laugh, a belly laugh, the most authentic kind. David joined them, not because he understood why it was funny but because it was the thing to do. After that the questioning was easier. Spring or her aunt would sometimes translate.

"Do you remember *Da Ge Ming*, the *Great Cultural Revolution*,...or *Shan Shang Xiang Xia,* the *Down to the village, Up to the Mountain* movements?"

It was with some caution that he asked such questions. After all, while growing up he had, like many Americans and Kenyans, read the books and newspapers that taught of the authoritarianism of Red China, where allegedly even asking political questions about taboo topics could land one in jail. The reality however, was that in many ways China today was no longer that other China. While public discourse was discouraged, at times punished, Chinese were remarkably open discussing the darker aspects of their history. In some ways this openness was so at odds with the unrelentingly negative portrayals of China in the Western press he wondered if he could be evenhanded in understanding the last fifty years or so of Chinese history, since the 1949 revolution. He wanted to know more of these famous times from people who had personally witnessed them, like Teacher Zhou and Nai Nai.

"No one from the villages went to the cities. Instead the children from the cities went to the villages."

She said it emphatically, as though no village folk in their right mind would have wanted to go to the cities anyway.

"We were so hungry, we didn't even have coconuts. Here, have some fruit."

She attempted to rise and pass him the platter of fruit on the table. The aunt quickly gave him the fruit instead and shushed the old woman back into her seat. When she sat down her back fit snuggly against the back of the chair, her hips straight and close against the seat, her calves flush against the foot of the chair. Her body was ninety degrees at three points and her hand was poised somewhere in front of her back and above the arch of the chair. Years of back breaking work had taken their toll. For decades she had hauled loads of up to 60 pounds as she had navigated back and forth over mountain paths often less than a foot wide. When she walked it was as though she were still sitting, her back and shoulders were so bent. Her thin legs supported her thick torso like the two parallel prongs of a fork as she waddled from living room to kitchen, from kitchen to living room. She nevertheless had some grace. Her hair, still long, dark and thick as a rich mass of seaweed, would escape her bun and tumble down her back. At such times she would almost look young, and a flash of youth and fragile tenderness would drape its magic about her.

"From 1962 to 1965 were the worst years. We had no food. Even the trees bore no fruit. After we lost the war with the Russians we had to pay them reparations. We were so poor. It was very hard."

He nodded his head. Auntie tenderly put a pillow behind the old lady's back. Encouraged, she continued.

"Some of the children here are old enough to remember, but others have full bellies and so they do not. Maybe they do not want to remember."

He nodded his head. The others in the room listened respectfully.

David, and perhaps Spring, were particularly attentive, perhaps because hearing others recount their personal versions of history gives us insight into our own lives and comfort us. We are instinctively drawn to the tales of struggle that bind us together through their simplicity and humanity. In his 'Ode to a Grecian Urn' Keats had declared

"Beauty is truth, truth beauty,"- that is all
Ye know on earth, and all ye need to know.

Others write of the connection between truth and beauty, such as when Ophelia asks Hamlet:

"Could beauty, my lord, have better commerce than with honesty?"

Or Plato in his *Laws* declares

Truth is the beginning of every good to the gods, and of every good to man.

Spring, perhaps faced by uncomfortable truths like the suffering children in the orphanage, sought a falsehood of sorts in which she could dream. David, on the contrary, perhaps sought a different comfort, somewhere between falsehood and truth. Camus in *The Fall* had declared that truth, like light, blinds, and falsehood is a beautiful twilight that enhances every object. David wondered if he was a blind fool, a vain seeker after beauty who happened to find truth as if by accident. He didn't know.

What was indisputable was that listening to the old lady recount her life was, like Ida's reluctant and terse statements about her bitter upbringing, strangely soothing. And in this serenity of sorts one could learn more about oneself, indeed a worthy goal. As the ancient Greek sages had said:

Gnothi savton

Or

Know yourself

"Every evening we had one steamed bun to eat. We split it evenly into seven pieces among our five children, every person had one piece. And even then these *man tou* were a treat."

"Did the smaller children get a larger piece?"

"No, every piece was the same size. The smallest child ate the same as every one else. Otherwise someone would cry and say it was unfair. Each day we got two food tickets. Each ticket could be exchanged for rations. The more one worked the more food one got. If someone did not work hard enough, it was very hard for them."

"Nai Nai, you had a very hard time I see."

"For forty years I carried heavy loads on my back!" her eyes lighted up and her voice was momentarily louder.

She didn't seem proud of her hardships, in the way one hears fat generals and rich tycoons talk of their raising themselves by their bootstraps, red jowls bouncing and gold rings flashing. She was neither happy or sad. Except for her perpetual smile, she was like Ida, deadpan and laconic, as though reading from a script that was beyond pleasure or pain.

"Have you ever traveled outside your home town?"

Spring and aunty seemed to shake their heads. The room was very quiet, except for the sounds of a clock ticking in the background, somewhere behind the sofa. The sounds of cars outside and children playing could faintly be heard. The old man had left on errands long ago. The old lady shook her head slowly.

"I'm from Henan. I lived there before I came here."

And she smiled gently, her eyes bright and her wise face wreathed with a glow from some ineffable source. David wondered, *How did she have the strength to continue for forty years, in those darkest of moments? Religion? Something else?*

"How did you keep going Nai Nai?"

"What? What did you say?"

Spring leaned forward and gently explained to her. She nodded.

"My children. I had to support my children. They kept me going."

"Do you remember the Second World War?"

She didn't understand, but after Spring explained. Nai Nai quickly continued without hesitation, her mind nimble and alert. Aunty, now less agitated, was quietly leafing through a fashion magazine. From time to time she would pick up her head, listen, and help Spring translate for Nai Nai.

"I was 16 when the war began. My father and mother were villagers. They were just simple farmers. We didn't want this war. But many people died. Our village was in the middle of the fighting. The enemy and our soldiers fought on either side of us. We were in between and we could hear the shots and the bombs. At night we heard the cries of wounded men. The fighting never came directly to our village, but sometimes I saw my father carrying wounded soldiers on his cart. They were hidden under the turnips and the green onions. Sometimes my mother treated our soldiers' wounds. One day a tall soldier whose hand had been wounded by shrapnel was brought home by my father. He smelled of blood and turnips, but his face was so handsome and his hands were so soft…"

She stopped for a few minutes, rubbed her eyes and continued.

"I helped my mother look after him for a few days. My mother was never very gentle with dressing wounds. The soldiers often wanted me to tend to them instead of her. But he treated us both with great respect, even though my mother hurt him a lot. Then, as if she knew, she let me stay at home to tend to him on his last day. I was so shy I said nothing. 'Do I still smell like a turnip?' he asked me and I giggled. "Yes." I said. He laughed. It was a rich, happy laugh. After that we talked a lot. He told me how he missed his family and his little dog. He hated the war but knew he had to fight for China. He was eager to go back to his comrades but said he would miss talking to me. He said he would come back to see me after the war. I even thought he would marry me. I was only 16 then."

"Did you marry him?"

"Goodness no. My parents chose who we would marry. This had been decided by them years before. My husband was a man from a neighboring village. I had seen him only once before the wedding. He didn't know me either. Before the wedding he sent his brother over to get a description of me! Things are different now, but then we had no choice!"

"Did you ever see the soldier again?"

"He didn't come back after the war, but I never have forgotten him!"

"Do you regret that?"

"Life is too short for regrets. I had a happy marriage and I love my children. And when I work in the kitchen and help around the house this is what makes me happy."

The old lady was eager to say more but it was late and she was gently escorted to bed by her daughter.

"The younger people are too busy to listen to my stories." She protested.

Escorted by Spring's aunt, she slowly left the room, her head bent as if to creep under the door.

He found some time later to check some of the mail he had received just before they left. He opened the PAR AVION envelope. It was a reply from his mother.

Dear David:

I found a very supportive lawyer — John Roberts of Shaw & Fillis — and he helped me to petition for a divorce from your father. This process was much easier in those days and I soon acquired a Decree Nisi. The Decree Absolutum would be granted in about three months time. I continued to work and live in Woodley with you and then he came back. He begged me to drop the divorce case, and he was always persuasive with me — I was a sucker in those days — and except for Mr Robert's steadfast encouragement I would have dropped the case. Mr Roberts convinced me to go ahead with the divorce because if he did change, it wouldn't matter. I could still live with him. During the final trial I remember being more undecided in my mind than at any other time in my life. I didn't want to go before the judge; then I did want to go before the judge. Anyhow, finally I went through with it and we were legally divorced.

I continued to live with him but told him that legally he had no hold over me anymore but of course he didn't really listen to me and thought I would always stay with him. He was mistaken. I finally got so fed up with his abuse and cruelty that I found an Indian male friend who brought a pick up to our house one day. I loaded whatever I could into it, and fled to a flat in Westlands on East Church Road with you. I had legal custody of you.

Esther my devoted Ayah followed me and took care of you during the day when I had to work. We lived in fear as your father came sometimes, knocked on the doors and windows, made a terrible racket, and threatened to kidnap you, and called me a prostitute. It was a very difficult and scary time. However, help was next door. A young woman named Ruth Dena lived next door to me and we became friends. She is a mixed woman (African mum, Swiss dad) and she is a fighter. She knew my story and I remember to this day her saying "If that bastard comes here I'll cut his balls off!" That sort of talk was what I needed to boost my courage. She also had some sisters living nearby so there were a group of women who supported me and helped me. Also she worked for the record company run and owned by your step father.

More later,

Love,

Mutter

He slowly folded the letter, thinking. *I forgot about Esther,* he thought. David remembered the last time he had seen their ayah. That afternoon in 1999 during a brief visit to Kenya, an old Kenyan lady, her broad forehead beaded with sweat under a blue and black scarf, sat humbly on her old employer's sofa, her legs bent primly side by side.

"Habari, David. Habari" She had said joyfully when she saw him.

It had been more than twenty years since they last seen each other. He remembered how she pronounced his name, DaVID, DaVID, always with the accent at the end, as so many Kenyans do by habit. That accent, he thought, how it got him into trouble at times. David remembered how he had mispronounced an old friend's name. His friend had said,

"You old son of a bitch, after ten years and you can't pronounce my fucking name. You old sod!"

He had never thought much of names, preferring to dwell on quirks of character and faces, which he never forgot. So he remember her face too, long and plain, teeth as white as ever, and her wrinkles hidden in her youthful blackness. Esther was of the Luhya tribe. This tribe is not as black as other tribes, such as the Luo, but is still very dark, almost a deep half-scorched brown. Sometimes it seemed as though the color of her skin varied with her moods or the seasons. A dark rich Indian chocolate in the summer, or, (particularly when he was next to her or she was mad at him) a warm raisin bread sheen. He had forgotten much of his Swahili and just said

"*Jambo* Esther."

He understood everything she said to him but he felt speechless and regretted he couldn't say more to her. He sat down beside her and gently held her hand. This had been the woman whom he had grown up with, who had fed him *nyoyo*, chapattis and cheese toast, scolded him and argued with him. cleaned his room and, whether he liked it or not, been part of his family. At times he had hated her.

"He doesn't want to eat with his own mother"

Esther had once said of David once long ago. And it was true. David's mother ate loudly, crunching chicken bones and slurping tea until it drove him mad. At times he had refused to sit down with her. Esther had regarded it as an affront to the *memsahib*, whom she loved and respected. Yet he hated the fact that she told her friends of these family conflicts. There are some things that are just not said outside, he complained to his mother. And his mother had gently chided Esther, and that was that.

He heard *Jambo* from her lips and it was as if he was hearing her voice like those countless mornings when she and the other help woke up and chatted. It would be early in the morning, when the birds just start to whistle and a distant rooster is well into its morning song. Her voice carried sharply through the sound of dishes being washed just outside his window in the outdoor spigot and concrete tub all the help used. The sound of water falling was like a shower that cleansed the fog of sleep from his eyes

She had what his mother still calls *Boston Reserve*. Her passions, though deep, were profoundly private. During the fifteen years that she was his *ayah* David never remembered seeing her cry. When he cruelly lashed out at her for some trivial thing like learning water on the kitchen floor, or not properly washing the dishes, she would quietly listen, nod her head, and 4 or 5 days later do exactly the same thing. Her emotional displays were in response to more substantial matters and even then were subtle, like a tear glistening behind her black eyes or her head turning quickly away

Esther was like a small light in the heavens. Surrounded by myriads of brighter stars, her lone firmament was David's family. Through her devotion and uncomplaining hard work, she showed her love, without ever demanding an acknowledgement. Such are the simple and good people who flash across our bows as we journey through life, like fireflies that give us light during their brief lives but never see the glow themselves.

She often wore dark blue and black clothes. Her legs were a secret thing, never to be seen. This was normal as most middle aged Luhya women wear long dresses as if in matronly, conservative rebellion at the younger, leggy *skanks* that prance across Nairobi's streets.

David remembered her smile clearly, perhaps because she didn't smile that much around him. It was broad and toothy, wrapped in good feelings and the fruit of simple pleasures. When she saw him with a good friend she would smile and say to all around her with a proud and slightly bewildered merriment,

"These two boys are so tall. He is David's friend!"

She believed it was a good thing to have a friend, and David had few.

Once or twice a week she cooked *chapatis*. These fried dough cakes that were introduced to Kenya by ancient Arab and Asian traders would turn a crip golden brown in the griddle. David's fingers would glisten with oil as he stuffed the peeling, golden flakes into his mouth, gorged.

"Make more next time!" he used to plead with her. "Let's have these everyday!".

But it was always only once or twice weekly, and each time there were too few.

As a result of a miscarriage early in her life which was never fully treated, she suffered frequently from a recurring infection. For many years she would lie in pain in her alcove room after work in the servants quarters that lay off the main building of our home. Until that day when Mom found her in her dark privacy, doubled up in a fetal position on the floor. 'I didn't want to bother you, Memsahib', Esther said.

He remembered a solid, stocky women, a salt of the earth type, not pretty but not plain. Always in control of household matters, from cleaning the furniture to preparing food, scrubbing, shopping, cooking, smiling, laughing, chatting, bustling about, scowling – being his mother in reserve.

What was the essence of this woman? A back-breaking acceptance of her role as servant, and yet also as a member of the family? He never ate with her, slept with her, or even played with her – yet there existed an invisible but unbreakable silver thread that binded the skeins of her life to his. *How does one pay tribute to a life?* He asked himself. In the end it all seemed like a series of random noises, never divorced from the his ego, linking the merest fragments of the truth – *perhaps that was enough*, he thought. To David the truth about Esther lay somewhere in that last visit.

Here, on that day, she was diminished. Here he was just the visitor and she was the subject. He hugged her small body awkwardly. For the first time he saw her cry.

" Hello Esther." he said in Swahili, for she never spoke English.

"David, David *nina rudi* (you have come back).", she said half smiling, half crying.

"She always asked after you." His mother said, sitting beside the little woman, her hands gently bit firmly holding the other's.

He wanted to say so much, but he was speechless. His Swahili was so poor and rusty after years of prancing around America's ice-cream world.

He remembered how long ago, growing up as a child in their Nairobi house, he had been locked in a dark cupboard by the man who cleaned the house when his mother was away at work. He remembered the dank smell, dirty towels and how he had cried a lot in the darkness. He had been about 6 then and the man was a prickly, easily enraged type.

"No one treated my children that way.", his mother told him years later. "So I got Esther, and she was the best. She fed you *nyoyo* every day and you were never ill."

His delicious *nyoyo* was as natural to him as breathing. Luscious yellow corn kernels mixed with burgundy red kidney beans, all fried to a delicious, mouth watering golden perfection.

His childhood was dominated by Esther's delicious food.

In general she was a terrible cook, but when it came to *nyoyo*, *chapatis* and *sukumawiki*, she shined with the spark of genius. Her chapatis were his holy bread, and nyoyo and sukumawiki were his manna from heaven. In the kitchen she would grab steel pots of boiling water or sauce with her bare chapped hands without flinching. He once grabbed her hands, as though on impulse. They were very rough, callused – like her shoeless feet – and hard as matted rubber. Hunched, with the bandanna tightly wrapped Manchu-like about her coarse black hair, her stocky body would dance in a marvelous lurching rhythm with the condiments and tools of that childhood wonderland that was her kitchen.

. "She couldn't get long with the other ladies and she was too old", his mother told him, "But I kept her on because she was family. Finally I told her it was time for her to go back home I gave her some money to by a few acres in Kakamega And she now grows her vegetables there and is quite settled down."

She died soon after that last visit.

He thought back to his mother. She too had had great setbacks. She had overcome adversity and was the major reason he had achieved well in school and had had the fortune to experience living and working in foreign lands. His mother had not had much money and had the misfortune of a bad marriage. In spite of these setbacks she had had the fortitude and drive to devote everything to her son. She had always encouraged him to go beyond the limits and tried to make all the best opportunities available to him. From the moment he was born they had bonded, and her culture and own ambitions had fused inseparable with his own. Her own experiences and education had given her a broader perspective on life and a willingness to challenge dogma. These were the foundations to becoming a citizen of the world, a man for all seasons, a perennial traveler in a murky universe.

She too had her faults and biases. Occasionally she had spoken disparagingly of Kenyans, particularly Kenyan men,

"So many are corrupt, and don't tell me they don't get enough sex. They get plenty. And the men sleep around and bring home diseases to their wives. It's often the women who suffer."

She would be adamant in her opinion. It was not surprising therefore that she had counted herself lucky not to get AIDS. Indeed, at that time, sexual diseases, such as gonorrhea and later, AIDs were rampant in Kenya. Men refused to practice birth control as it not only was un-traditional but it limited pleasure. Many also didn't believe the magnitude of the threat. Education initiatives began slowly. Even for the women, worried about getting enough clean water for their families, birth control was a distant, even extravagant thought. Furthermore, among the many Catholics, their religion forbade them any type of birth control, and when AIDs appeared, babies started to die too. Education programs set up by government started slowly, but messages were mixed. Some advocated total abstinence from sex, which was unrealistic. Others wanted to distribute free condoms.

David's mother knew her husband was sleeping around but she stuck it out for many years. She, like many white women married to black men, harbored no illusions about the frailty and willfulness of their African mates. It was a hardheaded skepticism coupled with boundless ambition for their coffee colored children that shaped their difficult lives. The many wrinkles in her face were like radiating cracks on an iced up lake, every one a mark of painful experience and a symbol of creative destruction. They were testaments to her experiences of pain and suffering, unrequited love and betrayal, cultural dislocation and painful integration, rebirth and redemption.

David compared these women, all ostensibly so different and yet so alike in their enduring hopes. On the one hand, there was a strong sense of unforced duty to work or family. On the other hand it was a dedication to betterment, such as in music and education. Without these, how poor and insipid would their lives, and his, have been.

Follow your passions and you will never fail

This was the dictum of David's life, but it could have equally applied to them. As he sat in this little apartment in Kunming, and saw the little old lady so bent that she could not stand straight, he marveled. Thousands of miles and many years separated these women. They were in profound communication with the very rhythms of life itself, and whether it was a woman who had eloped to Africa, a woman who had been born there, an old Jewish lady who forgot the pain of her arthritis when she played piano, or the old villager from Kunming who had shared her single *mantou* with her five children, all were linked, were whole, and gave life its tremendous justification.

*"They would consider such children as white niggers or black **mzungus**. They were too black for whites, yet too white for blacks. To survive, my son would need to be strong. In my imagination, with a little encouragement, he would put the pedal to the metal and zoom ahead - alone and self-reliant."*

- From David's father's journal

THE TOUR BEGINS

That afternoon they visited a traditional Kunming tea house. The building was set on about two acres of beautifully tended gardens. Lofty tree branches shaded goldfish in the ponds below and draped arbors and stone walls behind whose runic shaped peepholes unseen eyes lingered. Inside they saw rooms decorated with exquisite redwood furniture and traditional calligraphy and paintings. Sitting outside on a small pavilion beside the pond they were served the famous local *Pu Er* tea. This tea has a strong, deep, almost fishy taste. It is prized by Chinese for its medicinal properties, in particular in soothing abdominal pain. Stored for years on end, it gains in richness and value over time, much like the appreciation of red wine. David recalled how once he had seen a TV program about the history of tea in China. One section described tea's rich history in the province of Sichuan. In the demonstration brass tea pots of boiling water with meter long spigots were deftly handled by young men in tight fitting traditional yellow silk clothes. With great dexterity, they twirled pots about their bodies,, stretching and shrinking their limbs into fantastic positions, never spilling the boiling water. Finally, in a *coup de grace* they would pour the water from the long spigot in smooth elegant streams into the tiny tea cups on the table.

When they were about to leave the tea house, Spring and Auntie fell into a heated discussion. Spring turned to David.

"We can now take you to the hotel."

"What hotel?"

"Where you will be staying?"

"I'll be staying in a hotel?"

He had all along thought they would be staying together. Spring saw his disappointment. After a more lengthy discussion with her aunt she turned to him again,.

"Don't worry, you can stay with us an auntie's. They have a spare room that you can sleep in."

He was more relieved than embarrassed. Spring smiled at him and took his arm.

"Now let us take a look at the tea shops!"

They returned to the house soon after doing some shopping. David had bought Spring an elegant Chinese chess board, even though neither knew how to play. The board was of brass and reddish white marble and the set was packaged in a brown leather case. It had looked too elegant to ignore. Since he didn't want to look cheap in front of Spring and the others he didn't try to bargain down the outrageous price of 300 Yuan.

After they had had dinner at a restaurant they returned to the house. The coach to Lijiang would leave the next morning.

His room belonged to Spring's aunt's daughter, who was in college. Cloth dolls, teddy bears, vases of paper mache flowers, picture books, big fluffy shaped pillows were scattered tastefully around the pink painted room like a pretty scene from *Seventeen* magazine. On the walls were hundreds of photos of celebrities, such as the footballer David Beckett, actor Andy Liu and others. He paid little attention to these and flipped open his notebook. His mother had this time sent him an email.

> *Dear David:*
>
> *After we married, your stepfather got rid of your father for me. This was a tremendous relief.Your father, being a coward, was afraid of your stepfather.*
>
> *After our Malindi honeymoon we looked for a better house to live in.We found it on Ardwings Kodek Road, the house we live in to this day. A very comfortable, peaceful house it has been and I shall probably die here.*
>
> *I loved your father once. In some ways it was among the most intense love I've ever felt.Then again he maybe didn't need, or even love me in return, the same way. I had to break away. He made it easy for me.*
>
> *We haven't heard much from you.Well, I guess that's the way you like it? How did things go with that girl you wrote about? I worry about you.You are in some ways like your father. I think maybe you just don't need people as much as they need you?We know you are strong and self sufficient, but its nice to share one's life too. Is music enough? Is China enough?*

Dad had a cold for a few days and had to stay in bed (doctor's orders!). Now he's fine and out and about.
Love,
Mutter

David pondered awhile.
How could she love someone on the one hand and call him a coward on the other?
Perhaps she had expected him to fight for her, like the knights of lore and heroes of legend.
Had she been disappointed in his retreat from the field of battle?

David guessed she had found him lacking in that adamantine core, that her mother loved her father more than he loved her. She could forgive him anything, but he had lacked the will, the courage or just the desire to fight for her. If a child or locked door blocked his way, he could break them down or swat them aside, but if it was a armed rival, he could fall back on drink and the solitude of the wolf.

They left on the tour coach for Lijiang the following morning. The focus of their visit, Lijiang lies in northwest Yunnan province, about 360 miles from Kunming. The surrounding country is hilly and varies in temperature with the altitude. The locals often say,

"There are four seasons on the same mountain, and climate changes at every 10 meter walk."

Designated by the UN a World Heritage Sight and located in the center of Lijiang proper, the Old Town is a marvel to behold. Wooden houses with intricately carved walls and banisters huddle together over cobbled streets that are frequented by tourists, artisans, merchants and the local *Naxi* people, many of whom dress in brilliant azure garments and hats. From morning to evening the air is filled with the sound of their singing and the tinkling of water from streams and fountains.

Water from the *Yu Long* glaciers melt into the *Yu Quan Shi* river that flows through the city, emerging into three streams flowing east, west and in between. Drooping poplars seem to fall from the sky onto the five colored stone canals that in places have been rubbed a deep silvery hue from the countless feet and vehicles of Mongols and Christians, Taoists and Buddhists, lovers and merchants, families and strangers, the possessed and dispossessed. Like young love, rushing water finds its way around barriers and flows between buildings, a unifying and ineluctable force that turns driftwood into moonbeams and fountains into music.

During the Ming dynasty (1368-1644AD) the ruling family of *Mu* decided, at the urging of the Emperor not to build a protective wall. This made it unique among Chinese cities. The reason was based on the symbolism of the Chinese characters for *Mu* (meaning *wood*) and *Kun* (meaning *difficulty*). If a circle (representing a wall) is drawn around the *Mu* character, it becomes the inauspicious *Kun* character. The Chinese aristocracy, always superstitious, therefore decided not to build the wall. It is said that this contributed to the relative openness and tolerance of the Naxi people.

However, as they sat in the bus on the way to a town famous for love and music, openness and unity, they seemed anything but in love and united. Spring was pensive and reserved, never pressing against him or showing any affection. She was thinking of her mother and father, and particularly what a friend had told her when she had gone out with David one evening in Shenzhen. Some of her friends had accompanied them. While they were sitting together at a bar, David had put his arm around her.

"Don't do that!" one of Spring's friends said, as though stung.

"People will think she is a bad woman." she said to David, frowning.

David had laughed and brushed it off, but he had removed his hand. Spring wondered if she should have said something. David's gesture had seemed natural to her. It was as though all the rules of traditional China were once again invading her tranquil life in Shenzhen. She knew that her friend only wanted to protect her, yet Spring also wanted to break out of this amorphous, web that threatened to drown her. She had impulsively swung her leg onto his lap and planted a kiss on his cheek. Her friends laughed nervously, a little astonished. At once Spring felt uncomfortable. She removed her leg, sat up straight and blushed.

Irritated at her remoteness, David fell into his own thoughts. He remembered a long time ago something his father had said to him when they were making the long drive to Alego.

"White women who married black men were sometimes thought of as prostitutes. Their children were often considered unclean."

Long ago Bob Dylan had sung, *the times, they are-a-changing.* Now, decades later, on this bus surrounded by strangers, in spite of all the barriers of race, culture, class and superstition, the two of them were together. They were living proof of changing times, the intersection of cultures, and the sublime possibilities of requited love.

But today her behavior was puzzling and David felt wounded.

He hated her sometimes, for he was an individualist, something of a free spirit and the idea that one person could hold such power over him, that is, to make him insanely miserable one minute or blissfully happy the next, was a living torture. He comforted himself by reminding himself of the night after the Shenzhen performance.

He also remembered how even the aloof and reserved Spring seemed to care for him. For example, walking back to the school one night they had come across a street person selling attractive trinkets. He had offered to buy some.

"30 Yuan"

"You're joking!" Spring said. "That's terrible quality."

"25 Yuan." the peddler said as they turned away.

David started to hand over the money. Spring suddenly snapped at both of them, glaring at the peddler.

"Don't buy it. It's poor quality!"

They ignored the peddler, who nevertheless pursued the foreigner and Spring for a few yards, smiling obsequiously, his few remaining yellowed teeth gaping like bad and broken ornaments.

"Get out of here!" she said furiously and hurled a stream of invective at the astonished trinket seller who scurried away.

"*Ta Ma De! Pian zi!* Bloody cheat. He was going to cheat you. They do it all the time here. You buy these things, and two days later they shrivel up or stop working or poison you."

He felt strangely exhilarated that she had rebuffed the man so brazenly. He liked the sensation of caving in to her and knowing she was somewhat protective of him. He just nodded.

From time to time Spring too had recalled that incident. At that time her own reaction had somewhat surprised her. She hadn't let loose like that for a long time. In fact since her relationship with David had begun (he was her 'boyfriend' now, although she still found it hard to admit) she had been much less high strung than before. But with this trip, there were glimmers of the old Spring that occasionally came back to haunt her. She did not know why, but she was wondering what, if anything, they really had in common. And with this lessening of affection, she felt guilty. But she did not recognize this guilt for what it was. Instead an anger and helplessness surged slowly inside her, and occasionally vented when she least expected it. David too was somewhat bewildered by her mood swings and he dimly sensed that all was not well in paradise.

They arrived in Lijiang later that evening. The Old City was beautiful at night. Established hundreds of years ago, its cobbled streets and alleys and intricate wooden buildings speak to the artistic genius of the Yunnan people. Many artisan shops and cafes lined the streets. It bustled with people, cafes, bookstores and inns. Later they would even discover WCs that provided 5 star service for men and women (half a Yuan per use) – essential for foreigners in a country where the toilet is often just a hole in the ground. The first time Spring visited and saw the plush sofas, intricately carved tables with magazines and vases of roses she thought it was a café.

Their Naxi hostess, a prim, stocky woman in her thirties or early forties, met the tourists at the bus stand outside the Old City. Cars were not allowed to enter the Old City so she led them through the town, each carrying or pulling their luggage over the ancient gray cobblestones, past the brightly light wooden artisan shops, right into the central square, where the inn was located. Unaware of Spring and David's true relationship Spring's aunty had reserved separate rooms for them. As a result they had the option of sleeping separately, to keep up appearances. Spring was unhappy at having deceived her aunty, but relieved at not having to explain further. They would remain there for the next few days. Their rooms were simple and Spartan, clean and well ventilated.

The next two days were spent in Lijiang with day trips to the nearby village of Dali and the Buddhist refuge of Shangri-La to the north. David recorded the experience in his notebook.

Dali We visited the ancient village of Dali. The native Bai Zhu people were reserved and in general did not like me taking photos of them. We rented bicycles and rode about the narrow streets. Many Yunnan province buildings and houses, particularly in Dali and Lijiang, have roofs with upwardly pointed corners, like scrolls of calligraphy. The outer walls are often decorated with murals of landscapes and flowers. The older people generally wear blue tunics and hats and the younger people loosely wrap themselves around with bright red, yellow, white and blue cloth — mostly for tourists who pay for shots they can boast of back home. My impression was of a people who love to be surrounded by sounds, sights, shapes and colors. In particular the Bai Zhu love music, dancing and painting. 'Aren't the young women lovely?' I asked Spring. She nodded. 'What do you think of the men? Do you think they're handsome?' 'Oh no! They're too black!' Then she looked at my astonished face and giggled nervously. We took the local bus number 4 back to the Dali city center (a twenty five minute ride), promptly got lost, and limped back to the train station (for the trip back to Lijiang) with the help of a grumpy *taxi driver who (rightly) complained that a 5 Yuan ($0.50) five minute ride had turned into twenty minutes of u-turns and mistaken directions.*

Lijiang Opera *'You must visit the opera in Lijiang a Chinese friend had advised us. The performance started at 8pm. The master of ceremonies, a man named Xuen Ke, prefaced each piece with descriptions in Chinese and English. They went something like this:*
(In Chinese, very long)
"This piece is 1025 years old and very famous. Almost as old as us." (all 37 musicians on stage were in their seventies or above).
"The piece was written by an emperor while he was in prison after being deposed. Note that the music is sung with great attention to detail. Rather like PAV...VVARRR... OOOTTT...IIIII." (He cups his hands in front of his belly).
"When Pavarotti sings he is very still and only the music comes out, no dancing, moving and so forth." (And he cups his hand in front of the belly, evoking both the opera singers' stillness on stage and his great paunch)
"Now how do I say this in English for our English friends?" (and he smiles wickedly)

(In English, very short):
"Ladies and Gentlemen, this piece is 102 years old, written by a deposed emperor. It is very beautiful."

Although Spring tells me that he was very respectful of foreigners, I cannot help but think otherwise. In many ways the Chinese, including a man as learned as Xuen Ke, seem to look down upon foreigners. Their language, dense to non-Chinese, is often a very convenient mask that obfuscates a mild sarcasm of foreigners. Although it is true that many Chinese have a great fascination with American culture and fashion, ardently mixing criticism with praise of American society and politics, their government and many citizens bridle at American criticism of China's 'internal affairs'. I read, for example, in a newspaper once about foreigners who had been deported for telling their Chinese friends about their government's infamous policies. Then again, I also see the popular police, nurse and teacher television shows, every one of them without a bad thing to say about government and its workers. Chinese are often simply unaware of the many injustices at home, and, when called upon to be patriotic and xenophobic, often rally behind the flag and against those of others.

✳✳

On the third day, after the Opera performance, the two of them decided to break from the other tourists and head off for dinner themselves. Their tour bus would leave Lijiang the next morning.

They walked into a small restaurant. It was really just one room with a huge stove and steaming griddle surrounded by small tables and low plastic chairs. Evidently a popular place, almost every seat was occupied. Nevertheless, as though from out of nowhere, the proprietress quickly found them a table and chairs and returned to her stove to continue cooking.

"This is very traditional." Spring smiled at him, her chin resting on her hands.

They sat close to where the proprietress was flipping a steaming griddle of pancakes and fried vegetables.

"Not bad. Hello!"

He smiled at the group of waitresses who were hanging out in a group by the wall, ogling at him. The young girls in the restaurant were excited to see a foreigner. In this restaurant, most of the customers were elderly traders from the north, uncouth truck drivers and villagers looking to scrounge a cheap meal of noodles.

"Hello, Hello!" One of them bravely said, her chin thrust out defiantly.

"How are you?" he continued, looking at Spring, who frowned slightly.

"I am fine thank you. And YOU?" The girl with the chin smiled happily, pleased as punch at the chance to try out her English.

Her friends laughed and giggled. She took courage and defiantly came over. She poured hot tea into their glasses.

"Where you from?" she said, her eyes sparkling.

"I am just like you, from China too."

A look of confusion flashed over her face, but she quickly recovered.

"No. No." she stood primly as though at attention.

"OK, I am American."

"American is good." She replied, raising her thumb.

"Your English is very good. You are very smart and beautiful."

She gave a huge smile, blushed and giggled, then scurried back to the group of girls who plied her with questions about their conversation.

He turned to Spring, wondering why she had been silent. The smile on his face vanished when he saw her compressed lips and blazing eyes.

"What's wrong!"

She had expected him to at least understand. But that he didn't was beyond tolerable. She was now furious. And when she was furious she tended to internalize. Some people berate others. Some lash out physically. But she was the seething type. Her anger was like flowing lava, seeping slowly into amorphous places where it would harden and dash ships and break drills. Her face took on the expression of an ice queen.

"You don't know what's wrong? What's wrong with *you!*"

To tell him how insensitive he had been - how this very public flirting had humiliated her in public – was beneath her. She was a woman. He was a man. It was not her place to explain the basic respect a woman requires from her lover. But she went ahead and did just that.

"How could you talk to that woman that way, as though you want to screw her?" she still had an icy look and the red tinge around her tight lips revealed her unhappiness.

"What? What are you talking about? I was just having some fun."

"Chinese women are not like American women. When you talk and tell them how great they are and flatter them like that, they think you are serious."

"Why... You're kidding. Why that's silly! I was just being friendly."

"That's the way we are. And you did that with me sitting at the table with you. What do people think about me now!"

And she picked up her bag and walked out. Just like that. Embarrassed he placed some bills on the table, excused himself and followed after her. He could hear the sniggers and giggles that followed their retreating backs.

The incident rankled. Unlike him, she saw it as a major *faux pas.* It had for the first time revealed a part of him that she wanted to forget but couldn't. It was like the Sichuan Opera masks that appear and reappear in an instant, making the actors' faces a strobe of confusing dreams and mirages. She also realized her affection for him didn't blind her to his faults. And the faults were many. He was insular. He was perhaps incapable of trust. Like many smart men, he would calculate and intuit outcomes, then convince himself the outcome sprung from *trust.* By so doing, he was like a gambler, or a risk investment specialist, always banking on a low risk premium before he tossed the dice. He would use the right words when appropriate, correctly judging consequences, but intuitively, without understanding their deeper meaning. In another life, he might have been a superb politician, she sometimes thought, but now is now, here is here. She was not an intellectual but she knew there was love and then there was love. She was confused about her feelings but the idealist within her wanted a higher love, one untainted by small jealousies and petty putdowns. Their relationship definitely wasn't just friendship, she realized, since, after all, she was jealous. Love is blind, people say, but she wasn't. Perhaps, she mused, this love was simply not enough.

She remembered the one time her father had cheated on her mother. That day long long ago she had received a tearful phone call from her mother. Spring had at that time just arrived in Shenzhen.

"Bao Bei, Bao Bei, how could he? How could he?"

She would call her daughter Jewel (Bao Bei) whenever they shared something intimate.

"Ma, what is it…what happened?"

"I smelled the perfume…on his neck. He thought I wouldn't know."

"What perfume… who…"

"When he came back he went directly to the bathroom and showered. But he wasn't fast enough."

She was thunderstruck. For a few seconds she did not say anything.

"Father…you mean father…"

Her mother left Henan and came to stay with her in her little apartment. The father had come shortly afterwards, pleading and contrite. While the mother heaped abuse on him he had just stood there without a word, arms limply hanging by his side. Not a word of defense. Then, exhausted, his mother had rushed to her room to weep her eyes out. The father had quietly gone to the kitchen, prepared some food and remained there for the next two hours. He only came out to give his daughter his handkerchief.

"Give this to your mother."

And then he went back into the kitchen. The daughter couldn't see his face but his back was shaking. He stayed in a hotel and would dutifully come to the apartment three times a day to tend to them. For the next three weeks he did many household chores. He bought groceries and cooked for them. In time the older lady forgave him.

Her daughter, on the other hand, felt as if a hole had opened in her heart that would never be filled again.

Perhaps it was from that time that she decided she would never undergo what her mother had gone through. Her parents had the virtue of patience and the shackles of age. They would eventually reconcile. She was, on the other had, young and had time to choose. But she didn't want her future family to ever go through what she had gone through.

It seemed to Spring that they were an odd, unsuitable fit, but she didn't think, even then, of leaving him. She was vain for his attention, she admired his mind, they had slept together, and there was an undeniable emotional attraction that she just couldn't wave away with a burst of anger or a fancy pirouette or two.

They returned to the inn in silence and headed to their rooms. The rooms were located along an open corridor on the second floor. From the corridor one had an unhindered view of the cobbled street and surrounding buildings. The fresh breeze brushed against their faces and the sound of music drifted gently through the air. From over the railing one could see some of the local young women in traditional costumes dancing jigs. The music was coming from a gourd shaped flute called the *Hu Lu Sheng*. They moved slowly, almost as if they were swooning. Their hands swayed slowly over their heads, as though they were threshing wheat and hailing the moon in one smooth, graceful gesture. In the darkness of the plaza, lit only by a small fire that flickered its gold dust in the dry air, faint lights from the hotels and the dark purple sky overhead, they seemed like ghost dancers, involved in a ritual that stretched back thousands of years. It was one of those nights when the past and the present seem to collide and are swept up and discarded by thoughts of the future. In the gloaming everything seemed young and fresh and the air was thick with the heady smell of flowers. On such nights music revolves in one's head until, like a surprise, one realizes one is singing along with it. Yet this evening, as they stood on the terrace, brows furrowed and at a loss for words because words were not enough, they might as well have been on separate continents.

David turned to say something to her. He saw in an instant that she was very close and looking at him with something in her eyes that seemed like uncertainty and fear. He moved his lips to her almost without thinking, and it was in that instant that he brushed her lips with his that she turned away. She fumbled for her keys and said goodnight. Somewhat embarrassed but with the stinging feel of her touch on his lips he also mumbled something. She started to open her door. He did not understand this sudden anger and his own ambivalence. He was torn with a desire to hold her in his arms but also felt that this was not the time – or was it?

There was something almost spiritual in the air. He was terrified of losing her respect. He realized this fear was holding him back. He had the curse of thinking too much of consequences - for all his *joie de vivre* and devil may care attitude. He thought of consequences in greater detail than the actions that preceded them. 'You think too much!', an old girlfriend had once told him. He realized now how true this was and that until he let go and broke away from this tyranny of thought and caution he would forever be destined to skirt on the edge of ecstasy.

"I'll see you later"

He mumbled the words half heartedly. But she pretended not to hear. Her back was to him. He thought she hesitated for a minute as though to turn around and say to him *I love you. Come to me now and make passionate love to me. I forgive you all your mistakes and you forgive me mine.* But there was just silence. She silently closed the door and he was alone.

A few minutes later Spring heard a gentle knock on the door. She suspected it was David. She hung back and didn't open it. The next knock was louder and more insistent.

"Spring, let me in. I want to talk to you."

She relented and opened the door. He stood in the doorway, contritely, silently. She looked at him coldly.

"Well?"

"Can I come in?"

"No, you can *not* come in."

The moment she spoke she relented. She did want him to come in but she couldn't say it. He flinched visibly, as though wounded.

"What's wrong?"

"Ask your new Lijiang friend."

"Baby..."

"Don't say that!"

He looked at her. She was furious. A bright red glow spread over her cheeks.

"What the fuck is wrong with you!" he finally burst out.

He was shocked by his outburst. It was the first time he had cursed her. It felt good. It gave him a sense of power. He felt as though a barrier had been broken.

"What did you say?"

She couldn't believe what she had heard. *Who was this guy?* she thought. Something in her hardened. Repelled she stepped away. David tried to enter but she pushed him away without a sound. He felt the ice in her limpid eyes burn a hole through his face.

"Spring..." he tried to push his way in.

Or perhaps it was she recoiled from him too fast.

She felt what seemed like a sting on her neck and shoulder, as though from a blow. Then it was as though he was standing over her, his hands outstretched, his eyes wide open in a dumbstruck gaze. She realized she had fallen, or had been pushed, and was gasping, struggling to get up.

"Bab…Spring…"

"Get out!" she screamed, holding her shoulder as she raised herself up.

He stumbled towards the door. She slammed it shut behind him.

David stood alone on the corridor. The music now sounded harsh and the wind from the west seemed cooler than before. He wondered if it was raining.

The pain in her shoulder had gone but another remained. It was like a hard canker lodged deep in her belly, somewhere between her heart and the pit of her stomach. It would take only the slightest memory of the flash of anger that had swept over the two of them to resuscitate it. *He is not a bad person,* she thought. She remembered her mother's admonitions about infidelity and domestic violence.

"Chinese men beat their wives and sons. It's normal." Her mother had said.

Spring remembered how in the classic story *Dream of Red Mansions* the boy Bao Yu is beaten to senseless by his father who explains: *I am doing it for my son. It is for my son's education!* while tears stream down his face.

Spring's father had never laid a hand on his wife. *Maybe it's me. Perhaps I'm a bad woman*, she considered before quickly rejecting that thought. Deep inside she realized that something wrong had happened, that a hostile thing had punctured a hold in the smooth rhythm of their script, that the two of them had reached a watershed, something to do with betrayal, safety and a loss of trust.

In the confusion of emotions that rushed over her after David left she felt that she could forgive him. She nevertheless decided she would not make the first move, or even talk to him. It was not that she didn't want to hear from him. It was that she didn't know what she wanted or worse, what she might do. She also didn't want him to think she was an easy woman. *He probably hates himself now*, she thought. *Let the bastard suffer.*

✳✳

It was still early in the evening. She expected him to come back. She imagined he would beg her forgiveness. She would then be magnanimous and take his hand and forgive him. She lay on the bed in all her clothes and waited. She looked forward to escaping the grim confines of her hotel room. In spite of the warm wood of the inn the interiors were Spartan and cold. An enveloping gloom slowly washed over its cold façade. Spring shivered.

It was now half past eight and the enveloping darkness outside had not yet penetrated the hotel room where she was watching TV.

She wanted him to return. After their argument it was as though they had exposed a side of each other that they had not seen before. The side of him that she had seen, though thick with the potential for violence and conflict, was weaker than the gentler, poetic and caring side of him she had known. She half listened to the sounds outside, hoping that it was he. As the minutes ticked by she consoled herself. It would be a submission. It would be her victory. She would be magnanimous and forgive him. She suddenly spoke out loud.

"Where did he go?"

"I want to take a walk? Shall I come with you?"

She said the words out aloud. Then, realizing there was no one else in the room, she instinctively put her hand over her mouth and blushed. She said it again in her mind, as though it were an obligation.

He doesn't care. she told herself.

She shivered. She didn't know if it was from the cold wind that blew down from the mountains or came from the strong emotions within her.

She watched the TV and asked herself the question. *Why didn't you tell him what a bastard he is?* She looked at the TV. It was a music concert beamed from Beijing. Casts of thousands singing elaborately choreographed and patriotic songs paraded on a stage. Some well known actresses were lip-syncing (as is customary) some popular tunes. But she wasn't listening to the music.

It was now past ten in the evening and he still hadn't returned. She again looked out the opening in the center of the window. Under the elegant street lamps, dark scripted characters could be barely seen over some cafes and shops, some lit within, some dark. Always there was the faint sound of the gourd music in the background. On the TV a girl in a wheelchair was saying something to the presenter. Shots of audience members flashed across the screen. Some of the audience members were crying, their faces welled up with emotion.

"So your parents continued to support you?"

"Yes, and eventually I got into college."

"You tried and persevered. The doctors said you would die. What did your school teacher say after the operation.?"

They said something else, more people sobbed, and then the young girl's teacher came out onto the stage to a burst of applause.

But Spring was not listening. She was thinking about David.

Why hasn't he called? She looked anxiously at her cell phone. Rebecca had sent her one of meaningless emails, some joke about a guy with a large penis and a girl who farted. She smiled faintly. At other times she would have roared with laughter but this time it seemed meaningless to do so. She quickly sent a reply. She was hungry and felt the room was like a jail. Her mother had also sent her a small message but she one person she really wanted to hear from hadn't replied.

She finally sent David a short message. All her inhibitions had vanished. It was as though the preceding events had been a mirage, like the trembling air that creates sheens of water above dusty desert roads.

Are you coming or shall we meet tomorrow?

After a few minutes he replied. Her heart leaped.

Wait, wait.

So she waited. And waited. He didn't return that evening. Very late she eventually left the hotel and walked the dark streets looking for some place she could buy some instant noodles. She asked the proprietress, a middle aged lady in a polka dotted pajama suit, the price. She turned her swarthy face to the young girl

"What?"

She squinted and looked with some suspicion at her clean, expensive clothes. *What ridiculous earrings. The price is 2 Yuan but she surely can afford 3?* She thought to herself.

"3.5 Yuan."

"That much?"

Spring knew she was being duped but she didn't have energy to fight. She paid the money.

As she left the old woman shrugged to her husband behind the counter.

"Shenzhen?"

He nodded.

After she had returned she checked her cell phone again. He still hadn't called. She quickly ate her noodles and prepared for bed. The air-conditioner turned on and off. The room was very cold and she slept fitfully. She was no longer hungry but she felt abandoned. She would never tell him so. The direct approach foreigners take, particularly Americans - that wasn't her way. She was worried about him. Was he safe? Had something happened? She sent him several short messages and called his number.

No replies.
Nothing.

After they had argued David had wandered aimlessly around the hotel. He was nursing a huge sense of guilt. He felt he had diminished himself and in the process had lost her. *Perhaps it was meant to be this way*, he thought. When she texted him later he felt elated and yet disappointed, elated that she had made the first step, but sad because he now respected her less. He quickly replied. He did not want to return but couldn't tell her. He wanted to be alone.

In the distance he saw people grouped under a large streetlight. The large courtyard where they were standing was whitish orange in the faded evening light. As he came closer he noticed they were a group of women. Some were dressed in traditional costumes and they were lilting back and forth to music, their hands linked in a ring. This was the same group he and Spring had heard from the balcony.. Scarlet, blue and purple skirts merged with jeans and T shirts. They were so happy in their tranquil motions they seemed to pulse like a fish's mouth, ever opening, ever closing, drinking in air and giving out a rich, silent energy. The women were of all ages. A woman passing by stopped, looked at them for a few moments and joined in. A middle aged lady with kind eyes smiled at him and held out her hand. Wordlessly, he took her hand and joined the ring. He could not dance well and at first felt awkward. But when he saw no one was paying attention to his clumsy motions he started to relax.

They danced like this for almost an hour. Perhaps it was longer, but he didn't care. Meanwhile the sky grew darker and the moon slid across the sky like a drop of mercury slowly rolling over a black marble slate. As he looked at the moon and the mountains it seemed as though they looked down on him with a tremendous compassion. He thought of the poem Spring had taught him:

When I look up I see the bright moon
When I look down I remember my family

A wave of sadness passed over him. He remembered his mother and wanted so much to talk to her. He remembered the kind face of the man who had become his step father and who had taken him as his own son. *Where were they now?* he wondered. It was probably afternoon back in Nairobi. Mom was probably shopping for food and her husband was taking his afternoon walk at Parklands. He also missed Zhen Rui. Someone had given the boy a mobile phone and they now communicated often by SMS. While most of the messages were about scheduling when to meet he now remembered the one that the boy had sent to him during a long trip a while back.

Teacher, Thanks for always supporting me and teaching me to play piano. I am so thankful to you. You are not only my teacher, but you are also my best friend. Don't worry, I will study very hard. I will not let you down.

The letter had been so mature and honest, he thought. *What had Zhen Rui been afraid of?* Then he realized that the boy was bound to him and he to the boy. He had not realized how a separation of a few weeks would leave such a strong impression. He realized the boy was afraid the man would leave him. How could Zhen Rui think he would let him down?

He broke away gently from the group. He followed the small river that runs through the Old City.

"If you follow this you will never get lost.", the proprietor had told them, "It always leads to the Old City entrance."

Indeed, soon David found himself at the main gate of the Old City. He headed towards the faint bulge of the mountains. He took no note of what street he was on. Above him the moon was so large and radiant it seemed to be dripping milk into a sheet of black ice. Before him a broad road stretched in a straight line across the level plain. In contrast, small single storied houses and shops lay along it in orderless clumps. Solid and liquid waste was visible, spilling out of hidden corners. The rusted corrugated roofs looked like the broken wings of dismembered metal birds. Occasionally shards of broken tiles would be scattered across the tops of the roofs and on the sidewalks. An old one story schoolhouse lay a little ahead to his right, flanked by two scraggly trees. The school was constructed of stones and straw. Beams of rotting wood leaned against its stone walls. The front door was missing, exposing a dark hole. On a lone pink plastic swing that was bent at a sharp angle a little girl in a parka lazily drifted back and forth. A teenager, perhaps her sister, stood by and from time to time gave her a reassuring push. Other than the three of them the area was deserted.

David remembered how much of China was still poor and how cities like Shenzhen and Shanghai displayed only the brighter, more optimistic parts of China.

"400 to 500 million people lifted from poverty in just thirty years. What country can match that?" One of his Shenzhen friends had told him.

David had retorted that according to experts, China still had over 130 million people in China living on less than a dollar a day.

Yet in this broken wasteland, the road gleamed. Probably built or paved in the last year it symbolized, like the TV in the peasant's hut, the ineluctable opening of China. No matter how poor and forsaken a village might seem, there was always the *new*, a hospital, a school, a road, even a café, something that had not been there months or years before, but was now part of the great evolution of China.

"Mr David, where are you going?"

The voice came from behind him. Startled, he looked back. It was one of the men from the tour. A pudgy, gregarious man, he had wanted to meet David but had been to shy to approach him while in the group. He had been traveling with a young woman whom David remembered vividly because that first day she had worn jeans with a large hand printed over her behind. She probably didn't know the meaning or thought no-one else knew. She didn't speak English (he had tried to strike up a casual conversation), was young and constantly talked to Spring about the bright yellow jeep her boyfriend would buy her. As for her boyfriend, he was a rich car salesman from Guangzhou. In his mid forties he had the look of a man whose life has been spent trying to make lots of money and now feels that pleasure and young women can compensate for the drooping lips, sagging skin and wispy remnants of hair brushed carelessly across his scalp. He didn't have much interest in David but Spring attracted him, like a stringed ball attracts a cat. She had no interest in him, giving him a cold stare when he had smiled at her. He had gravitated towards David in the way that a moth avoids flying directly into the light but circles around and eventually settles on a cooler surface. But he wouldn't approach the American in public. He was afraid he would be rebuffed and lose face. But this time they were alone and there was no risk. The foreigner also looked downcast and lonely, and this gave him more confidence.

"Just walking."

"Where are you goin? Is your wife with you?"

"Heading back to the hotel."

David didn't correct him. He liked the sound of the word *wife* but then remembered Spring and was at once despondent.

"Come with me. I'll treat you to a beer."

He thought of heading back to Spring. Then he remembered her angry face and his guilt returned. *Why go back now?* She had texted him but he wouldn't be rushed. He wouldn't be cowed by her.

"No, I'm fine thanks."

"Please, let me treat you."

He refused once again, but he knew that the offer was real. In China generally offers from strangers to eat or drink out are refused as a matter of course. Foreigners sometimes accept the offers the first time with alacrity, to the exasperation of the other person. However, most Chinese politely decline the second or the third time and then, if they really want to hang out, accept. He accepted.

"Where?"

"I don't know, but there must be a place close by."

Most of the restaurants were closed or closing, but a seafood restaurant was open even at this late hour.. Two hostesses stood outside in their long tight scarlet *qi pao* dresses The harsh neon streetlamps overhead seemed to soak up the life from everything below, making their white faces look like pale bloodless heads bobbing in the haze. Day after day, like vampires in a vigil, they would stand in their totem like positions for hours. Their hands were gently clasped above their bellies to make a square of their arms and elbows. They beckoned passer bys with calls of '*Huang ying guang ling!*' (Welcome Honored Guest). Next to them were racks of glass tanks filled with frothy, bubbling water. Inside were fish, squid, eels and various other sea creatures. David turned to his companion.

"I'm sorry but what's your name?"

"Hely."

"Harry?"

"Hely."

"How do you spell that?"

"H-E-L-Y."

"Oh, *Hely.*"

David wondered how Chinese people got their English names. Sometimes they were so bizarre. There was the time he met a girl called Himen. Then there was the man called Botom. He couldn't forget the male restaurant host called Merry. A friend once told him these names were often casually selected by their foreign friends. Often the spelling would be poor and the Chinese would fiddle with a letter of two to make it sound more appealing. For example many women didn't like the name Ashley because of the sound *Shi* which means excrement in Chinese.

"This place is so far from the sea. And there are no nearby lakes. How do they survive? Does it make enough money?"

"Of course, look there."

Hely pointed to a spot next to the entrance where on a small stand next to the fish tanks was a rack filled with car tires.

"What have car tires got to do with food?"

"You don't understand, my friend, in China, it doesn't matter, as long as you can sell and make money."

When they were seated inside he went on.

"Have you heard of *Yan Shen?*"

"No, what is it?"

"Yan shen is about using your face to communicate."

"What do you mean?"

"Big bosses use it all the time. They don't say anything. They just move their eyes. At once the people around them know what they want."

"But if there are many things on a table, say lots of fruit, and he looks at all of them, how can they possibly know which one he wants."

"They just know. Maybe his eye looks a little longer at some fruit. No one teaches you how. We Chinese just know."

"I'd love to know how."

"Many foreigners think they just need to know Chinese. Yet in China many things are understood and cannot be explained. *Gang Bei!*"

They toasted each other.

"Show me an example."

Hely hailed a caddy filled with different foods. Barely glancing at one of the dishes on the lower cart and without saying a word, he let the waitress know what he wanted. David shook his head.

"That's amazing."

"You see. You foreigners are so direct. All of us understand what you are thinking. When you walk down the street and see something you like, you don't need to say anything. The street person already knows what you want. And today, for example...when I saw you on the street, I knew you did not want to go back to the hotel."

David nodded. The other man nodded sympathetically.

"Women?"

"Well...Chinese women."

"I never have problems."

"You and your wife seem to get along well."

"That's not my wife!"

Looking at the foreigner's puzzled face he went on

"You do not understand. In China one is married and one also has many girlfriends, maybe even a second wife in Hong Kong or Taiwan. It is different in America. These girls in Shenzhen want to have a good time. Some nice dinner, maybe karaoke, a rent and clothes money each month..."

"Don't they care if you're married?"

"They know but they don't care...they just want a good time."

David was astonished at his brazenness. But his face was serious. Then again, he thought, Chinese men are remarkably good at hiding their feelings. He had much to learn from them.

"So I met this girl. And she is only 18, and that is what I like most of all. She helped me care for my father one day at home. And she gave me her phone number. Then a few days later I sent her a short message. Then I said would she like to go out for dinner. And she said OK. So a few days later, she took a train to Shenzhen and we had a very nice dinner but she didn't let me kiss her. I spent over 500 Yuan! A few days later when she came again to Shenzhen. I took her out and we decided to stay the night in a hotel. It was a first class hotel. But she insisted on having separate rooms. But she let me kiss her and let me hold her breasts a bit. 2000 Yuan. *2000!*"

"Man, you blow your money on the babes. That's why they don't let you go all the way. You have to hold back a bit."

"Yes, but she was so young I couldn't resist. But I spent so much money on her! Now this other women - *she's* a different story. She's all right."

"The one you're with now?"

"Yes, you have to search long and hard for the right woman!"

David nodded sympathetically. The other man went on, his face gloomy. Then, as if remembering something, his face darkened.

"And then there was another one. I met this TV broadcaster and flew her to Jamaica. We stayed in a five star hotel, went swimming, made love, ate expensive food and drank champagne. And then when we got back to Shenzhen she never called me again. I must have spent over 5000 American dollars on her!"

Then his face brightened and he lifted up the glass.

"That was then. Out with the old, in with the new! Gang Bei!"

They toasted each other again and again. Then the other man impulsively said,

"Now you're my friend. We have drunk together and you are now my GOOD friend."

But David just smiled. He did not know why many Chinese men had to drink themselves to a stupor to prove friendship. He prided himself on his ability to swallow liquor without becoming drunk. It was as though he would get a brief rush, and then his sense of equilibrium would return. He saw another man at another table fold over in a drunken faint. A slight feeling of contempt coursed through him. *They are so weak. It's so easy to control and yet they cannot?* But then he second-guessed himself. *What is weak about letting yourself go, revealing your weaknesses? Isn't it the mark of a strong man to show his flaws, come what may?'* And in that instant he realized that his weakness was not that he couldn't free himself from himself, but that he had such limited means to do so. His way was not the way of beer or of women. It was something much loftier, much higher. In his mind the great dictum of Keats

The Truth shall set you free

Had, for many others, become

Beer shall bring you happiness

Now, as if in a eureka moment he realized

Music shall set you free.

At that moment he longed for his piano, that marvelous metal beast of the thousand claws and hammers that ripped one's soul apart and stitched them together in ever changing tapestries of sound. The incongruity of his thoughts and his circumstances struck him. He was stuck here in a seafood restaurant in the middle of a desert, next to a pile of price marked tires, rejected by his girlfriend, drinking beer with a stranger who nevertheless professed deep friendship, and thinking only of his piano. And he remembered the sick child who also had found a way to be free, to fly beyond the walls of the orphanage, into a rarefied space where dreams and music intersect. For the boy hope was like a sphinx - many times burned, and in its latest incarnation, revived as the muse. They were both dreamers and prisoners locked in their own jail cells, and art was their sole key to the outside. For the older man, love was a quirky thing, as powerful as his music, but unreliable. His piano was a constant. It was his plane of meditation, his cone of solitude and peace, from whence he could clearly see the world. But he put aside these thoughts, comfortable in his new awareness of himself, and lifted the tumbler high.

"Gang Bei!."

⁎⁎

The next morning when she woke up she remembered the previous evening. She had already experienced this empty feeling in her stomach. She had had a broken heart before. It had been one of the worst experiences in her life. She looked at her phone, as though it held something hopeful, an elixir of rejuvenation. There was a message from Rebecca. No other. *Perhaps something had happened to him*, she thought. *There must be a reason. He would have called me or contacted me somehow. He couldn't have ignored me.* In her heart of hearts, she realized that unless he had a very good excuse, they had crossed the Rubicon. Perhaps...perhaps he had been with another woman.

She didn't trust him. All sorts of little hates and misgivings were now percolating to the surface. He was selfish. He didn't care about anyone other than himself, but she had allowed herself to fall for him. To him, she was probably just another conquest. She hated herself for her weakness. *Weak.Weak. Weak.* She despised herself for her vulnerability. But to all intents and purposes, no one could have seen her beautiful, placid face and sensed the roiling within. She got up from the bed, dressed as usual (in a stunning dress that her aunt had long ago given her as a birthday present), and prepared her bags to leave with the bus. They would reach Shangri La today.

She knocked on his door.

"It's time to go. The bus will be leaving in a few minutes."

Her voice was mechanical. She didn't hear his reply. She didn't even know if he was behind the closed door. She did not care. She was already on her way to the lobby.

"Where's your friend?" the tour guide asked him.

"He's coming."

Spring was one of the last to enter the bus. Everybody was waiting for them.

"Where's your boyfriend?" someone asked.

"He's having fun somewhere!" another man laughed.

His companions burst into laughter. Spring's face turned a deep red. They waited a few more minutes in silence and some murmurs and whispering. The tour guide came up the aisle to her.

"I think you should ask your friend to come. We have to leave."

She stood up, her mind in a daze. She was furious at him. It was a black, terrible anger that seeped through every fiber of her body. She stumbled out of the bus, avoiding the stares of the other passengers. The tour guide went with her, barely keeping up with Spring, who resented her presence. It was as though she was back in school and she had done something to bring shame upon the school.

They reached his door. The guide knocked on the door. There was no reply. Spring knocked.

"David, we must go."

There was still no reply. Her anger turned to puzzlement. She knocked harder.

"David, we MUST go. Are you in?"

They both hurried to the front desk. The women on duty looked at their anxious faces.

"Excuse me. My American friend is not opening his door. Can you help?"

"Oh the foreigner. I'm sorry, I should have told you. He left this morning. He was in a hurry and could not stay."

Then seeing Spring's shocked face she added,

"Don't worry. He took care of the bills. Yours too."

"All around us people were screaming and running around like headless chickens. The street was empty. I was saying where are the police? Where is the ambulance? No-one came. Bwana, they wanted the Old Man dead! Several minutes later the police and the ambulances came."

- From David's father's journal

ZHEN RUI

The morning after David left Spring, she was in shock. Her skin tingled and her soul burned with an icy, cold fire. It was a slow burn, seeping through every pore of her body, ineluctable, without pity. He hadn't called her. He had left her alone in this strange place. *What did I do to him? Why has he hurt me so?* She did not know why he had not called her. However, to those around her she appeared impassive.

"I see, did he leave any message? Is there a bill?' She had asked the receptionist, casually, as she would order a cup of tea. As though seeing herself from afar, like a disembodied spirit, she wondered how she managed to maintain this sense of distance. Even now she was like the placid eye at the center of the storm."

"No. The bill is paid in full."

Spring didn't seem to hear. She just stood at the counter looking at something on the wall. It was a kitschy painting of a huge dragon flying over an impossibly blue lake. *I've seen this picture somewhere before*, she thought.

"Are you coming?"

The tourist guide asked again, impatiently, with the vaguest hint of a threat. Spring snapped back to attention. With a start she realized she was crying. She quickly wiped her eyes with her hand. She reached into her bag and grabbed her sunglasses. She dumbly nodded her head. Inside she was humiliated, angry, and sad — like all the four seasons co-existing in one turbulent maelstrom. She quietly followed the other woman to the bus. She would defend him from the taunts of the fellow Chinese tourists, but she felt she was changing no minds, and was deceiving herself.

Hely would see her despondent face and when he did not see David he realized he had an opportunity to make inroads with this attractive woman. He would not mention anything about the previous night. Instead he would spend the rest of the trip trying to ingratiate himself to her. As it happened she got so tired of listening to him she moved to another seat, leaving him to cope with his ignored and irate girlfriend.

Outside the sound of traditional music floated through the air from the nearby town square. She had always wanted to hear the songs of Lijiang. A woman was singing a beautiful, plaintive folk song. Sunlight bounced off flecks of golden dust suspended in the cool air, as though dancing with the sad, rich and powerful tune. The voice was perpetually young and eternally wise. Spring didn't understand the words but she intuitively felt it was about happiness and loss, loneliness and love, permanence and change. Spring was in uncharted territory and was searching for a path to resolution and peace. There were no rules or signposts to guide her. In her solitude she would have to forge her own path. The Naxi woman might as well have been singing the lines from Swinburne.

The wind of change is soft as snow, and sweet
The sense thereof as roses in the sun,
The faint wind springing with the springs that run,
The dim sweet smell of flowering hopes, and heat
Of unbeholden sunrise; yet how long
I know not, till the morning put forth song.
Save his own soul he hath no star
And sinks, except his own soul guide

Some women are strong and reliant. They can take great hardship and abuse from their lovers, and bounce back up again, bruised but ready to lick the wounds and still love. She was not that type of person. She was fragile, like a china doll without soft packaging. David had wounded her and she felt she could not recover. The wound was deep and would fester for a long time. It was like a man's dashed honor - almost impossible to resuscitate and never again fully whole. She decided it was over. David was too self-absorbed. There was no earthly reason he couldn't have contacted her by now.

He had her number.

He knew it was the right thing to do. He must have been afraid. Or else he...If he had been hurt, even that was unforgivable. He had still left the hotel without a mention. Cold logic consumed her. It was as though she instinctively knew they were incompatible, but she just had to prove it to herself, to rationalize it.

The song continued. She had stopped hearing it. She stepped into the bus. It was time to move on.

The previous evening David had drunk like there was no tomorrow. After he had emptied several bottles a dullness seeped through his body. He wondered how Chinese workers survived these daily beer binges without succumbing. He was dizzy. The table was spinning. His companion's ruddy face had become a huge scarlet mask, from which spittle dribbled onto the table. They were the only customers left in the restaurant. They both felt a warm glow inside that seemed to grow with time. They were reluctant to leave. Hely suddenly looked accusingly at David.

"We Chinese don't respect foreign teachers. I tell you this frankly."

"No please, go on."

Behind the smiles and courtesies there was always the threat of sharp teeth and pointed claws. David instinctively braced himself.

"It's the women."

David nodded, a bemused smile on his face.

"They think you just want to sleep around with Chinese girls. And you lose respect. The best professions in China are business people. They have wealth and fame. But foreign teachers..."

"But that's all you give them! You make it very hard for them to get other jobs."

"What do you mean? There are many jobs in China. "

"I'll tell you. One of my friends is a brilliant engineer. He complains all the time that the Chinese only want him to teach their children English. He loves China and wants to live here. What choice does he have? "

"That's because Chinese people are smarter. They also work harder. Westerners are lazy. They don't know what hard work is. "

"They have different approaches to life, but they aren't necessarily lazy."

"Chinese people know what it's like to be poor. One day we will be very rich. We will be a great country. Can you imagine what it will be like when we succeed? It will be because we work harder than you. You want art, and music, an easy life. Americans want TV and long vacations.... "

Hely's voice trailed off. He felt he had said too much and was embarrassed. But he was more irritated by the other's silence. It was as though these foreigners looked down upon him.

But David didn't reply. He just uncommittedly nodded his head. The beer was soaking in and a dull lethargy was stealing over him. In his dazed condition something was ticking in his head, a recognition of some truth in what the other man had said. The Chinese were no doubt among the thriftiest and most hard working people he had ever met. In so many streets, in so many cities, it seemed as if merchants were on steroids. In China the business of making money was more contagious than the flu. The Chinese are fond of saying that in emptiness there is substance, that falseness and truth co-exist, like *ying* and *yang*. But next to the *yang* of commerce was the *ying* of exploitation, environmental deprivation and a loss of quieter, simpler and more wholesome times - when one could read poems, practice calligraphy in one's spare time, even be with one's family instead of across the country working in a factory.

Glasses and bottles were scattered on the desk. The hostesses looked at them impassively from across the room, their hands nonchalantly by their sides. A buzzing feeling traveled up his legs. He swatted his leg, thinking there was a bug traveling up his pants.

"What's wrong?"

"You're fucking me man."

The Chinese man burst into peels of laughter

"Fuck, fuck."

He cursed without conviction, as though the four-letter word was being read from a dictionary. It was a low toned curse, out of sync with the atmosphere of beer and joviality. David wondered why it was so hard for Chinese men to curse in English. Whenever they cursed it seemed somewhat apologetic, even with a hint of fear, as though they were charting a road through a territory without rules or laws. Indeed, in a land where saving face was the modus operandi, such curses were like stone axes in place of fine scalpels, just as to foreigners, the tools of Chinese etiquette could be like tea cups in a gorilla's hands.

The buzzing feeling had stopped.

"Why are you a teacher?"

The other man said it casually, but in a thoughtful way.

"Because I thought it was an easy way to start understanding China, through its children."

Hely laughed.

"No, that's not true. You only are looking for Chinese girls."

He snickered and went on.

"I'll tell you a secret. Chinese people look down on you foreign teachers you know. They think you just want to sleep with Chinese girls. The job is easy for you, like a vacation."

He took a swig. David was half listening. His leg was buzzing again. He answered with a note of irritation.

"Maybe you're right. The job is easy... sometimes. I also like Chinese women, but why not? If you were in America maybe you would like American women too. "

"Yes, but they wouldn't like me. You know..."

"Why?"

"You know why!"

"No I don't!"

"I'm not big enough! Maybe it's different for you! But I'll tell you a funny story. I made love to a foreigner once. She was Russian, you know. Big tits. Very pretty. I paid a lot of money and she was very nice. But when we got to the bedroom I couldn't hold back. That's right. I tell you, she was so fantastic and pretty. Only 5 minutes after we entered the room. What a waste of money! I was so embarrassed. "

David laughed. He took no offense. Hely laughed too, but with some embarrassment.

The buzz was now annoying David. He had an image of a vibrator traveling towards his crotch.

"What the fuck are you doing?" he said to the server, who gingerly stepped out of his way.

"It's your phone man! It's your phone! " The server pointed to David's trouser leg, where he had squirreled away his cell phone.

Sure enough his cell phone was ringing and buzzing. He picked it out of his pocket. It was from Shenzhen. He flipped open the lid.

"David, David, is it you?"

He recognized Mr Ma's voice.

"Yes, who is ...Mr Ma!"

His mind snapped back to attention.

"David, I'm sorry to call you so late. It's Zhen Rui. He is very sick. They think he is going … He wants…"

Through the haze and dizziness, his heart jumped. It was as though a cold blast had tunneled though the phone into his head and gripped his stomach. He was now very sober.

"What's wrong? What happened? "

"He had a relapse. He was OK yesterday when I saw him. The doctors say he was reading and then he couldn't breathe. He is now on a respirator but very weak. "

David didn't say anything. His mind was trying to digest the information.

"Hello, David. Are you there? "

"Yes, I'm listening. Please go on."

"They think he will not last the night. But he asked for you. "

David was already on his way out the door, Hely looking after him with a silly, befuddled look.

"I'm coming."

With a quick farewell to a flustered and confused Hely he jumped in a taxi and sped back to the hotel.

At the hotel he had a very cold shower and quickly packed his things. He would call Spring later. He checked out, took care of both their bills and took a taxi for the 2-hour ride to the airport. It was 4 in the morning when he got into Kunming. The 2-hour flight to Shenzhen left at 5am. He barely had paid for the ticket and checked his bags when he had to board. Just before he boarded he tried to call Spring but there was no signal.

Maybe I'm out of range. Anyway it's probably too late. She'll be sleeping he thought. He thought of sending her a text message but decided things could wait until he was back in Shenzhen later that morning. By then she'd be awake.

✳✳

It was 8 in the morning.

David hated hospitals. They reminded him of weakness and decay, and the failures in his own life. They were a symbol of pain and desperation, a scab on the face of an otherwise generally reasonable universe. Above all, they represented the weaknesses and frailties that forever would lurk in others and in himself. He remembered long ago how his mother had one day hurriedly woken him up.

"Are we going to school?"

"No, not today. Brush your teeth and let's go. "

His mother's face was strained, as though she were shouldering a large invisible burden. But the boy didn't worry. After all, her burdens were not his own. That's what mothers were for - to carry one's burden. In any case they were not going to school and that pleased him to no end.

They had taken a taxi to Nairobi hospital, the largest in the city. In a crowded ward he saw the broken body of his father. Surrounded by the bustle of visitors and patients his father's bloody bandages and crooked body was splayed out for everyone to see. The car accident had almost killed him. By now the odor of formaldehyde and disinfectant had replaced the smell of Tusker Label beer.

"How are you, boy?" His father's voice was so weak the boy had to listen hard.

He refused to directly look at his father. From the periphery of his vision he saw a black object shrouded in whiteness.

"OK."

The boy's tone was curt, almost angry. He did not know why he was here. He would rather be back in school. He was ashamed to see this man. He did not know why he had to be part of this scene. He was tired of grandiose, cataclysmic, debilitating, histrionic, humiliating and overbearing scenes. The man didn't care anyway. He might as well be greeting himself for all the boy knew.

"Make sure you keep studying."

He tried to laugh but it was painful. The sound that emerged was weak, like dry paper dragged over bamboo sticks. How different from that confident, deep baritone that had commanded both of them. The mother looked on grimly with an *I told you* so look. The boy took her hand and whispered,

"Let's go."

But she wouldn't go. Her eyes were red and her face was flushed. He looked at his mother and father. She was so pink. He was so black. Compared to his broken body she was so strong and together. They looked so different, so *abnormal*. And yet they were his parents. When he saw her red eyes he felt angry at her too. *How can she be so weak? Everyone can see?* He thought. The African faces around them in the ward looked dumbly at the three of them. How he hated those stares, those wide-eyed, sullen images of accusation. He remembered other times her face had been flushed and angry; when she had been beaten, and when he was beaten and she tried to defend him.

The father rolled over on his side and tried to say something else to the boy but he was too weak. The boy sensed that he was ashamed, but he didn't care. He just wanted to leave this theatre of pain and humiliation, these scenes of shattered bones, lost dreams and broken people.

"Let's go Mum."

This time he said it more insistently and tugged her hand. She looked at him in the eye, gave a bittersweet smile, and quietly said,

"Say goodbye to your father."

For many years David had banished that scene to the back of his memories. Now, seeing the clean white sheets and breathing in the inescapable odors of a busy hospital, all the details of that meeting surged to the front of his thoughts. His father's physical weakness and mortality had been exposed. His affair with alcohol and family battles had led to this. He had been like a baby on that hospital bed, weak and vulnerable. David the man now wished that David the boy had had the courage to go up to his father and say:

"You and I will forever be apart but I forgive you."

What would he have said? How would he have replied? How liberating that dialogue might have been, David thought. Now an adult, David didn't hate or blame his father. Nor did he love and admire him. He realized he was just human, although a vaguely defined man. He had sought a love of sorts and been denied it – perhaps because he had been unable to offer it. This saga of unrequited love in David's family had slashed a great scarlet welt across the canvas of his father's story. David was now asking himself what was the value of brilliance without humanity or passion without commitment? David wondered if he would ever answer any of these questions. He felt there was so much he didn't know about this man and perhaps never would.

It was the same hospital and the same ward he had visited before when Zhen Rui was ill. This time it seemed there were less children than before. The heart ventilators quietly stood like white pillars beside the beds and the electronic eyes of the monitors flashed their cryptic red characters above the quiet prone bodies beneath. The metal beds were neatly arrayed about 4 or 5 to a wall. Except for the children, everyone wore gauze caps to cover their heads and feet. One child lay sideways on his bed, kicking his feet and silently opening and closing his mouth, like a fish out of water. David recognized Zhen Rui immediately. His small figure lay straight and still on the bed, a white gauze bandage covering his eyes. It was the Maasai bracelet on his thin arms that drew David's attention.

This time David viewed the hospital differently, as a place of people who were trying to save lives. And more than anything he wanted them to save the life of this boy. The strong antiseptic odor and bright neon seemed less invasive now. He forgot about Spring, about Lijiang, and about the orphanage. When he entered the ward the nurses and doctors seemed to flit across his consciousness like disembodied ghosts. He steeled himself and headed to the boy's side.

Zhen Rui was used to pain. Ever since he was born it had been part of his DNA. At such times he would find a place in the back of the orphanage by the stairs and the toilets to be alone. Once someone had found him doubled up on the floor. He didn't remember that time. But recently the pain was excruciating. It seemed as though there was a great weight on his chest. He would feel cold and shiver. The pain was amplified by the public nature of his treatment. He did not like people to see him like this. He could not care for himself. Others did it for him. Sometimes they did not help the pain. Sometimes they did. But always there was that flip flop feeling in his chest, as though there were a great fish jumping within him, trying to escape the confines of his small body. The medicine the doctors had given him had helped a little. Nowadays he was very weak. He would come in and out of consciousness. One time he heard faint sounds of music. He couldn't tell where it was coming from. Perhaps it was from a radio or TV further down the hospital corridor. It could have been imagined. He instinctively moved his fingers. He wanted to touch the piano. How he missed his piano!

"It makes me happy." he said to Mr Ma.

A few hours later someone had brought him a small electronic keyboard. It was light and it helped him relax. He missed the black wood and metal *Pearl River* upright piano he had grown used to, but even this small keyboard helped him reduce the pain.

Mr Ma was sitting by his side on a small stool. He stood up to greet David. Mr Ma's face was thinner than David remembered. The skin around his lips was tight and lent them a pinched look, like one who is scrounging within himself for the energy to continue life's mundane and not so mundane duties.

The boy rolled about on his bed, weakly, like an exhausted creature thrashes on a beach for the last time. The voices of Mr Ma and David floated in and out of his consciousness. They seemed very far away. Their voices were disembodied and hard to understand. *Congenital heart disease. Very worried. Too weak to operate. Mr Ma crying. Crying. Crying.*

He heard David's voice and weakly called out. At once he saw the man's dark swarthy face looming above him. He felt him gently touch his hands.

"I'm here Zhen Rui. How are you son?"

"*Lao Shi*, where did you go?"

"I was with a friend far from here."

"I thought...I thought you left me." the boy said, his voice barely audible.

He held David's hand tightly. David suddenly remembered the big black eyes of the baby whose fingers had gripped his so tightly that first time he arrived at the orphanage. His body shuddered involuntarily.

"*Lao Shi*, I'm afraid. I feel cold and I cannot see."

"Don't worry Zhen Rui. I'm here. You'll get better soon."

Zhen Rui saw a white hazy light above him that seemed to warm the gauze wrapped about his eyes. He thought it was so welcoming and beautiful. David's voice flowed in and out of his consciousness.

"Flying."

The boy muttered again.

"Flying."

He imagined himself on the wings of a bird soaring over a vast landscape of trees. Their autumn foliage was a mix of golden flakes and green carpeting laid across broad mountain ranges with snow capped peaks in the distance. Just like the pictures he had seen in the book his American friend had given him.

Zhen Rui died that morning. David remembered the time because the doctor called it out just before Mr Ma started sobbing. 10.31.

When they covered the child's thin, frail body with a white sheet his arm dangled from under the sheet. David dumbly looked at the Masaai bracelet that was still on his wrist. The ruby red beads were glowing under the harsh gaze of the neon lights. The bracelet fell on the ground with a harsh clatter. He leaned down to pick it up and saw something under the bed. He pulled out two flowers, one red, and one blue. They were examples of the traditional *bu hua* style that uses simple metal wire and colored paper to form delicate, lifelike artificial flowers. He looked up in consternation at Mr. Ma, who was sitting beside him, his head in his hands. Mr. Ma looked up. Seeing the flowers, his eyes lit up.

"Oh, those were Zhen Rui's. He made them the last time you came to the hospital. He wanted to give them to you but couldn't find them."

As the nurses gently set aside the Roland keyboard David felt the cool wind that entered the open window from the direction of the South China Sea. *Strange, it's hot today*, he thought. Then he realized his cheeks were wet with tears. It will rain soon, he thought.

The passing away of a child is an unnatural thing. Like a great tree shrinking into a leaf or water flowing up a mountain. When the child has particular promise to give the world it becomes an obscene event. The scales of justice, if they ever exist, are spun in all directions. Those left behind grope for meaning where there is none to be had. What is worse is that nature and God, are not necessarily evil. They are much worse than evil. They are downright indifferent. David had never believed in God, nor had he disbelieved in His existence. He was Jewish by birth only and proud of it. A secular Jew he was nonetheless a spiritual agnostic who had long waited for proof of God's existence. Now the scientist within found proof by negation. It took only Zhen Rui's death to turn him from an agnostic to an atheist. A thousand theorems and miracles might validate the existence of God. But it would only take one awkward, contradictory cog in the hubbub of life to disprove Him. He had inwardly prayed the child would live. Now that his prayer hadn't been answered, he felt like a weak, gullible fool.

Afterwards whenever he heard the sound of the pianos they had used together, he would see the boy's tousled hair and those huge spade-like hands grasping the keyboard like a boy grabs the handlebars of a bicycle the first time he careens down the road by himself, elbows akimbo and knuckles white as ash. He would remember the boy's talent. Mostly he would remember that sweet smile that was touched with the scent of angels. How could such a blend of passion, gentleness and skill just vanish into the ether?

He remembered how, a long time ago, he had asked a catholic priest the same question. The priest, a hulking old Irishman with balding wisps of hair and the lope of a gentle bear, had smiled quizzically. "They don't just disappear, you know. God has a plan. These souls are still here, around us." He didn't remember how he had answered, but at that time he had felt somewhat comforted.

So he comforted himself with the thought that Zhen Rui was still somewhere around, like one whose intellect disproves but whose soul rebels. As one grows older, one tends to become more skeptical and bitter. Life seems harder than it used to be, and dreams fall by the wayside. Sometimes the spark of hope and the stuff of dreams are still within, but they need a gentle hand to coax them forth. The hand can be love, ambition, even hate and fear. In the past he had found music to be its own momentum and justification. When he made music it was as though there was no goal and no cause. It was a state of perfect balance. Everything was as it should be. But now, after Zhen Rui's death, even the music he coaxed from the small fingers of orphanage students had a grating sound. He would play for himself and the pain of the boy's passing would abate temporarily. He continued teaching but it was different than before, as though something was missing. Bit by bit, his students fell away. He was driven and sometimes harsh with them,. He expected much but they were looking for something else from him, something he could not give them. After a few months he stopped visiting them.

That first day he arrived in Shenzhen David broke away from Zhen Rui's bed for a few moments and remembered Spring's text messages. He called her number. At the same time Spring saw her mobile phone light up her heart skipped a beat. Not knowing Zhen Rui's situation, Spring pondered whether to answer but, remembering the humiliation of the past few days, she held back. She reasoned that since she was with the other tourists in the bus their discussion wouldn't be private. Inwardly she wanted desperately to talk to him but was too proud to admit it – bus or no bus. She turned off the phone.. She would turn it back on later. She needed time to think.

Despite his blinding and over-riding concern for Zhen Rui David now regretted he hadn't called her earlier. He thought back to his actions and realized how rash he had been. A cold terror swept over him. Spring's abrupt response seemed to confirm his fear. *What have I done*, he thought? Although his first preoccupation had been with the boy, he tore himself away to go to Spring's apartment. He was sure her father would still be at Spring's place and perhaps might convey a message from David.

The older man looked surprised to see David. He didn't ask him in. He saw the man's disheveled clothing and nervous eyes and knew something was wrong, perhaps terribly wrong.

"What, why are you here? I thought you were…" he asked.

"There was an emergency. I had to come back to Shenzhen alone. I had to leave suddenly and I have been trying to reach Spring. Is she OK? Can you contact her?"

The father only heard the words come back to Shenzhen alone. At once alarmed, the father wanted to seize David by the throat but held back, his tight lips barely masking his growing anger.

"Where is she? Who is looking after her now?"

"She is still in Lijiang."

"Can't you call her yourself.?"

"I tried but…"

"But what…"

"She isn't answering my calls."

Spring's father nodded his head. He wanted to immediately call Spring but not in front of the *lao wai*.

"I see."

David was about to say something when the other man interrupted.

"Why?"

"Why what?"

"Why won't she take your call?"

David didn't say anything. He realized then that the father wouldn't help him, even pass on a message. His voice mechanical, he continued.

"Can you phone her to tell her to call me?" David finally blurted.

The father frowned. He now understood it was probably a lovers' quarrel. He nodded his head slightly and mumbled something. In calmer times David might have realized that a *no* in China can be a *yes*, and a *yes* many times means a *no*. He thought it was a nod and relaxed. Eager to be away from this man whose tight and angry lips resembled those of his daughter in her worst moments, he nodded regretfully and left.

Spring's father called Spring immediately after he closed the door.

"*Ba*, what's wrong?"

He was relieved to hear her voice. He wondered how she always knew there was a problem even before he said a word.

"Where are you?"

"Lijiang. Of course Lijiang. What's the problem?"

She sounds fine, he thought. *Better not to say too much.*

"I was just a little worried."

"Worried! About what?"

"Is everything OK?"

"Of course everything is OK." Spring could barely disguise the slight tremor in her voice.

"How's your friend, David?"

"He's fine." she said cheerily.

"Your voice sounds different. Have you been crying. If it is him…"

"I'm fine. Listen the bus is arriving, we have to go. Give Ma my love. Bye."

Spring understood her parents. She knew that her father had something serious he wanted to discuss with her but for some reason couldn't so directly. In such cases he would call his wife who would then call Spring. So when her mobile phone buzzed about half an hour later she knew it was her mother. The bus had stopped and Spring could now talk more freely.

"Ma, what's wrong. Did Ba just call you?"

"Where are you?" Her mother's voice was curt and worried.

"Lijiang. Did Ba just call you?" she repeated.

"Your father is worried about you?"

"What do you mean?"

"Bao Bei, Bao Bei," her voice suddenly was soft and gently, "What's going on?"

"Ma…"

"Your father told me. He's worried about you."

Spring's heart melted. Her mind was in a maelstrom of emotions. She wanted to confide in someone but to do so would force her into decisions, freeze her thoughts into opinions, and lead her into uncharted territory. She was scared. Everything she had so elaborately prepared, the masks that she had so rigorously constructed, about David being just her teacher, that she was above the sticky web of love and all its confinements, all would be exposed and revealed, deconstructed and scattered to the winds. Her protective sphere of dreams and allusions, love and disappointment seemed to be imploding under the candid stares and speech of those around her and close to her.

"About what? Everything's fine." Her voice was weak.

"Where is David, Bao Bei?"

"Who?"

"The American, David, where is he?"

"David, David…"

"He left you didn't he?"

Spring realized her parents knew she and David had argued, but she was still shocked to hear her mother say it so explicitly. How did she know? Worse, how could she answer?

"Who told you that?"

After a short silence her mother replied.

"No one needed to tell me. I know more about you than anyone in the world."

"We argued. I was jealous. I don't know."

"You've argued with people before. Is this any different?"

Spring couldn't tell her mother how she felt. In China there is a saying

He Jiu Bi Fen

Or

After a long time things must separate.

She couldn't tell her mother that David had hit her, or come close to hitting her. She did not want to hurt her parents. She had to maintain face. She also couldn't admit her own failure.

"Do you love him?"

"I...I don't know." Spring stammered then quickly added,

"Maybe..."

"So...what's the problem?"

The two of them didn't say anything. It was as though they were both motivated by love but lacked empathy or strength: that one couldn't forgive certain things and the other hadn't the strength to affirm her commitment to the man she had loved just hours ago.

They had made small talk after that. And just as her parent's dialogue had forced her to recognize important facts about their relationship, so she felt something of her attraction for David begin to ebb away. She now knew he wanted to contact her, but she decided to wait. Little did she know that waiting becomes a decision in itself. Days passed and his calls became less frequent.

For David it was as though the death of Zhen Rui had also exposed his vulnerabilities and weaknesses. The hurt within him was so great at the loss of the boy he didn't want to confront the possibility of having his heart broken again. He convinced himself that Spring did not want him anymore. She wouldn't return his calls. He wouldn't give her an opportunity to break his heart. He was returning to the way of the wolf.

✳✳

Spring had returned to Shenzhen alone. Now the cooler winds of Autumn had begun to blow across Southern China. In the fields the farmers prepared for the mid-Autumn Festival and leaves began to fall off trees and spread their natural confetti over the derricks and construction cranes of Shenzhen. The cold breeze that had swept through her heart after that morning in Lijiang had only deepened with the passing of time.

Since he did not know exactly where Spring was working David could only reach her by phone. He had called her several days after the Lijiang incident but she had screened his calls and not answered. A few times he managed to catch her on the phone. The first time he did so she had picked up the mobile unconsciously, before screening it.

"Spring, it's me. David."

She didn't say anything. She did not know what to say.

"Spring , are you there…"

She hung up the phone.

It had been the first time she had heard his voice in a long while. She should have felt something powerful, she thought. However, listening to him was like a bad dream, something unwelcome.

Finally Rebecca persuaded her to take his call. She had explained the situation with Zhen Rui.

"You should talk to him. He really wants to see you."

Spring had been shocked at first. It explained a lot, but not enough and now a momentum of quiet alienation had begun. Her parents' opposition to their relationship, the violence in Lijiang, Zhen Rui's death were too much to bear. Spring wanted simplicity, a quiet life. As T. S Eliot had written, It was as if she was in a tumultuous place

> With the voices singing in our ears, saying
> That this was all folly.

Finally she called him. He answered at once.

"Spring, what happened. Why won't you take my calls?"

 David's deep voice seemed to dig into her slim frame.

"I've been busy, that's all."

"We haven't seen each other so long. I want to tell you so much."

He sounded different to Spring, less confident. His voice was weaker, as though he was reading from a script he didn't believe in. There was no blame in his voice, just traces of sadness and regret.

"I'm very busy now. Maybe some other time."

"When?"

"I don't know I'll call you."

David's heart sank. Finally the words burst out.

"Why have you been avoiding me? You know I care but a lot has happened."

"I know, but I can't say…" she cried.

At that point Spring would have perhaps relented. She knew a lot had happened and his directness was at once irritating and appealing. David didn't let her continue.

"Please, please…I must see you."

Perhaps it was the pleading in his voice, a tone of supplication that she had never heard before. All at once her sympathy seemed to vanish. She couldn't explain why.

"I will call you…now isn't good. I have to go…"

There was a long silence on the other end. She wasn't sure if they had been disconnected.

"David, are you there?"

"Yes."

"I have to go now."

"Spring…"

With a sigh she hung up the phone, her heart beating.

But she had almost closed her heart. It was as though she had seen a part of him, a selfish, willful part that could never be excused. Some people can accept the ingratitude, infidelity and inconsiderateness of another as a one time thing, repair the hurt and move on as though it had never happened. Others, like her, mold the experience of hurt into a key that can lock and unlock the door to their soul. Unless they hand over the key they remain hardened to that person. In time the mold hardens and becomes part of their character. She was young and would recover, but even though part of her understood his decisions and actions, her reaction was like the remorseless and illogical fury of vendettas. What could have once been solved through an act of kindness, or even a harsh, sudden, forced revelation, simmered, boiled and burned into something bigger than it ever was. Like an emotional osmosis it sucked in and accumulated all the little hurts and pains of their months together. In time, unless arrested, it would indulge in itself and became a justification for going down separate paths.

David eventually stopped calling her, although the hurt remained in both of them.

Then one day, months later, he was walking on the street beside Lian Hua Park. He saw brightly colored kites high overhead. They were fluttering in the breeze. *They must see everything*, he thought. A woman passed him by and smiled at him. It was a glance, a passing smile. Like that of the Mona Lisa it seemed both sad and happy. He turned his head and looked after her retreating body. She walked like Spring.

He had not thought of her for a long time. He reasoned that she had eventually tired of him and decided that they had no future together. He had also withdrawn more into himself after the boy's death and tended to avoid those who knew him well. Now when he saw the woman's back and remembered the way Spring had smiled, he felt a pang of regret. It had not been one of the bubble gum, half artificial smiles that people casually give to friends of a friend. It had been a bittersweet smile, one that made him think of something that happened to him on a safari road trip long, long ago in Kenya.

That safari long ago he had joined a group of fellow tourists and they had driven to the arid north of Kenya. When they came to Lake Turkana they had encountered a number of local tribes living on the shores of the great and ancient lake. They were from a distant past. They lived in small communities of thirty to forty people. Their wooden houses looked skimpy but were strong in a place where nature demanded resilience. They were a vanishing people. Sickness and the onset of Western culture had made them an anachronism. The children were beautiful. Their skins were a polished brown and their eyes twinkled with a sad and sweet merriment. Brightly colored beads dangled over their faces and across their chests. The people were shy before him and his tourist group. David felt he ought to have been shy before them for he and his group were the real interlopers. They were the gangly hairy foreigners dressed in rude khaki with clunky cameras. Behind the rattan of a hut he saw an old man who was mumbling silently in his solitude. The guides told them he talked to himself even into the deep night hours. He was a member of another ethnic minority, and he sat alone in his hut because he was slightly mad and his dialect was unintelligible to those around him. What was more astonishing was that he was the last surviving member of his tribe. This village had taken him in and sustained him with their charity. He would talk as the people around him slept, uttering his words into the cool night air. Day after day he would do this. He could have been sharing great thoughts and ideas, stories of ancient warriors and heroic epics of vanished races and love stories. And yet fate had been savagely indifferent to this man who had so much to tell about his life and the extinct people who had left him forever unable to communicate. But the man could still smile. It was a wide smile, guileless, bittersweet - like those of the children. It was a smile that said more than words could express. Like Spring's. Like the woman by the park.

One day, as he was walking to an errand he noticed a couple walking on the sidewalk in his direction. The woman's easy walk and the way she held her head seemed familiar. He started. It was Spring. She was walking faster than the other man who, chatting on a cell phone, was nonchalantly strolling, forcing her to slow down so that she would impatiently look back at him, as though urging him to hurry up.

"Spring, is it you?"

They almost bumped into each other. He peered closely at her face. It was indeed Spring. She looked the same as ever, though a little thinner. Startled, she gazed at him wordlessly, a smile frozen on her face.

"Oh, David!"

"How are you doing?"

"Great! Great!"

She moved jerkily, closer to the other man, as if for protection. David nervously grasped the strap of his backpack. It was all so forced it was embarrassing for both of them.

She was conflicted. All of her emotions came back in a flood.

"I tried to call you, many times…"

"Oh yes, yes…"

"Who's this?" The man was off the phone. He was Chinese and spoke English with an American accent. He looked warily at David, smiling all the time. He was taller than the American. He wore jeans and a tan open collar shirt, buttons open at the neck, giving him a roughly western Marlboro man look.

Spring just bobbed her head, her bright smiling white teeth contrasting with bright eyes that had turned strangely, remorselessly cold. . This was not the smile he remembered. She was distant, unreal.

"He's my old teacher."

"Oh."

There was an awkward silence. A few yards away an old man carrying some plastic bags of food shuffled by, looking curiously and suspiciously at the two foreigners. On the curb a bicycle fixer squatted, sunk in thought. A bicycle pump with a broken handle patched with white tape stood upright before him. Further down, two young woman made futile attempts to flag down cabs. They didn't know that at this time of the late afternoon, Shenzhen taxis rush to take a break, spurning all fares for at least half an hour.

"And you…" said David

"Well, I guess I'm her current teacher."

"How's she doing?"

"She's a terrible student. So damn lazy." The other man avoided David's eyes and casually looked at his watch.

"I see."

He looked at Spring to see if she had anything to say. He looked for something in her eyes, although he did not know what. Perhaps an old spark, a note of contrition or forgiveness, something, anything! But her eyes were cold as she smiled that fake, unnatural smile. It was as though there was a part of her he could not, perhaps could never, reach.

"Well, mate, I'm off. It was good meeting you."

The two men shook hands. He hadn't finished his farewell before the other two were on their way.

David looked after them for several seconds. Their shapes became smaller and eventually were lost in the crush of buildings, vehicles and pedestrians. David was standing on Ai Hua Lu. He remembered this place. When he had first come to Shenzhen he had seen the words but not recognized the Chinese characters on the street sign above him. He easily translated. *Love the Homeland* Street. Love. *Ai.* He shrugged. Faint odors of burnt charcoal and hyacinth blended in the late afternoon air. He turned and walked in the opposite direction. If the old man had looked back, he would have seen the American stumble once, recover, and quickly move his arm as if to brush away something from his eyes. But he didn't see this. He was too busy thinking how the price of pork had jumped by 3 Yuan in just the past 6 days.

Africa treats the challenges of the dreamer with little subtlety or partiality. Her world brooks no nonsense, is proud and brave, driven and enduring. To view for the first time the lion kill is humbling. To see the sky that stretches forever, or witness the sanctioned murders of the Savannah—this is a fascinating journey. And it does not stop at these national parks at the edge of the cities. It can be seen in the Nairobi and Mombasa, in Nakuru and Voi, in the limping traffic and the sweaty vendors jammed on sidewalks with their wares spread before them. One finds it in the small-minded bureaucrats and the whores and the cavalier expatriates. In these places one observes and lives death, transfiguration, and unrequited love - all cheap and as common as the dust of the Sahara. Though seductive, Africa requires of its people a special and unflinching persistence.

- Mark Ndesandjo (Diaries)

EPILOGUE

A few months later David received a package in the mail. It was from Nairobi. Accompanying it was a short letter from his mother. His name was scratched in her chicken feet script across the envelope, as though as an afterthought. Inside was a single sheet of lined stationary paper in which she had written the following in longhand:

Dear David:

Haven't heard from you in ages - how are you?

While rummaging through some old things I came across something your father wrote. I hadn't seen it for a long time and had forgotten about it. But it would be of insight to you. Read it and go on with your life. Leave the past behind if you can.

Love,

Your mother

P.S. I also found some of your old books and have sent them to you hereby enclosed.

David looked at the package. Two old cardboard *Blue Band Margarine* boxes were sealed and bound together with several strips of sisal rope and white tape. Inside were several books from his teenage years (those deathless years!). They now carried an odor of age and decay. He recalled ancient memories and for a few moments forgot about the computer and the tasks waiting for him at work. The books poured out like dusty gems, fragile and virtually shouting out FLIP OPEN WITH CARE!! *La Nausee, Les Mots*, Sheridan's plays, *Doctor Faustus, Lysistratus, Modern Studies on Augustus of Hippo, History of Philosophy, Myth of Sysiphus, The Castle, America by Camus*... The list went on and on. So much in just two small boxes.

Giddy with nostalgia, he flipped through some pages and read ancient annotations he had long ago scribbled into margins. His crabby signature was proudly scrawled on the first few pages of a few of the books. Thoughts of those confident early years in Kenya passed through his mind like an ancient, powerful, and unexplored river. In this surge of recollections David seemed to relive thoughts and feelings, once so assured and part of his dreams, now so penumbral. He rubbed these yellowed, gritty, worn pages between his fingers, reflecting. Then he noticed a small notebook. It seemed to be hidden in a corner of one of the boxes. Thin white pages could be seen sandwiched between ragged corners of the blue cover and binding.

He gently lifted it out.

With dry bureaucratic clarity, the cover's bold black script read as follows:

Jamhuri Publishing Company Limited
Notebook
Primary Level
Kenya Board of Education

He opened the book gingerly, with great deliberation, as though a careless gesture might flick into oblivion the dust of fragile memories. His father's elegant but almost unreadable script pressed heavily into the paper, such that one could feel the impressions on the flip side. Many of the sections were without order, and sections of paper had been clearly torn out of the notebook, leaving ideas disconnected and random. But there was a rough chronological order to these recollections. He started reading.

I am writing this journal because I am lost. Last night my wife and child left me. My son does not understand me. He fears me. The demon drink is my best friend now. Someone said to me "Take up a pen for god's sake and let it out!" Now is the time to see where I came from and what I have become. So I will write about some of the most important moments of my life and what they mean to me. I am not reflective, but I will try to be. To understand me one must understand Africa. I am an African, a Kenyan. This is where I was born.

Reading these words, David felt as though he was reading about himself. His mind returned home. *Both our journeys had begun in Kenya. This is where I was born too. I too have been searching for meaning. We both failed our women. Are we that different after all?* He continued.

My father was a guard, an askari, for the English. He was a harsh man. He was tall and strong. His ancestors came from the northwest of Luoland, from southern Sudan. They crossed Lake Victoria in search of places to fish. Many also grazed cattle and raised crops.We Luos are dreamers.We are good at telling stories, and talk and talk. Many of the other tribes, such as the Kikuyu, call us big mouths. Among we Luo bombast is everything, for the pretence of power is more important than power itself.We are proud and arrogant.We are not modest. Here no false modesty, bless your heart! But my father was unhappy. He often complained to us that the whites took all the best jobs."Why do they look down on us? They are stronger than us but this is our land.They treat us like cattle. For many years I have lived among them. And although I have a few cows and some wives it has been too slow and too hard coming." He buttoned up his lips outside our home. He spoke little. He chose words carefully and was respected in the village. Frequently he would drink **kong'o**. *Since he often worked during the day and only part of the evening, many evenings were free.When he came home he would appear in the door of our small hut, standing very straight, swaying a bit. We would smell the* **kong'o** *."Give me my food, woman!" My mother would smile gently and make him his food.*

When I was five, or maybe it was six (I don't exactly remember when), my mother left me. My memories of her are in bits and pieces. Her skin was soft. She never raised her voice to me. I remember the faint smell of her smooth skin when she suckled me. Her eyes were at once sad and happy, as though she would never be satisfied. She was strong willed and often fought with my father. He beat her many times.When she didn't clean the house properly, he would beat her.When she raised her voice in irritation at him, he would beat her.When he had no reason to fault her, he beat her. She was a dreamer, and he hated it. He knew that he could never make her submit. She would bend her head, but her eyes would flash and once she said," So, old man, you think you can beat me and crush me. Never, you will never beat me down!".That day he beat her until her back dripped blood. I remember this because my white shirt turned red and she had to clean it.

In another time she would perhaps have been a doctor or a lawyer, even a politician, for she was smart, charming and beautiful. But she was a woman. She was my father's property, like a high-grade cow. In those days men could have many wives. The richer one was, the more wives one had. It was common practice to beat one's wife. Many women would say,"Yes, men are hard. They beat us. But they also feed us.We often are to blame for our misfortunes.We serve them.They protect us, and it is not our place to fight them or argue with them. That is the way of our people." I think my mother had many regrets. I think of what my father used to say about women. "You can beat them, you can love them, you can buy presents for them, but they are still your property, like the cattle that feed us." My heart did not agree with him but my head listened.

My earliest memory is of following my mother through a field of maize just after the harvest. She was walking very fast and I couldn't keep up with her. "Wait! Wait for me!" I must have shouted though I do not remember. The sun was very bright and the maize was taller than me. I think I was about three or four years old at the time. I was frustrated trying to keep up with her. I only saw big and fat legs in front, no matter how hard I tried. I wanted to walk faster than her. Perhaps this is why I became competitive. I wanted to move faster than my mother in every way.

I will always remember the day my mother left me. I was about 5 or 6 years old then. Many things that happened that long ago are unclear but some are as clear as yesterday. I can imagine some of the things she said and what my father and I said. I mostly remember the wetness of her face when she said goodbye. That day I was playing outside. I had collected some old pieces of wire that had been lying by the roadside where the big cars and trucks used to drive past on official business. Twisting them together I had made a little wire grooved wheel that I could push along with a stick. The children of the village had never seen something like this before. "Let me try, let me try!" they cried out. But I kept away from them because my father hated to see me play with them. "They are dirty and filthy. They will make you dirty and filthy too." That day I heard a sound and looked back over towards our hut. I saw my mother carrying something large, maybe a cloth sack, on her thin shoulders. She came over to me. She bent down and said:

"My son, I must leave you. "

"Where are you going? When will you come back?"

"I will not come back, my son."

"Can I come with you?" I did not cry.

"I cannot live here anymore. It is very hard to live with your father. He has found another wife." I saw welts on her upper arms. On her dark loamy skin they looked like sergeant's stripes. Tears were falling from her eyes.

"I love you, my son, and when you are older you must come to me. I will wait for you."

"Mama, mama!" I saw she was sad. I did not understand.

She placed her cheek on my cheek. I could feel the wetness.

"These are my tears. Remember my tears. I cannot take you with me."

I didn't understand what was happening. She quickly walked away.

Then I started to cry. Later my father came to me as I stood alone on the street. I don't remember what he said but I think it was something like:

"Don't worry. Be strong. She was no good. The woman who bore you will soon be forgotten. You are older now and do not need her. She will be forgotten, for that is the way of our people."

How could I forget my mother? How could I forget she who had bore me in her womb? What could I forget about her with whom I alone had shared unspoken secrets! I missed her for a long time. But my father was right. Eventually my heart grew hard and I forgot about her. The only other thing I remember about that day is that my father complimented me on my new toy.

He shouted out to the neighbors.

"You see my son's toy! This boy has a head that is as clear as the lake and as strong as a stone. He will go far!"

Years after she left I banished thoughts of her to the back of my mind. But sometimes she appeared in my dreams. One night, when I was about seven, I dreamed I was walking through a field of tall grass and she was walking too fast. I was crying and got lost. I woke up in a sweat. But this is not what scared me. I couldn't remember what her face looked like! I decided then that I would go and find her. I was 8 years old then.

A few nights later I left. That night there was complete silence. It was cold and I only had a thick cotton shirt with some missing buttons and my hand-me down shorts that didn't reach all the way down my leg. I wore some plastic sandals. In the distance I could hear the faint sounds of men drinking **kong'o** and laughing. I had a few pieces of cassava in my pocket. I thought that I could go as far as the missionary school in Kisumu, forty miles away. Once there I could find my mother's sister who had a job as a teacher. I didn't know what she taught or where she taught, but I knew I just wanted to leave and find my mother. I told myself I did not want to forget what she looked like.

David stopped reading at this point. He had heard how his father had been separated from his mother when he was young. He had not known the details. He tried to imagine how the child had felt that night. In his mind's eye he saw what the young boy must have seen: the great cathedral of an African sky filled with thousands of sparkling stars and the faint blush of a lingering sunset spreading from behind the hills of Alego until it was absorbed by the oily blackness. Most of the villagers would have been in their homes, asleep or preparing to sleep. When someone passed by outside the hut, it might have sounded like calico cloth brushing against the ground, urgently, impatiently. The rich smell of dung would have hung in the air like incense from the fields. The luminous moon would have washed its light over the village calmly and softly, as though life had no beginning or ending. How beautiful, yet how terrifying for a young boy! He continued.

*That night the road was empty. Shadows moved in the moonlight. I was afraid of the shamans. These witch doctors travel at night and change shape, killing travelers and bad people. I shivered. I held my machete, my **panga** tightly. It was my father's. He called it **Pesa** after **Juma Pesa**, the Luo witch hero. He carried it always and used it to cut away brush and clear land. I walked through bushes and trees, along the small dirt paths, terrified but determined. At one point I started crying, but I did not know why.*

"What's that?"

I heard a voice, and I saw some black shapes heading towards me on the narrow road. I quickly rushed into the bushes and ran and ran until I could run no more. The night was quiet again but I had lost my sandals. I was too frightened to sleep. In any case the crickets and sounds of the animals would have kept me awake. I was glad when the sun came up and covered the earth. I could see the white waters of LakeVictoria in the distance. I sat under a tree and ate some cassava. I had never been this far, and I did not recognize the place. Exhausted I fell asleep.

When I woke up, my face felt wet. It was a dog licking my face.

"Holaaaaaa!"

I jumped up.When I saw that it was just a small stray dog I felt better and gave it some of my food. After that the dog followed me. I did not know how far away I was from Kisumu but eventually found my way back onto a large road.

"Which direction is Kisumu?"I asked some old men who were passing by,

"In that direction, towards the sun and those hills. Just follow the road."

I passed many other people. None recognized me. But I felt it was too risky to travel during the day. My father must have already known what had happened and might be searching for me. It was very hot and I was very thirsty.

"Mama, give me some water please,"I said to a lady carrying a big pan of water delicately balanced on her head.

"Where are you from, child?"

*She stopped and looked at me."Aren't you a little small to be alone on this road?"She let me drink a little water from her gourd. Feeling her suspicious eyes on me I thanked her and quickly left. I slept and walked, slept and walked. Soon three days had passed. The third night I almost gave up. I wanted my comfortable bed. My cassava was almost finished. I now hated the taste. I was so hungry. I missed my tasty home cooked food. I could smell the **nyoyo**, tasty **njugu**, long sweet yellow **rabolo** from the trees, **rabuon**, **ring'aliya**. I wanted to eat delicious **ngege** or*

mbuta *from the lake. But I imagined my father's angry eyes and the rod that he would lash me with. In my mind's eye, I now remembered my mother's kind gentle face. Her warm lips and eyes were as clear as the day she left me.*

"Mother, mother, where are you, why did you leave me?"

That gave me courage. The dog had befriended me and now followed me wherever I went. At first I had tried to shoo him away, then I welcomed his company and would even talk to him. He also liked the cassava and that pleased me. I had never met a dog that ate cassava.

"Where are you from, Dog? Have you left your family too? "

But he would just look at me and wait for some cassava. I would have stolen food but did not know how, so I started to beg strangers for a piece of kwon here, a slice of fish there, and some water here. I had survived this way for five days now.

"How far is Kisumu?"

"About 50 kilometers in that direction."

Some strangers replied. What was "50 kilometers?" How many steps in 1 kilometer? I had been walking for ten or more hours each day. I somehow calculated that I had 30 to go! This would take forever! I counted each step, each breath with regularity. Just twenty steps. Just another twenty steps. I would count the number of trees I passed automatically, as though they were markers that would determine the success of my journey. I do not know how I managed.

*One night a hyena, an **ondiek**, came across me on the trail. Its fur was yellow in the bright moonlight. I first thought it was a leopard. It growled and I knew immediately it was an ondiek, and hungry. I was deathly afraid. It was about half my height and snarled ferociously. It looked at me and crouched. In an instant Dog jumped in front of me, snarling at it. Its teeth latched onto the wide-eyed Dog's neck.*

"Go away, go away." I screamed.

*The mauling of the little dog continued. Its painful yelps cut my heart. I felt helpless. I used **Pesa** to taunt the hyena, and even hit it a few times. I picked up loose stones and threw them in desperation at the animal, but it ignored me and ripped away with its teeth.*

I screamed. I felt as though part of me was being ripped out, as though someone you love is being tortured and is dying before your eyes. Then the yelps stopped. The ondiek seized the limp Dog in its teeth and bounded back into the forest. I cried all night. My friend, my companion had been taken from me. The wet tears that poured down my cheeks fell to the dry ground. No one was there to lick them from my face this time.

The following day the sun was high in the sky. The road stretched out before me, shaking in the heat. There was no one around. The ground was so hot it burned my feet. I had to walk on the cooler grass, even though there were scorpions. I found some palm leaves and made a hat. I also used some of the thicker leaves to wrap my bare feet.

While I was traveling my throat was often parched and I wanted to drink very badly. I had broken my promise to walk only at night, but now the night truly scared me.

"Where are you Dog?" I heard these words in my mind and imagined his small yelp.

But when I looked around there was no Dog. That day after Dog died was the loneliest of my life.

I found a small copse hidden beside the road and fell back on the grass. Soon I was asleep. Around me the trees shaded me from the heat. In the distance a lightning blasted tree stood alone. I still remember its dead shriveled branches. I dreamed strange things, of wild animals, of my father, of Opiyo, of my mother's farewell, all confusing dreams that gave me no peace. Then something knocked my feet. In my dream I felt it was my father hitting me with his cane. I woke up in a sweat.

"What are you doing, child?"

"Don't hit me. Leave me alone!"

I shouted and jumped up. Alarmed, I thought for a moment that she was a shaman, her face looked so strange, like an old orange, in the setting sun.

"Gor Mahia, spare me!" I called out the name of the great shaman who could turn invisible or into an animal or even an old woman.

" **Nyathi matin**, don't be frightened little one. I'm just an old woman. When I saw you lying under the **mirembe** I thought you were dead!"

The old lady gently smiled.

"What is a little **jakogelo** like you doing out here all alone?"

I relaxed a little but said nothing.

"Don't worry child. I'm just an old lady. I won't hurt you!"

Shrugging her shoulders, the old woman went on her way. Then she turned around.

"Here, have some water child, and some **nyoyo**." Before she had finished her sentence I was already greedily drinking. As I ate the **nyoyo** she looked at me.

"Where is your village? Are you from Alego?"

"I'm going to Kisumu." I said.

She laughed. It was a throaty, honest laugh. "Kisumu! And how are going to get there. Fly? Kisumu is far, far away. And you must have a car or take the train.

But only whites can take the train, and you certainly don't have a car. Have you a car, child?"

I didn't say anything. She tried to make me say more, but I was quiet and just ate and drank from a distance. She mentioned my village. Maybe she would take me back. I was cautious. Eventually she walked away in the direction from where I had come, shaking her white head.

Unknown to me the old lady knew my father. When she entered Alego she told him the news. He and some friends set off to look for me. They discovered me hiding on the road, filthy and half-starved. I looked up at my father's grim face. It was thinner than I remembered. His eyes were angry, ashamed, relieved and regretful. Anger at my disobedience. Shame at how the village now saw he couldn't control his son. Relief that I was still alive. Regret that things had to come to this.

"Do not beat me, father! I did not mean to steal **Pesa**.*" I remember how I handed the panga to him with trembling hands.*

Instead he cried. It was the only time in my life I ever saw my father cry. He didn't touch the panga. I never forgot that journey. I later discovered that although I had traveled a long distance. Kisumu was still far, far away. Many never understood how I had survived for so many days. My father never again spoke of my sad adventure. He had revealed his love and that shamed him. "People should never show their weakness. If you vanquish your enemy, do it completely. Mercy is for fools." To him love was a weakness.

Afterwards, I think I lost my love for my mother. Something hardened "hy did she leave me? Hadn't I tried hard to see her again?" I had shamed my family and my village. My love for her now shamed me. Just as my father's love for me shamed him. The pain slowly died. I still hear Dog, however - that foolish dog.

David stopped reading. He reflected on how this adventure must have changed his father's life. In moments of great personal change or transfiguration, David thought, one often doesn't see the wood for the trees, and instead reflects on how inconvenient change is. Memories of his father's journey had become inconvenient, like laundry that must be washed, or folders that must be processed, but then are forgotten. It is said that the most important moments of one's life often pass by imperceptibly, like wisps of cigarette smoke that vanish in a puff of wind. For better or for worse these moments define our lives for long after. Only years later do we recognize them for what they are — the sparks that make great or lay low a kingdom, bring glory or shame to one's family, or form the apex or nadir of one's existence. From that moment on, one's life begins to climb upwards, or creep downwards, often unnoticeably.

David realized that his father, normally an unreflective person, had, like David himself, often been unaware of these arcs and curves of life. David's father had seen his own father cry. Afterwards his heart hardened to his mother. The father's love had been grudgingly exposed, like a glint of gold wedged among chunks of charcoal. That instant had been life-changing. He continued.

I decided my father was correct. Women are soon forgotten. "That is the way of our people." he had said. I removed her memories from my mind. I would never let a woman be close to me again.

. . . [Several pages were missing]

As I wrote above, my father was a police guard, an **askari,** *for the British magistrate assigned to Alego and its district. At that time the courts were a mix of colonial and tribal establishments. Most disputes involving locals were settled by the village councils, of which my father was a member. More serious crimes such as murder and anything involving a white man, involved the magistrate. Mr Reynolds was a strict man. He always left his neat little red brick house for work at 6 each morning and returned promptly at 10 each evening. From our hut a few hundred yards away we could always hear the honk of his driver's horn at the gate. We knew that my father was then opening the gate and would return home later that evening. Once there was a big party at the magistrate's house. The music could be heard all across the village. The music we did not recognize but I remembered a few words:*

The sound of her laughter
Will sing in your dreams.

Only later I learned this was from Roger's and Hart's Film **South Pacific.** *I remember that music well because the Reynolds family would often play the record or sing it alongside their piano. They all seemed so happy. They were like aliens.*

I remember that song because it sang about dreams. My father once told me, "Without dreams you are like a bird with a broken wing. You cannot fly. I want you to dream, as I dream for you." My father had many evil thoughts and did many cruel things, but he said many truths.

I made friends with the magistrate's son. Rodney was a red haired boy who was taught by his mother at home. "My mother is French and she doesn't like the British teachers." he told me once. We were lying on our backs side by side outside the village by the **ober** *(oak) trees looking at the sky. He looked bored.*

"What are you looking at?" I asked him.

"I am looking at God." he said.

"God is in your ass." I replied.

We laughed. We were both ten years old. Everyone in the village thought I was mad to befriend a Briton. But I was headstrong and didn't know understand what it was to be poor and black in Kenya. Furthermore I was at the top of my class and my English was good. Why should I be afraid?

Rodney was my best friend. We used to do everything together. From time to time he would come to our hut and even try some food. He liked the **chapattis** *my stepmother (I called her auntie) made and the delicious tilapia and kwon. We always laughed at his manner of eating. He would sit in our circle. He, auntie, my uncle and I (my father was often out when we ate) would surround the large bowl of kwon and side bowls of meat and fish. He would scoop out the kwon so delicately we laughed.*

"Not that way, Mr Ronald!" My uncle would laugh heartily. His big hands, tough like black rubber, would gently form a small round ball with the kwon, press it in the middle to make a small hole and then dip it in the sauce to scoop the gravy. Finally in one smooth motion he would gulp it down without spilling a drop.

"See that's the way you do it!".

But Rodney was awkward at such moments and always spilled food and gravy. Sometimes I would scoff at him.

"You **mzungus** *can't eat like real men." I once joked.*

My uncle didn't laugh. Ronald just looked down. My uncle shook his head. After that I didn't make fun of him, even though he always spilled the food over his clean clothes.

"I'm used to forks!" he would sputter.

One day his father came walking over to our hut and spoke to my uncle and my father:

"The boys should be doing their own things, John. I'm sure you understand."

He stroked his moustache as he looked paternally at my father. My father understood. He bowed his head: 'Yes, Bwana.' I had never seen my father so humble or so quiet. I also saw the shame in his eyes. He thundered at me that night.

"Have you been seeing the white boy?"

"Yes father," I said. I never lied to him.

He beat Auntie and me until we were very sore. Afterwards, of course, I saw Rodney less and less.

I progressed very fast in school. I was placed two classes ahead. Most of my fellow students at St John's missionary school were older than me. Our class was so full that sometimes we had to sit outside under the trees. Our classes were math, history, civics and PE (Physical education).

We had few teachers, for we were a poor village. I do not remember them well. Occasionally Father Odhiambo, the headmaster, would teach us. Father Odhiambo was a big man, but was never angry or harsh. He lived in a small brick house not far from the classrooms. He wore baggy gray clothes and we often saw him walking slowly across the fields on his way to school. He would always look down, at his feet, as though afraid he would fall. He had curly white hair and wore thick glasses. He had a fantastic memory, and knew his books, particularly history books, inside out. His smart eyes would look at us while his hands flipped through pages. He loved history and the one term he taught us really opened my eyes to the world outside.

*His syllabus included not only British things like the exploits of Kipling and Gordon, but also mixed in African history, including even Kikuyu material. At that time we were not so split along tribal lines. We and the Kikuyu often mingled and were friends. Then the British jumped in and did their best to force us apart. That's another story. For example, one day he discussed Gordon's "Liberation of Khartoum" and heroic death. Afterwards he jumped into a discussion of our Luo heroes too: like **Luanda Mangere** who fought the **Kipsigis** and turned into a great stone when he died. He also mentioned **Ng'onga'a Makodima** of **Alego** who could talk to the elephants, the witch hero **Juma Pesa** of **Karachuonyo**. I learned more details about other heros like **Nyakiti Kogutu**, **Oyama**, even **Chege wa Kibiru**, the great Kikuyu prophet who had prophesied that "frog-like white people will come from the East, carrying magic killing sticks and wearing clothes like the **cuhuruta** (butterflies)". Kibiru had said they would bring to our land "a great iron snake that spits fire. Snaking across the land it will eat people and spit them out, always hungry, never satisfied." The prophet had said " Learn from these people. That way you will conquer them." Or something like that. Father Odhiambo said the 'snake' was the great railway the British built across Kenya in 1900.*

He would be shouting and whispering passionately. I would sit spellbound under the mango tree.

He proceeded into a discussion of the search for raw materials in Africa and the partitions of the continents among the European Powers. Meanwhile I would be taking much notes, wondering how I would remember everything. . .the influence of America, the British

Several pages seemed torn out. Others were yellow and so faded that the words were illegible. David continued.

. . .not only had a photographic memory but I was able to calculate numbers

and visualize complex abstractions and shapes easily. At twelve I developed a method to instantly mentally multiply ten and 12 digit numbers in my mind. But I was not just a calculating machine. I early realized that the sciences and arts were linked. Mathematics led to [...] physics led to the study of cause and effect, which in turn led to God, philosophy and religion. But I had a big problem: while I was good at all these subjects, they were not my passion. There was no love here, only duty. Instead, the subjects were...

...Here there was another gap.

We [...] discriminate among ourselves just like black and white Americans in the United States. Our clans or tribes flaunt power arrogantly. Our arrogance in managing power was a parting gift from Britain. [...] symptom of tribalism and nepotism - the twin sicknesses of the continent. The bureaucrats are worst. And their display of power is wielded against whites as well as blacks. As one comes into the airport, for example, all disembarkees must line up with their passports before three Kenyans, it used to be three whites, seated on a five foot high pedestal. These three men don't look at the people before them. They just say "Passport." "Here you are..." A solemn pause... "Hmmm..." A longer pause. "Hmmm... What is this?" The scared tourist thinks he's going to be sent back to England or dumped in a jail with the blacks. "Uhhh. What? Ex- Excuse me?" Ignoring him, the officer shows his workmate the passport in question. All is silent in the terminal. It is late at night. This proceeding is strange. Many in line are silenced with bewilderment. The two men speak for a minute or two in Kikuyu or Luo. The Englishman is sweating. Finally, the bureaucrat hands back the passport, as though it carries germs. The Englishmen grasps the little book with relief. "Thank you." With a slight gesture the Kenyan waves him on. "You can go." The Englishman is lucky. There have been stories of people delayed for hours for no reason other than an official's dislike. The process repeats many times each night.

. . . [Several pages were missing]

Why did I befriend this boy? Part of it was that I was lonely. Boys my age were often herding cattle and doing their chores. My family, on the other hand, encouraged me to spend time on my homework and less on other things. I was entranced by the ideas of the whites. I liked their books. I realized their knowledge was superior to ours. They also had power. I had to respect them, even if sometimes I feared them.

"One day you will go to university and achieve more than them."

My father words still ring in my ears. I wanted to understand the whites. I could prove them wrong. I would exceed my father. I would not have to kowtow to the whites. They would kowtow to me. Africans mistrusted Indians and Europeans. They, on the other hand, all believed Africans were incompetent or needed guidance like children. This racism based on colors and ethnicities was everywhere. I had, however, other challenges. School and solitude were the twin pillars of my existence. They provided me direction. My dreams were color-blind, full of hopes and dreams. Books about philosophy, war and business were my daily friends. They shaped my imagination. Plato, Napoleon, Walter Raleigh, Adam Smith, I was like a wolf or a snake — I kept away from the racial conflict. I just wanted to explore books. But it was hard to close my eyes. Before independence my father muttered about the greed of Indians and Europeans. After independence, he would add in the corruption of Africans in the civil service, "Those civil service bastards, they just drink and whore, wasting our money and demanding bribes. They have forgotten the country and think only of their families and tribes!" Teachers at school cursed African youngsters, just as the whites had done to some of them long ago. Our own African teachers seemed to look down on us, even though we were their children.

While we were friends, I was curious about Rodney. Perhaps he held the secret of escape from my backward existence, like [...] I must have appeared as a freak. I discussed philosophy and the art of war at eleven, spoke perfect English and was to all intents and purposes, a stranger to my people. Sometimes I would grab a stick and play swords with Rodney, pretending I was Napoleon, " Down, tremble before me!" I would yell across the fields. Only Rodney and the cows would look up at me.

Once Rodney introduced me to his friend Sarah. When she saw me she looked taken aback but didn't say anything. Later I would hear her whisper to Rodney,

"Why are you friends with him?"

"He's my mate."

"But he...he's not..."

They whispered but I could hear well enough. He's not one of us, she was saying. In my mind I finished the sentence for her, but I pretended not to hear.

Once in a while we would walk to our favorite place, a small copse in the wood not far from the village where there was a small brook. Rodney always brought along his mongrel Bruno, half bull terrier and half something else. He was white with black spots and made fought or screwed (excuse my language!) every dog or bitch in the neighborhood. He was macho, a king among canines, and a good friend. Rodney and I would follow the leashed dog as he trotted along. Some Africans, walking back home from work or women carrying shopping bags of twine on their heads, would stare at the two boys and the dog. Some would recognize me and smile. Others frowned, either at my companions or the panting dog. In those moments it was again as though my people were strangers.

"Jambo, Master Rodney ! "They cordially greeted him and they would nod distantly to me.

*"Jambo, **Habari gani.***"

He happily returned their greetings. Normally I would nod respectfully. I would avert my eyes. This time the girl made me even more uncomfortable. Our favorite spot was a small valley filled with trees and a brook that could be heard from up on the ridge. We used to fall back on the moss and dreamed. Perhaps the forest is still there.

David imagined the three alone in that space in the woods. He could see the thick green leaves that shrouded the muddy path. The path must have seemed like a drunken swab of brown paint that curved through the emerald landscape. They would have dreamily looked up at the mosaic of leaves pasted against the cerulean sky. It must have been a special place, one of solitude and freedom from obligations, where one could move ever deeper into oneself and away from the castes and privileges of Kenyan society.

[…] ill at ease. I was awkward […] She was very pale. Her hair was brown, her face round, freckled. Actually she was quite a plain girl. She was thin, with a rail-like body. Her body seemed to shake every time she laughed. It was clear she liked Rodney. Looking at the two of them I suddenly felt very lonely. I suddenly realized there was a big difference between me and them. I wanted to be friends with this girl. But something had come in front of me and said 'No way!' It had nothing to do with intelligence or character. It had to do with my skin. From that day I took comfort knowing that my father, my uncle, our women and families were the same blood and culture. This was our country, the whites were the interlopers. Nevertheless, even at that young age, living in a white man's world, in the shadow of colonialism, I always felt trapped. It was as if there was a place high on a mountaintop, and I would never climb up to it. Magazines, books, the easy lyrics on the radio, all these things were stamped with pigmentation.

. . . [Several pages were missing]

I got along well with most of the teachers, except for Mr Otunda - our biology teacher. He was unpopular and often hit the students. When he wasn't using it to give us "six of the best", he clipped his belt with the buckle facing left – the way cowboys sometimes do. He would stand still on the balls of his feet. His sharp black eyes would coldly survey the class. His clean shaven face was almost devoid of motion. He took no nonsense and spoke in clipped sentences or monotones. When he taught biology all was dead silence." Six of the best" lashes were for students who didn't pay attention.

"Good morning Mr Otunda!" The students were required to stand up when teachers entered the classrooms.

"Good morning!"

Once he asked me a question. I didn't hear him. I was looking out the window or something.

"I say! You there, what the hell is wrong with you."

I jerked up.

"I asked you a question, goddamit. Did you hear me?" He looked directly at me.

*The **goddamit** bounced around inside my head. His eyes were cold behind the steel-framed glasses.*

"Excuse me , Sir, I didn't hear you." I said meekly.

"OK, let me repeat it slowly for your benefit, What is a principle use of plants in Latin America?"

I had no clue. I didn't like biology. Mr Otunda was still standing there.

"Well?"

There was silence in the classroom. And then it hit me. It seemed a perfect answer.

"Furniture?"

The whole class laughed. Mr Otunda did not. His eyes were like fire.

"Get out. Right now!"

I stood outside in the corridor for the rest of the session. To this day I still do not know why he was so angry.

. . . [Several pages were missing]

David was now remembering more and more of Kenya. To some Kenya is just another developing country on the eastern edge of Africa; to him it had always been a mood. It was a place of dithyrambic excess and silent beauty.

The land in which father and son had been born is about the size of Texas, and filled with people of many languages and ancestries. Nairobi, the capital, is metropolitan in nature, with almost all the amenities of any international city. Cafes, five star hotels, drunken taxi-cab drivers, whores, and fat, overdressed politicians spill out and over the street like bright and dull marbles ricocheting on a glass table.

The African sky stretches above like a colossal sheet of suspended blue liquid. It is the most magnificent skyscape in the world. When the rainy season begins the drops fall from its gray and furrowed mien, like the tears of a dark and alien God. At once accosted and beguiled, one shrinks before this monstrous circular and all-encompassing universe. Thus, the petty bureaucrats and the unwashed prostitutes and the arrogant expatriates and the sweet and cooing young mothers become tiny characters limned against nature's great reality.

The African sky is huge, and the sea is even more vast. He remembered when as a child he had visited the Indian Ocean as a child. There the water meets the great receptacle of an inimitably huge kael, the world seems to reach its limits, and one never forgets the experience. So even in the dark of night, when the air is full of love and death, one pokes one's head out of one's hotel window and senses a huge unnamed spirit. And when the cool cotton pillow strokes the cheek, the mantra of the waves crashing again and again upon the distant shore puts one quickly to sleep. All reflects the spirit of vast spaces. Even shells that formed the homes of long-vanished creatures sing the music of the sea. One holds them up to the ear and the sound of waves sing their mysterious song. In Africa the world is rhythm, and rhythm, brutal and unadorned, becomes an ineluctable force.

Once when I was about 12, my father took me to go bird-hunting. We were very poor and my father liked to spend most of his money on kong'o so there wasn't much left for food. He was a wonderful athlete. He could throw and run faster than anyone else in the village. I always loved to see how his muscles gleamed in the sunlight as he strained to make a perfect throw to hit a rabbit or a slow pigeon. He would take care in picking up the right stone, then he would roll it in his calloused hands.

"It must be just a little round, not too much." He would slowly and seriously advise me. If the stone was not right he would throw it away with disgust and start searching again.

Then before I could even see the target his hand would hurl the stone in a magnificent sweeping motion.

"AAYYYYOOOOOOO...."he would yell with joy when he hit the target, often a bird, sometimes a rabbit.

"That's the way to do it!"

I would share his happiness. At such times he smiled a lot. His teeth shone like ivory and his eyes sparkled with merriment. I realized then that my father was a man who loved life, but he loved being free even more. I always remembered that broad smile. Although there were sad moments, these happy memories seemed to redeem my father.

One time we were heading back to the village from hunting. We came across a car parked beside the murram road. An African and a white man, a **mzungu**, *were standing next to it. The white man saw my father and shouted from across the street, "Hey! I say! Come over here!" My father looked at me, his face suddenly serious, as though the time for play was over.*

"Stay behind me."

The white man nodded at my father, pointing to the flattened tire. He was a young man probably in his early thirties. Bony arms and legs stuck out from his khaki shorts and shirt. His bright blue eyes quickly looked us over. He looked at me.

"Is this your son?"

"Yes, Bwana."

He nodded slightly. Wiping the sweat from his forehead he pointed again to the tire. His sharp, thin mouth quietly asked,

"I say, can you fix this?"

My father looked at the other African, but he just shrugged his shoulders and looked away. He was well-dressed, one of the thousands of clean young men turned out each year by the missionary schools to serve in the civil service. My father despised such Africans. "They accept everything the British say. Their religion, their customs, their clothes. And then they look down on their parents and their ancestors. But," he shrugged, "...one day they will run the country."

The white man shrugged.

"He's useless. See if you can do it."

My father took the tools and after a few minutes, with me helping, he had replaced the flat tire.

The white man looked angrily at the other man.

"See. He knows how to do it. You bloody Africans are so damn lazy. And..." And he didn't say any more.

My father bowed and made to leave. The white men just nodded his head. When we were further down the path a voice called out from behind us, "Hey, boy! Wait!"

It was the African. He was running after us. My father stopped.

"Here's some money. Mr Fernandez wanted me to give it to you."

"I'm not your boy!" My father coldly replied. The man looked after us in amazement as we quickly walked away.

Rodney and I did not meet as frequently as before, since our parents forbade it. Once in a while, however, our paths crossed. We were both passionate readers, and from time to time we would discuss the Western classics. Once, the magistrate secretly overheard us as we discussed the Japanese fable **The Tale of Genji** *I said.*

"It's a story about love and sacrifice, not politics."

"Of course it's about politics. It's about women and how they had to struggle for equality using all the tools at their disposal."

"I know what tools you're thinking about." I said, smiling (We already had a reputation as a lady-killers at that young age). "Seriously, its about how the oppressed fight back. – love becomes a tool more powerful than the sword...or the gun."

"The only reason you're saying that is because the author was a woman."

"Supposedly, but the stories of love, betrayal, loyalty - all these are about power. Even in our Luo stories, the concept of power through love, not the love of Jesus, but sexual love, is common."

Rodney later told me that his father had by chance overheard our argument. Rodney had expected a beating but his father had merely said,

"You whippersnappers are studying some interesting things in school these days, eh?"

One day the magistrate was leaving his car to enter the house after a busy day at work. He turned to face the old askari.

"How is your son doing?"

"Very well, Bwana, thank you!" If the father betrayed any surprise he didn't show it.

"How are his studies coming along?"

"Very well, Bwana..."

"I see. Tip top." And the magistrate turned back to the house. My father hurriedly followed up,

"His teachers say he is the smartest boy in the school, Bwana".

The magistrate didn't turn, but he paused, bent his head slightly as though listening to an inner voice,

"I see...I see...good...tip top."

Later that evening I overheard my father recount the story to my aunt.

"The Bwana asked me some questions about the boy. He seems interested in his studies."

"You should encourage him. Maybe he will help him get work?"

My father didn't let her finish.

"He will do more. You remember old Wilson from Kisumu? He found a rich American who paid for his son to go to college in America."

From then on the magistrate would from time to time ask after me, and my father would unfailingly reply, each time with more details.

"...He got A's in his civics class, Bwana."

"...His teacher tells me that if he keeps up he should do well in mathematics, Bwana."

"...The headmaster thinks he should go to college, Bwana."

"...He was the only student to get 100% in the end-of-term exams, Bwana."

And so forth. Each time my father would afterward tell auntie and I what he had said, word for word. It was Rodney's father who persuaded the district council to enroll me as a scholarship student. He also had rich friends from America whom he persuaded to support me. I remember what the magistrate once told me like it was yesterday.

"Your father works hard and he is too smart to have been an askari, so he drinks and beats his wife. You think I don't know what goes on in your huts? Maybe you can do better!"

He said just these few words. They were [...]erica.

At this point a number of pages were torn out of the book. In the chill draft from the open window the frayed edges of paper trembled like dry grass on a hill. Sections appeared in pieces, unwhole, unformed, with no central conclusions or main ideas. He skipped over many such places. Then the following segment appeared abruptly.

When I lived in the States many of my friends were white, a few were black. Partly because the elite educational establishments were mostly white and the civil rights movement was a nascent, ongoing struggle with few tangible success stories in higher education. Partly because by temperament and culture I was quite different, I knew few African Americans. They were ostensibly so close to me, and yet in fact were far apart. Hundreds of years of discrimination by the majority damage a race in ways that Africans find difficult to understand. Under the British, Kenya had been a colony for many years, but we Africans had always known that this was our land, and one day we would be independent. The American writer Mark Twain had said that African Americans 'masculinity had been ... ground out of them.' While this was an exaggeration, there was some truth in it. I sensed among the many poor American blacks an undercurrent of despair and recklessness — a recklessness of people who have given up on life and throw it all to the winds (something which in my later years alcohol has caused me to experience and understand).

"They bewilder me...I don't know about them..." I had heard many of my fellow Kenyans studying in America say to me.

"They have this craziness about them..."

and so forth. I didn't sense craziness among the well educated and successful blacks, but I felt they were in a perpetual battle against their own apathy. They reminded me of Sisyphus, always struggling to roll the stone over the hill, never managing to push it all the way to the peak. Finally, it would roll back again. I was sometimes reminded of Leopold Senghor's words ."Emotion is Black. Reason is Greek" According to Senghor, Africans are characterized by their emotional faculty, through which they trump reason in understanding certain things. The language of African Americans was of the heart. Their dark history energized it. Spiced with religious fervor and musical abandon, it moved back and forth between self praise and self ridicule. Yet, though I was African, I found this language hard to relate to.

To American blacks, everything was a win or a loss in relation to the whites. As far as relations with their African brothers, many looked down upon them. Others saw in Africa an ideal place that in fact didn't exist. Yet others couldn't be bothered. They had enough on their plate without having to judge black foreigners. Whites (those in my circles) saw me first as a foreigner, only secondly as black. I was thus somewhat separate from the racial antagonisms that had percolated in American society since its inception. They discussed with me things they would never discuss with their fellow dark skinned Americans.

"Why are you people so hung up over race here?" I once joked, "You should just treat people as though they are the same. We are all like potatoes, maybe a few different spots here and there, but delicious never the less!"

"Exactly, that's the way I see it. There's so much fucking sensitivity about these things. I have to be so careful about what I say." The talker, a fellow white student, seemed relieved. It was as though a weight had been lifted off his shoulders. He continued.

"They just can't let it go."

I had been joking but I was naïve. In America, among whites and blacks, discussion of race is not a joke. It is a ticket to a place of code words far too complicated even for me to understand.

. . .

I met my wife at a party a few months before I graduated. I had had white girlfriends before. The novelty of dating and making love to white women had long passed. I was no longer a child. I had achieved much, coming from a childhood of poverty and want to a world of plenty and unlimited opportunities for the ambitious. Proud of their supposed anti-imperialistic leanings (Which was a self-delusion) Americans regarded the Kenyan independence struggle with attitudes ranging from amusement to passion. Among the young this idealism was mixed with much curiosity. They saw me as black, but I was a different black, one unstained with [...] slavery. In their relations with African Americans, whites were self-conscious and defensive. It was as though my being there gave them an opportunity to save themselves, explore a new world, or be a part of political change. In addition, my university pedigree and my confidence in stating my opinions drew them to me. It didn't hurt that I was a good dancer. The girls had fun with me. I smiled a lot and was charming. They saw in me what they wanted to see: a happy, good looking, smart, confident and lively exotic. I was a statement of their independence. To these lonely girls trying to escape the boredom of their middle class lives, I was their exit ticket.

We went out a few times. She was pretty and young. I felt the world was my oyster. But I also knew I had to return home and work to change the country. I also had other women waiting for me. I did not love this woman, but I needed her. She needed me to escape the drabness of her own life.

"I'll just get married to a nice Jewish boy and spend the rest of my life in Brookline." she once said, half joking.

"And I'll get married to a beautiful Jewish girl and we'll spend the rest of our life in Nairobi." I replied, smiling.

She laughed.

"You're a real lady killer. You think I trust you?"

"Of course, you can trust me. Come to Kenya and we'll get married." I meant it partly as a joke. I could see the hunger in her eyes, that naive understanding of life that relies on trust and is overwhelmed and blinded by emotion. I had seen it so many times in young women. But I was horny and that was that, I had said it.

"We'll see."she said, sounding distant and remote, as though she wanted me to think she didn't really care about something she actually cared about.

A few months later I returned to Kenya. I got a good job in the government statistics department. I was busily involved in trying to train people and prepare for the independent Kenya that was coming. I had left love behind and was convinced that my work would be good for the country. She followed me there.When I heard she was in Nairobi looking for me I was surprised. She was stronger and more persistent than I thought. A few months later we got married. It was an ordinary thing, an official ceremony performed in the district magistrate's office with one friend attending as a notary. Some words were muttered, a ring was slipped on a pink finger, a kiss was exchanged and so forth. Papers were signed and the event seemed to represent a merger of sorts. So in some ways, this woman, great dreamer that she was, lowered herself for me, and I was grateful to her, but there was no love in me- at least I think not, but I'm not sure. I know she wanted a more traditional wedding, something like the catholic weddings in white, or whatever the Jews do, but, just as she had forgotten her whiteness in marrying a black man, she let that go too. Ever after, she would cry and sniffle whenever she saw weddings, even on TV.

David remembered once when he was very young the three of them had visited the Bomas of Kenya, a tourist trap of a place with dozens of huts and villagers specially imported from the countryside to spend their days dancing and entertaining the white tourists in front of their neat, decorated, authentic huts. "You will divorce after three years." an old medicine man once told us. He was crabby and squatted before a plate filled with beads. "You must be joking." my mother said with a little laugh when she heard the translation. David's father just grunted and motioned her on. The medicine man had rattled his fortune-telling beads and grimly looked after the coffee colored boy as though he were the scum of the earth. "Three...three....three years." He said, shaking his beads furiously.

When I married this woman I knew that my children would be half-castes. I knew that my son would have a difficult life. To my face, society would call them names I hated. 'Half-caste', and 'chotara were the most extreme. Chotara was a term of the purest abuse. Some people used it with the casual familiarity with which one might say **rose** *or* **chair***. They would consider such children as white niggers or black mzungus. They were too black for whites, yet too white for blacks.To survive, my son would need to be strong. In my imagination, with a little encouragement, he would put the pedal to the metal and zoom ahead - alone and self-reliant.*

. . . [Several pages were missing]

My father was Muslim. I am not. Neither am I Christian. My wife is Jewish. My son is free to choose or not. All these religious things spill over and confuse. I am too intelligent to be part of this religious thing. I chart my own path. I create my own destiny without any spiritual crutch. If people are happy believing in God that's their business. I wish them well but don't impose it on me thank you very much.

. . . [Several pages were missing]

I remember the day Tom Mboya, a great Luo benefactor, a man who tried to change government for the better, was assassinated. Things were crazy that day. A friend of mine who had been with him told me the following. I remember his eyes were so angry but his voice was cold. "Tom fell into my arms. As the blood rushed over his white shirt, my arm felt wet. He was still alive, and was trying to breathe. The fucking blood just kept spraying out. Then he breathed gently and closed his eyes. All around us people were screaming and running around like headless chickens. The street was empty. I was saying where are the police? Where is the ambulance? No-one came. Bwana, they wanted the Old Man dead! Several minutes later the police and the ambulances came." My friend couldn't go on, but I knew how he felt. With Tom's death, tribalism had arrived in Kenya. I wanted to scream. Instead there was just silence. The next day life went on. The Kenya I loved died that day. Political change went into a deep sleep. Politics had always been in my blood. We Luos are talkers. We say what's on our mind, whether its nonsense or fact. That's what did me in. The Kikuyu bosses wouldn't accept a Luo loud mouth. I had no mentor. They did everything they could to silence me. My speeches moved from government auditoriums to grimy beer joints in Woodleigh. Since deeds were out of the question, I used my mouth to curse and to drink. The shamans took hold of me. Soon I lost my job.

I had always been a heavy drinker. I found that it helped me break away from my serious self. I was aided by tradition. In my home and among my people it was common for men to drink late into the night. My father was an exception. He kept tight control over everything in his life, including drink. "Clean this, clean that." He would demand his wives and children maintain order in the house and in their lives. He would drink much but he never let it affect his kazi (work). He used to say "Drink lets loose my demons. It is hard not to drink when you swim among fish." As I was growing up, my friends would dare me over the bottles of beer, "Just a sip! True friendship is measured in gulps." I was willing to risk my health, but not my friendships. I felt free to think and say what I felt after the warm liquor warmed me up. When things turned bad at work and at home, it was a good friend. Too late I found I couldn't let go.

. . . [Several pages were missing]

"It's Christmas." The police officer said to me. In Kenya, Christmas in July means only one thing. I had been returning home from my government job when she pulled me over. I gave her about 100 shillings. She waved me on. The British had left but now they were replaced by the corrupt bureaucrats. At least the English were reasonably strict on corruption. "Let's have a drink." My boss would say, even after turning up for work red-eyed and smelling of Tusker beer. "Let's go and have a beer, my fellow workers would say to me. All this on the government tab." Eventually I also started to say "Let's go and have a beer." This was not a sip from a martini. We would stay up all night until the foam leaked from our mouths. We would go dancing, sleep around with women, and then put it on the department bill (except the hospital bills of our beaten wives). I remember how one night I returned home, yelled at my wife and terrified my son. I saw my face in the bathroom mirror. It was creased with lines of anger and worry. I looked really bad. My eyes were red. My head stooping. I looked just like the people I had been running away from all my life.

. . . [Several pages were missing]

I hate to see defects in people close to me. The problems of strangers are distant things, of little importance. Charity is voluntary - easy if I have money - and I can forget it quite fast. However, when my wife needs an operation or there is something about her health that has to be cured, I must do something. These are not choices. They are obligations. These obligations irritate me. I feel I'm wronged. You see, these sorts of things force me into action, but I hate being forced to do anything. She's unlucky. I blame her. She looks bewildered, and does not understand why her 'Thank you' makes me angry. Her meekness reminds me of my selfishness. "Give me, don't take from me", I think. It is as though my heart is a bank account in deficit. She is my perennial debtor. She draws from me. My heart bleeds. I am trying to understand this guilt, I wonder if I really love her. After all, how can a true lover [...] Damned if ...

The words stopped abruptly, as though someone had snatched the pen from his father's hands. A slight jagged trace of ink leapt leftwards into white space. It reminded David of the last page of the composer J.S. Bach's *Art of Fugue* manuscript. Written on his deathbed, the great work ends mid phrase after scores of pages. A bare note or two dangle over an empty page like a black raindrop over a vast expanse of virgin snow. His father's notebook was no *Art of Fugue*, but it was a revelation. That day and for days afterwards he read it over many, many times. It was as though his father was finally telling him all the things he had wanted, but never managed, to say. Ever since they had been separated those long, long years ago, he had wondered who this man was. He remained a mystery, but some of the veils had now been swept aside. A man with his weaknesses and all too human vulnerabilities had been exposed.

His father had died in 1976. Perhaps it was 1977. He didn't remember exactly. He had been in America at the time. No one bothered to let him know. No phone call. Nothing. It was as though he had been in a separate universe, and information would later reach him through filtered rumors and off hand recollections.

It was now many years later. In David's heart there was no bitterness, but only regret at what might have been. Were it not for this slim diary he might never have known the other side of the harsh man who he had once feared so much. Now he had a fuller picture that, though ragged in places, helped him to understand himself a little more. His difficulty in falling in love, his fear of being hurt emotionally, and above, all of letting himself go – all these were products of his upbringing. He had never loved his father. That was for sure. But he could now understand and forgive him his sins. The rest of his life would continue to be a journey defined by solitude and family, two concepts that, like *ying* and *yang*, had no beginning, no ending, and alternated between brightness and shade. If not love *what* then linked him to his father? He was indeed his father's son. The proof, he realized, was the ability to see in one's actions and history an image of the other's thoughts and dreams, and to recognize in one's thoughts and dreams the consequences of the other's actions and history.

David realized that in reply to all those things that separate a man from his brother, a woman from her mother, or a person from his neighbor there are things that bind across races, cultures, religions and nationalities. His father had broken economic and racial barriers in his dogged march from Alego to the New World, but his journey had been an incomplete one, for love had been lacking. David had come to realize (his father had alluded to this in his notebook) that life is like a mirror in which one sees oneself. From time to time the mirror is shattered, but love often reconstitutes it. Through another's guiding hand or gentle caress it brings the pieces back together like a marvelous glue, until finally one sees one's true self. His love of Spring had been that glue. He realized that what some called miscegenation, black, white, poor, rich, represented arbitrary divisions which his whole life repudiated. His identity did not lie in a place or a culture. He was a citizen of the world, straddling cultures and countries, at once an exile and a observer, a participant and a member, but with roots in the global community.

Later that evening he cried for the first time since he had left the hospital. The tears were copious. It was as though great waves of energy pulsed through him. The face in the bathroom mirror was old. There was a stubble of growth around the chin. Loose strands of hair dangled from his ears. Once bright and alert eyes were now puffy and listless. The wrinkles would increase in the coming years. His hair was already receding. Where was that flash of youth, that bright smile? He remembered the birds and kites soaring over Lian Hua Park. In his mind's eye he heard the music that Zhen Rui had played and saw the smiles of the children of Nairobi and Shenzhen. Once he had shared a beer with a stranger in the lost restaurant. Once he had loved a girl. He knew then that he still loved Spring. The school and the music were less important. Shenzhen was empty without her, like dust on an old gem. He wanted to wipe off the dust. For that he would do anything. He didn't care what others thought. He would walk out amid their denunciations. He would seek the woman he loved and not rest until he found her again.

I leave tonight
My life has spun its course
Like silk from dead worms
Or the candle's final smoky tears.
Beneath the cold moon
You sing your love for me.
I'm not far, indeed,
You're the lark that seeks me,
The hundreds of flowers
The East Wind blows
Into my soul.

- Mark Okoth Obama Ndesandjo (An adaptation from a Tang poem)

THE END

LaVergne, TN USA
09 November 2009
163512LV00004B/7/P